KEZIAH'S SONG

A NOVEL

DARYL POTTER

Paper Stone Press
Oakville, ON, Canada
www.paperstonepress.com

March 15, 2021
Oakville, Ontario, Canada

Paperback: 9781777307301
Mass Market Paperback:
978-1-7773073-8-7
Hardcover: 9781777307325

Large Print: 978-1-7773073-1-8
eBook (Mobi): 9781777307332
eBook (ePub): 978-1-7773073-5-6
Audio: 978-1-7773073-6-3

Grateful acknowledgement is made for the quote used as the epigraph for this novel. The quote is by Tom Waits, as told to Terry Gross on Fresh Air in 2002. Fresh Air is produced at WHYY Philadelphia and distributed by National Public Radio, used with permission.

Quotes from Homer's Iliad are based on:
Samuel Butler, 1898. *The Iliad of Homer*. Translated by Samuel Butler. London: Longmans, Green and Co.

Quotes from the Biblical prophet Nahum are based on:
Robert Alter, *The Hebrew Bible: A Translation with Commentary.*
W.W. Norton and Company: New York, 2019

Edited by Diane Young and Amelia Wiens
Proofreading by S. Robin Larin / Robin Editorial
Map created by Daryl Potter and Jackson Potter
Cover design and typeset by Damonza

For Keziah.
The first two, and this one.

I like beautiful melodies telling me terrible things.

Tom Waits

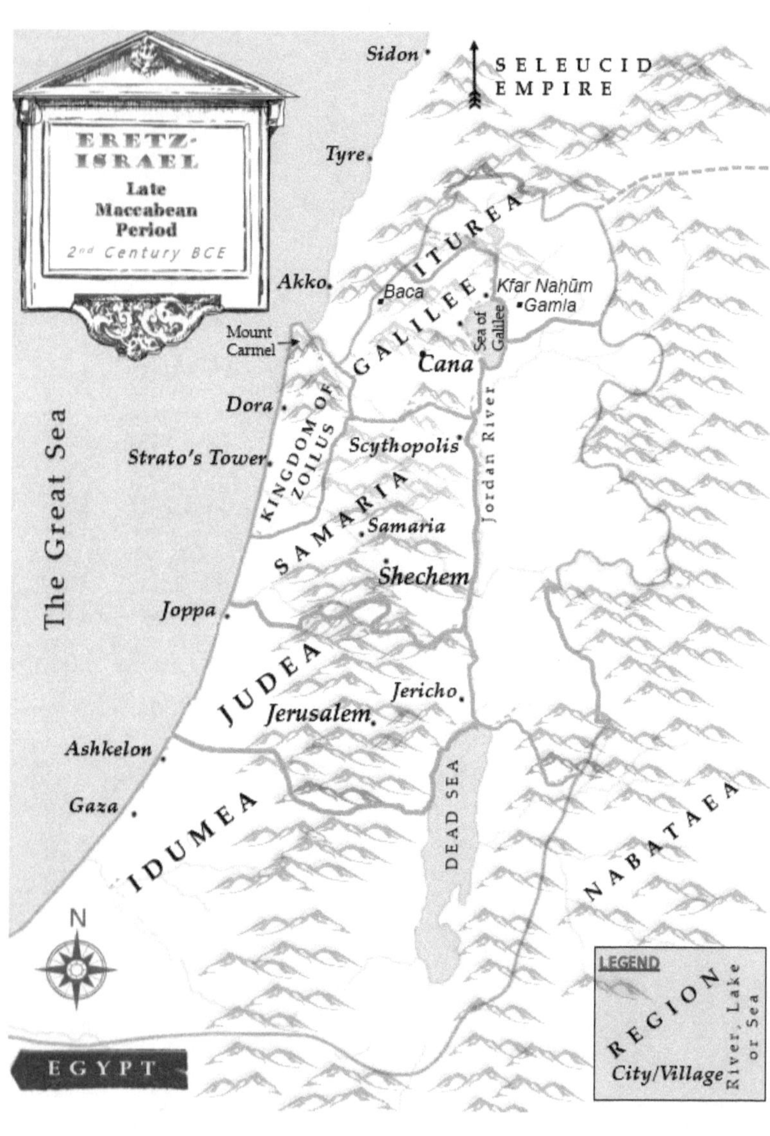

ERETZ-ISRAEL
Late Maccabean Period
2nd Century BCE
Sidon
SELEUCID EMPIRE
Tyre
ITUREA
Akko
Baca
Kfar Naḥūm
Gamla
GALILEE
Sea of Galilee
Mount Carmel
Cana
Dora
KINGDOM OF ZOILUS
Jordan River
Scythopolis
Strato's Tower
The Great Sea
SAMARIA
Samaria
Shechem
Joppa
JUDEA
Jericho
Jerusalem
Ashkelon
DEAD SEA
Gaza
IDUMEA
NABATAEA
N
LEGEND
REGION
City/Village
River, Lake or Sea
EGYPT

Keziah's Song

1

135 BCE

CONSIDER THE GIRL. On a star-littered night, she rides a cart among empty crates, facing the way they have come. She has no seat but the uneven boards of the cart's bed, no padding but a polluted blanket. She stares into the night and sees only black. There are no other travellers on the road. The girl is dark-eyed and hollow. Her hair is matted to a glassy forehead, cheeks, neck. Hours after the event, her hands still tremble. Her legs dangle listlessly. A dip in the road jars her heel, and she flinches. She draws her legs up under her, slowly, unmindful now of blood.

The rattling crates drown out donkey and driver. Her village is gone from sight. Cresting a rise, she can see the far-off city of Jerusalem. It shines in the night, though it grows ever more distant. She will never see the city again, nor her village.

Her mind bounces with the movement of the cart. It is the mind of a child becoming a woman. She cycles through scenes of violence, uncomprehending, events out of order. She is beyond scared. Her world has ended. It ended in fire, in death, in this orphaned exile in an Iturean's cart.

At the village, he had gripped her arm. Hard. "Do you know where you are going?" he asked. He loomed over her while her childhood home burned. "Do you know where to go?"

"I'm just a girl," she whispered into the nearly black face above her as firelight flickered across his cheeks.

They had fled the village: the gentile man and the Jewish child. He had spread a blanket so she would not stain his cart.

Beyond the cart was darkness and hidden there a harsh Judean landscape of rock, sand, scorpions, and snakes. She had a vision of herself escaping only to wander in that waterless place until death found her, otherwise alone and unknown. She would spend her last hour begging the sun, hands reaching with stilled fingers, a wordless cry to a sand-sea. Her ghost would forever be tethered to unburied bones.

The Iturean's cart was taking them through northern Judea toward the land of the Samaritans. There she would be despised for being a Jew, a girl travelling with an Iturean, in public during her time of blood.

An owl hooted. It prophesied her fate as well as any jackal.

The cart bounced again, and she gasped and leaned into the crates, which were abrasive against her back and shoulders. She heard the driver shout at the donkey. Her throat constricted around ragged breaths, and she hunched lower in the cart, tasted the saltiness of tears. She was an animal, a thought that had never occurred to her before.

She slept in brief intervals, wedged between towers of crates. She woke at bumps and slept again but roughly. As dawn approached, the cart stopped. She awoke.

The Iturean came around to the back of the cart. He looked at her in the dim light. He had a sack in one hand. He pulled her to the road. She stumbled. Her knees were weak and shook. Her back was stiff as an old woman's. He pushed her forward. She felt her way carefully in the dark, and they came to a pool. The sky grew lighter, the sun minutes from the horizon.

"Take off your things and clean yourself." His Aramaic was thickly accented.

She looked around. There was nothing there but the pool. "Where?" she said. She could barely hear herself.

He stared at her. "Wash."

A whisper: "I cannot."

"The Samaritans will not accept you, or me, with your blood. Clean yourself and your clothes, or I will leave you for the jackals and lions. You will wear this." He held up the sack, which had a torn hole in the bottom. "Until your clothes dry. And this"–he held up a strip of linen–"between your legs and keep it there until you stop bleeding. Do you understand?"

She nodded but did not move.

The Iturean snorted. He dropped the sack and cloth on the rock at her feet and walked away.

She worked quickly, bathing in full clothing. The pool was not deep, but the water was cold and swift. Her feet slipped on rocks that were the size of her father's fist. The place where she bathed was just a wide spot in the stream. There were large boulders downstream and up. Her toes slid between rocks, and she twisted her feet sideways, felt forward, tried to find a place where she could crouch, and finally sat in the water. She scrubbed at her undergarment, at herself, at her hair, her face. She silently cried as darkness gave way to dawn.

She heard him with the donkey around the bend. He talked to it. It came to her that her mother and father would only know this existence now. Even less than this. They would have no hope of a cart, another human voice, a village, a house. They would die of exposure. No one would clean their wounds. Father's arm. Mother's back. She started to shake in the stream and then splashed more water on her face. Forceful. Desperate. Finally, she stripped out of her wet clothing and stood shivering, naked, as the sun peered over the horizon.

She pulled the dry sack over her head. There were no holes for her arms. With her hands emerging from the bottom, she grasped her dress and awkwardly rubbed the bloodstained fabric in the dust at the side of the stream. Once she had created a puddle of mud in the bank, she began scrubbing the stains even more vigorously. Back in the water, she rubbed the cloth hard against loose stones and fine sand just beneath the surface. She dipped it again and again, deeper in the stream. She worked hard and focused on her task until his voice behind her made her leap in surprise. She stumbled into the water, nearly fell without the ability to throw her arms out for balance. One bruised foot stayed wedged underwater. Her hands pulled the sack down.

He held the cloth out to her. "Here," he said. "You'll ride in the front with me. I don't want your blood on my cart."

She stepped fully onto the shore. She could not see his

expression. The sun was behind him, his face a shadow. He pulled out a knife. The blade swung toward her and stabbed at her left shoulder. She staggered as he pulled her roughly around and made a cut on the opposite side. He reached into it and pulled her arm through the hole in the sack. Then both arms were free. She was uncut.

"Here," he said again and thrust the strip of linen at her.

The blanket she had sat on through the night hung from his load of crates. Water dripped from the cart. He had washed it himself. He arranged her dress so it too would dry. She sat in the front as he commanded. The cart moved again. She shivered with cold and emotion, too ashamed to look at the road ahead. An ache clamped her skull tight and squeezed her eyes.

Everything that mattered had happened before the Iturean. She wrapped her arms around herself and tried to remember yesterday. All that came before. What started it.

Her mother had leprosy.

The disease had come more than a year before. Mother and Father kept it secret. Mother became an excessive cleaner and a slow cook. She stopped touching the children. She was distant with Joazar when he came from the siege at Dagon. "You're a man now," she said by way of explanation, as though mothers did not embrace their grown sons.

When Joazar returned to defend Jerusalem, Father and Mother told Keziah and her little brother the secret. It had spread to Mother's left hand, where she could conceal it no longer. She had cut herself, and it would not heal.

Keziah knew what leprosy meant. Her mother would be banished to the wilderness. A cave would become her new home, and then an unmarked grave would follow it.

Her father looked at his two youngest children with red eyes. "We're not going to let that happen to your mother. We will protect her here and pray for God to heal her of this disease. We will hide her until then."

Beyond Keziah's village, throughout the region of Judea, a terror reigned that had nothing to do with leprosy. The Seleucid Empire, the northern Greeks, besieged Jerusalem. Their war machine of cataphract cavalry, with each breast and horse dripping in thick chain mail, thundered through the countryside with spears twice the height of a man, and behind them came the densely packed infantry with their even longer sarissa spears and small shields. Behind them farther yet, the war wagons, followed by terrifying creatures, the scent of which panicked even Seleucid cavalry mounts. The professional Seleucid army came in coded colours and phalangite formations.

The Jews had no professional army to respond to the invasion. Like Keziah's brother, volunteers manned Jerusalem's walls with what weapons they could find or fashion. King Simon was dead. His son, Hyrcanus, was no Simon.

The family kept Mother's leprosy secret throughout the winter. The local people lived in fear that the Seleucids would relent against Jerusalem or conquer Jerusalem and, in either event, turn on the surrounding villages. Fear, it seemed, served as a great distractor. The disease remained a secret well into spring. Until yesterday. Leprosy, it turned out, was a village-sized problem.

Keziah first knew of the village's discovery when she saw the house wearing a hat of fire. She was returning home. She had crossed a wet field and walked a strangely quiet road. Then she saw the flaming roof and saw a man walk from the house and toss a firebrand back inside, saw the crowd, the entire village assembled. They paid no attention to the man or the burning. The man joined the crowd; they all stood with their backs to Keziah.

"She will die out there!" Father shouted.

"She's already dead."

"Stay back, Keziah! Stay there!"

She was halfway through the crowd when her father stopped her. He stood in an open space, hunched like a dog surrounded by tormenters. His opponents spread out before him. Behind him were several men from the village with long poles. They prodded at Mother. Father backed toward them, glanced behind him, then returned to his accusers.

"Get that woman moving!" a voice said.

"Let her be!" shouted Father. "Let her be!"

The villagers surged forward, and a man with a threshing flail led the way. The end of the flail was a thick, knotty branch, crudely fashioned and unsmooth. The man was long-haired and large. Keziah did not recognize him. She saw him walk past Father, between the men with poles, and carve a path through the air with his tool. It came down across Mother's shoulders with a sickening, dull sound. He retracted the loose end to himself and tore a strip of clothing from Mother's upper body and with it a gouge of flesh.

Mother screamed, and Father screamed and ran. Keziah had never before seen her father run, never seen her mother's blood. Keziah ran toward them, her vision blurred. She made it into the clearing, staggered, and then fell, palms to the ground, as the sky swung overhead. She looked toward her parents. The long-haired man raised his tool again, and as it came down, Father inserted himself in between, arms up. One forearm cracked, and a spike of shorn branch penetrated flesh. It came back to Father's attacker red with both Mother's and Father's blood. There was a moment of pain violently revealed, and then Father was beside his wife, covering her with both his broken and good arms, pulling clothing over fresh wounds that would never heal. A child's wail rose in the heat.

"Now you are cursed as well! The blood from her is in you." His accusers pointed at Father's bloodied arm, wrongly bent at the place of the puncture. There was blood in his beard and on his face. "You too are unclean. You are never to see another human being until God takes your life!"

"We will starve."

Keziah cried out, and their eyes remembered her. She was on her knees. Twenty steps separated her from the arms that had held her from birth.

"She's bleeding." A woman's voice from the crowd. "She was down in the village, and she's bleeding. It is her time of blood, and she's been out in the village!"

There was a roar. Hands reached for her, and then her little brother shouted with his small child's voice and ran across the open ground. He sprinted toward her as fast as his fat legs would carry him. A man in the crowd cocked his pole. "Moshe!" Father shouted, and the boy stumbled. As he fell, the pole shot forward. Instead of finding a waist or legs to stop the boy, it found his falling head. The sound snapped through the crowd like another flail crack. Moshe fell, face into the ground. A dent lay at the base of his skull in place of missing bone. His legs twitched excitedly while his torso and head were still as death.

The crowd surged past Keziah. The men with poles

blocked Father and Mother. Keziah rose unsteadily and found herself behind the crowd as it surrounded her brother's small body. Then a rough hand closed over her mouth. An arm dragged her backwards, past the burning house, down the street, and around the bend in the road. She twisted and clawed at the big arm. They passed for the last time the houses of her childhood. She struggled harder when they turned at another bend in the road, and a growl came in one ear. "Quiet, girl! They'll take you next." Other words were said that she did not remember until later.

A gentile shopkeeper came up beside her assailant, holding a large blanket. She recognized him from the outskirts of the village.

"Get her in!" Her kidnapper rolled her into the back of a cart. She could see her attacker now. An Iturean trader often seen at the gentile shop. Then the blanket covered her, and she saw only late-day sunlight diffused through a coarse and threadbare cloth.

The shopkeeper moved to the front of the cart with the Iturean and talked quickly in a language she did not understand. The cart swayed as the driver entered. She could hear the shopkeeper's quick steps as he kept pace beside. The men came to an agreement. The shopkeeper drifted to the rear, and then his voice spoke above the blanket. "Stay hidden."

The Iturean did not check on her until just before dawn when he told her to wash. She could have slipped away at any point in the night, and he would not have known. She did not leave the cart. There was nowhere to go, and no way to get there.

2

135 BCE

HOW HAD THE great blind bard put it?

With the besiegers came Strife and Riot
and came also the goddess Fate,
dragging three men behind her:
one wounded, one fine, one dead.
All three were dragged by their feet
and her robe was muddy with blood.
Strife, Riot, and Fate went in and out together,
each hauling away the other's dead.

Jugurtha considered Homer's words as he watched the war horde before him. A bedraggled crowd was trapped in the no man's land between his Seleucid besiegers and Jerusalem's walls. They were common people, expelled from the city, not equipped for war. When word was given, Strife, Riot, and Fate would have more than they could haul between them. The whole of the Greek pantheon would be required to harvest these dead. If it came to that. He did not think it would. He had a colder idea.

"He's coming," the bronze-clad man atop the dais announced.

What had Homer said? *Bronze-shod.* Bronze since the days of Homer.

From beneath the great tree
there welled a stream of pure water.
Then Jove sent a fearful serpent out of the ground,
with blood-red stains on its back,
and it darted from under the altar
and onto the great tree.

The death of innocents followed in that tale: a screaming mother and her young. The snake was an image in Jewish lore as well. Homer never explained how the snake got to be bloodstained before the killing started.

Here, outside Jerusalem, death was less personal. There was the smell of horses, of camels, of elephants. There was the light clatter of arrows being stacked and the heavier sound of spears, the great boom of stone launchers, catapults that brought down thousand-year-old walls. Here there was accounting for wages, time, plunder. This was no myth. He'd seen no snakes. The only tree in this story served as a battering ram.

Jugurtha knew the source of his own blood, unlike the blood on Homer's strange serpent. He was among the Seleucids, but he was not one of them. His grandfather had been the chieftain of an African tribe skilled in medicine, art, and agriculture. Slavery came to Jugurtha's homeland following a failed war. Jugurtha had been born a third-generation slave but was better educated. Father told him his history, how his blood was not that of a slave. He was of a chieftain's line; where he led, people would follow.

Sold north as a boy, Jugurtha passed through several masters who learned to value him. Jugurtha spoke more languages than were needed. He was good with numbers. He understood how things would end before the events got there. He impressed his owners.

One day in the royal palace at Antioch, he found himself owned by Demetrius Nicator, king of the Seleucid Empire. Had events not otherwise conspired, Jugurtha might have risen to the role of personal assistant to the king. But events did not unspool that way. Demetrius went to war, as Seleucid kings did, and the Parthians captured him. He had owned Jugurtha for only a matter of months.

"Where is the runner?" Jugurtha asked.

The man above stood as tall as he could. "Near the swill pit. He'll be here soon."

For years now, the Seleucid king had been held captive in Parthia. His brother, Antiochus Sidetes, held the throne in his place. Kept it in trust. Naturally, he also took responsibility for Demetrius's slaves, including Jugurtha. Also, Demetrius's wife. They had children together now. Such were the ways of Seleucid kings.

Jugurtha's bearing, languages, skill with numbers, and attitude towards money did not go unnoticed. Sidetes assigned his young slave the task of auditing the treasury. Jugurtha found a modest dividend in the books by exposing certain bureaucrats as careless with financial details. Their carelessness made them wealthy, as clever carelessness often did.

Jugurtha's discoveries were reported. Sidetes rewarded his careless bureaucrats with a careless swordsman who took many attempts before he completely severed their heads.

For his part, Jugurtha was manumitted. Free. He was given an elevated role in the treasury, and his ascent began from there. Now, responsibility for the financial management of the Jerusalem campaign was his. Treasurers simply counted. Jugurtha forecast. His job was to ensure that each adventure was profitable. Each expedition proved his numbers as surely as they tested the general's tactics.

Today, he awaited a runner. He studied the lookout again but did not make another inquiry. He just scowled and waited. It was not Homer but another poet, Nahum the Jew, who captured it best.

The city, like a pool of water,
drains away.
"Stop! Stop!" is the cry,
but none turns round.

Something would drain, either Jerusalem or his profits. They had camped outside Jerusalem's walls for too many seasons now. Long sieges became expensive sieges. Expensive sieges were hard to justify. This one was approaching a dangerous line in his ledger columns.

The runner finally came glistening through the dust, and two Chalkaspides, bronze-shielded soldiers, stepped into his path. One tilted his shield towards Jugurtha's tent.

"The news," said Jugurtha.

"The Jews have expelled the common people from Jerusalem. They are not armed. Many are old or children."

"Don't harm them. Send them back into the city."

"The generals will want to—"

"Do these people pose a threat to us?"

"No, sir. They are useless to the cause of the Jews."

"Then you don't need the generals."

"Sir—"

"There are limited resources within the city. That is why they have expelled the commoners."

He studied his nails for a moment and then spoke again. "Their mouths will help eat the food that remains inside the city until those inside starve. Or they open the gates."

He looked up at the flushed man before him. "They might have water and patience to spare, but they cannot grow grain on rock. Do not let the exiles pass. Do not harm them. Let them starve within sight of their own people. Or let the Jewish king readmit them." Jugurtha gestured to regain the messenger's full attention. "If you find any lost Jews on the way back to the lines, take them with you. Add them to the population. This is not a matter for the generals. This is an accounting matter. Go!"

The runner turned away. Footfalls faded below the sound of wood clattering and the milling of troops.

Homer understood.

No man can do battle without food.
Hunger and thirst will find him out;
limbs will grow weary beneath him.

Jugurtha smiled. The solution in Homer's great poem was to delay battle for the sake of a meal. The view was that of the attacker. At Jerusalem's wall, it was the defender's meals that were delayed. Homer's lesson was applied with the opposite application. Nahum came to mind again.

The city is stripped and distraught and despoiled,
fainting hearts and buckling knees
as all faces lose their lustre.

Jugurtha's smile morphed into another expression. Slaves in the Paradise of Daphne feared that look. Those that had been trained to it survived. Others floated, and the river in that place disposed of them in the sea.

Slavery was not a warm growing ground, and neither was bureaucracy. Jugurtha returned to his tent. As he did so, his hand passed over a page of figures, and his expression changed again to something approaching serenity.

3

135 BCE

SHE WOKE DISORIENTED.

The morning air was wet and carried the scent of donkey and almond blossoms. Opening her eyes, she saw an elevated view from the cart. A shielding screen of trees leaked light; a dark well absorbed it. The Iturean sat nearby and with him the gentile shopkeeper.

She sat up, and the shopkeeper came over. He gathered her dried clothing from the cart and handed it to her. "Change now. I've come to help you find others who will take you in."

She took the clothes from him. She stepped down from the cart and circled behind it. Tension from the previous day bound her. Her chest, ribs, and back ached as though tied by shrinking bands. She pulled the ruined sack over her head, hesitated, then hung it on the cart. She held her real clothing, stiff now but dry. Mother would shake it out to soften it. Mother. Keziah froze and slipped into memory. Mother's wounded shoulders came before her. The way Mother tried to conceal her hand. Her pleading eyes, and the violence of the flail, the blood, the sodden sound of impact and rage's release. As Keziah remembered, her mouth gaped. Quick, shallow breaths passed slack lips. Her eyes locked onto the pattern in the rock before her. Her vision blurred. Her attention skittered away from the image of her brother's poleaxing, returned to the flail, the shoulders, the implications. Mother.

Standing naked behind the cart, she felt herself falling down an internal shaft. She became aware of the present again only when the shopkeeper stepped around the cart. She could not move. Violent memory filled half her mind; an awareness of the gentile man invaded the rest. She held her clothing to her chest and stared forward. She was immobile and did not flinch when he touched her. She was not a near-woman anymore. She was just a child.

The shopkeeper dressed her silently. She saw him pick up the bloodied cloth from the dust and walk it to the treeline, kick away some soil, bury it. She was shocked to see him touch her blood, the second man in the last day to do so. He returned to the cart and rustled among the Iturean's belongings. Then there was a tearing, and he returned.

He gestured with a clean strip of cloth, and she took it. When ready, she climbed onto the cart as directed. The Iturean sat on one side as the shopkeeper settled himself on the other. They squeezed Keziah between them.

The cart did not move.

"What do you see, Keziah?" the shopkeeper asked softly.

Her eyes swam and resisted focus. She waited.

"What do you see?"

"I don't understand," she whispered.

The shopkeeper pointed in front of them, past where the ridge was white-edged and broken. Dust hung dry and resistant to transient dew. She returned her eyes to the cart and the road below them.

Mid-morning sun was behind and flowed past them. There were miles of trees in the lit valley below. Green showed as far as she could see, bisected with irregular lines like the pattern in the boulders around her. Not lines of granulated mineral, but bright lines, smooth like glass or silver sheets hammered into a pattern, flashing light and then dark. It was a valley crossed with water. There were canals between olive trees and vines and beside geometric fields with emerging yellow crops. There was a mountain to the right and another to the left with only a mile between. There was a well here and water in the valley below. A small city before them had been built with the same white limestone that shone in mountain scars.

The shopkeeper brought Keziah's attention back to the nearest walls and rooftops. "Do you know the name of this city?" he asked.

She did not respond. She felt the presence of the two gentile men on either side of her as strongly as she felt the spectre of her family's murder.

"Shechem," the shopkeeper said. "This city is like a woman forever beset by—"

The Iturean stopped him, reaching across Keziah, a hand on the shopkeeper's arm. "She's just a girl," he said.

4

135 BCE

There is an animal that breathes very lightly out and does not breathe in at all. Resigned sighs of gas escape and flesh spreads as it settles.

Long knives separate the meat from offal. Soldiers turned scullery workers turned butchers pant as they labour. Elaborate pavements run red.

❧

"Do you know what you're doing?" Joazar asked.

Ebed looked up and appeared to consider the question.

A cow on its back stared dully down the room with sightless eyes. The room itself was a makeshift butchery, a place designed in years past for finer things.

"I've done a goat before," Ebed finally answered. He straddled the dead cow's chest, facing its gut.

"The butchers use some kind of hooked knife," Joazar said.

"You got one?"

"No."

"Then we'll do it my way."

Joazar shrugged.

Ebed made his first incision into the skin just below the rib cage. Once the cut was large enough, he stuck his free hand in, followed by his second hand with the blade.

"Don't cut your fingers," Joazar said.

"Yeah."

"You need the hook knife so you don't split the gut sack."

"That's what my fingers are for. A guide." He worked his way forward slowly, opening up the skin.

"Too much blood," Joazar said. "I think we're supposed to let it cool longer."

Two-thirds of the way down the animal, the gut appeared. It swelled up white and blue and grew into the open air.

"Phew," Joazar said and put an arm over his nose.

Ebed kept working until he was down between the cow's rear legs. The gut sack grew out of the animal to nearly twice its original size.

"Good thing you didn't cut that thing open. How do we get it out in one piece?"

"I'll show you something." Ebed got off the animal, circled the bulbous gut sack, and then straddled the carcass again, facing the opposite direction. He reached back in at the place where he'd made the first cut. He pushed up into the chest cavity with both arms. He grunted, and Joazar grinned to see the swollen gut press against his friend's backside. The sixteen-year-old began to roughly saw with the knife deep in the cow's chest. Then there was more grunting and pulling, and soon Ebed's gore-covered arms emerged from the cow's torso, gripping an enormous flexible shaft.

"Looks like the world's largest chicken neck," Joazar said. "Or a bull's penis skinned out."

"Throat," Ebed said. "Help me with this." He got off the animal and motioned to Joazar. The two boys grabbed the white and blue windpipe and then pulled and peeled it out of the animal. Soon its attachment to the gut became evident, and it became a handle. They kept backing up until the wobbly gut spilled from the carcass and with it a tangle of white and blue intestines and streams of escaping blood and yet more parts unrecognized. The boys laughed and pulled until they both fell and slid across the mosaic floor and then stood up again.

From there, they worked fast. They cut away strangely yellow and hard white tissues. They pulled objects of black and dark reds from the cavity, and a smaller sack burst and kidneys spilled, one of the few parts they recognized. They were shirtless and blood-smeared. They worked to outdo each other as they emptied the cavity, bantering, laughing, talking over each other. They were nearly done with the organs and ready to start the proper butchering of bone and meat when the captain came. They heard his approach. They heard him talking but did not immediately register what he was saying.

"You can have these two. They are useless to our cause otherwise."

Both boys looked up as a group of a dozen men entered the room. The captain stood at the head. Behind him were not regular soldiers but members of the palace guard with several officials and Hyrcanus himself. Jerusalem's king.

"What in Hades have you done?" the captain asked.

"Butchering the—" Joazar stopped himself. The answer was obvious. Their orders, vague as they were, had come from this man.

"The skin is still on." The captain looked both angry and confused. "It wasn't left to cool. There is blood everywhere. You've ruined the skin. What is this?" He pointed to a lumpy mass at his feet. It was one of the unknown dark objects, nearly the size of a man's head, but flattened and flabby. "What is it?"

"It came from the cow."

"Where in the cow?"

Joazar looked at the animal, then at Ebed. His friend was a mess from head to foot. Not just his arms–even his face. It looked like they had massacred an entire army themselves. They were both breathing heavily. Joazar looked back at the captain and his palace guests.

"Where in the cow?"

Joazar shook his head.

"We don't know," said Ebed.

"It all just came out," said Joazar.

"You're supposed to—" The captain stopped himself. He seemed to consider his guests. "Hang it. You're supposed to hang it." He gestured at the hooks in the ceiling.

Joazar looked up. He wanted to ask how they were supposed to get hundreds of pounds of cow up onto those hooks but remained silent.

"Recording what you take out. Where it comes from. Clean parts in one place. Unclean . . . " The captain turned back to his guests. His face bore a clear question, though none was stated. Joazar wanted to point out that this exact lack of clear communication was to blame for whatever they had done wrong. The king seemed to understand.

"They'll do fine. Clean them up. They'll go out within the hour."

The palace guests departed. The captain stayed in the butchery and looked with tired eyes at the boys.

Everyone was thin. This cow was one of the last in the city. Proper butchers were among the exiled, trapped between the city's walls and the unyielding Seleucids.

"Got a new job for you," the captain said. "Cleaner. You might survive it."

᪥

Joazar and Ebed rode out on horseback as the first of the exiles were let back into the city. The two boys were at the rear of a group of seven riding unfamiliar and thin mounts. One horse's mouth dripped a relentless trickle of foam. All the men wore new armour and old footwear.

"You don't look like much of a soldier," Joazar said. "The horse is skinnier than you."

"The foam from yours is attractive," Ebed responded.

The leader of their party slowed and twisted around. He gave the boys a long look. He had a veteran air about him and said nothing. Rode on.

"Should have stayed with the half-naked, covered-in-blood look," said Ebed.

"You can both shut up now," the veteran said.

Joazar looked out at the Seleucid ring that surrounded Jerusalem and then looked away, contemplating the near ground instead. They crossed a plain of rock and shattered pottery, discarded clothing, human waste. Fragments of wooden arrow shafts stuck upward from cracks in the ground. There were bowls and rags and unidentifiable shapes in browns, greys, and yellow-whites. A blanket smeared with orange and green substances was left on a pile of debris that loomed and stank of unliving flesh. The detritus of war proliferated like the refuse of an apocalypse. The trapped population had burned, consumed, and abandoned what little they had as hunger and fear raced among them in that no man's land between armies.

Joazar looked up again. The phalanx that awaited them displayed the iron points of sarissa spears that were three times the height of a man. The weapons looked heavy and unwieldy. Tightly packed, the first four rows of soldiers lowered their points while those behind kept theirs in reserve, pointed at the sky. The most heavily armoured cavalry would be ruined against such a barricade.

They came to the weapon wall and stopped. The seven riders sat on their mounts and tried to look unawed.

The vertical forest suddenly shifted and parted down its middle. The front rows raised their shafts, moving aside and completing the channel.

The seven Jews shifted, uncertain, then the veteran moved his horse forward, and the rest followed. They passed through a canyon of red fabric, silver shields, and thick shafted weaponry. Joazar brought up the rear.

They came to a clearing. The guards here were bronze-shielded with standard spears and short swords. They waved the seven into the clearing, and then another round of the overly long sarissas greeted them. Their spears were points skyward until the Seleucid army surrounded the Jews, and then the spears came down. Ebed and Joazar found themselves cut off from the others by sarissa shafts and blades before, between, and behind them. The long weapons crisscrossed and created a lattice that pinioned them in place.

"Your horse has killed us," Ebed said. "It's slobbering everywhere."

They were in the midst of the army now, an olfactory sea of sweat, rank leather, and horse. Dark eye sockets peered from under shining bronze helmets topped with blood-red plumes. The helmets were lined with leather that was blackened by age and sweat. These helmets, with dangling cheek pieces and thick nose guards, not always centred, made the soldiers look like deranged creatures of some sub-human variety set upon this Jewish landscape like a plague.

The other five Jews rode on while Joazar waited with Ebed in this sudden thicket. They could do nothing but wait. With the spears a mere handspan from his face, Joazar was struck by the poles' thickness. The great pikes would weigh, he guessed, more than his little brother. The thought made Joazar want to go home. He wanted to see his family, probe more deeply into his mother's odd behaviour, and spend time with Keziah.

"For the sake of Zion, get your horse to dry up before it gets us killed," Ebed said.

Joazar's horse stepped uncertainly, as though it had somewhere to go.

"Your horse is pissing, isn't it?" said Ebed.

The blade points suddenly rose, and the soldiers parted, forming a new path through the crowd. At the end stood a large tent and before it a tall, strange man. The boys turned their horses in his direction and advanced.

The man was lean, taller than most, his skin both dark and oddly grey. His hair, close-curled and tight to his scalp, was also grey. The man himself, the smoothness of his skin, the shine of muscle, and how he held himself despite his greying hair and deathly complexion, looked young. Tattoos traced repeating patterns across his chest and up his neck to one cheek. His wrists bore the scars of old shackles cruelly worn, but the man did nothing to conceal them. He did not look like a slave. When he smiled, he had too many teeth. His eyes were blue. His entire appearance was unsettling.

"That man scares me to Sheol," Ebed whispered.

Jugurtha watched the young soldiers ride forward in their unmarked battle gear. He noted that the horses did not match their finery. He had the young men dismount and silently led them into the tent. Nearby, three bronze-shielded Chrysaspides stood guard.

"Why are you here?" Jugurtha asked.

Joazar wondered if it was typical for all men in authority to ask stupid questions. He looked at Ebed.

"Not just you two here. All seven of you. What is the official request?"

"A truce," replied Joazar. "For the festival. So we can celebrate the festival."

Jugurtha started at him. Then at Ebed. Then back at Joazar. "A festival?"

"Every year. At this time."

"What else?"

"What else, what?"

"Why else are you here?"

"You're supposed to see that we're healthy young lads who will hold up a lot longer under this siege," Joazar continued. "We're not to be trifled with. Maybe this truce for the festival can start a conversation."

"You don't know all that," Ebed said.

"I heard the captain talking to . . . to the other captain."

"You're not supposed to tell him."

"You were supposed to hang the carcass—"

"Stop talking," Jugurtha said. He studied them. "I don't care about that, whatever it is. I want to know about this festival."

ర్

When the time came to depart, an understanding bound the boys to the tall, strange man. The delegation of five Jewish soldiers rode up. Even the veteran leader seemed to find Jugurtha's appearance unsettling.

"These will remain with me for one day," Jugurtha declared.

"How can we celebrate the Ingathering when we have left two of our own behind? With gentiles. As captives."

"I understand." Jugurtha seemed to consider the captain's concern. "Take their horses. We will return these men with new and better horses when the time is right."

"I cannot," came the reply. "We won't leave these two."

"You have no choice."

There was silence in the square of soldiers. Walls of sarissas on all sides barred the Jews' exit.

"Did you get what you came for?" Jugurtha asked.

"Yes."

"Tell me your request."

"I don't explain myself to—" The veteran stopped himself. It was clear that he did not know who he was talking to. His eyes strayed to Jugurtha's scars and then the standing soldiery, the scene. "Peace for the festival. A truce."

"Did you get what you came for?"

"Yes."

"Then you can leave with what you came for," Jugurtha said. "You will trust me that I will return these two safely tomorrow or the next day." He looked at the old soldier. "I might keep my word, or I might not. Either way, you get your festival. Or you can fight for their release." Jugurtha looked at the assembled army about the square and then back to the five before him. He smiled. "I see now that I was wrong. You do have a choice. What is your choice?"

"It will be all right," Ebed called out. "We will come before Hoshana Rabbah. God willing, we will come with additional cause for celebration."

The old soldier regarded Ebed and then turned to Joazar. "And you?" he asked in the old Hebrew.

Joazar blinked. Not many understood the old language anymore. Aramaic was now the language of Israel, and Greek used for formal writing. Only sages and careful students who preserved the old ways used the traditional tongue. It was a guess on the part of the old soldier. Joazar was able to answer him in kind. "The Greeks will tire of us and want rid of us soon enough. We'll be there by Hoshana Rabbah."

The captain said nothing in reply. He waved his men forward, and the group rode toward one towering wall of weaponry. It parted, and the company passed onto the debris field that churned with miniature whirls of dust and the remains of old fires, echoing centuries of disorder in that place. The wall of sarissas closed again, and the five were blocked from sight.

"Further conversation is in order," Jugurtha said in the old Hebrew to his startled captives. "We'll start with this Hoshana Rabbah."

~

There is a man who does not seem to breathe. What comes to him relentlessly accretes; accounts calm as he settles.

Long experience separates gold from mere stories. A slave turned free man turned royal official smiles as he labours. Long columns promise black.

5

135 BCE

FROM JERUSALEM'S WESTERN wall, Joazar watched the dip and detour of a dog in the wasteland. It travelled in the empty distance with its nose to the ground. The animal was darkness in twilight and disappeared into shadows. It reappeared for a moment but then faded to a suggestion, a cipher on the landscape.

"You have a dark look," Ebed said.

"Yes," Joazar replied.

The great city had been battled over since David claimed it from the Jebusites nine centuries earlier. Now it faced the Seleucid Empire's army of Greeks and their conscripts. The only celebrants of the festival this year were the hungry trapped within its walls.

"A year ago, Simon Maccabeus was murdered," Ebed said.

"Yes."

"This past Sabbath year has been all war instead of rest." Ebed looked over at his village friend. "Do you remember the Ingathering Festival from Simon's time?"

"Of course," Joazar said. "Do you remember the time you came with us? We arrived this time of night."

Back then, the trumpets in autumn air had been clear, and night's darkness nearly complete. Jews had come to Jerusalem with their branches of willow and myrtle and palm fronds. They built shelters outside the city walls that leaked rain and light. Sprigs of leaf and berry strayed off the tent roofs in random directions like boys' hair. Happy families had celebrated the holiday, the travel, the feasts.

As Ebed and Joazar had approached Jerusalem, they had passed the sound of cooking and conversation, children without bedtimes, endless chattering in dim light, the crackle of fires, and the smell of meat and spice and roasted vegetables mingling in the air. By the time they arrived, the daytime festival din was subdued, and voices in the dark were like night birds' gentle calls. They heard snapped sticks and the collapse of a too-hasty booth and quiet laughter and community assistance with light and hands and directions and the footsteps of other travellers along the road searching the darkened day for one booth among thousands. It was a city outside the city, a clever wonder, a child's delight, a cheerful throng, a maze without markers. Most of the year it sat as an empty plain.

Father had led them amid the carnival of settling families, through the gates, and inside Jerusalem. They found the same atmosphere inside the city: residents had abandoned their houses in favour of booths on roofs and rooftop fires; voices carried with elevation, echoing on stone; everything was overrun with children, everywhere the same loose conception of time and social order. All Israel had lived in temporary shelters like their ancestors leaving Egypt. They called it variously the Ingathering, Sukkot, the Festival of Booths.

"I remember," Ebed said. There was darkness below where green booths should be leaking light and laughter. The dog could no longer be seen. "The ox was good."

"Yes," Joazar said.

Ebed spoke of this year's ox. It had been a gift from Jugurtha for this year's festival. The boys picked it out, and a Seleucid metalsmith gilded its great horns. They returned to the city on fresh horses and led the shining ox across the empty wasteland accompanied by gentile escorts, Jugurtha among them. The strange and fearsome man observed all that he could from the Court of the Gentiles. He tracked the celebrants in their ritual rounds, a strange sight with his escort amid thin and hungry people re-enacting old rituals.

"This year was not an Ingathering," Joazar said. "None of the rest of the nation came. The family that owned that ox lies smoking somewhere up the coast."

"Don't say that."

"I don't think it walked from Antioch," Joazar said. "And I regret what we're going to do to make this truce last."

"Do you believe Jugurtha?"

"We gave ourselves up for his promise."

"Do you believe him?"

"I don't know. I hope. We each have a job to do as part of it."

❧

Hyrcanus had five more days to deliver on the Jewish terms for peace.

The Seleucids waited outside Jerusalem's walls.

∽

Joazar rode alone through the Seleucid camp on a Greek warhorse. He wore his village clothes and carried a sword that Jugurtha had given to him. The sword's red-trimmed sheath was a stark contrast to his otherwise modest garb. He was expected. The Seleucids had agreed to this personal mission. Jugurtha watched him from a distance. The young Judean rode through and on.

When he got to his village, instead of his last family gathering, blackened shadows confronted him. Night crouched at midday where his home should have been. Charcoal image, charcoal substance, the splash of sterilizing lime shame-labelling new ruins. Doors were shut all along the street, and nothing moved in his childhood village. Public places were empty. The silence was visual.

He rode to the ruined house. There was a hollowness without and within. He stepped down from the horse and touched a blackened and gutted mezuzah frame dangling from a charcoal post. In this way, he began his discovery.

It took the better part of two hours to patch together a clear picture of what had occurred. Conflicting and reimagined memories from lifelong neighbours exposed a village traumatized by its actions. Joazar stood alone at his brother's graveside, his tears flowing. There was just one grave. Little Moshe represented his entire family. Neither Father nor Mother could have survived long after the events of that day, but no place marked their passing. None of the conflicting stories about Keziah could be true. Whatever the truth, she was gone.

Joazar discovered details regarding Moshe and his parents from various people in the village. He pieced together these fragmentary accounts into a tentative whole until he determined the identity of the long-haired man with the flail. He decided that man would stand for all.

The sages say that the pores of men leak a substance that animals can scent and interpret. From it, they read fear, dominance, intent. If the sages spoke true, then behind Joazar trailed an invisible tail that smelled of charcoal dust and ash and the scents of something breaking, something evil thrusting up from within, something stirring that would not be stilled but, correctly read, would inspire fear. Joazar welcomed this new hate. It came with purpose and took him over so that even his hands did not feel like his own. He saw through the eyes of another and did not question who.

Joazar rode to a fork in the road and took the left-hand path. His immaterial passion revealed itself in muscular tension. Near long, low sheds, he stopped to clear his mind, which refused to calm. He studied the problem as he might have one of his father's lessons. He rode farther.

A large man with a broad back and long hair walked around a corner, carrying a barrel on one shoulder. "Who are you?" His manner was brusque. He looked at Joazar's sword and belt and horse but also his clothes and hair. "You're not a Greek."

"From Jerusalem," Joazar said. "We are looking for supplies."

"For who?" the man barked. "The Greeks?"

"Hyrcanus."

"Riding a Greek horse? Wearing a Greek weapon?"

"Won killing its rider and bearer. The war goes slow, but well. Hyrcanus will prevail."

The big man snorted again. "He's no Simon."

"He is Simon's son. He needs grain. Men must eat."

"How would you get anything through the line?" He stood before Joazar, still holding the barrel.

"There are routes through the Kidron Valley the Greeks leave unprotected. They cannot be everywhere."

The man regarded him for a moment. Then he spoke again. "You might be worth a story. And you have a hungry look. Eat with me."

He turned his back to Joazar and stalked toward the squat, square house.

Joazar dismounted and followed him. At the house, the big man bent down and lowered his barrel to the ground. He grunted as it touched down and then sighed again, a barely audible loss of breath, as Joazar's sword struck from behind, slipped between mid-back ribs, punctured through flesh, and then slid through into the open air. The big man stood, turned, and looked down in shock at the sword tip protruding like a miracle from his chest. He looked at Joazar with wide eyes.

"Little Moshe," Joazar said as their eyes locked. The big man's hands reached and came together like a supplicant's at prayer. He made a weak grappling attempt with the sword's tip. He touched it as though to push it back into that unthinkable place from which it had emerged. "Little Moshe," Joazar said again.

The big man did not talk, but his face sorted through a multitude of expressions. He knelt before Joazar. He started to hiccup, and it became a full-body spasm. He put one hand on the ground. The other floated below the sword tip as though unsure of his next action but convinced one needed to be taken. The hand weaved back and forth oddly.

Joazar stepped around and pulled on the sword handle. He nearly pulled the man over. He put a foot on the man's back and tried again, and the sword released and slid back to him. The man was strong and did not topple.

When Joazar left, the farmer was still on his knees, leaning on one hand. The other hand wavered between chest and ground, no purpose left to it in the air, catching what ran from his chest and, having intercepted the flow, letting it run over and onto the ground. When Joazar rode away, the man was frothing, weakening, head nodding under its weight, eyes on the spreading pool below him.

An hour later, Joazar came through the Seleucid camp like one of the *Furiae* on horseback. He stampeded the unwary in the gathering dusk and then onto the wasteland before the city. He rode hard and brought his finished mount to a halt before Jerusalem's implacable walls.

6

135 BCE

KEZIAH STOOD BEFORE a window, briefly outlined by the surprise of distant lightning. She was quiet in the space, and then thunder rumbled through and over. This house was her mother's cousin's home, now her own home since the Iturean's departure. She stepped outside before the rain came.

The Galilean air lay thick about the farm, and Keziah felt the same thickness and suspense within. She passed across the courtyard, tried the gate, eased it open with just a bit of lift to check the squeak, and exited into the broad landscape. She moved quickly with no purpose and no light. She ran an aimless circle in front of the gate, passed dangerously close to the wellhead in darkness, clipped the edge of a resting jar, returned moments later to the gate and with haste eased it open and closed, mastering silence, and then raced the rain she could now hear pattering across the ground behind her. She slipped into the house and quietly closed the door against the night, damp on her skin, humidity hanging in the air. Rain sluiced against the sides of the house, and another brief line of lightning illuminated her stage.

Other than the fading echo of thunder, the house was soundless. The children from this house were all grown but one.

Lightning flashed again, and this time Keziah knew that Little Jacob was there. He was like an only child, his brothers and sisters long since gone to make families of their own. He worshipped Keziah, a new older sister, so much closer to him in age than his natural siblings, but still older and out of reach and mysterious. She was able to hold him the way she had held Little Moshe, the only one in her Judean family she had held that way. Little Jacob observed her tears and asked her questions that no one else dared to. He touched the exact place in her heart that needed him. She told him what happened, wept, told him again, and he had the wisdom at eight years old to just listen.

By brief lightning, she confirmed the location of the lute. In her village, she had been one of the few who were musical. She had learned to play the long-necked instrument in another family's home in the neighbourhood near the western oak groves. She never took the delicate instrument home. She played it across the village, in its own home, as often as she could. She had played less during the time of her mother's illness. She had not played at all this past year.

In darkness, there is no apparent deceit when pretending not to see a loved one. The eye wanders where it will, without interruption. She pretended not to see Little Jacob and focused on the lute.

She crossed the room and removed the linen cloth draped over the lute. An older brother had played it, a brother lost in Simon Maccabeus's time. One son of this house had played the long-necked lute. When he was lost, it was left behind as a hollow invitation–until now.

She lifted the instrument from its holder, counted the loose strings in darkness, and felt for the pegs. She touched the sharp curves of its profile and the swelling of its plain back.

She tuned it in darkness. She adapted to the new design. Blind fingers found the strings, the curve, the right position. She tried a quiet chord. A second. Single notes. Her fingers were wooden stumps at the strings, responding slowly, fingertips uncalloused. The softness of her fingers added to the unresponsiveness of her movements. Everything was delayed. She adjusted. She modified her expectations and approach. Different chords were used. She tried something less demanding of speed and precision. Again. The instrument was beautiful. Its provenance was unknown to her, whether it had been turned out in a Galilean, Judean, or gentile workshop.

As she worked quietly, the dark room gradually filled with a quiet and simplified melody.

❧

When lightning flashed again, the boy, wise beyond his years, stayed still. He observed her cheeks glistening in the sudden light, tears flashing their message to the darkness. He listened to the sounds from his lost brother's lute, the new sounds from his new sister. When the bassline of thunder followed the light, her chord changed. She anticipated the timing and responded to it. She played with the universe in a way that made Jacob's hair prickle and awoke excitement within, and the boy suddenly understood that his new sister had a gift.

Lying in the inner room, a grey-haired woman was also listening to the girl play the lute. The woman did not just hear the sounds, she understood what she heard. The notes faded quietly with the reduced background noise, considerate, beautiful, intuitive. A tear escaped across the woman's temple and into the bedclothes, and she knew now that the child would mend.

Beside the woman, an old man slept, unknowing but for a faint refrain that invaded his dream. When he awoke in the morning to survey his rain-shined farm, he felt a new lightness and life. He left before the others were awake and found that he loved the land beyond the gate again as he had not in years.

7

135 BCE

EBED HEARD THE call to halt but did not stop. He gave one more swing with the pickaxe. It came down hard and brittle as iron bit stone. He straightened and then dragged the heavy tool across the stone floor to where Joazar watched.

Dust settled and water jugs were unstoppered by sweat-soaked men bathed in torchlight. They talked in short, declarative sentences punctuated by soft barks of aborted laughter.

"Going to help?" Ebed asked.

Joazar took the water jug back. Grunted. He looked at the progress on the wall, at the men, at the fog of dust hanging in stale air.

"Did you at least talk with Keziah?"

Joazar gave no response.

When he had returned early from his village trip, men

from the gate said the horse slid and fell there and was ruined. They reported more: Joazar had picked himself up, unsheathed his sword, turned, and driven his blade into the Seleucid animal. He pushed it to the hilt as though this were an act common to men. The creature stared at thunderclouds with a wild-eyed glare.

Joazar now sat in the tunnel with Ebed and the others. He said nothing.

Ebed felt that his mission would similarly collapse. The mortared stone wall blocked the tunnel, but beyond it lay a sacred treasure, long buried beneath the city. To loot that treasure would invoke a curse and a shame that would forever rest on the men who toiled now in the dark. This adventure would be another Dagon. Another decision by Hyrcanus that implicated the rest. This mission proved that Simon Maccabeus was the last of the great Maccabees and that Hyrcanus was no Simon.

The captain spoke a word, and the grunt and chunk of men and stone and metal began again as picks bit into the mortar between rocks. Great mauls struck iron bars lodged in precarious niches, each blow only penetrating a hair's breadth into the stone. The men wore bronze infantry helmets, and amid the percussive tones of the operation, there was the occasional ringing of small chips striking their helmets and a curse when the thin muslin covering their eyes was violated. They worked through a haze of fabric, dust, and sweat. A serpentine track of blood arced from one man's shoulder to elbow. The scarlet streak shone brightly and then faded beneath a layer of fine dust. The bloody mark darkened, grew black, nearly crumbled in the dry air, and then melted again with the mingling sweat, blurring once more.

None would have been in this place but for this war and its proposed resolution, concocted in the African-Seleucid's tent. Joazar and Ebed had been spellbound soldiers with no blood on their swords, mere sucklings in the business of surrender and unconscious betrayal. They ceded all they knew of ritual and prejudice and history to the man named Jugurtha. Joazar betrayed even himself. He agreed to be part of the contingent of hostages that the Seleucids were to take with them when they left Israel. With Joazar and his fellow hostages, there were to be another five thousand Jewish soldiers drawn from Judea and Galilee. They would be sent in armour to support Antiochus's Parthian wars. All this to save Jerusalem.

These were only two of the betrayals. In addition to hostages and soldiers, a third betrayal lay behind this underground wall of stone.

Torches blazed from three sides. Shadows overlapped in triplicate along the floor and walls and faded towards the ceiling in a shaky cross light. In the spaces between men, in suspended dust, hung three-dimensional ghostshadows. The shadows were like wraith envoys of the pagan gods worshipped by the gibbering gentiles in their smoke-saturated camps outside Jerusalem's walls.

Ebed swung his pick yet again, and it struck a softer gap in the mortar. Approving voices cut through the roar in his head as he levered and pulled and dislodged a chest-sized wedge of stone that had been unmoved for nearly eight hundred years. It fell into the room beyond with a boom. They had breached the wall. A few more stones were now loose and were pushed through by hand to open the hole further.

Ebed was the smallest. They boosted him through, and

he disappeared into the dark. The captain passed a torch through. Ebed held it before his eyes, looked back at the wall with faces crowding the opening. They were not looking at him, but beyond. Heat from the torch radiated off the wall and warmed Ebed. The heat contrasted with the cool emptiness behind. He turned away from warmth to face the dead.

The hall was very tall, and the ceiling curved. The arch above was twice Ebed's height. The room was shaped like an elongated barrel on its side; the curved walls and ceiling grew increasingly wider and taller toward the room's middle. At the far end, the room tapered again. When Ebed got to that end, he turned back to mark his progress, and the flickering hole he had been lifted through was a mere dot in the distance. Even narrowed at this end, the arched space above was cavernous, the niches and notices legendary. Here lay Israel's first kings.

Ebed walked slowly to the end and found a ladder. It rested against the far wall. It led to a ledge and the target of his mission. He put one foot on the ladder to test it, and then he quickly stepped away as the wood disintegrated and collapsed before him. After the clatter came a plume of dust like smoke rising before his torch. He returned to the others and framed his face in the opening.

"I need a ladder."

"You broke Solomon's ladder?"

"Eight hundred years will do that," Ebed said.

A new ladder was delivered and passed through the wall. Ebed carried it to the far end, kicked the old ladder's remains aside, and set up the new one. It was Solomon's ruined ladder, but not Solomon's tomb. Solomon's tomb was to one side, clearly marked along with those of Bathsheba,

Rehoboam, Abijah, Asa, and others. The first kings of Israel. One king's wife. David's royal bloodline was entombed here beneath the city that bore his name. Ebed was startled to see the name of Naamah over one opening in the side wall. An Ammonite woman buried with Israel's founding kings. Ebed looked suddenly about and was relieved to find that the pharaoh's daughter had not found her final resting place in this room. Wherever she lay, it was not with her husband.

He turned back to the niche that was his mission: an elevated room carved farther back into the rock above him. He climbed the ladder, torch in hand, until he was shoulder-level with the new floor and surveyed dust-covered mounds.

"What do you see?" called a voice from far behind him. Ebed did not yell a response from David's tomb. He was eight hundred years away and beholden to a different hierarchy.

The first cask he opened gave his answer.

Breaching this place of the dead brought disgrace to all who participated, but to none more than Ebed for entering so deeply. However, the shame briefly fell away as he touched what had remained untouched since Israel had laid their second and greatest king to rest. But Ebed had not come to honour King David. He came to loot David's tomb. His heart sank as he thought ahead to the avaricious multitude outside Jerusalem's gates to whom this wealth would be given. This was a holy treasury destined for a pagan horde.

Back at the opening in the wall, Ebed leaned into the torchlight and tossed gold coins out onto the dust-drifted floor. They did not ring but sank silently.

"Twelve coins," the captain said. "That is all?"

"It seemed a good number. What is our debt?"

"Two thousand pounds of gold. Is there enough?"

"Yes. There is enough."

The captain motioned for the coins to be collected and then brought to him. He handled them. "Some are not Israelite." He held one up that had caught Ebed's eye as well. Egyptian. "But they are all gold." The captain motioned again, and one of the priests handed Ebed a small, thick sack with shoulder straps. "Fill it three-quarters full. Bring it back here, and we'll dump it into the larger carriers. Then go back and fill it again."

"How many times?"

"Seventy-five. Three-quarters full. A bit more to be safe."

"I'll help him," Joazar said.

"No. We don't have another strapped sack. The measures must be consistent. You have other duties."

"None should be here at all," Ebed said. "One is enough."

He disappeared then from the opening, and those outside heard only a whisper of his feet in the dark. Then there was silence.

Coming down the ladder on his sixty-eighth trip, he fell. Gold spilled across the tomb floor, and the flash of pain in his hip set him on the edge of a scream in the darkness. He bit down hard to quiet himself. He swallowed with knotted throat muscles and found himself weeping and gasping frantically, nearly sightless as he fought back flashes of pain that radiated from hip to back and down one leg. Gradually, he was able to summon the will to roll over and then to stand. He limped down the stone hall until he came to the illuminated opening.

"I need another torch," he said.

8

135 BCE

The Seleucid egress: a mass migration of donkeys and oxen hauling dry goods and men on war wagons, elephants carrying equipment, horses with chariots, the cavalry of heavily armoured cataphracts and lightly armoured archers and camel riders, the unmounted bronze Chalkaspides, the golden Chrysaspides, the token silver Argyraspides, the red-fringed mercenary Dahai, the foot soldiers from Lycia, Thrace, and Galatia, and beyond this vast, salaried horde came the mule trains of the commissary—a great host, a ground-hugging invasion of giant locusts, a single rapacious, slow-moving, relentless war machine, late fall fields and trees stripped and torn apart, homes and villages plundered, meals taken from tables, stores from barns and bins and cupboards, leaving a pavement of excrement, this multi-member beast choking through natural bottlenecks—a plodding, sullen congestion diffusing in open spaces to make broad roads from meagre pathways that were never designed for such an enterprise, swamping fresh water holes, damming streams and rivers.

Dysentery knifed into weak pockets, dropping soldiers to the sides of the road where they fevered, suffered, and died in their filth. The dead bodies were graphic markers, the only signposts left behind that pointed to the cause of this transit of carnage. Like giants found in myths, the elephants alone stripped, consumed, and evacuated four thousand pounds of grass, crops, bushes, and tree branches. The army was like an unholy plow, and in this peace, the Seleucids' exit from Israel was a vector of destruction indicative of total war.

The prize awarded for the Herculean re-establishment of empire came to twenty-three hundred pounds of gold, twelve hostages, and two thousand Jewish conscript soldiers with more to follow. The trip to Jerusalem and back had revitalized the entire Seleucid enterprise.

Four days from Jerusalem, fever and nausea climbed into Jugurtha and Joazar's cart.

"Do you want to die, fastidious Jew?" Jugurtha asked.

He directed the driver to the right flank, manoeuvring through the masses. They came alongside a group of camel riders and held pace until Jugurtha ordered a sudden stop while the cart was at an angle, forcing the populace behind to swing around them like a parted river of flesh.

"Observe," he said, stepping from the wagon, waving for Joazar to follow. "What do you see, Jew?"

"Dung."

"Camel dung. Very fresh camel dung. I watched it made just now. Watched that nothing stepped in it. It is ours alone." He picked up one of the soft balls and contemplated it up close. He made sure Joazar was watching and then theatrically ate it. "Now you." He laughed loudly at Joazar's reaction. "I'll ask you again, Jew: do you want to die?"

Joazar did not answer. Could not answer. Every Jewish distinction about what was clean and unclean, every purity law principle that he had ever wrestled with, the mere fact of him riding with this pagan, sitting near him, picking through his food with the prophet Daniel on his mind, passing the borders of Israel both present and ancient, and submitting to his fate while tortured with functional, practical, religious confusions–all of these cultural and moral internal debates were run aground on this single cross stroke, this beyond-the-pale act of inhuman grotesquery.

Jugurtha was still talking. " . . .and some of these Greeks and the others will die as well. Campaign fever plays no favourites. Some will lie beside the road for days and recover and catch up on their own. Many will be consumed by animals or buried by locals who find them. Some, mysteriously, are immune, will never catch the plague. But my grandfather's people survived bad water and bad food long before these Greeks and Carthaginians came to trouble us. I suggest you follow the way of Grandfather. Eat fresh camel dung and live."

He picked up another soft ball and extended it to Joazar. "So again, Jew. Do you want to die? Or do you want to live?"

"How can this help?"

"You have a very pretty temple. If you get back to Jerusalem one day, you can ask your god." He waved his offering in front of Joazar again. "You Jews deal with disease by banishing the infected. No different than these Greeks. You are not in Israel anymore, Jew. Try the way of my people. We cure our sick. We don't discard them. I chose you. I would rather you live."

For the rest of that afternoon, Joazar was unable to cleanse his mouth. Of the eleven other hostages, nine died. Two recovered after several weeks of illness, weakened but alive. Joazar improved by the morning after Jugurtha's dung treatment and three days on was not weakened but as healthy as those never infected.

The great host halted its northern advance two days short of Antioch. Soldiers began to unpack equipment untouched for the past three weeks, setting up camp in a formal grid layout. Their efforts amounted to an afternoon of town building.

"A successful enterprise," Jugurtha said. "Nature alone was our enemy. The losses were few. A very successful campaign, though a grim failure in the eyes of some."

"How does your view differ?"

"I don't care about glory. I care about wages, supplies, and the replacement of animals and men and equipment. This was a great success. We've come back with more men than we left with. That, as much as your gold, means a profit instead of a loss. And now we have time for this training cycle, which will set us up for victory against the Parthians. A complete success." He turned and studied Joazar for a moment. "It is how empires persist or fail. They succeed to the degree that they do not out-consume their income."

The next day's morning offered a cold mist that invaded tents, sleeping clothes, even breath. Joazar emerged to find his Seleucid captor nearly naked in the makeshift street between tent rows. Jugurtha's breath swirled about him. It gave the tattoos on the side of his face, down his neck, and across his chest a detached, disembodied aspect. Jugurtha threw over his shoulders a fur coat, and the illusion vanished.

"Are you ready for an adventure, Jew?"

"Why do you call me Jew?"

"You don't like it."

"No one calls you African."

"I am not. Grandfather's blood was cut in half when he made Father. Father's was halved again when he lay with Mother. I am, above all, an Arab, though I don't know much about my mother's bloodline, nor my grandmother's."

"No one calls you Arab."

"Nor Parthian either, thank the gods. So, you don't like Jew. Joazar is not likeable."

"Neither is Jugurtha. Should we invent new names for one another?"

"People will think we're friends."

"Are we?"

"I'll show you an adventure today. Friends are only known in retrospect. Today I'm going to show you something about elephants."

ର

Light faintly pierced the morning fog. As the mist faded, elephants began to appear, bodies of grey skin snaking their way through long grass in one massive row. First, there were only twenty in sight, then twenty-one. Twenty-two.

Twenty-three. More were revealed as the mist thinned. Soldiers attired in overdone cataphract armour appeared on platforms mounted on the elephants. Some riders seemed to be floating on a sea of fog. Behind the elephants came the disembodied heads of foot soldiers who emerged slowly from the low fog with a few lit torches, but none had the tall sarissas, spears, or bows.

Drums sounded, and the elephant line moved. There were half a hundred such beasts, energetic, edgy, like intoxicated monsters. Up and down the terrain, the animals moved in an uneven line. Their positions blurred in patches of persistent fog.

From the far right, an opposing force rose from the grass and with them, faintly, the thin sound of human voices in contest. Then a strange shadow-filled sky and the volley of slung stones fell in on itself like a flock of minute and silent birds. From his observation post on the hill, Joazar saw the cloud of stone fly across empty space before striking the elephants. He could hear the ringing of stones bouncing off cataphract armour that now seemed sensible and not overdone.

The elephant herd panicked. It was an unschooled force, untrained, untested, and it wheeled about in alarm, surging back towards the army behind it. The foot soldiers there raised torches and beat drums and launched a counter volley of stones at the beasts in an attempt to turn them back on course. This black cloud was thicker than the initial assault. It rang off armour louder, and the retreating elephants were punished harder, and the drums and the fire and the second wave of stones drove them back around towards the real enemy. The battle was not a fight between men but an exercise to train the elephants. The beasts were meant to learn that trampling the enemy in front was the right and good path and that retreat was no option at all.

Before being trampled, the attackers fell into prepared holes and covered the pits with hefty planks that carried the stampeding terrors' weight, leaving behind only dummies of stuffed armour and sticks and false heads to be crushed and savaged and gored.

The beasts were triumphant, jubilant with their swinging trunks and trumpets and nodding heads and swaying towers. The army arrived behind and emptied sacks of fruit. Then they led the satisfied creatures across the field for another trial.

"Too easy," said the one that Jugurtha had identified as Pericles of Crete. The Greek official grinned and displayed a missing tooth and caught Joazar's eye. "Have you ever rowed at the oars of a quinquereme, just one of three hundred damned souls, when the sea rolls up and down?"

The man looked hard at Joazar with not just his eyebrows raised but his entire forehead. Then he turned his attention forward again, inspecting the field generals as the generals studied the training masters and the training masters watched the army.

"Pericles is like one of those Arabian dancers who take their time revealing what they intend to show," Jugurtha said. "You have to wait."

Joazar was at a loss to know what to make of either Pericles or the mock battle. The idea that elephants needed to be trained had never before occurred to him.

The reassembled forces formed up as before but with less fog now, and the elephants conducted their second charge with focused energy. The trainers set up the exercise a third time, but the elephants lost their nerve on this round and turned against their own line once more. This time, a section of the supporting army was distracted, lulled by recent success and slow with slings and torches. The elephants trampled dozens before the soldiers could correct the creatures' course. The trial went on despite the tragedy. Drums and stones drowned out the screams of the injured until the elephant line successfully chased the proper enemies into holes, abusing the fresh dummies and relishing their reward of fruit.

"We're here to teach beasts," Jugurtha said. "Men, by this point, if they haven't learned already, cannot be taught."

"An apple tree then," Pericles said, eyeing Joazar with his forehead compressed. "Too high, too far up a limb, swaying back and forth, trying to grab your prize, that perfect apple, while the world around you goes in the opposite direction. You've done this, no?"

The field generals waited until the field had been cleared of the dead and wounded. Once all were ready, they signalled the fourth round. The trainers signalled in turn. This charge recreated the second: the soldiers spent less time wheeling about in uncertainty, and there was no trampling of allied forces. It was a complete success.

"Drunk out of your head," Pericles said. "You know that?"

"I have never been drunk. So no, I don't know that."

"We'll need to address that deficiency, Jew," said Jugurtha.

"You've not been drunk," Pericles continued. "But you've seen it, though? Ah, good. Like that. Somewhat.

Like a drunk man, almost but not quite falling down. No more drink than that. It's just like that."

The fifth round started, and the elephants now understood the surest path to a successful conclusion. They charged across the field in an alarming manner, and the air felt alive. Thunder resonated through the ground to the onlookers' feet and legs.

Past the holes, the elephants wheeled about and trumpeted and stomped their victory. A disturbance near the front drew Joazar's attention. One elephant suddenly went down. There were two beasts in conflict. The smaller rose, and then the monsters battled each other again. Riders in buckling towers flailed as the creatures went mad. Their trunks lashed with tusks tilted for advantage, their bulk bulling forward and falling back. There were head shakes of anger. One rider flew into the long grass. Then a swarm of men surrounded the creatures. Joazar couldn't make out what the men were doing until the battling giants began to topple, their legs entangled with rope. The last rider fell awkwardly, struggling with his armour and heaving his way off as athletic and suicidal trainers flew over the great beasts. Finally, a calm came over the battlefield. The other elephants gathered around, standing guard, standing witness, and shaming while consuming trunk-clutched caches of fruit over their disgraced peers.

"On a good day, ten elephants are worth five thousand soldiers," Jugurtha said. "More. They feed themselves and don't get paid. They terrify the enemy before the battle even starts. Horses unused to them will bolt the field. One good charge ends it all. When not fighting, they carry massive loads, move obstructions, even reproduce and feed their own young. But after years of training, they still go rogue, fight each other, trample the wrong army. A cost-effective but unstable weapon."

"A log on the river!" Pericles exclaimed, staring out at the field. "Staying upright on a log on the river. Fighting from that position." He seemed to have forgotten Joazar. "That is what it's like to ride an elephant to war."

They eventually quit the soldiers' camp and moved on to Antioch.

9

134 BCE

THERE WERE THREE cushioned chairs at the back of the war wagon. Jugurtha held down the central chair with Pericles on his right and Joazar on his left. Some ambitious artisan or slave had upholstered two of the chairs in a green fabric embroidered with animals, demons, and stars. The third, Pericles's perch, was purple and patterned with figures of warriors and jars. Jugurtha was naked but for his furs. Pericles wore the red tunic and winter cape of a silver Argyraspide and the coarse woollen pants and stout footwear of his native Crete. Joazar wore clothing from Jerusalem. It was not his military clothing, but his best robe with a cape in severe blacks and whites and browns. The three looked like buffoons in their unmatched costumes and gaudy upholstered chairs set in a row. Pericles grinned with his missing tooth at any females they passed while Jugurtha pontificated, hands augmenting words.

"Mount Kasios," Jugurtha said, pointing to the western mountain. "The Mitanni of the Hurrians called it Hazzi. . ." Jugurtha went on lecturing Joazar about all the different names and gods various peoples had ascribed to the gargantuan mound of rock. "But it has always been Kasios, home of Zeus," he concluded.

To the north sat another mountain range. Jugurtha identified it as the Amanus range and explained how it stretched northwest towards the farther Taurus range. The mountains were white-capped and rugged, with threatening passes through which Alexander the Great had ridden some two hundred years before. Between Kasios and Amanus lay a valley. Through that valley flowed the river Orontes, and on its western bank sat Antioch.

"After Alexander the Great's death, his generals divided up the Greek empire between them," Jugurtha said. "Seleucus Nicator was one of them. On Kasios, Zeus himself told Seleucus where to build Antioch, and Seleucus obeyed. The city became the capital of his empire, and he named it after his son, Antiochus Soter. Antioch. Our present-day king's great-grandfather's great-grandfather."

"The present-day king, meaning Sidetes," Joazar replied.

"Yes, Sidetes. But don't call him that. Some can. You cannot."

They were quiet then. Pericles looked as if he wanted to say something but decided against it. He grimaced instead at an ancient, hunched woman standing by the side of the road.

Antioch lay alongside the river, with northern mountains acting as a violent martial backdrop. Joazar learned of peoples he had never heard of, nations not recorded in the Torah, peoples who had climbed Kasios's peak in times before Abraham made his trek to view the sea and worship. Beyond Kasios, to the south, was Israel, forever lost to the Jewish boy.

Joazar shifted in his seat and looked out the window. The city's flora was still alien to him. Every part of Antioch seemed slightly askew. The width of doorways, the height of windows, and the angle of rooftops were all built according to the conventions of another civilization. He had only ever known the villages and towns of Judea and the city of Jerusalem.

"I don't eat that, Jugurtha."

"You will," said Jugurtha from beside his mistress. They were in a room just a short walk from Jugurtha's house, wife, and children. The ex-slave, manumitted into respectability, had bought both his wife and his mistress from a reputable dealer, and he kept this suite of rooms on a second floor for his other life.

The city's flora was also alien. The Greeks were unlike the Jews who gardened for practical food production. The Greeks had gardened Antioch for ornamentation. There were ilex bushes and trees with their sharp, waxen holly leaves and fatal berries. The arbutus was everywhere with its peeling bark and impatient new fruit forming beside the overripe, left intentionally to ferment naturally and later eaten for taste and intoxication. The red fruit was the size of giant figs and served as Joazar's stealth introduction to alcohol in volume.

"I don't do this, Jugurtha."

"You do now," said Jugurtha, exiting, leaving Joazar as both captive and free man with the woman.

Everything was different in Antioch: the purple of sumac mixed with onions and kefir over slow-roasted meats; yellow, red, and orange cumin blends baked into thick, rich stews; saltwater fish clothed in rosemary and oregano and lemon powders, or hot with red, yellow, and black peppers, or sometimes even spotted with golden-brown cinnamon in sweetened, warm goat's milk with the fermented red berries of the arbutus.

Soon these addictive new tastes and smells blended with offerings of forbidden foods. These seductive flavours became associated in Joazar's mind with the exotic architecture, the nearby ocean, the mountains and their stories, the city's history, and finally, the strangely clothed and unclothed women. Usually, Pericles was with them, grinning and feasting and talking in periphrasis, and Jugurtha was always there, too, a careful host, a serpent, Joazar's netherworld guide, captor, mentor, corrupter. The taste of the curries entwined with the sight of the darkest of Jugurtha's women, and the arbutus berries became associated with a single fair and plump woman who favoured Joazar in ways that shamed and consumed him.

Amid the onions and the debauchery, Jugurtha had gradually introduced more unclean and forbidden foods. First had come the pig's whitest parts, deeply darkened in its stew, passed off as beef. Then camel. Eggs of forbidden species. Among the lawful kinds of seafood were slipped eels, and then crabs and clams. Once the lines were consciously crossed, there was a return to pork's more dramatic cuts. At last, Joazar had picked his own woman, and his captor had paid for her and kept her as well in the rented rooms near the family home, making Joazar's counter conversion complete.

The ocean to the west pleased him. With a small offshoot that ran through the city before returning to the main stream, the river Orontes was a wonder. "Was this river branch and middle island always here?" Joazar asked. "Or was the river diverted into the city by engineers?"

Jugurtha and Pericles did not comprehend his questions. They did not understand his wonder at this city of fountains. The open river within and alongside the city, the lake just a short walk away, the bridges and wetness, and even the smell of saltwater on the western wind overwhelmed him, but only him. Antioch was a city of water. Jerusalem had no water. No river, no lake, no ocean, no stream, no reason for its persistent presence for one thousand years. Destroyed and stubbornly rebuilt, treasured yet eternally dry.

Joazar took his woman in silence to the water's edge one night, threw her in, and was delighted to see that she could swim. She walked back with him, silent and fearful, dripping in the street. For him, the rich abundance of water was as overpowering as perfume.

10

135-134 BCE

KEZIAH FILTERED EVERYTHING Galilean through dislocation and loss. Everything in Galilee was foreign to her. Judea was barren and rocky, pocketed with only discrete and limited oases. By contrast, Galilee displayed endless miles of greenery in valleys lipped by magnificent rock. It was as though the entire land was composed of vast, connected garden bowls whose fertility ran up the sides of one and spilled over into the next. Some markets sold not select imports but endless varieties of the same item. Multiple types of olives. New grapes. Sarah taught Keziah which wheat strains were better for yeast-raised doughs and which were for unleavened bread recipes. In Judea, there was just wheat.

That summer, Keziah also worried continuously about Joazar. When she heard of the Greeks' elephants, she searched for someone to draw one for her. None could be found. Some tried to describe the creature to her, but she did not believe what she heard. The dimensions and features were imaginary and could not be real.

In the fall, none were able to go to the festival because of the siege. When the Seleucids departed, winter followed. News spread regarding the robbery of David's tomb. The people of Galilee could scarcely believe what they heard, and the region churned with bitter families bereft of both sons and honour. No veterans of the Jerusalem siege told tales of heroism. Love for the Maccabees vanished, and throughout the land, people repeated the new refrain: "Hyrcanus is no Simon."

Ephraim, Keziah's adoptive father, took her aside and broke the news to her: her brother was one of the hostages, a human deposit to guarantee Jerusalem's future submission, sacrificed along with David's gold.

The rest of the winter was darker than her summer and fall. The early storms had been fast and unpredictable; they caught people unprepared in fields and markets, soaked through their clothes, and then they were gone just as quickly. Fall storms required adaption to volatility but little endurance. The fall matched Keziah's internal weather in those days. She could be rescued by Sarah, by Little Jacob, by the responsiveness of the lute. The winter, however, was different. Winter was a sky of blackly oiled metal that descended upon the earth as a curse of cold and gloom. The weight of her winter grief threatened more than the fall's thunder and lightning and dramatic rain. Winter's dark days refused to end. One day followed another, and a dull horizon crept evermore over her, into her, exposed the immovability of what had been and could never be again.

Each new day produced no revival, no relief. She would never see her mother again. Never again her father. She would never unsee the killing of Little Moshe.

It was beyond her imagination that, on top of all that had happened, she had lost Joazar as well. Her mind struggled to grasp the idea. The unrelenting pain was all that she would remember of that first Galilean winter.

"How could this happen to me?" she whispered one night to Sarah.

"Child," the woman said by candlelight, "why did you think it couldn't?"

Reports circulated of Seleucids and Jews dying on the road to Antioch. Keziah dreamed of Joazar among the dead, unburied beyond the northern borders of Israel. When she awoke, something lodged inside her and would not leave. It coiled in secret places, fed a burning in her throat, and wrapped itself in a cloak she called fear but knew to be something deeper. She did not speak of it to anyone. Madness did not run in their family.

It was some months after the dream when Keziah found something special in Galilee. It was a place near the house. She found it after winter had passed and when spring was just beginning. Stepping out the front door into sunshine, she made her way through the dusty courtyard gate, past the rough-hewn stone well and its old jar, into the glistening field on the left, across the field, over a wall of gathered, tight-grained stones, and into the almond grove beyond. That first day, the white blossoms had just begun to drop. Past the almonds were pomegranates, their red and extravagant flowers starkly contrasting with the almond's pristine white. Then came a small creek. Beyond the creek stood a sagging, lordly oak.

Before the oak, in the midst of the creek, lay a flat rock. The water divided around the rock in separate channels. The rock was three times Keziah's length and sat slightly above the flow of water. It was a simple matter to step across the creek's nearest branch to the small flat-topped platform. From there, she could simply leap from the rock to the far bank and be in reach of the great oak's shadow. It was on this small rock island, surrounded by the music of the creek, that she first began to feel something approaching hope.

Little Jacob had shown her the creek and the stone the first time. He taught her to pick the unripe almonds, shed the green husks, and consume the future nut inside while still a clear jelly, formed but not hard.

A day came when Little Jacob burst upon Keziah to tell her he had a surprise for her.

"Just come," he said. "But it's a secret. We have to be quiet."

He led her out of the house and through the courtyard, past the well and its forgotten old jar, and then left across the field, towards the wall of stones and over it. "Careful," he said, as though she had never been this way before.

He did not rush toward their usual path through the now green and lush almond trees but steered her to a different route on the left.

"Don't make any sound. Don't let him see you."

He crept along, hunched down, and she did the same. The little boy was all drama, and she supposed that there must be a deer down at her rock island or maybe early pheasants.

She saw the deer first. A stocky example. Too stocky. It was a donkey, standing in its tracks, grazing and unaware.

"Careful now," the boy said. They crept along a line of bushes that were beginning to bud.

There was noise down at the creek, the grunts of hard labour followed by the dull bass note of something heavy settling into position.

"We nearly missed it."

Little Jacob pushed through a tangle of branches and new leaves, stopping at the edge of their hideaway, and sat down. Crouching over him, Keziah peered at her little island from an unfamiliar angle. A man was there on her rock. And a tree. Or rather the delimbed trunk of what had been a great tree, propped up horizontally on temporary braces. She looked around and confirmed that none of her trees had been cut down. The donkey cart was empty; the tracks behind it were deeply rutted. The man must have brought it on the cart. Wherever the tree came from, its thick bark showed that it had been an old tree.

The young man worked on the opposite side of the tree, chopping at its underside. After several energetic swings of his axe, he then applied himself to a saw before stepping back to inspect his work. As he turned, Keziah felt a jolt of recognition: Joseph. The set of his jaw caught her breath as it had when she'd first seen him in Cana. The hard hollow below his cheekbones where his beard was thin contrasted with the warm smile that always revealed itself, simmering below the surface, even when he was serious. He was often serious. His smile, however, did not change the physically imposing presence that he shared with his brothers. Like them, he was built a bit taller and broader than most. The woodworker's trade shaped his shoulders. Joseph could have stood before the long-haired man with the flail, her mother's assailant, and stopped him. He could have halted the entire crowd. His seriousness, his smile, his size would have saved the lives of Mother, Father, and Little Moshe.

Joseph kicked casually at his braces, and the log thumped down onto the stone—it was the same sound she had heard before—and then he leaned on the trunk, trying to roll it. The early spring air was cold, but he worked without an overcoat, his bare arms flexing. Once satisfied, he gathered up the metal bar and thick poles he had been using as braces, and he hopped across the creek and set them in the cart. He gave a word to his patient donkey, which let a ripple of muscular tension pass from his withers to haunch, and then Joseph returned to the island carrying a leather-wrapped bundle.

Keziah could not see him as he knelt behind the log, but when he re-emerged, the leather bundle hung across one shoulder and from it hung several chisels and a mallet. He was holding a smaller axe with a blade on one side and a spike on the other. He set to work on the log's centre, facing away from Keziah and Little Jacob's hiding place. First, he stripped bark from one area and then began to attack the trunk with fierce and steady strokes that pulled material away in crude triangles. Most of the curls and butchered chunks fell on the far side, hidden from Keziah's sight, but occasional pieces escaped onto the visible side where they lay like creamy curls on black rock.

She could not tell what he was doing. She could only observe his efforts and the glisten that highlighted the shape of his arms. He seemed unaware of his audience. His face wore an expression that Keziah could not read.

An hour went by, and then he paused, knelt over the creek, drank deeply, and walked back to the cart with another word for the donkey. He opened a small package and began to eat. He walked around to the front of the cart and seated himself before the donkey, which regarded him with a placid expression.

Keziah felt a cramp in her side, and she stood uncomfortably, still half-crouching, and motioned Little Jacob to follow her. The boy followed until they were well away from the worksite. "What is he doing?" she whispered.

"He's working on a log," Little Jacob whispered back.

"What is he doing with the log? Why has he put a log there?"

"He makes things. It's what he does. Metal and wood. He's a maker."

"I know that. What is he making?"

"I didn't ask him. How would I know? It's Joseph from Cana."

"I know it's Joseph." She shifted uncomfortably, her emotional irritation becoming physical. "What is he making?"

"Maybe he's making a boat."

"Why would he make a boat? The creek is too small for a boat."

"His cousins live in Kfar Nahum, and they make boats."

"He's not making a boat."

"Maybe he's making an idol!" the boy said, his eyes suddenly alive. "Maybe it's one of those—"

"Stop it!" Keziah said. "He's not making an idol."

"You *hope* he's not making an idol. Because if he's making an idol, then there is going to be a big fire down here, and then there's going to be another big fire when his father's shop is burned to the ground, and—"

"That's enough, Jacob. He's not making an idol."

Evening came and with it the family meal. Ephraim and Sarah made conversation with the children, and then Keziah and Sarah cleaned up while Ephraim took his son outside to attend to a chore. There was never a good moment to go back to the stream and investigate the log—the sun set on a quiet house.

"Why is Joseph without a wife?" Keziah asked.

Sarah looked at her through the lamplight with an inscrutable expression. "She died."

"I know she died, but how?"

"Giving birth. She was too small."

11

131 BCE

At night they roamed Antioch like mercenaries fresh with blood. They craved drink, tavern noise, and cluttered speech. The three criss-crossed the city with a Greek guard trailing.

❧

"You can't go home to your wife tonight," Pericles laughed. "And your concubine won't have you either."

Jugurtha scowled and pointed to a new establishment. Pericles and Joazar followed.

"Captives and professional whores," Pericles said. He leaned in, face to the table, eyes upward to view Jugurtha through a tangle of overgrown eyebrows. "A lot simpler." A crooked smile slowly formed on his lips. "Do you disagree?"

"When Alexandrus quit his contest with Menelaus,"

Jugurtha said, "he was transported back to Helen. She hated him, and he wanted her even more."

"What came from it?"

"He ordered her to his bed, and she went. Homer says it so simply. Consummation as the final word. Satisfaction and conclusion."

"Ignore the hate. Keep the action." Pericles barked loudly, the Cretan's laugh, and then drank with a gurgle and wiped his face.

"Bathsheba was our Helen," Joazar said. "Also stolen by a king. Her husband murdered. Our story led to no good either."

Jugurtha raised his eyebrows in exaggerated surprise. He turned to Pericles. "The Jew joins our debates."

Pericles barked again and pounded his now empty mug on the table, caught the attention of the sweat-soaked jug-bearer, and then turned his attention back to his friends. "Hera and Aphrodite put Zeus to sleep with sex so the rest of the gods could get on with war. Some fighting for Troy. Some fighting for the Greeks. Those kinds of gods I believe in." He laughed again and scanned the room. "Enough of this place. I have somewhere else to show you."

They went to the Serpent and then to the Four Heads Tavern. The Crossed Sword. The Half Leg. The Iron Heel. Each place had its beer, its wine, its crowds. Some crowds were raucous and others thin. Some hung their light in cages, others from chains mortared into boreholes and drilled through timbers. There were tipping oil spouts and glassed wicks and candles. In one place, a roaring fire billowed light and heat that drove the men out into the streets in search of cooler air.

The Trierarch was the largest. It crowded the shore of the Orontes. Befitting its namesake, it was built to look like a timber-braced galley that overlooked the water. More particularly, it resembled a great trireme, with two hanging sails and three rows of oars protruding on each side, all wood, hung with lanterns, and vented with more windows than any of the previous places the trio had been. Sailors and watermen filled it along with soldiers and men who Joazar presumed were brigands or mercenaries. Or both. The sort of women that Pericles preferred came and went and returned.

Despite the smell of the river and the lighter air, Joazar's stomach was unsteady. An illness grew, a creeping tension, a rise of acid, weakness in his hands. The name of the Serpent should have been a sign. With each new place, each fresh drink, each shift in conversation, his neck wound tighter. His skull became brittle. He felt a chill.

Carousing with gentiles no longer troubled him. It came with money and discourse, oblivious to the boundaries of Judean propriety. He ate pagan food freely, and sweet overcame sour. Old repulsions faded like childhood foolishness.

When it came to women, he spent his lust at first in Pericles's manner. Then he had settled on one and Jugurtha's role in the purchase no longer bothered Joazar. Captor had become host. There were no Jews to render judgment, no Greeks with better morals.

When his woman became pregnant, he found someone in need of a wet nurse and sold her. He never saw the child.

The next day he purchased a new companion of a different complexion. He did not test to see if the new woman could swim. He no longer cared.

When Jugurtha's concubine bore a child, it was taken to the river and slain and sent to the fish. This was the way of the Greeks. Others in the same situation took their infants to one of several temples and sacrificed them to whatever god there called for human blood. In this regard, Joazar's solution earned a more tangible profit. His friends in Antioch hailed him as a man who could teach his elders.

In the Trierarch, the feeling of unease continued to grow within him. He watched his companions drink and refill, watched them soak their bread in spiced fat and chew, watched them tell stories. He tried to chase illness away, but bread would not absorb it, drink would not drown it.

All were the same, like soldiers in heat, even old shopkeepers and retired bookmen and boys at their lessons. Every man cultivated crude relations around a core of greed, and the same spirit lived in every chest, the heart of Alexander, David, even Zeus. Every man hoarded the narrowest advantage and bred in the cruel pleasure-markets of the city. They were limited only by their means.

Pericles drank deeply and spat into a dark corner, then described some foul deed committed by another. Joazar did not catch who. Jugurtha laughed and passed judgment. Pericles continued, head down, eyes up, dealing out old or invented memories to fill the evening air.

Joazar focused on the space between the two men. He saw neither. He swallowed what rose within and took a dark drink to chase it.

The religion of Jerusalem had failed. If it had ever wielded power, that power was gone. It sold itself to the Seleucids, and in doing so, sold him into this new life. The ease with which he discarded childhood superstitions was proof of something he chose not to name.

Antioch offered alternatives. Unlike Jerusalem with its strict morality, the Seleucid capital gave men choices. If a child posed a problem that needed solving, then the market offered a solution. Or the river, or the temples. A man had only to choose. There was no wrong.

Joazar squinted, squeezed his head, stared through lamplight at the table. Tripe was mounded there. Cups scraped tabletops, lips glistened, voices spoke.

He felt tightness in his stomach. He felt heat rise within. He struggled as whole cartographies of ancient custom arose within him, the overwhelming feeling of his Judean boyhood trying to reassert itself.

Pericles laughed. A joke about deeds recorded in archaic poetry. Pericles postulated, and Jugurtha countered. Abrupt syllables softened, laughter deepened, expressions opened. The sound of gentile friends, the room, people coming and going, it all poured into Joazar like a bitter potion. Beer soured. The room bloomed with an air of must.

"Listen, you need to hear this," Jugurtha said. He pulled his friends closer. His short black beard glistened against gaunt cheeks. "All the literature of the Greeks tells the same tale." He started to explain himself and then coughed. Pericles pushed a mug forward, and Jugurtha drank. "The same tale." He launched into an account of gods seducing other gods.

"Hera blamed Poseidon for crimes she herself initiated," Jugurtha continued. He changed stories again without finishing his thought. He told of Zeus's son Sarpedon, slain by mortal Patroclus, while Zeus looked on. "He made it rain blood. Blood rain on the Trojans."

The light in the room shone yellow. People came and went. The air of the Trierarch hung warm about them.

Jugurtha continued with tales of gods at perversions, in hatreds, displays of spite, and pursuit of revenge. "Listen, you need to hear this," he said again. He scraped his mug against the heavy timber of the table, drank, studied the remaining liquid, and then looked at his companions. "Listen to this."

There was nothing new. Jugurtha toured treachery, lechery, tragedy, false friendship, and betrayal, told stories of mythic mortals as well as deities. The stories marched in parallel. No difference existed between mortal actor and divine except the particulars of reach. Neither man nor god aspired to anything holy. Holiness did not exist.

Through the window of the Trierarch, moonlight shone on dark water. A rippling path of bright white light led directly to Joazar, its cool glow contrasting with the Trierarch-lamplight's flickering yellow. No smoke stood against the moon. The moon's light held steady, shone with white purity, lay calmly on ripples of liquid darkness.

Jugurtha's discourse turned towards dim circularities. Mangled quotes and incoherent explications gradually became a match for Pericles's verbal disorder. The gods were all liars entertained by cruelty, wallowing in the capricious treatment of devoted subjects, the rapes of their peers, and the abuse of children. These were the ones that Pericles and Jugurtha followed. These were the gods that drove the Greeks and Romans. They were the version of gods that drove the Parthians and Arabs and all the nations of the world as well. All except for those of Joazar's abandoned homeland.

Joazar had been to Heraclea, a place four miles to the west of Antioch, close to the sea, where Apollo's Pythian temple rose from its park of wood and water. They called that place, with its temple, the Paradise of Daphne. There, he immersed himself in formal debauchery as part of his initiation into non-Jewry. There, he gave himself over to Jugurtha's way. Now, on the Trierarch, in the white light of the moon, Joazar found himself unable to bear it any longer. Their forbidden attractions freshly repulsed him.

Apollo was a rapist, a kidnapper, the murderer of his male lover, the murderer of his pregnant wife. He gave his son to a Cyclops, was a curse to his lovers and a petulant loser of musical contests, and used divine powers to humiliate his betters.

The woods and waters of Daphne's garden swam into memory. The grass there ran in long stretches between beautiful trees, the fields spangled with flowers and light and life. In it, he saw the Garden of Eden abandoned by attendant angels and overrun by a debauched mob, blood spilling amid beauty. The filth of Cain and all his moral descendants polluted paradise. Even the women, captivating as they were, wore masks suited to their purpose in that place.

In the light of the moon, Joazar reached for the edges of the table before them. He wanted to see the innocent expression of a Judean girl, the rosy cheeks of his mother and Keziah. He released the table and drank from his mug. It soured in his throat.

Jugurtha's stories were not the source of Joazar's unravelling. The drink, the food, the culture, this bestial view of humanity was not what stirred acid within.

"So similar," Pericles said. "Very, very similar." He was

comparing a woman he had once hired to a local statue of a goddess. Joazar missed which.

He thought of the woman he sold, the mother of his child. Her tears had not been real tears. Not the tears of a Judean girl in love. She cried as one might cry for a lost piece of jewellery, the frustration of having to adapt to a new master. There was no soul there. Nothing in this empire cultivated the possibility of a soul. Only power and hatred and pleasure thrived, with no room for souls.

"I don't need to experience a goddess to know," Jugurtha said. "The gods keep coming down for ours. That's proof enough." Pericles roared, and both men grinned at Joazar. They talked at once then, over and against each other, building on Jugurtha's discovery.

Joazar looked out, confused, into the darkening room. Nothing there spoke to him. He took his hands off the table. Put them in his lap. Calmed his breathing.

"What do you think, Joazar?" Jugurtha asked. His bloodshot eyes shone, and he did not wait for a reply.

It is not their philosophies, Joazar said to himself. *Not what we've done. It's the gods themselves.*

He looked out again at the river. A bat darted erratically in silhouette, an unclean ellipse in moonlight, and then was gone. He gazed at the white light that remained and knew the nature of the thing that would not give him peace: there was no purity here. Not in their temples. Not in their relationships. Not in their gods or even in the ambitions of their gods. Stripped of poetic metre and oratory art, the divine tales exposed a degraded form of bestial humanity. The house of deity was a madhouse governed by mad gods. Nothing holy existed in any variation of the pantheon. Humankind's role was simple: skirt the attention of the gods, seek their clemency or succour only as much as needed, and revel in as much godlike madness as circumstance allowed. The only difference between slave and king was means. Their wallowing and their end were the same.

The night at the Festival of Booths appeared to Joazar again in his memory. He and Father with Ebed between them. So many years ago. The walk through those temporary dark paths between branch huts became as real to him as the Trierarch's yellow light. He could hear children playing in the night, and husbands and wives in intimate conversation, varieties of mundane tenderness revealed. Then he had only witnessed the scene. Now he understood it.

A fundamental difference shaped Jerusalem's festival fellowship, a difference born of beliefs not found in any branch of the Greeks' empires. A degenerate tangle of warring gods could never create such a festival as Sukkot, the Ingathering, the Festival of Booths. Such a thing required a different god. A holy God.

As these thoughts and memories surfaced, his rejection of all things Jewish came to Joazar like a wraith of condemnation. Bright moonlight exposed him, and he saw himself as a garden self-trampled by whoring and drunkenness. His guardian angels were lost. There were no heroes anymore. Ebed crawled about in the dark, looting David's tomb. David was a lecher and a murderer. The universe was either all Greek and empty or something that was once good and now abandoned, forever unrecoverable.

"If there is an ideal that fails but is still true, should a man pursue it?" Joazar suddenly asked.

Jugurtha stopped. The question collapsed his latest loop

of thought, and he turned his puzzled and drunken face towards Joazar. Lamplight flickered.

They were on to a stronger wine now, and it made Joazar's eyes slip off focus. He pushed both hands firmly against the table again.

"It's the Stoics now, is it?" Jugurtha said. "Stoics don't do what they say. And they live miserable lives trying to mend the gap."

"The ideal is in the third room," Pericles said, pointing. "She's not cheap, but she's worth a pilgrimage through the crowd to get there."

12

132-130 BCE

Two men leaned over Joseph's shoulders. Oren and Peretz. His older brothers. Only the three were present in the family workshop at the foot of Cana's hill. His brothers crowded around Joseph as the early evening sun illuminated his work. He turned the blade within a recess, nearly erasing the curve marked in charcoal.

"You're putting too much into it," Peretz said.

Joseph grunted and shook both shoulders, a move that should have cleared space. Like Joseph, both his brothers were big, and neither stepped back. Oren leaned closer. "I didn't need to build a fancy box to find a wife," he said.

Joseph put his chisel down and stepped back with his arms out, forcing the others to make room around him. Anger rose in Joseph, betrayed by a smile's shadow. He looked at the case, at Oren, and then at Peretz. "I need a solution for a hinge," he said. "Something to match this inlay."

"More complicated than they have to be," Peretz said, "those joints. How long did it take you to cut? Simple joints would be just as strong. Take a quarter of the time. And the inlays . . . " He didn't finish the thought.

"It's for her," Joseph said. "For the hinge, I'm going to go back to my original idea."

Peretz's hand twitched. He glanced at the box and then back at Joseph. "You've been working on this for two months. You're going to dismantle it to redo the hinge?"

"Does this hinge match the rest of the case?"

Peretz looked around the shop. "We make wagons. Carts. Plows. Big things. Heavy things."

"She's like a songbird," Joseph said. "Her with the lute. She makes beautiful music. The case needs to be just as good."

"Nests are made of mud and sticks," Oren said. "That's good enough for a bird."

Joseph turned and raised a hand, and the brothers scattered, laughing. They left the shop then, and he watched them walk up to the hill. Joseph returned his attention to the bench. The olivewood case waited, strapped tightly to the table. He held the chisel in two hands and carefully guided the tilted point around the unbalanced curve. Rough became smooth as the curve deepened. The charcoal line disappeared. When he was satisfied with the cavity, he tested the premade inlay piece. It fit perfectly this time but rocked on a high point. He removed the inlay again, set it aside, chose a different tool, and began to work the recess, blowing each lifted layer away, gradually flattening the seat.

He worked the recess and thought about a new hinge. One mind on two tracks.

❧

His heart-stopping excitement throughout the engagement and wedding was not in any way diminished for having done it all before. If anything, he was more aware. Of himself. Of the others. Of her. Especially her.

When they closed the door on the world, just the two of them alone, he was surprised to discover the case in the room with them. Firelight cast a glow. The olivewood case seemed to not merely reflect that glow but cast its own light into the room. Her beauty was distracting, but Keziah led Joseph to the instrument and directed his attention back to the case. He had not seen it since the night of their engagement.

The closed case was a work of art. Oiled and waxed, the olive grain traced shades of creamy white, tawny hazel, and deep, dark brown in wild and scattered patterns. The lines of wooden waves evoked movement, energy, and life. The mid-tone figure in the wood grain caught the light when tilted; those sections seemed to move, to reveal a liquid and shifting subsurface.

He stood behind her, against her. She leaned back against him. Her hands reached out and trembled as she touched the case. She felt where the natural wood tones transitioned sharply between hues. "I expected it to have ridges here," she said. "The light plays tricks. I can see right into the grain, but to the hand, it is smooth. The wood is alive."

She turned into his chest, looking up at his face. "You made it," she said.

He touched her then, where he had never touched her before. She stopped him, a mischievous look in her eyes, one he had never seen before.

She motioned him back and seated him on the bed. Then she returned to the case with her back to him. She opened the case and took the lute out slowly. She turned to him then and began to play, the same look in her eyes. She motioned for him to stay where he was when he tried to stand. She remained near the case and played for him. She played as he had never heard her, or anyone, play before. His eyes took her in as his ears absorbed the lute, and such was his desire that he didn't understand what he heard at first. She repeated it. He looked at her hands, her fingers, and then her face. Her eyes. Then he began to hear as well as see. He understood that there was a call, an invitation in what she was playing, a language in the notes, the shifting melody, the follow-on bass tones, the peculiar way she brushed and tapped the shell as she played its strings, a language that made promises. When she saw that he understood, she stopped. She smiled at him. She put the lute away and unbound her hair, and it fell down her back and shone in the firelight. It was what a wedding night was supposed to be.

In the years that followed that night, she did not give him a specific song, but there were patterns in some of her melodies that alluded to their first night—a minor key, a rhythm, something in the tune that he was not musically gifted enough to articulate but was man enough to recognize. It was her way of calling him. Throughout the years, she never used words for this. She often used music. He never misunderstood her, never misread the notes. There was a secret countermelody that only she knew how to call out of the strings, and only he heard, even when she played with others in attendance.

The first time he heard that subtle music within the music in public was only a few months after the wedding. He looked up in surprise during the gathering. There were nearly two dozen present and five at instruments, a night of laughter and friends. Then came that sub melody, a version he had never heard before but knew was part of the same suite of sounds. Her fingers touched strings and tapped in a manner too complicated and fast to follow completely, always creating a second pattern beneath the music's main course. No one could ever imitate it if they even heard it. He heard her in that full and social room and understood. He looked across the room in surprise. She caught his eye, looked away, repeated the call at the strings, and then looked at him brazenly, the way a wife should never look at her husband in public. Her eyes twinkled, and then she glanced away again, but as she did, she let that secret melody slip out and across the strings one more time. It faded, lingered at the forefront of his mind for the rest of the night as he tried to maintain focus on the good people of Cana who had known him since he was a boy. The girl from Judea stole his focus from across the room without saying anything. The others present were oblivious to their silent discourse.

He led her home that night in a dream of distraction, and they came together with a passion that, if it were not for Solomon's famous song, he would have believed they, just the two of them, had invented for the first time. Something new in the history of humankind. It was private, between the two of them, and was more than either could have hoped for or imagined. She rarely made music in public, but she played nearly every day, and he always knew when she was just playing and when she was calling him. He never misunderstood.

13

129 BCE

A RIDER CAME TO Antioch bearing news. The three friends were on Jugurtha's second floor while the women were away.

"Not even a Seleucid," Jugurtha said. "Some Cretan messenger." He looked at Pericles as though it were his fault.

"The message?" Joazar asked.

"The Parthians have freed Demetrius," Jugurtha said.

Pericles stood up, his face a mask. He took a step before Jugurtha put a hand on him.

"Not now, my friend," Jugurtha said. "Not now."

Pericles stayed standing.

"What is it?" Joazar asked.

"Politics," Jugurtha said. "Strategy. Damnably good strategy." He stared out across the balcony and on towards the distant sea.

"I don't understand," Joazar said.

"Sidetes holds the throne in trust for his brother," Jugurtha said.

"For Demetrius."

Jugurtha nodded. "The Parthians are losing the war. So, they've released Demetrius. He'll come back to Antioch and reclaim the throne. From his brother."

"And?" Joazar looked at both men, who seemed to be reading more into these events than he could decipher.

"And Cleopatra Thea. His wife."

Joazar still didn't follow. "But Sidetes and Cleopatra Thea have children now," Joazar said.

"You're catching on."

"No, actually, I'm not."

The three men waited. Pericles seated himself again. The three sat on the floor, near the balcony but not on it. They kept to where there was shade. Someone, somewhere, was smoking a pig, and the scent drifted through. It was an invitation without a location.

"You're going to have to explain this to me," Joazar said.

"The Parthians have released Demetrius," Jugurtha said. "He'll come back and want his throne and wife back now."

"Do the Seleucids have rules for this kind of thing?" Joazar asked.

Pericles barked with laughter and gave Jugurtha his attention.

"If the queen had managed to keep herself out of Sidetes's bed—" Jugurtha started.

"Her brother-in-law's bed," Joazar said.

"Yes. Without that indiscretion, the brothers would be able to work it out. Sidetes steps down. A co-regency. Something."

"Greeks aren't Romans," Pericles said. "They don't share women."

"I've been here six years," Joazar said. "Seleucid morality eludes me."

"He still talks like a Jew," Pericles said.

"There'll be civil war then," Joazar said. "Between brothers."

"That's the strategy part. The Parthian strategy. They release Demetrius and start a civil war between the brothers. Such a war will put our fight with the Parthians back at least four years. All unproductive expenses. A waste. Instead of finishing off the Parthians, we're going to fight among ourselves now and see which brother comes out on top."

࿐

Joazar found himself at the Trierarch two days later with Pericles.

"Jugurtha will be along shortly," Pericles said.

The early evening light was grey, the room a third full and filling more quickly than usual. They claimed a place in a corner.

"News?" Joazar asked.

Pericles shrugged and offered a few words that Joazar could not make out. The Cretan spoke Aramaic as clearly as anyone, but at times he spoke with no meaning. If Joazar failed to understand on the first try, he no longer asked a second time. It would be worked out later, or never. Cretan restatements were pointless.

When Jugurtha arrived, the tension in his jaw forecasting his mood.

"Stupid man," he said.

"Who?" Joazar asked.

"Sidetes. King of stupidity."

"What is it?"

Jugurtha looked at Joazar and then at Pericles. "You don't know? Sidetes is dead."

The details came out between deep swallows from a large mug. The king had not known about his brother's release and tried a final military push against the Parthians before returning to winter quarters. A lucky arrow found him in a crowd. The king in trust was dead.

"No civil war then," Joazar said.

Jugurtha downed two fresh mugs as soon as they arrived and then held onto them like weapons in white-knuckled hands.

Pericles joined Jugurtha with the double-fisted mugs, rapidly swallowing and forcefully finishing. Joazar looked to each man and waited. Two more rounds passed before he broke the silence. "I suppose with Sidetes dead, the Parthians will regret releasing Demetrius now."

"I don't care about Parthians," Jugurtha said. "I'm not going back to being a house slave."

"What do you mean 'house slave'?" Joazar asked.

Pericles launched an orderly row of syllables, forming identifiable words that, strung together, did not communicate anything intelligible.

"House slave," Joazar repeated, looking at Jugurtha and ignoring Pericles. "Explain yourself."

"I provided a valuable service, and I have continued to manage—"

"Jugurtha!" Joazar interjected. "What do you mean 'house slave'?"

"You can't manumit someone else's property," Pericles said. Suddenly he was perfectly clear. "Sidetes set him free, but he belongs to Demetrius. Not Sidetes."

"Manumission doesn't hold now," Jugurtha said. "Not with Sidetes dead and Demetrius back from the dead."

"You're a slave again?" Joazar said. "Under Demetrius?"

Jugurtha's answer was a very long swallow from Pericles's mug.

"Let me see if I've got this straight," Joazar said. "The manumission cut you entirely free, even after Sidetes's death. Right? Those were the terms?"

"Yes."

"And Sidetes is now dead," Joazar said.

"But Demetrius is not."

"Is Demetrius king yet?"

"He will be." Jugurtha looked away from Joazar. He cast his gaze about the Trierarch and then contemplated an empty mug.

"Is Demetrius back yet?" Joazar asked.

"He will be."

"You are Sidetes's freed servant for now. Right?"

"For now."

"You're still in charge of the treasury."

"For now." His tone became increasingly clipped.

"Then you can do anything you want," Joazar said. "You serve no one but yourself right now. You are freer today than ever before."

"Except Demetrius, not Sidetes owned me, and he didn't agree to any—"

"Jugurtha, for the love of Zeus, pay attention. Demetrius is not in Antioch yet. We need to leave! Now!"

"The Jew wants to run," Jugurtha said with a wry smile for Pericles.

"We need to leave," Joazar said again. "We! Us! You included."

Jugurtha paused and focused more closely on Joazar. "What are you trying to say, Jew?"

14
129 BCE

TWO DAYS PASSED during which Jugurtha introduced his wife and children to the idea of a trip and brusquely packed them off to the dockyards. He ushered the harried woman onto a ship with her children and bid them goodbye. Jugurtha had paid the captain handsomely to speed their departure. The women in the second apartment were freighted with freedom papers and money, for which they expressed an appropriate amount of both gratitude and feigned sorrow. A final demonstration of manufactured bedroom passion ensued, and then they too were gone, departing with barely suppressed glee.

Joazar looked around the vacated rooms. Discarded clothing and furniture lay scattered about in disarray. The scene evoked many emotions, but not one of loss.

"A calculation," Jugurtha said. "All of life is a calculation."

Pericles entered, carrying empty saddlebags. He

gave his fellow conspirators a brief look. "Still discussing philosophy?"

Neither answered.

Distraction ruled the city. Seleucid mourning for one king conflicted with celebration for the other's imminent return. The queen of both kings did not indicate which mood should triumph. Tension prevailed. Opportunity for offence gleamed at every corner.

"Work," Pericles said. "Debate the meaning of it all later."

The boxes from the treasury did not belong in Jugurtha's private apartment. The transfer of their contents into saddlebags went far beyond a mere accounting irregularity. The men got to work quickly, and when they left the apartment, they had to work in pairs to carry the bags down one at a time. They left one treasury box behind, still filled with the weight of wealth they could not accommodate.

❧

"Avoid Apamea," Jugurtha instructed.

"West then," Pericles said. "Along the sea."

At noon they encountered grey mud. Cold and viscous, it sucked at sliding hooves. Hours passed before they found a solid track that led them through the marshland and closer to salty air. Before dark, their route began to climb. They passed through stunted oak and sycamore. The ground grew soft again. Between trees, thick vines draped downed limbs, spread over all, climbed neighbouring trees in a wild tangle. The wood beneath the vines was softer than the ground.

The horses stepped on twitchy legs and swung their heads from side to side in low-energy protest while the two saddlebag-laden donkeys protested with more vigour. They were cured of resistance by way of a green switch.

They set up camp in a place where a grove of oak had been flattened in times past by some vast devastation. Only a small residue remained of the forest. The chopped fuel held water, smoked in the fire, produced neither heat nor coals. They ate a cold dinner.

"Enough," said Pericles.

They put out the fire and, in doing so, raised a billow of smoke. Each slept dissatisfied in the vine-covered field without putting up the shelter. It rained in the night. They departed at daylight, wet, with empty stomachs.

"Better hungry than caught," Jugurtha said.

"He's still a long way from Antioch," Pericles said. "And once he does get there, it'll be days before he learns of your treachery."

"Theft. Not treachery."

Pericles did not answer. Joazar resolved not to be drawn into Jugurtha's mood. They rode without further conversation.

For three days, the sky swirled, soaked, dried, and blew with impunity.

On the fourth day, they were, by Pericles's calculations, only abreast of Apamea, maybe twenty-five miles to the west of it and the Orontes River, their trail occasionally giving them glimpses of the Great Sea. They were well on their way to Judea now, but not nearly as far south as the trio would have liked. They came down off a long, sloping hill strewn with loose rock that made each step slide and each heart race. Pericles was the only one of the three not to shout or curse on the way down. They crossed a shallow stream at the bottom, refilled their skins, let the beasts water themselves, and then advanced on a field of high grass. They had come down the slope single file, but they drew abreast of one another as they approached the grass.

The grass was taller than they were. A crowd of elephants could have been concealed in that field. They entered it slowly, parted tall green walls, and made horse-wide paths. The green stood pristine between the three horses. Their paths created hallways for the two laden donkeys to follow. The horses and donkeys expressed alarm with wide, rolling eyes, as though fanged beasts might emerge from this strange forest. It reminded Joazar of the towering fields of sarissas outside Jerusalem just six years before.

They camped amid the tall green sea, unable to discern how far they had come or how far they had yet to go. The ground below was a great mat of dead grass, compacted in years gone by and parted only by strands of new crops that rose on tremulous green stalks. If the mat below caught flame, the earth itself would burn. There would be no high ground to flee to. Their imagined pursuers would find their bodies blackened on the bottom and uncooked above, smoked all through. They slept without a fire.

At dawn, Jugurtha agreed to a cold morning ration, and then they pushed on through the grass as they had the day before. A few hours later, they found themselves walking out onto a rocky place.

"It feels too open," Joazar said.

They came to the road again far south of Apamea. Halfway to Sidon, two others joined them. They were rough-looking men who also rode horses.

The two groups exchanged nods and formalities. The strangers looked at the pair of donkeys burdened by small but heavy bags. They looked only glancingly at each other. They engaged Pericles with bright eyes, but their movements were careful and slow.

"Going to Joppa?" the taller man said. His head was misshapen like the product of some accident in childhood, easily distinguishable even by evening light. "Good port. Good town. Plenty for men like yourselves. But you don't need to go that far. Sidon is also good."

"Tyre," said the other. He was stockier, the shape of Pericles, a handsome head on a brute's body. "Or Strato's."

The two stopped when the three stopped that evening. The strangers watched Joazar and Pericles unload the donkeys. Their eyes shifted away and then back again; conversation around the fire had no rhythm. Jugurtha offered none of his usual philosophies, and Joazar was silent while Pericles did most of the talking. His speech lacked its native chaos as he addressed practical matters of immediate concern. No one offered anything genuinely conversational.

The three slept uneasily through the night. In the morning, the shorter, muscled man was gone with his horse.

Pericles and Jugurtha lifted one pair of heavy bags onto the first donkey while Joazar and the tall, misshapen man looked on. The two finished with the second donkey and then stood with the others.

"Where's your friend?" Jugurtha asked.

"He had some personal business to attend to."

"Did he leave this morning?"

The man shrugged.

"In the night?"

The man said nothing.

"I believe you need to speak for your group."

"He's not my group," the man said. "Just a traveller on the road. I was glad to have his company."

"When did you notice he was gone?"

"Same as you."

"When we were all up and around?"

"Same as you."

"He was a quiet riser," Jugurtha said. "Leaving in the dark. You two sleeping so near each other."

"Didn't hear anything?" Pericles said.

"I sleep well. A fault."

They each mounted up but for Pericles, who led the two donkeys to his horse. He seemed to lose control of the three beasts as they swerved in front of the group and created a traffic jam of animals on the road. He cursed and made a commotion amid the creatures, steering them in a wide arc to straighten them out and point them back towards the road. In this way, he came out near the tall, misshapen man but concealed by the trio of animals. As Pericles was about to pass the stranger, he ducked under his horse's jaw and was suddenly below his opponent. A sword shot upward and slipped into the man's side just above his hip bone and deep into his internal organs. Pericles shoved hard and then pulled the blade back and out with a twist and a slice, his other hand quickly grappling for the animal's reins.

The big man fell from his horse and hit the ground with a gasp and crack of bone. In a moment, Pericles had all four animals in hand. He gave over the fistful of reins to Jugurtha and returned to their visitor.

Pericles knelt and studied him while the man looked back with wide eyes, clearly stunned at this sudden adjustment. A white bone projected starkly just above his elbow, but the man's other hand attended only to his opened side. "I had no part in no conspiracy," the man gasped. He held his stomach wound closed, but fruitlessly. The damage was not so much in the opening as all the cutting done inside.

"Maybe," Pericles said.

"Get me to a surgeon."

Pericles laughed. Quietly. He removed the man's sword and inspected it. It was of inferior quality to what they'd taken from Antioch, rusted in one long patch, poorly polished, not oiled. He tossed it to one side. He removed a dagger from the man's waist, but it too was of poor quality and maintenance. Pericles thumbed the blade and then met the man's eye.

"You sure you've said all you can say?"

The man hesitated. It gave Pericles his answer.

"On with it."

"Five others."

"Which way?"

"The way we came."

"Behind us?"

The man nodded.

"Why?"

The man's eyes strayed to the two donkeys with their load and then back to Pericles.

"I mean, why are five coming from behind? What were you two about?"

"That's our camp. We were to get supplies."

Pericles moved closer and opened up the man's shirt. There he found the money pouch and removed it. He snorted at its contents and then put it inside his own shirt.

"Zeus's mercy," the dying man groaned.

Pericles spat in the dust and eyed the moisture that glistened there. "Never heard of it."

While the man lay bleeding, they emptied his belongings onto the ground and took several wrapped packs of coins from each of the donkeys' bags over to the dying man's horse. When they rode out again, they were three men with three pack animals trailing. The misshapen man's gaze was steady and sightless, taking in a day that had barely begun but for him was now over.

"You going to find a home to welcome us, Jew?" Jugurtha asked. "Or are we going to wind up like that man back there?"

"We'll find something," Joazar said.

The road home was turning out to be as long and strange as the road away had been. The sun stood just above the horizon, but the day felt prematurely aged. They did not stop until long after dark.

15
129 BCE

KEZIAH AND JOSEPH'S first child, their own Little Moshe, was two years old when the hammer fell.

No. A false telling.

The blow came long before. Before Joseph. Before Galilee.

It fell in her Judean village, at the poleaxing of the first Little Moshe, her mother's leprosy discovered, a flail cracking bone and opening flesh. It fell when her Judean life ended.

What came this day was not the original hammer, but its echo on a long delay.

&

She stood at the door of their home in Cana. She held the new baby at her side, their second, a girl wrapped up, suspended in a sling. Moshe, her son, played in the yard. She watched him, and she saw her little brother within him, both souls in the same boy. Inside, she carried a sister's still grieving heart mingled with a mother's anxious one.

I'm just a girl, she said to herself. She remembered saying those words to the Iturean. The first year with Grandma Sarah had been a year of tears. Then came Joseph. So many changes since Joseph.

Moshe looked up from his play, saw her there, then returned to distractions.

Looking at Moshe, her little brother's image, Keziah's other memories emerged: the pole, the chunk of missing bone, the cry of her parents, the flail, the fire. Images appeared and skittered away like speechless ghosts flinging bright darts. Her arms loosened until just the sling held her new baby. Her face grew slack, lips parted and hung loose. She said nothing.

Past Little Moshe, she could see Cana's hill but could not bring it into focus. The sky shone blue. A push of heat washed around her and into the house behind. Beyond the yard, she knew, were cultivated fields, and beyond them, the valley and the river. She could not see any of it now. She saw fire. She saw the coarse weave of a blanket thrown over her, threads made brilliantly clear as light shone through its thin weave.

Something carnivorous loomed behind her confusion. It lurked like mountains behind a mist. Weight was present without detail.

She leaned against the door frame but did not feel it. She felt the bite of the cart's empty crates against her shoulder. She sensed fangs bared around her, could smell wild and rotted saliva. Jaws opened wide.

Her mother's voice came then. It diverted her from

the thing she should not see, whether memory or imagination. Her mother's voice steered her inner gaze elsewhere, away from a pit's edge. Her mother spoke about flour and about cream from the goat, how it differed from the cow's cream, and how she should use it differently with flour. The voice was unmistakable. She knew the soft leather of it, the smooth quality of Mother's sound, recognizable even when muffled and from another room. She could not grasp all the words, but that voice's texture filled her and was clear as colour.

Flour and cream instructions mingled with recent memories. Something about blending. Grandma Sarah had many flours but made no distinction between creams. Grandma Sarah's intrusion took Keziah too far from her distant memories. She lost her mother's voice in the fresh memory of Grandma Sarah's sound and was once again in the present. She straightened up in the doorway, refocused on Moshe's voice in the yard, the association with her long-gone little brother, and as tears formed, she tried with a breaking heart to find her way back to her mother's voice.

She could not recover it. It was gone.

The hammer landed in her Judean village many years before.

The memory of her mother's voice today was a distraction. It rescued her from something terrible: an echo of that first blow, the salivating jaws of something that knew her and wanted her and sought her. Something waited. Something needed to be seen fully to be fully born, and today had nearly been that day.

Keziah turned back into the house with the baby and forgot the shadow that her mother's voice had driven away.

❧

"How was the day?" Joseph asked later. They lay in the night together.

"Just rain clouds," Keziah said. "So dark in the middle of the day. And cold."

Joseph lay beside her with a frown. Her answer was strange, and the entire day had been hot and dry. The workshop was mere steps from the house. There had been no clouds, no cool, no darkness at midday.

16

129 BCE

NIGHT LIGHTNING PASSED from cloud to cloud over Cana's hill and its quiet inhabitants.

At Joseph and Keziah's home, windows let in the early fall night air as the day's heat lingered. The flicker of light in the sky complemented the flicker of the hearth. Lamps about the room were steady.

In the house, Uri hunched over his lyre. His great bear-like shoulders and round, muscular arms dwarfed the instrument. He was bald, with an extravagant beard to compensate, and always red-faced. Tonight, he laughed as his wife, Mahlah, played her shepherd's pipe with her right hand and the timbrel against her leg with the left. Keziah's lute traded the melody line with the lyre's harmony, and then both instruments faded into the background. The pipe moved the melody forwards, and then Rehavam's wife, Basmat, filled the room with the sound of her full-throated voice, offering low vocalizations without words. When the pipe turned to pass the melody line on to the singer, words spilled out at last. A love song. Unrequited love.

"Always unrequited," Rehavam said mournfully. The song concluded with a haunting echo of his wife's voice. The room burst into laughter, and she flicked a slip of cloth at her husband.

Joseph, too, sat listening. Like Saul from Kfar Nahum, Joseph was unable to contribute.

"I'm sorry Anna could not make it," Saul said.

"How are the babies?"

"Two at once is a lot. She doesn't sleep."

"At least she has the help of the older ones."

"We know someone's love isn't unrequited," said Rehavam.

"Well, four times at least," said Saul, and the room broke into laughter again.

Keziah touched the strings of her lute, then began to play again, quietly. It was music that explored the room and pulled conversations closer. The night air remained warm, entering and leaving the house on invisible currents.

They spoke about children, the events in Kfar Nahum, and Cana's news, and the rest of Galilee. All the while, Keziah played her lute in the background as Basmat's daughter slept with her head in her mother's lap, her hip against Keziah. The lute notes changed to match the discussion, never intruding, sometimes pausing if Keziah needed to contribute an explicitly spoken point to the conversation. Then she would pick up the melody again. Only the occasional sharp note penetrated like the fading flicker of outside lightning.

It was getting late, and all the children were asleep. They had yet to broach the reason for Saul's visit.

Saul turned to Uri. "I presume you've made something you'd like me to sell."

"We all did," Uri said.

"You've all become winemakers, then?"

"Not wine."

Saul's eyes lit up. "You're experimenting again."

"He's done more than an experiment," said Mahlah. "He's perfected it."

"This is different," said Uri. "You liked the distillation I came up with before."

"I've begged you to make more than just samples for friends. I need volume. There is a market for your wine in Alexandria and elsewhere that would make Galilee a destination for certain types."

"Rich types."

"I'm telling you I could—" He paused. "What is it that you've made?"

"Well, it doesn't have a name yet, but I can tell you it isn't easy to make. It's more than just a wine."

"Yes?"

"It's distilled more times than I care to admit. And I'm not using grapes."

"You tried apricots before."

"Quince," said Uri. "And a few other bits."

"Quince? Awfully sour—"

"Not when it's overripe."

"Unpleasant to handle."

"Perfect for my process. But not easy. The labour is high. Just separating the stems and the seeds takes time.

Not like wine. With quince, everything has to be carefully prepared. Then it has to go through multiple fermentation cycles. It can never be a large batch."

"How many then? A dozen jugs?"

"A dozen jugs or a few dolia at most. If I can access more trees, then within a few years I'll be able to make maybe two or three dozen each season. Maybe."

"I can sell it," Saul said, "but you'll never make money at it."

"I will if I sell it to you for ten times the price of my wines."

Saul choked and then laughed and then looked puzzled at the set of six serious expressions about him.

"Try it," Uri said. He took a stone jar and poured a small portion into a tiny cup.

"Bread first," Mahlah said, handing Saul a piece.

Saul tore off a small chunk, chewed it slowly, and then accepted the cup.

"Slowly," Uri said.

"I know how to drink wine," Saul said.

"This isn't wine."

Saul studied first the dark liquid and then his friends. Keziah stopped playing. Saul sampled the cup, and a soothing ripple seemed to spread across his features. He pursed his mouth but made no sound. Then he swallowed slowly and breathed in deeply. He still made no sound. Only the crackle of the fire filled the room's silence. He took another drink, eyes closed, and something like a tear formed at one eye. Finally, he opened his eyes again and looked past Uri to Mahlah. "You are right. He's done it." He sat silent for a few moments and then spoke again. "Tell me more."

"The formula is a secret. The process is impractical."

"But the product is something from heaven," said Saul. "Can you repeat it?"

"This is our third batch."

Saul started. "You've been sitting on this for years?"

"We need to sell more than just quince. We've been discussing this among ourselves for over a year. To make it profitable for us, we need to sell it to you at an enormous price. And for you to sell it in Egypt, we need to sell more than the taste."

"Alexandrians buy dried and pickled Galilean fish because it reminds them of home," said Joseph. "For some, it reminds them of a home they've never even visited. They pay a high price for the preparation and shipment, but in the end, it's just fish they are buying."

"Uri's creation needs to be different," said Rehavam. "When someone buys Galilean wines, they look like all the other Galilean wines until tasted. You sell Uri's wines at a premium because they are better, and the satisfaction comes when it's tasted. This new creation needs to sell for a lot more than just a premium."

"For this creation," Joseph said, "the satisfaction needs to start right away. The purchaser needs those around him to know what he's purchased even as he's bringing it home."

"At home, it needs to sit on a shelf and inspire desire just as an object," Rehavam said. "It should last a great deal of time. A specialty item. Not a wine to consume in one sitting. Not an everyday item."

"Small tastes," Mahlah said. "Special audiences."

"An audience?" Saul said. "For a drink?"

"You've tried it."

"I have."

"And?"

"I told you it tastes like something from heaven."

"Show him," Keziah said.

Joseph reached into a cupboard and pulled out a rough sack. He handed it to Saul, who removed from it a small, square box. "It's beautiful," Saul said. "Well made. Like something I'd expect you would make for Keziah."

The room watched him. He tried to open it. He discovered he could not. "You've glued it shut."

Basmat stroked her hand along the edge of the box, and it opened.

"We're only interested in your richest clientele," Joseph said. "We expect that you would sell these personally and show them how to open it. This is not a normal item."

Basmat closed the box again and handed it back. Saul turned it over, puzzled, and Basmat directed his hand to the concealed release. The box opened. Inside was a glass jar. Not stone. Not fired clay. Spun glass.

"You can't sell your product in glass jars," Saul said. "It's beautiful. Rehavam, you've always done beautiful work, but they'll break between here and . . . and anywhere."

Joseph and Uri stood up, went to the other room, and then returned carrying a crate between them. "There are twelve of these wooden boxes in this crate," Joseph said.

"And one glass jar in each box," Rehavam said.

"I filled and sealed them myself from the same batch you just drank from," Uri said.

Joseph and Uri raised the box to waist height. Saul's eyes widened, Joseph nodded, and they dropped the box.

Saul called out and jumped to his feet. All the commotion inadvertently woke Basmat's daughter. Joseph and Uri picked up the crate, placed it in the centre of the circle, and carefully removed and opened each box. Each glass bottle was cupped in packed straw. There were no cracks, no chips, no loosened seals, no leaks.

They passed the bottles around.

"Each one is different," Saul said.

"I didn't use a mould," Rehavam replied. "I made each one by hand. They all have the same general shape and scale, but I used different sands to make each one's colour unique."

"I could sell the bottles alone," Saul said.

"They're thicker than they look," Rehavam said. "A trick of the eye."

"They're beautiful. And they contain the nectar of heaven."

"We'll sell them to you by the crate," Joseph said. "The individual boxes are precise, and I made the crates so they all fit tight. You should keep the crates out of the rain. The boxes are oiled, but they will still swell if left out in the weather, and the straw inside should not get wet."

"None of that will affect the liquor," Uri said. "The bottles are sealed well."

"But the presentation is still part of the product," Saul said to Uri before turning back to Joseph. "I understand. You're reteaching me my own business. How much?"

They told him the price. It turned out that Uri's original quote had been an understatement. In all, the price was nearly twenty times the cost of Uri's usual wines.

"How much do you have?"

"Three cases plus a few extra bottles that we will keep locally."

"I'll take all three cases," said Saul. He looked both flushed and pale as he said it. "And I need one of your extra bottles. For samples. Special patrons only. To get them talking among themselves."

❧

"Since boyhood," Joseph said in the late-night dark, "all four of us have been working towards a project like this."

"You've trusted him with a fortune," Keziah whispered.

"We've already trusted him with a lifetime of friendship. The quince is just quince."

"Until it's sold."

"Until then. Then it's just money."

17

129 BCE

THEY PASSED SOUTH through Tyre, then Akko, and then farther south along Mount Carmel's dry slopes and the coast. Twice more, Pericles's blade found the insides of a fellow traveller.

"We're in Eretz-Israel now," Joazar said.

"The Land of Israel," Jugurtha said in translation.

Pericles nodded. The two men dragged a body off the road and hid it in the scrub there.

When they set out again, Jugurtha turned to Joazar.

"Folks are curious about the packs," Jugurtha said. "They're too heavy. They advertise what's in them. Where will we be able to settle in peace?"

"Well, we can't bring Pericles into Jerusalem," Joazar said. "Nor the money."

"We'll go to the port, then." Jugurtha turned to Pericles. "You can start setting up shop there."

"In Joppa?" Pericles asked.

"Yes," replied Jugurtha.

❧

The first time Joazar and Ebed had spoken to King Hyrcanus was shortly after he had ascended the throne. They had just been boys then. Shirtless, foolish, blood-smeared. Now Ebed wore clothes made with Egyptian cloth and reported directly to the king. The two old friends sat in Ebed's house in Jerusalem. Jugurtha was present for this strange reunion, and Joazar felt the bizarre vertigo of two incompatible worlds colliding. Servants passed by regularly.

"I need to understand the Seleucid situation," Ebed said.

Joazar was distracted. Servants didn't usually distract Joazar. Jugurtha's households had been full of them. He was distracted, though, by finding servants in Ebed's home. Even more so, he was distracted by the news that Keziah was still alive. A stranger had abducted her from the village and so saved her life. He found it hard to meet his friend's eyes. He found it hard to focus. He instead followed the movements of people he did not know.

"Jerusalem is in an uproar," Ebed said. "I need to know about the Seleucids."

"Sidetes is dead," Jugurtha said. "Demetrius is free and will reclaim the throne. There is a pretender to the throne: Zabinas. How the queen will respond to the competing claims is unknown. I presume she will throw her lot in with Demetrius, her former husband."

"We know all this," Ebed said. He leaned forward. "Our soldiers in the Seleucid army have returned for the winter."

"What about Keziah? Where is she?" Joazar asked.

"In Galilee."

"You should keep the army here," Jugurtha said.

"They are obligated to return in the spring," Ebed said. "The Seleucid war with the Parthians will continue once winter has passed."

"Where in Galilee?" Joazar asked.

"To who?" Jugurtha said. "The army will return to who?"

"Sidet—" Ebed stopped himself. "The Seleucid king. I see." He frowned.

"Where in Galilee?" Joazar asked again.

"Cana. She's in Cana," Ebed muttered before turning back to Jugurtha. "What are you suggesting?"

"Sidetes is dead. Why be involved in the fighting between Demetrius and Zabinas?"

"What else do you know about how she's been doing?" Joazar pressed on, but Ebed's attention was now fully fixed on Jugurtha.

"You're suggesting that we don't pick a side?" Ebed asked.

"Why would you?" Jugurtha said.

Ebed sighed but said nothing.

"You won't be able to convince King Hyrcanus to stand down and let the Seleucids fight among themselves if you cannot explain why," Jugurtha continued. "Why stay neutral? How does that benefit Jerusalem?"

"I don't know."

"What do you know about Keziah?" Joazar asked.

"Later, Joazar. You're suggesting we should let the Greeks fight among themselves, then throw our lot in with the winner?"

"Why throw your lot in with anyone?" Jugurtha asked.

"If we don't pick a side, we go to war with both of

them. They won't ignore us if we renege on the terms of our treaty." Ebed flexed his shoulders. "You're the one who negotiated the terms."

"Why did you accept?"

"Back then? We were doomed to lose."

"Why were you doomed to lose?"

Ebed stared at Jugurtha. He waved his hand in a circle, indicating Joazar, indicating the world beyond the room. "We were outnumbered, unprepared, starving behind our walls." He threw his hands up.

"Why were you outnumbered, unprepared, and starving behind your walls?"

"You were a nation equipped for drawn-out battles and costly conquest. Still are. And we were trapped in the city and running out of food."

"Ebed. Think." Jugurtha looked around and then back at Ebed. "You're a captain in an army."

"King Simon was dead," Ebed said. "You came right after our king was murdered."

"Not good enough. What was the first excuse?" Jugurtha asked.

"Excuse?"

"You were unprepared."

"We were unprepared. Our king was dead."

"It was just him who was dead," Jugurtha said. "Why was everyone else unprepared?"

Ebed stared at him. "It's Simon Maccabeus's fault now? You're saying what happened seven years ago was Simon's fault?"

"Where was the army when Simon died?"

"There was no army. Israel doesn't have an army. Its people are its army. When there is trouble, the nation rises."

"Arises from where?" Jugurtha asked.

"Everywhere."

"Where does it go?"

"To Jerusalem."

"To the defence of Jerusalem?"

"Of course." When Jugurtha did not respond, Ebed continued. "The temple is here. David's city. The palace."

"Everyone rallies to Jerusalem?"

"Yes," Ebed said.

"And leaves the rest of the country open?" Jugurtha asked.

"What else are we supposed to do with it?"

"Well, that depends on your objective. Do you want to win or starve behind Jerusalem's walls?"

"What would you have us do?"

"Why isn't your army at your borders?" Jugurtha asked.

"There is no army. We're volunteers. There are fields and boats and shops to attend to."

"Except when there's a war."

"Yes."

"When they are in Jerusalem."

"Yes." Ebed sat back now.

"With all their families and livestock and crops, of course."

"No." Ebed looked like he needed a backrest. "Of course not."

"You plan quite well," Jugurtha said. "You plan to lose. Whether that's Simon's fault or something in your collective habits or Hyrcanus's doing, I cannot say, but it's definitely a plan to lose. You give your enemy the entire country to feed and clothe themselves with while all your soldiers—your poorly armed, poorly trained volunteer soldiers—are cooped up in Jerusalem. Waiting to starve."

"You think we can post an army at the borders," Ebed said, "a professional army, with forts, equipment, training regiments, and maybe even a sailing fleet. That out of the desert shall miraculously rise an army supported by a thriving homeland industry to keep them armed, fed, clothed—" He laughed. "Let me know when you work that out."

"What would you need to do what you just said?" Jugurtha asked.

"Not much. A hundred thousand men, an entire manufacturing industry, a few buildings full of money. Some way to keep the harvest and shops and everything else running while our soldiers spend their days playing games of dice in border region outposts in case the Egyptians or the Seleucids or the Parthians or Nabataeans invade."

"You have a lot of enemies to defend against."

"We have a lot of greedy neighbours. At least the Seleucids keep everyone else away."

Jugurtha looked at Joazar with a flat expression. "You misled me, my friend," he said. "Your god. The stories of David. A holy nation. All of that."

Joazar said nothing.

Jugurtha turned back to Ebed. "So it's better to be the vassal of a pagan nation."

Ebed's expression darkened.

"Better to let your sons die in Parthian wars to enrich the Seleucids."

"What would you have us do?" Ebed replied.

"You already said what you need to do."

"We don't have a hundred thousand men or the industries we'd need to do anything differently."

"Why not?"

"Our women are no more robust than the women of any other nation. And our babies take the same amount of time to grow."

"How many soldiers are home for the winter?" Jugurtha asked.

"Five thousand. That's not an army to take on the Seleucids. Or anyone else."

"It's a start. How could you get more?"

"Mercenaries," Ebed said, "but we don't have that kind of money."

"How much do you pay the Seleucids in tribute each year?"

"That won't work. If we stop paying the tribute, the Seleucids will go back to war with us instead of fighting the Parthians."

"When is the tribute due?"

"You know the answer to that. Six months."

"Who is it due to?" Jugurtha asked. "Which king?"

Ebed opened his mouth. Then he closed it.

"How long will it take to resolve the Seleucid succession problem?" Jugurtha asked.

Ebed said nothing.

"Who is in charge of the Seleucid treasury now?" Jugurtha asked.

Ebed stared at Jugurtha. Finally, he spoke. "They've been at war with the Parthians for half a decade without winning anything. Can Demetrius afford to pay for a Seleucid civil war and a Parthian external war and still deal with a Jewish rebellion as well?"

Jugurtha smiled. "Now you're asking the right questions."

❧

Two days later, they met again. They used the flat roof of Ebed's house. Servants had been banned from the roof. Sunlight came aslant, reaching for them beneath the shade of the canopy. Tea cooled on an otherwise warm day.

"Tell me how this Sanhedrin operates," Jugurtha said.

"It's a court of seventy men," Joazar said. "They meet in the temple. They are an advisory body to the king and the supreme court for all of Israel. They oversee matters both religious and civil."

"And is it the Sanhedrin we need to convince or the king? Which one?"

"Both," Ebed said.

"Who has the power?" Jugurtha asked.

"They both do."

"They can't be equal. Who decides?"

"The king," Ebed said. He tasted the tea, then put it back down. "Based on how the Sanhedrin advises him."

"Seventy people advise him?"

"Yes."

"You can't have a conversation with seventy people," Jugurtha said.

"Their consensus advises him."

"You don't get a consensus from seventy people. I thought you said it was composed of two groups."

"The Pharisees and Sadducees."

"You don't get consensus from seventy people split between two different factions. Who is in charge?"

"The high priest," Ebed said.

"Then it's the high priest and the king we need to persuade. Who is the high priest?"

"Hyrcanus."

"Another Hyrcanus?" Jugurtha asked.

"The same one," Ebed said.

"John Hyrcanus is both high priest and king?"

"Yes," Ebed said. "It's not allowed, but he's doing it anyway."

Jugurtha studied Ebed. He shifted his gaze to Joazar and then back to Ebed. "Hyrcanus is the head of his own advisory body?"

❧

A day later, near midday, they walked the olive groves outside the city's eastern gate. The servants stayed near the road. The three men shared a bag of almonds, picking off the flaky husks and eating them one at a time as they passed through dappled light between trees.

"Hatred of the tribute is unanimous," Ebed said. "Start there. The Pharisees are against it based on the Torah. The Sadducees just like money."

"Then it's straightforward," Jugurtha said. "You keep collecting the same taxes but stop paying the tribute. Starve the Seleucid treasury. That's your income to run the new army."

"And we loot what remains of David's tomb for the upfront investment."

"Yes."

Ebed looked at Joazar.

"You're going to have to empty it," Joazar said. "All of it this time."

"There was enough left behind. Mounds. No one has been there since. It's all been resealed. How long do we have to get ready?"

"As long as the civil war runs," Jugurtha said. "Plus, whatever Parthia supplies by way of distraction. The Seleucids were winning before Sidetes died. The Parthians released Demetrius to create division. Sidetes's death was unexpected, but Zabinas's claim to power is stirring up the same civil war anyway. We have a few years. Maybe more. Long enough."

"Gentile mercenaries in Eretz-Israel won't be popular," Ebed said.

"Keep them at the border outposts," Jugurtha said. "The whole point is not to have all your forces in Jerusalem. Use the Jewish soldiers in Jerusalem and Jericho and the other major centres."

"And you're going to run this?" Ebed asked.

"Just the money part. Pericles will do foreign recruiting. We can't send Jews, and Pericles has experience with that kind of thing. Jews can serve as commanders once the mercenaries are here."

❧

"You're having doubts," Joazar said. It was just he and Jugurtha. Ebed had returned to the city for the evening sacrifice. For centuries, these olive trees had listened to the temple's call and heard disparate tongues carry across its slanting landscape, the languages of the Assyrians, Babylonians, Persians, Greeks, Nabataeans. The trees were gnarled into grotesque forms as though all they had witnessed had distorted, truncated, regrown, and damaged them in an endless cycle.

"The history of the Jews is that of overthrowing nothing," Jugurtha said. "Your people only know subjugation."

Joazar did not reply. There was nowhere to sit but the ground. Jugurtha seemed to have endless stamina, so they continued to walk.

"The freedom of your people has always been gifted or rented at the pleasure of greater civilizations," Jugurtha said.

"I wouldn't say greater."

"Subjugation implies lesser. They subjugate you. That makes them greater."

"What did you say coming down from Antioch?" Joazar asked. "That it was 'a plan to change history's unalterable trajectory'?"

"Yes, I said that. Probably around the same place I made you eat camel dung when we were going in the opposite direction."

"Make your plan work. Tomorrow, talk the Sanhedrin into throwing off the Seleucids, and you will launch an entire nation in a new direction."

"Let's hope it's a good one," Jugurtha said. He stopped and looked up.

Joazar followed his gaze. The sky above was cloudless. Blue darkened as the day lengthened. The smell of burning flesh came faintly across the valley from the temple. "It will be what God makes it," he said.

Jugurtha turned and looked at Joazar. "You've become quite the Jew again. I hardly recognize you."

"I have always been a Jew. I may have chosen to pass on this evening's sacrifice, but I have always been a Jew."

Jugurtha raised an eyebrow.

Joazar held his gaze. "I would advise you not to forget our agreement."

"I have forgotten nothing. We bury the details about your failures in Antioch. In exchange, you help me here. You get your old life back. I get a new one."

"Just persuade the Sanhedrin."

It took two days for Jugurtha to sell the Sanhedrin on his plan for Israel. The Pharisees supported him from the beginning. The Sadducees came around when they grasped the opportunity for profit. There were many ways that they could administer taxes that didn't leave Eretz-Israel. Such thoughts could be read in their eyes.

There was a final recess. Support was in hand, but there had not been a firm decision yet. The agreement lacked momentum. "Decisions need emotion," Jugurtha said, but he would not share his plan with Ebed or Joazar.

In the evening, the floor was again his. He stood before the Sanhedrin as he had before—with his shoulders back and head high, as a warrior, the descendant of chieftains, a man in his prime from a bloodline of kings, a man of money with secret knowledge and skills that these religious provincials could not equal. And then he relaxed his shoulders. His chin dropped. His eyes warmed.

"I have come to know one of your sons very well these past seven years. I have come to view him as my most intimate friend. Of the captives we took from Jerusalem, Joazar was my charge. Just a boy then, but I have never known a boy like him." Some of the older men leaned in to hear more clearly. "When we offered him foods that did not agree with your laws, he would not eat. When we mocked him and gave him no other food, he starved. When we relented and fed him an acceptable diet, he thanked his god instead of us. We made a sport of him. We tempted him with wine, with women, with a new life of freedom and riches in Antioch and all of these he refused. Once I realized that he had a brilliant mind, I placed him on my staff, but I could not resist testing him. He would not change his obedience to your country's laws, even as he served in the treasury of my country. He was like your prophet Daniel's friends. We might have tried to rename him Shadrach, but he always remained his original Jewish Hananiah.

"One year, he grew sick. I thought he would die. I could not understand how his god could allow a young man like this to die in lonely exile, and then it occurred to me that perhaps your god would cause this young man to die rather than suffer the torments of exile any longer. In his fever, he spoke about Jerusalem and its temple, and I understood then that there was nothing in Antioch's riches to tempt him because his love for this place and its god was so great. Anything I might offer was rotten by comparison.

"In my sojourn upon this earth, I have been to Africa, Arabia, Parthia, and all the reaches of the Seleucid Empire, yet your son in exile was the first holy thing I ever encountered." There was a hitch in Jugurtha's voice, and he paused and hung his head. His audience was still and focused. Jugurtha looked up, took in the seventy faces, and then continued.

"He taught me the law. He taught me your language." Then Jugurtha repeated himself in the old Hebrew. There was an intake of breath among the scholars in the room. He continued in the old Hebrew. He spoke it haltingly, as though it were more difficult for him than it was. "I learned about your god, who cannot be named. I learned your ancient stories. From this young man, I learned about David and Solomon and the splendours of your country. He read to me from the Psalmist when I lost a child, and I wept for the comfort and truth I found in those holy words."

Jugurtha paused and then returned to Aramaic. "But I knew that those words were not for me. I was a pagan, a gentile, a worshipper of wood and stone. I was unclean. My captive had become my teacher. There was nothing in my empire I could offer him because he had your god, and all I had to tempt him with was the filth and disease of unholiness that no dressing could make more appealing and no physician could cure. So, I left my country. I gave up riches and power. I abandoned a home, a wife, a seat at the head of an empire where I commanded men. I chose to cast my fate with this young man and his god, just like David's ancestor Ruth. I did not just come here to build you a new bureaucracy for war and defence. I came here to become a Jew, to be circumcised, to immerse myself in the waters of purification, to bring a sacrifice to your temple, to abide by your laws. I will fight for your nation and live my life dedicated to serving this country as my own—not as one trueborn but truly adopted.

"This is what this son of David did for me. One Jewish boy. Through him, I know what holiness is. I lived like royalty in Antioch, second only to the king with a Jew as my captive. I left everything behind to be one of you."

Jugurtha bowed his head, and the Sanhedrin remained silent. The king was present and seemed to be holding his breath. A priest finally came and escorted Jugurtha out.

18

129 BCE

"I SEEM TO RECALL him speaking old Hebrew much more fluently in the camp seven years ago," Ebed said. They were back at Ebed's home, alone again on the roof. "Your tutoring seems to have degraded his command of the language."

Joazar said nothing.

"You must be the holiest of men to spend seven years among the Greeks and remain pure."

"Are you going to be the one to re-enter David's tomb?" Joazar asked.

"Someone else can have that distinction. The old captain is the one remembered as the leader of that expedition. Will you go see Keziah?"

"Yes. You said she has two children?"

Ebed nodded. "She will be glad to see you. What will you do after Galilee? Will you come back to Jerusalem?"

"There is nothing for me here. I will make a home for myself somewhere far from these sorts of places. I am no longer drawn to the centre of the action."

"Will you witness Jugurtha's circumcision? Help him through the temple process, the immersion? He could probably use you in the new administration he is setting up."

"You can take my place."

"Would you put in a recommendation for me?"

"You are known by the Sanhedrin. You talk directly with Hyrcanus. You don't need my voice to get a position."

"With Jugurtha."

"He already knows you from before. You helped him with the Sanhedrin. You don't need my recommendation with him either. Are you becoming a Sadducee?"

Ebed shook his head. "No. The Pharisees need to maintain access to Hyrcanus's ear. Sometimes purity of intent needs a bit of shrewdness to assist it."

"Which is why I need to go north again. I'm glad Keziah is in Galilee. It's a long way from political intrigues."

"A man must never forget Jerusalem."

"I didn't say anything about forgetting Jerusalem. I fled the Seleucids to come straight here. I brought you Jugurtha with a plan that can help us regain our sovereignty. But intrigues are a part of it. I see that now more clearly than before. Father used to speak about it sometimes."

"Then he would go to his parchments and papyri," Ebed said quietly.

"Yes, you remember."

"He taught me. After my father died."

"Did you know he was an unhappy man?" Joazar asked.

"He wasn't unhappy."

"Melancholic then."

"I could see that," Ebed said. "He sought solace in texts."

"Always after a trip to Jerusalem. After the councils and debates and alliances and compromises. After the relentless scrutiny of others."

"He spoke more about that to you than me."

"I mostly just observed him. I only later understood the strain I had seen on his face. I felt that strain after the siege at Dagon. Then I understood my father. For the first time, I understood. I talked to him once more. Then I never saw him again."

19

129 BCE

JOAZAR LEFT JERUSALEM on foot across ground that had once been a wasteland filled with scavenging dogs, starving refugees, and refuse fires lit by Sidetes's army. Now, the land lay dressed in springtime grass, wildflowers, and the twiggy remains of last year's Sukkot. No discarded mementoes of occupation remained to prove the past. Seven years had erased all records. Likewise, his time in exile was unknown to any on the road that day.

The way north through Samaria offered the shorter route to Galilee. On that path, it would take two days to reach the border and another partial day from there to Cana and Keziah. Alternatively, there lay the eastern path near Jericho. The journey across the lush land beyond Jericho and following the Jordan River north promised something to Joazar that he could not put into words. The length of his trip would double on the Jericho route, but he needed quiet and time. He took the Jericho road.

He joined a company of Jewish travellers starting at the plain just outside Jerusalem. They passed through whatever remained of the invisible ghosts from David's armies, the Assyrians that came after, the Babylonians, Persians, Greeks. The imagined throng was a great crowd from the past. Revived, they would have buried the road with the people of a thousand years.

A wind rose soon after they started. It carried a stash of dry yellow leaves and crumbling white flower petals pulled from some formerly protected hollow. The suddenly blown petals scattered in ten thousand spangles over the travellers, and then the wind died away. A girl, just a child, walked with her family. She bore, unbeknown to her, one leaf and one petal lodged in her loosely bound hair. The thin leaf and wispy petal seemed to glow in the sunlight as though they were shards of coloured glass, a holy symbol marking the little one as separate from the rest of the company.

The travellers stopped at midday near the ruins of a small village, the final remnants of a people marked by the faint remains of circular stone walls. The stones were white and crumbling, the circles smaller than towers. Perhaps the buildings had been nighttime stockades for a few animals, or tight sleeping quarters, or a place of defence, or storage for provisions or loot, or the remains of a messenger post from some forgotten civilization. Unlike the plain exterior of Jerusalem, which bore no trace of its abundantly recorded history, this site left indications of its past inhabitants but no records to describe them.

The road steepened as they set out once more, with

stone walls rising on one side and an open chasm widening on the other. The region was a wilderness of twisted canyons and layered cliffs. The cliffs were dressed in faint shades of yellow, blue, and red and cut by inexplicable vertical clefts, the work of God's own chisel. In some slashes, water trickled.

When the route allowed, the company spread out. When required, they gathered into a narrow formation. A lone goat across the way stood isolated against vertical stone, appearing to perch on nothing. It watched them traverse the road with either curiosity or contempt–Joazar could not tell which.

The sky above offered no additional garlands of miraculous petals, no clouds, no relief from the year's new heat. The ubiquitous smell of dust permeated hot, still air.

At a treacherous turn, a scrabbling of hooves on rock broke the silence. There was a scream of voices, and then a donkey went over the cliff edge. Its rider, the young girl, was lost immediately as the beast turned over, hooves still trying to connect with the vanishing cliff. It tilted out into emptiness with a braying to match the mother's screams and the father's curses. The entire vision soundlessly faded far below. The girl never made a sound.

The mother did not relent with her voice or her body. The father wrestled her back from the cliff's edge. He held back the girl's siblings as well until the other travellers recovered and encircled the family, leading them around the corner, away from the edge, onwards, downwards. In a safe section of the road, they huddled. More voices joined with cries that echoed back from the cliffs in that place.

Joazar stayed behind. A tiny yellow leaf hung suspended

in the air over the cliff's edge. It floated, wavering in some heated updraft defying the void. As he watched the leaf, his throat constricted, and his feet rooted. He memorized every vacillation, each shade of light shifting through the thin yellow membrane. When it finally succumbed to nature and began to fall, he moved closer as though to catch it, as though he would step out into the air where the girl had passed and seal memory with an artifact.

A hand grabbed his arm and pulled him back. "I don't know where you're going," the gruff old voice said, "but that can't be it."

He looked at the old man. He was big, with a beard in disarray and the hands and arms of a miner, woodsman, or stonemason. The face bore its own model of cliffs and clefts behind which eyes swam in weak pools. A thin, stubborn line of saliva joined upper and lower lips.

The old man turned Joazar with a hand on his back and guided him along the way of the others.

The mother stood apart from the father. Through snatches of choked words and the shades of insanity that drifted across her features, Joazar could see that she hated her husband. The man was answering practical questions posed by fellow travellers. She stared with eyes unfocused and unstill. It seemed to Joazar that letting her fly off the cliff would have been a mercy. The three surviving children stood together and alone. Joazar found that he despised the mother in her grief in a way he could not explain, just as he could not explain his need to walk the Jordan route north.

Later in the day, the mother spoke to her children in a cracked whisper. Later yet, she rested her head against her husband and wept openly into him. She defied convention with that revealed intimacy.

They came upon an anticipated place of pools, but none stopped to rest or let the children play. Soon the lights of Jericho showed in the distance as the sky began to dim.

The next day, he took the Jordan River road alone. He walked north through rock-bottomed ravines and honeyed forests that gradually led into farmland that sloped into the river. He tried to follow the tilt of the land without drifting into the slow water, but he was walking with tired legs, tired eyes, and a weary heart. He took shelter in occasional patches of pine. It was strange to be alone. He had not been alone in years. At night he watched the stars wheel overhead. He heard the grunt and bark of creatures finding their rude way along the water, unconcerned by the small fire and shelter and the traveller's single-voiced conversations with the dark.

He bathed before entering Bet Yerah. The city stood at the southern tip of the Sea of Galilee. The Persians had taken it first, then the Babylonians, then the Persians again, and finally the Greeks. The Greeks called it Philoteria. It was a strange city that overlooked the river and lake from its triangular platform of rock. Elaborate granaries signalled a place for storing wealth. Curved windows looked out over the lake. It reminded Joazar of Antioch but on a smaller scale. There were Greek mosaics, plaster covering brick, and water, wildly abundant water like in Antioch. He thought briefly of the woman who could swim, but then put her out of his mind.

He spent the night in a Greek-style bed and ate food made by a foreigner's hand. He bathed in a hot bath and took a Greek-style massage, the likes of which he had not enjoyed since Antioch. He felt like a repentant drunk spending one last night sampling abandoned habits. He was not drunk again, but tasting something exceptional, stopping before the fall. He refused the woman offered to him.

Galilee surrounded him now. The distance to Cana was one more long day. He had gone farther north than was necessary, but he had wanted to see the river to its mouth, to see the waters that the Torah called Kinneret and the Greeks restyled as Gennesaret. Though it was technically a lake, as he stood on the cliffs of Bet Yerah and was unable to see the water's end, he understood why others called it a sea. Galilee's Sea. It had the same view as a true sea: endless rippling waves, dazzling sparkles, and a blending of sky and water in the distance. There were no islands on this sea, and the water was not salty. No Greeks or Romans lurked over the horizon.

The next morning, he turned his back on the lake and walked westward to Cana.

20

129-128 BCE

In Cana, in a workshop at the base of the hill, hung five wooden poles that were three times the length of a man. Each pole had been boiled in a large vat until saturated, fished from the water with hooks, and then carried across the shop with hands wrapped in cloth. Thicker than a man's wrist, each softened pole sagged as the men moved them. The men bent the softened poles to the right shape, forced them into a mould, and then secured them in place with long leather ties. Once the mould was full of bent and still steaming poles, they hung the mould on the wall where it was left for a year to dry.

Joseph untied the first pole and brought it down. Dried, it held a stiff shape, straight over half its length, then it took a slight curve downwards before straightening out once more. He inspected the pole for end checks and surface checks. There were no flaws.

On the shop floor stood two wheels attached to the frame of an unfinished cart. Joseph fit one end of the pole into the padded iron brackets that were just above the axle. They would bite into the wood once he was ready to hammer home the pins. Once completed, it would be a wagon suited for both commerce and war. It was a new design. He could make five with the boiled, shaped, and dried parts already prepared.

"Satisfied?" Peretz asked.

Joseph turned to his older brother and nodded.

"It's big for a chariot," Peretz remarked.

"Small for a wagon," Joseph answered.

"Do we boil up more poles?"

"Let's fit it first," Joseph said. "Use it a few days. Take it apart. See how the wear plays at the joints."

Oren came into the shop. "You have a visitor," he said, "someone asking about Keziah."

❧

Joseph came up the road to a startling sight: Keziah embracing a man in public. It was something even a harlot would not do, but a sister could with her brother. As Joseph approached, he saw that she was weeping. The man's face wore a hard look that alarmed Joseph.

"Joazar," Keziah said through her tears. "Joseph." She left to fetch Avigail and Little Moshe.

❧

Joazar wiped his face. His sister's husband was a giant. Then a little boy came running.

Joazar had always taken after his father. He was taller

than Father, but his features were the same. Keziah and their little brother looked like Mother. The little boy running looked like Keziah, looked like Mother, like Little Moshe.

When she said the boy's name, Joazar dropped to his knees before the babbling two-year-old. The child had his lost brother's looks and blood and name. He said, "Little Moshe," as though it were a question. He wanted to hold him, to pick him up and run down the street in tears and promise to never leave for Dagon, for Jerusalem, to take the boy wherever he went. He stayed still, at eye level, and watched the ghost of his little brother talk excitedly. When Joazar looked up at Keziah, he saw that she saw the resemblance, son like brother, and then Joazar could not see anything through his tears.

The boy stopped talking as though waiting for Joazar to respond to his landslide of syllables. Joazar wiped his eyes. "You and I will look for treasure one day," Joazar said. The boy suggested several places they should look. Everything was a wonder at this age, even Joazar's wild beard, which the boy decided to touch tentatively. Joazar held the little puffy hand to his face, and the boy pulled away and darted back to the house.

Joazar faced Keziah. "He is the same—" he started but could not finish.

"I know," Keziah said. "And he has the same bad habit of running away when you're trying to clean his bum."

⁂

Days later, in the evening, friends crowded the small house. Joazar watched Saul and Uri sing a duet. Saul was bass against Uri's baritone in a song of history, of love, of Galilee.

The music mingled love for Galilee and the love of a woman together, and the women's instruments complemented the men's voices: Mahlah at the sistrum and pipe, Keziah with her lute. Rehavam and Basmat were there as well. When Basmat's voice started to echo quietly, harmonizing with the men, Joazar thought it a mistake. Then the perfection of the accompaniment grew on him. Hers made the men's voices better. The effect stole through him as nothing had in many years.

Late-hour light flickered, and Joazar sat uneasily. He watched the men sing with another man's wife. He took in the flashing, energetic brightness in Mahlah's two instruments and the wonder of Keziah's fingers on strings. He felt a new kind of terror creep through, something holy, something for which he had no prior experience. The Psalms were here, something of the Teacher's mysterious message, something of the ecstatic prophets, something of Israel's true meaning. He could not grow used to this. To do so, something irreparable had to be broken and removed; something vital had to be gouged out. He found it hard to breathe. He looked several times at the doorway.

The baby Avigail lay between Keziah's knees, the lute tucked up against Keziah's chest. Music flooded the baby's sleep. Little Moshe was talking in the corner, perhaps trying to learn how to sing or merely murmuring in a dream.

Joazar thought of Antioch, the Trierarch, white moonlight on the Orontes. The music and friendships here were akin to the purity of that remembered light. Nothing else of Antioch stained this room. This was why he had come. Now he was afraid to be here.

❧

Weeks later, Joazar stood alone in Keziah and Joseph's home. Keziah had gone up the hill with the children to see a friend. Joseph was in the workshop with his brothers when a man came into view, cresting the hill and running towards the house. Joazar stood in the doorway, watching him. He had the look of a messenger. Though it was only mid-morning, his hair stuck to his forehead and neck. Hair and skin shone as the man approached. It seemed as if the man had lost his ability to gauge distances accurately and would barrel into Joazar without stopping, and Joazar found himself putting up a hand either in defence or as a signal to stop. He was unsure which. The man put out his hand and used a fence post as a brake, finally stopping in front of Joazar.

"From Jerusalem," the runner breathed out. "They say this is the home of Joseph."

"It is," Joazar said.

"I'm looking for Joazar."

"That's me."

The runner nodded, breathing heavily, and began untying a pouch at his waist. He removed a roll of paper. "Do you need me to read it?" the runner asked.

Joazar looked closely at the man.

"It's in the regular Aramaic," the runner said.

Joazar said nothing in reply and held out his hand.

"Okay then," the man said and handed Joazar the message. "I'll be back in the early afternoon for your reply," he said and started to turn away but then paused. "Where's the market?"

Joazar pointed up the hill. The man turned and walked away.

The valley beyond the village had greasy clay beneath its grass. Here, beneath Keziah's house and Joseph's workshops, the earth held more sand. Up the hill, the ground turned to stone. When the runner reached that climbing slope, Joazar stopped watching. He considered going back inside. He considered the workshops. Then he walked towards the valley and sat some distance from the house in long grass where he opened the letter. It was from Jugurtha.

Joazar,

Greetings, my friend. The plans we have spoken of proceed well, and I regret your lack of engagement in these matters. Pericles is preparing to depart to begin the next step in our program. Ebed has provided valuable assistance. Cleopatra Thea, the wayward wife of Demetrius, has taken up residence in Akko. I do not like her proximity to Galilee. The war between Demetrius and Zabinas continues. Eretz-Israel is not in danger, but having the Seleucid king's wife on Israel's doorstep is unsettling. Send a sample of your brother-in-law's work. There may be a need sooner than planned.

Joazar rose from the grass, backtracked to the house, and then continued to Joseph's shop.

"I need to consult you on this," he said and showed Joseph the letter.

Sunlight had a golden quality here. There was something soft to the sweat on Joseph's face, neck, and arms, unlike the runner's gritty look in bright sunlight. Joseph wiped his hands on a rag and took the letter.

"Akko is straight to the coast from here," Joseph said when he had finished. "Less than a day's walk."

"The sample?"

"Not yet. The poles are too light. Broke at the connection. We've got a thicker batch that will be dry in a few months. Oren is redoing the metal fittings."

"I'll send a reply and let Jugurtha know you're still working on it."

"A herder toward Nazareth found a wagon in the woods. Not a usual design, probably Seleucid. Oren saw it. Abandoned all these years. Rotted from what Oren said. He took some measurements and scratched a drawing. How about we take tomorrow afternoon and go find it?"

❧

The next day, the men walked and talked. Nothing was said of Joazar's time in Antioch or Joseph's first marriage. They found the remains of the abandoned wagon late in the afternoon. After so many years in the field, overgrown with vines and disappearing into the ground, the wood frame could be pulled apart by hand. The metal components were heavily rusted. Joseph adjusted Oren's outline and made a few observations regarding the joint work. When done, they left what remained of the ruin and walked back to Cana.

"You're good for my sister," Joazar said. "You and your family and friends."

"They're your friends now as well," Joseph said. "Find a woman in one of the villages. You'll be a Galilean before you know it. And put some of that money you brought with you from Antioch into Uri's quince business. Make it work for you rather than just sit in a box."

Joazar took Joseph up on his Uri suggestion. As the months passed, to keep busy, Joazar also helped in the workshops where he could, but he had little skill for the woodworking trade.

"You're good for cleaning up and fetching things," Joseph laughed after they had wound down their work and returned for the evening meal. Turning to Keziah, he said, "But he can't saw straight."

"Your saw is dull."

"And he can't sharpen either."

Then there was a noise outside. It was not yet dark. The sound of footsteps warned of someone coming quickly up the walk. Joseph and Joazar both went to the door. The runner did not pause for introductions but thrust a new letter into Joazar's hands while eyeing Joseph. It was another letter from Jugurtha.

"Go ahead and read it," Joseph said and turned back to the tired runner. "Come inside. Keziah, get him a cup and a plate. There's extra."

A lamp shone inside, but it was still brighter outside. Joazar went out with his letter. Joseph followed him.

Joazar,

Greetings. I bring you troubling news and request your immediate return to Jerusalem.

The war goes badly for Demetrius. He fled the battle with only a remnant of his forces and made his way to

Akko for the security of its walls and his wife's guard, but Cleopatra Thea unexpectedly barred the gates.

"Looks like his wife betrayed him," Joazar summarized. "Demetrius will go to Tyre and then sail to Cyprus and clean out the available mercenaries there before Pericles arrives to deliver Jerusalem's offer. He wants me back in Jerusalem to work out a new plan."

❧

They put the runner up for the night in Joseph's shop. After they had settled the children for the night, the three returned to Jugurtha's message.

"Will you go back to Jerusalem?" Joseph asked.

"No. Judea is no longer my home."

"Are you a Galilean now?" Keziah asked.

"I don't know. Hyrcanus will raise his army however he can. I can do more good finding other Galilean workshops like yours to take the king's orders. I will write back to Jugurtha and gain a commission to recruit and pay more locals. Whether the war is against Zabinas or Demetrius doesn't matter. The money we've raised is to defend all of Eretz-Israel, not just Jerusalem. I won't go back."

❧

Less than a month later, the same runner came a third time.

Joazar,

Greetings. Demetrius did not make it to Cyprus. His men turned on him at Tyre and handed him over to Zabinas. Zabinas cut off Demetrius's head. Cleopatra

Thea is once again a widow. It is unknown yet whether she will join with Zabinas or continue her late husband's war against him. Egypt backs Zabinas, and Cleopatra is the pharaoh's daughter, so an alliance is more likely. This does not bode well for Eretz-Israel's borders. Once the Seleucids reunify, they will turn their attention back towards us to recover their revenues. They will have Egypt with them. Israel will soon be in a desperate war.

A commission has been agreed to, as you suggested. Hyrcanus has marked the necessary papers. The money delivered by this messenger should assist you to begin work. I recommend spreading production across many villages and towns to avoid creating a production concentration in any one location.

Ensure that your craftsmen only use well-dried wood. Arrows and spears prepared with green wood will curve in flight and twist as they dry. Accuracy matters in all phases of a battle.

Joseph grunted when Joazar finished reading. "Does he think we're fools?"

21

127-113 BCE

FOURTEEN YEARS PASSED. There was no war.

During those years, Joazar settled in Cana. He married Noadiah, Mahlah's sister, and became the brother-in-law of Rehavam, the glassmaker. Four children were born into his household, all girls. Joseph and Keziah had two more daughters as well.

During those twelve years, Nabataea followed Israel's lead and broke away from Seleucid control as well. Other nations followed.

For fourteen years, there was no war, but letters from Jugurtha continued to arrive. Joazar stored them in a box Joseph had made for him, each laid in the order of its arrival.

On a warm afternoon, alone, Joazar paged through the letters, reviewing the key events written in Jugurtha's drawn-out script.

Cleopatra Thea has surprised us and has not joined with Zabinas. She defies her father and put Seleucus Philometer, her son from Antiochus, on the throne as co-regent. The war with Zabinas continues. This gives us more time to build our strength.

The continuation of the Seleucid civil war left Israel in peace and had inspired Joazar's search for a wife. A few weeks before his wedding to Noadiah, another message had come by way of the same wet-haired runner.

Cleopatra Thea has killed Philometer. Her son. His ambition swelled, and so she now reigns alone.

Jugurtha did not write just about Seleucid affairs.

Hyrcanus is building the fortress at Bara, a short walk north of the temple. . . . Hyrcanus sent a delegation to Rome to re-establish relations. . . . Hyrcanus has started construction of the fortress east of Jerusalem near Qumran, where the monks have their settlement. It is to be called Hyrcania.

"Where are the northern fortresses?" Rehavam had asked. "Galilee is between Jerusalem and the Greeks. If there ever is a war, the Greeks will come through Galilee before they threaten the south."

Joazar wrote back to Jugurtha on this point. The response, carried by the same unhurried walker, did not please.

I have pressed Hyrcanus about Galilee's missing fortifications, but he and the Sanhedrin seem to be reverting to old habits and have only fortified Jerusalem. They don't understand Eretz-Israel's borders. Galilee remains the region beyond Samaria. I fear it is forgotten.

Standing before his box of letters, Joazar remembered the effect that message had on Cana's people. Joseph and the other craftsmen continued to accept the king's money, but they did not love him. This news had not helped.

"He's no Simon" was a refrain heard often.

Years later, the sweating runner had reappeared. "I had other assignments," he explained. "Messages to elsewhere." He accepted a cup from Noadiah. "I like the new place you've got here."

"We've been here a few years now," Joazar said.

"I still don't love the hill."

"Sit," Joazar had said as he did the same and opened the newest letter.

Cleopatra Thea and Zabinas continue their war. One wins a battle, and then the other wins the next. They weaken themselves without a clear victory, and years roll by. As the former treasurer, I can surmise that both sides must run out of resources soon. They cannot continue to spend on soldiers without anything to be gained from their expenses. The cessation of tax revenues from former vassals must make the bookkeeper's job there dire. They'll be paying their armies soon with promises.

Now sitting alone in his home, Joazar skipped through

several pages. There were details on orders and money. Half described matters of dire urgency in one letter disappeared from discussion later. Stories were started halfway through as though Joazar understood their context. He came to one letter he remembered well.

I believe the Seleucids' civil war is now over. One of Cleopatra Thea's sons from Demetrius killed Zabinas. Antiochus Grypus is his name. Presumably, Grypus will join his mother. Or he might not. He might turn against her for betraying his father and murdering his other brother. For now, the fighting has stopped.

Joazar paged forward again, skipping letters and months to reread the next chapter of the Cleopatra story.

As suspected, Cleopatra Thea has made peace with her son. She and Grypus have formed a joint regency together. This is in defiance of her father in Egypt.

Two months later came news that altered the picture.

Cleopatra Thea is dead. She attempted to poison her son, Grypus, who would have been the second of her sons poisoned. She failed in her attempt. He discovered her plot and forced her to drink the cup instead. She died horribly while he watched. Grypus now rules alone.

When the letter had first been read, Keziah had looked at Little Moshe, who was not so little any longer, and then at Joazar. "I don't understand. A mother tries to kill her son. The son kills the mother instead."

"You're not meant to understand," Joazar said. He thought about Antioch, about what he knew, and then chose to say nothing else.

More letters followed. The news became increasingly unbelievable.

Antiochus Cyzicenus, another one of Cleopatra's sons, has raised an army. He is a half-brother to Grypus and was brother as well to Seleucus, the son Cleopatra had successfully murdered. Whether Cyzicenus sees Grypus as his mother's murderer or his other brother's avenger is another unknown. Seleucid politics have always been a confusing storm of hatred. This means that a new Seleucid civil war commences, which is good news for us. Now, instead of mother and son at war, it's half-brothers trying to kill each other.

Joazar tried to remember how exactly the people of Cana had responded to the escalating chaos of the decade long Seleucid family war.

"You spent time with these people," Joseph had said.

"I was a hostage," Joazar said, "barely more than a slave."

"I'm talking about the Sanhedrin."

"What about them?"

"I thought Eretz-Israel was to be defended at its borders. Not a single mercenary outpost is on Galilean soil. We are directly in the path between Antioch and Jerusalem."

The Seleucids were descending into madness, but everything in Cana came back to Galilee's taxes and their lack of defence. The Galileans had started to read Jerusalem's inaction as a betrayal.

A page slipped out of Joazar's hand. He knelt to pick it up and then couldn't sort where to put it with the others.

The half-brothers have managed to murder each other's wives. This has somehow brought them to a truce, and now they have agreed to a co-regency. That the murder of each other's wives would result in an end to their civil war is something that you would have to grow up in the Seleucid court to understand. After all these years as a Jew, I confess I understand the Seleucids less than I would have previously. My intuition for Seleucid intrigues is fading. The reunification of the Seleucid leadership, though, is terrible news for Eretz-Israel.

Noadiah came into the room then as he stood holding fourteen years' worth of letters. He had not seen Jugurtha once during those years. His friendship with his former Seleucid captor had become a relationship with handwriting.

Noadiah put a hand on his arm. "Spending time in your letters won't change matters," she said.

He put the papyri back into the box and closed the lid.

"Moshe is not your little brother," Noadiah said.

"I know."

"He's not your son, either."

"I have no son."

"You have four daughters."

"And I have a nephew who is like my son."

He followed her outside and sat beside her. They were on the hill, but the courtyard walls blocked their view of the valley. This conversation deserved the roof, where they could look out over the valley, but Noadiah had led him into the courtyard.

"I visited Uri yesterday," Joazar said. "The new dolia for storing the liquor are installed."

"We were talking about Moshe."

"Jews are not going to war," Joazar said. "Hyrcanus's mercenary army is. Moshe will be in no danger. Jews are just observers, except for the few Jewish captains."

"Then why do you have to go?"

"This is Eretz-Israel. All of it. Not Judea in the south, Galilee in the north, and Samaria with its own temple in the middle. It should all be Eretz-Israel. One country."

"I understand one Eretz-Israel. Why do *you* have to go? Because Moshe is going?"

"Moshe is going because his father is. Joseph is going because he needs to see his wagons and weapons in action and put a face to our Galilean production. And to meet Jugurtha for the first time, the man who has been paying us all these years. And I'm going because I want to see Jugurtha again personally. I want to support Joseph. Ebed will be there, and Hyrcanus. I want to see these people again."

"And because Little Moshe is going."

"He's not Little Moshe anymore."

"He is to you. He's going to see a war, and you don't want him there."

"I was seventeen when I went to war at Dagon as was Ebed. It's a careless age."

"Moshe has a father."

"Who has never seen war."

"I think he would handle himself quite well."

Later, as Joazar walked down the hill to Joseph's shop, he was no less divided than he had been before opening Jugurtha's box of letters. For fourteen years, Israel had braced for a Seleucid war that never came. Rather than be grateful for the peace, it now marched out to an unprovoked war with Samaria. And he was going to Samaria just to observe.

22

113 BCE

THEY WERE IN the region of Samaria with ten men on foot and two donkeys pulling a pair of carts. Samaria was no better prepared for war than Jerusalem had been in the days before Jugurtha. Samaria had no army. With the onset of this new conflict with the Jews, the population fled to their cities and waited behind stone walls. The Jewish army had laid siege to the region's capital city, also called Samaria. The Galileans traversed an empty countryside on their way to observe the siege.

"This is the same route your mother took when she came to Galilee," Joseph said.

"With the Iturean," Moshe said.

"Yes. With the Iturean."

The valley stretched out long before them. Water revealed itself everywhere, supplying vineyards, orchards, and field crops. The soil was black. Uri stopped and turned over an unearthed square half the size of a man's head. He studied it, smelled it, tested the texture between his thumb and fingers, and then dropped the sample and brushed off his hand.

"Good soil," Uri said. "It should belong to us."

Joazar walked with them, wearing a sullen demeanour. He said little.

For a large portion of the afternoon, the conversation centred around who exactly the Samaritans were. All agreed that they were a plague within the land. Had been for centuries. Some described them as opportunists: during the dark days after the Babylonians burned the nation and deported its population, the Samaritans had slipped in and claimed what remained of Jewish homes and farms in the fertile valleys. Others suggested they were equal victims—Babylonian captives themselves, deported from their homelands to replace the Jews. Others held the view that they were the refuse of the original Jews—the ne'er-do-wells who came out of cowards' holes to loot their own people's land once the Babylonians were gone.

"They are all of that," Joseph said. "They are a mixed people, partly Jewish, intermarried and mixed with every kind of gentile."

The Samaritans populated the middle part of Israel and separated Judea in the south from Galilee in the north. Hyrcanus had decided that it was time for them to go.

⁂

A tent, like the one Joazar and Ebed met Jugurtha in more than two decades earlier, engulfed Joseph and Moshe. Others of the Galilean delegation followed. After a moment, Joazar entered as well.

Joazar embraced Ebed and looked around for the half-naked and tattooed terror that this tent reminded him of, but Jugurtha was absent. Ebed introduced the Galileans to Hyrcanus.

"You were a shirtless, blood-covered boy when I first met you," Hyrcanus said. The king was grey-bearded now, with lines around his eyes and arcs across his cheeks. "You and your friend Ebed here. A great service you have done for God and this country these many years. Many adventures. I see that you are well."

Hyrcanus wore his sword as though he had personally used it in battle. He finished welcoming his guests and then introduced the Galileans to three of his sons: Judah Aristobulus, Antigonus, and Alexander Jannaeus. Aristobulus was the oldest of the three. Antigonus was in his early twenties, Joazar guessed. Jannaeus was much younger, younger even than Moshe. Other introductions were made. The map spread out on the table was reviewed, and the work done around the mountaintop city explained. Hyrcanus's army, mostly Cretans and Cypriots, had built a ditch and double wall, imprisoning the Samaritans in their fortress. The region was called Samaria, and so was this, their capital.

"The perimeter of the fortress is five miles long," Hyrcanus said. The king paused to let the immensity of the project sink in. "One and a half miles across the middle."

Hyrcanus continued with his overview of the situation. There were observations about materials, supplies, timelines. Finally, he declared his intention to depart back to Jerusalem and leave the Samaritans' final disposal to his two older sons: Judah Aristobulus and Antigonus. The siege was expected to take months, maybe longer. Hyrcanus, in his dual role as both king and high priest, was needed at the temple.

"How is Jugurtha?" Joazar asked the next day.

"He looks older than his years," the king said. "He never found a wife. Perhaps none would have him. A strange man, your friend."

❧

The day after Joazar's discussion with the king, Joseph and Keziah's youngest daughter, Sarah, seven years old, played in the morning sun in tall grass far from Cana's nearest buildings. Boulders lay about the base of the hill. The field beyond was unfarmed and left for the perpetual, untimely floods. The grass now was long. Seated, she could see nothing but green stems. She leaned against cold stone that was taller than her. Its coolness drew heat from her. She considered turning and pressing her face to the stone.

She heard thunder. Felt it beneath her. Looking up, she saw a blue sky. Only blue sky. The stalks of tall, straight grass around her trembled. There was no wind. She looked farther, and still, there were no clouds. The rumble did not cease but swelled as though something was wrong with the thunder.

She wanted to stand, to investigate, to run for the house around the hill over a mile away. The boulder seemed harder now and colder. She wanted to follow her own warmth inside it. To hide there. Some great thing was coming. It was thunder that stretched as far as imagination, an organism of embodied roaring, like the sea, like a great wave that crashed and did not end but went on and on. It moved past her and her hiding place, not stopping, roaring in front and away. She was between Cana and a new river that raged in the valley.

She stood slowly, looking towards the river sound, and saw horses and wagons, thousands of horses and wagons, and men with them. The men carried shafts of wood, like Father's javelins but longer and thicker, and shields and helmets on their heads and red plumes, and she knew who they were. They were the Greeks, the Seleucids, the terrors adults spoke about in whispers. Her entire life, she had heard snatches about this northern army, lurid details from the older boys, her cousins, even her sisters, telling of dangers she was too young to understand.

The Seleucid army was heading towards Father. The Greeks would fight on the side of the Samaritans, and Father would face these many thousands. She would no longer have a father.

She stood, transfixed by the river of men and beasts and equipment passing so close. A veil of long grass hid her, one hand on her rock that joined the line of rocks at the base of Cana's hill. She heard nothing but the passing roar, saw nothing but the passage before her, imagined nothing but fear. Fear for her father.

She was not aware of the horse that stepped up behind her on the Cana side. She did not sense the leering face looking down, the large-knuckled hand that reached for her. She did not see any of this. The horse's snort finally alerted her, and she jumped, but too late, as a rough hand grabbed the cloth at the back of her *kethōneth* and hoisted her into the air. She screamed, and there was a responding roar from the man who eyed her with delight. He kicked his horse forwards around the rock, in the direction of the main force. She screamed and struggled, and the sweat of the man's wild and curled hair entered her mouth when he roared again, his kind of laughter. Then he released her with a violent thrust of his arm, and she sailed through the air, experiencing a shock of disorientation before she struck a new boulder. A flash of light was followed by blackness.

She was unaware as her body slid off the rock and back into long grass. She lay crumpled below the boulder. Her body trembled as the ground trembled. Her body kept trembling long after the army was gone.

❧

Hours later, in the dark, the girl moved, rhythmically shaking from her feet to her upper body. The lines of blood from her ear and nose had long since dried. Her legs kicked at the grass, and sweat from her efforts softened the blood on her lip, smeared it into a blackness that glistened in the moonlight illuminating the girl's shape. When the moon passed, she lay subject to the boulder's moonlight shadow. She stopped trembling. She was still and sightless in the dark.

A winged insect landed on her to preen and then rose again. A bat dropped out of the dark and plucked the insect from the air with an inaudible wingbeat, barely grazing the girl's cheek. The wind stirred the tips of nighttime grass, and a fox picked up the scent of a nearby human and escaped downwind towards the river.

❧

In the fading glory of late light, the shadows of the Galileans and their animals stretched across the valley that lay between Mount Ebal and Mount Gerizim. They approached

Shechem as its walls reflected the red sky. The donkey cart wove between uneven mounds—the remnants of tattered grapevines tangled with the bodies of men and animals. The occasional spear shaft or fractured arrow left standing in the ground marked the thinnest of shadows that stretched out and pointed in the direction of the army's passage. Aristobulus and Antigonus were succeeding at driving Cyzicenus and his Seleucid army back the way they had come. The Galileans followed the armies' path at their leisure.

Both Galilean carts moved parallel to one another and stayed within shouting distance. As they came upon remains, the men stepped down and scavenged swords. They were superior to anything the Galileans had produced during the previous decade of preparation. Belts were unstrapped and sheaths claimed. They also collected long knives and pole weapons with hooked axe heads and spear tips. An oversized quiver on an abandoned wagon was untied and remounted on Joseph's cart. The carpenter secured his javelins in this new carrier. When they found similar containers, they mounted them on the other wagon and filled them with more pole weapons. The wealth left on the field of corpses was extraordinary.

When dusk approached, they lit torches mounted to the wagons' sides and continued along the debris trail. Moshe walked ahead, guiding the donkey around obstacles of flesh and equipment. The second wagon drifted behind.

Turning away from Shechem, the men encountered land more treacherous for night travel. The route narrowed and ambush points became more numerous. They began to discuss setting up camp when there came a shout from Moshe. The shape of a warrior emerged out of the night.

Then two more. Moshe froze, and the men in the cart cursed, surrounded by weapons but unprepared for war in that trail of corpses. The men took what came to hand before it became apparent that the three strangers posed no threat.

The leading man bore an arrow. The shaft was still lodged in his stomach, draining his capacity for violence. The second Seleucid's arm was wounded, which he supported with a rough sling. His leg was also damaged and covered with a swath of bloody bandages. The last soldier suffered from a head injury, bandaged with the remains of a uniform. He, too, was lame, one foot bound.

"Moshe, get back here," Joseph said.

Moshe did not respond to his father. Did not hear.

The three soldiers limped forward, speaking in a language the Galileans did not understand. They drew closer. Moshe was alone before them.

≪

The village came out and searched for Little Sarah. Torches cast eerie shadows over the ground as they went well beyond the perimeter of the hill. Twice, groups of three or more passed on the wrong side of the boulder where the girl lay.

It was the old shoemaker who found Sarah. He had been a strong man in his youth but had outlived that youth and two wives. He was alone in Cana.

He found Little Sarah as he poked slowly through the line of boulders. He held a long torch in front away from his body. He found her when there was no one near. At first glance, it appeared that she was dead.

He did not say anything at first. He simply knelt over

the girl. As he watched, a tremor ran over her cheeks like a creature moving beneath her skin. One arm twitched. She was alive. He stood up and called out into the night, but no one was near. There were too many distant voices cluttering the night. His throat was weak. He knelt again beside her but could not awaken her. Blood streaked across her face and pooled in one ear. Her back was twisted as though she had tried to scratch an itch by rubbing it into the ground.

He stood tall in the darkness. He still could not draw anyone to him. He would not leave her. He could not be expected to carry her at his age, and even a young man could not safely lift her and the torch.

He set the torch on the rock where it would cast light in the direction he wanted to go, and then he knelt beside her again. "Come with me, Sarah," he said kindly. "Let's go find your mother."

He put his hands under her, one under her shoulders, one under her legs, and tried to stand. At first, he could not lift her. He tried again and was able to get her up on his knee. He found a way to shuffle his shoulder forward to support her head, and then with a gasp, he staggered the rest of the way to his feet. His arms immediately protested. He grumbled back and began to walk. The torch on the rock provided some light at first, but soon he and the girl were in darkness. He continued to walk. He followed the base of the hill by testing the ground carefully with each step, not daring to take the shorter route straight up the slope. He looked in vain for others. After a few minutes, he set her down again. He did not trust himself to put her all the way down and get her up a second time, so he knelt on one knee, taking her weight on the other. The arm supporting her was only partly relieved of its burden, and the thin muscles of his shoulders and neck burned.

"You've given yourself up to an old man, Sarah," he said hoarsely. "I don't have what I used to have. Lord, send Joshua to bear up these old arms." He stood again and groaned. His bottom lip hung slackly, a quirk of age his second wife had often protested, poking him into paying attention and tightening up the lazy drift. He could not keep from wetting himself, and when an eye began to water as well, he cursed the infirmities that made this moment shameful. He could no longer set her down on the soiled knee. He carried her farther than he believed he could. He planted his feet nervously, tilted forward, righted himself, and then took another step. When he could not carry her farther, he carried her anyway, one eye leaking uncontrollably. He was unable to see the burden before him, unable to endure the tearing in one arm, finally unable to continue, and so he stood and wept with only one eye seeing.

"Eli?"

There was a light beside him. He turned to see a face from the village. He knew the face but couldn't think of the name.

"Good Lord, Eli!"

"Eli found her!" another friendly face shouted. Others began running toward them.

"Over here!"

"Let me take her, old friend."

"We've got her. You can let go," another familiar voice said.

"We've got her, Eli."

"Hold on! Grab him!" He couldn't keep track of the

voices in the semi-darkness, and then he couldn't keep track of himself.

"Hold up!"

"I've got him."

"I've got her."

"Stay with him."

"Someone find Keziah."

The wounded soldiers approached Moshe in the weak light of a failed day. Stench rolled from them and sullied the night. The man talking, the closest one to Moshe, spoke his plea in a low voice. He held the shaft of the arrow protruding from his stomach steady as he stepped. Blood seeped and glistened in torchlight. He was tall even though hunched over. His beard was close-cropped over a cleft chin, his eyes small, nose wide, head partially shaved above a flat brow. The second man, the one with the head wound, had the pale skin and angular features of a Greek Cypriot and was wounded in one leg. The third man looked like a mason by stature—wide-spaced legs; thick, rounded shoulders—and one of his arms was supported in a sling and swathed in bloody bandages. One foot was also wrapped with red-soaked rags. All three wore swords, and the mason kept a hand resting near his.

There was a confusion of Jewish voices: Joseph tried to gain Moshe's attention, Galileans passed weapons, questions were posed in the dark. Some of the men later reported a howling, though there had been no such sound. There was just one soldier's plea. No wind. No night creatures. No chorus. The soldiers' halting steps continued to draw closer to Moshe. The light was poor. There was definitely no howling.

At least, there was no howling until the soldiers were nearly upon Moshe. Then there came a howling.

The mason moved first. He straightened and pulled his arm from its sling, revealing a dagger, and his other hand moved to his sword. There was a sudden movement, and then an arc of blood flew across the scene. The howl came simultaneously with the blood. The mason leaped forward with one leg while the other buckled sharply beneath him as it came apart in a welter of severed muscle. Joazar let his momentum propel him forward, past the falling mason. His sword dove into the undefended back of the Cypriot, the head-bandaged man whose lameness had suddenly been cured, standing with his sword half unsheathed. The tip of Joazar's blade pierced through the Cypriot's stomach the same way it had the killer of Little Moshe so many years before.

The tallest Seleucid was indeed injured. He staggered forward to grapple with Moshe as he tried to reach for his belted dagger. The boy parried the man's tackle with one hand and caught the embedded arrow with the other. As the tall man came down on him, dagger nearly out, Moshe twisted and pulled the arrow and then drove it back in at a fresh angle. An inhuman sound came from his assailant, a high-pitched inhale as he fell to the ground, curled up in a ball around the arrow shaft.

The mason was the only one of the three actively trying to stop his bleeding. He thrashed about, unwound the fake bandages from his foot, and shrugged off his sling. He tied both together and then wrapped them around his destroyed right leg. He worked frantically while the Galileans watched.

The tall arrow-wounded man attempted to sit up. He felt about for a weapon. His dagger sheath was twisted beneath him, as was his sword, and he could not get to either. Joseph pushed him back to the ground with a javelin's tip.

The Cypriot was the only quiet one. He knelt on the ground and held his stomach closed around Joazar's sword tip while a pool formed before and behind him. Joazar pulled the bandage from his head. His curly hair fell naturally, sweat-matted but untroubled by blood or injury. Joazar grasped his sword as he had done outside his childhood village years before and wrenched it free. The wound bubbled bright black in the night's light. He would not survive. "What will you do with us?" the man asked in Aramaic.

Joazar ignored him and looked over at the mason. He pointed his sword tip at the prone man. "This one could live. His leg is ruined. But he could live. Do you know where you are?"

The mason had gone quiet except for the panicked sound of his breathing. He had his dagger out and used its handle as a windlass to make a tourniquet about his leg. He held the butt with one hand and the blade's flat edge with the other. He twisted the knife to tighten the cloth and staunch the bleeding. "Judah, cursed of Zeus," he said in Aramaic, and he spat a long stream of phlegm in Joazar's direction.

Joseph lifted his javelin tip over the mason. His thrust came with the power of a man used to working wood. The bronze tip pierced the mason's hand and plunged through the bandage, into the side of the man's thigh, and then into the ground beneath him. The mason screamed and cursed and scrabbled at the soil to pull away, but he was pinned to the ground he would now die on. The dagger unwound on its own and then fell from the leg; the tourniquet went limp. The leg pumped freely. He shouted in whatever his language was and struggled for a minute, but Joseph did not remove the javelin, and soon the man quieted. He became still and developed a dazed look. His posture softened and began to list.

"They came from the north, through Galilee," Joseph said. "The trail has turned north again, back through Galilee."

A ripple went through the men present, and each understood.

When the Galileans were through with the three strangers, they continued in darkness until they came to a small, abandoned stockade. They brought both wagons inside, checked the perimeter carefully, and then bolted the gate. An orange-tinted moon slunk below the horizon. Bats appeared and fed on invisible delicacies by starlight as they did throughout Samaria and Galilee that night. As they did on most nights.

❧

Hours later, Joseph lay still, awake, looking up at an inscrutable sky. His son had participated in the killing of a man. It was the experience of a previous generation. It was the experience of soldiers in Judea, of mercenaries who sold themselves in service to Death. This was not a world for his son.

He thought about the workshop. He remembered teaching Moshe how to sharpen a blade differently for chopping and for shaving, how to find the grain and work with it, not against it. There was yet another way to sharpen a blade's edge for putting metal to flesh. He had never broached that lesson with his son.

He remembered a scene from when Moshe was eight years old. They had been in the hills north of Cana, felling a large tree. The tree had been dead for some time; it was tall, leafless, and dry—perfect for his purposes. It had been a strange tree, having grown tight and perfectly straight against a steep slope. The strangeness was its burden. At some early point in the tree's history, two of its lower limbs had grown around a large knob of rock on the upper slope. As the tree grew and the slope eroded, these two branches wrestled with the rock. The tree's trunk had not bent to the contest but remained unyieldingly straight. As the tree grew, the branches grew; they curved as they stretched down and under the rock, and then by erosion or some weakness in the mineral, the rock broke away from the slope. As the years passed, the cliff eroded further, and the rock remained resting in the air in its strange cradle. On this day, the rock was suspended in the air at a height taller than two men.

Joseph paid it little mind. He set work with the axe and the saw in the usual way. Then there came a moment when Moshe went down the slope. The tree was soon to fall, and there was little room to the sides for more than Joseph and no way to climb the cliff, so the boy went far down to be safe. Joseph applied the final strokes, and there came the creaking groan that signalled the tree's intent to fall. The trunk groaned, and then there came the shriek of cracks, of dry wood splintering and splitting and tearing itself apart. The trunk tilted more than it could bear, and then the tree crashed down. As it hit the ground, the imprisoned and elevated rock was freed and flung from its basket, a rock half the size of a man's torso, a catapult's missile directed downslope at the stunned Moshe.

The eight-year-old turned and ran, but the stone was on him in two steps. Joseph could only watch. It happened so fast that he later had to recreate the scene in his memory to understand it. The rock flew through Moshe. Moshe's upper body disappeared, and the rock flew farther downslope, where it smashed through a bracken. Moshe was gone. His feet projected from a hollow, but his upper body was gone.

The cry from Joseph's throat was a sound only he heard that day. Moshe had no later memory of it.

Lying now in the dark, resting in the barren, war-stricken fields, Joseph could hear that scream again. It rattled his head even now. He had plunged down the hillside to the body of his only son, crashed through the downed limbs of the stone-flinging murderous tree. He had fallen at one point, stood again, and chased the slope to see what remained.

Before Joseph got to him, Moshe sat up, unscathed and leaf-covered, with the craziest of grins on his face.

"I felt it whoosh right over me!" the boy exclaimed with all the excitement of a mind unaware of consequence. "It touched my hair! That close!"

The boy overflowed with uncontained excitement.

Lying in the dark within the Samaritan stockade, Joseph could taste the acid in his throat from that day—the elation, the horror, the restarting of life. A refreshed awareness of vulnerability. It had made his hands and legs shake as they were shaking now. Moshe had been happy and excited and could hardly wait to tell his mother and his sisters.

That night, Keziah said nothing to Joseph, but her eyes burned. He thought there might be something like hatred within her. It passed after a time, but he believed that a coal of that hate remained. Something had been exposed. Something deeper than he could compensate for. Something that predated him.

The lute case represented a vow of protection. His vow. He had understood that when he gave it to her. Had intended it to be so. Every careful joint was deliberate. He had designed it, built it, practised the words to present it with and with those words made more than a marriage promise. But he had not fully understood.

He understood now, lying in the dark. And he knew that he would eventually fail. The case had been a false promise. The promise had nearly been broken today. Again. Nearly. He was not enough. He would eventually fail.

࿐

The next day, within sight of Scythopolis, ten Galileans stood to the side of the path as Jerusalem's mercenary army passed south, returning to Samaria's siege. The captain stopped to talk. "There is no accounting for the Fates," he said. "God gives Fortune to rich and poor, however he chooses. All you can do is take what he has seen fit to give you and make the best of it." He hurried on to catch up with the others.

Joseph looked to Joazar with a puzzled expression.

"Homer," Joazar said.

"That is supposed to make it okay?" Joseph asked.

"They've left the Seleucid army on Galilee's doorstep. A bit of Homer?"

Scythopolis took in the remnant of Cyzicenus's army and closed its gates. Hyrcanus's sons had no appetite for two sieges. Samaria was the objective, not a corner of Galilee, and as far as Jerusalem was concerned, Cyzicenus could depart Israel at his leisure.

"Galilee has been left alone," Joseph said. "It's up to us. Jerusalem will never protect the north."

23

113-112 BCE

THREE MONTHS LATER, Joseph and Joazar, men used to walking and not riding, rode north from Cana's terraced hill towards Bersabe. With the last of the sycamore trees behind them, they crossed into Upper Galilee. On the Sabbath, they spoke in the synagogue at Baca. Across the mountains in Meronoth, they recalled the prophets Jehdeiah and Jadon to counter the anti-Jerusalem sentiment they found there. At Ramah, they used the words of Samuel. In Sepph, they spoke of Noah and the new moon signal fires, in each place using the locally significant stories to minimize north—south, Judean—Galilean division. Their goal was to raise a local army to defend Galilee against another Seleucid invasion. Uri and Rehavam were on a similar mission together, rallying the southern half of Galilee.

Joseph and Joazar worked eastwards through Upper Galilee in a sweeping arc, persevering through winter winds, stark exposure in the mountains, gloom in the valleys, and the slow to melt resistance of their audiences.

"Jerusalem starts the war, and we fight it" was a remark repeated in many towns. This was not at first a vote in favour of Joseph and Joazar's appeal. "We were better off with the Seleucids in control" was how those statements ended.

Joazar's contacts through Galilee included trades- and craftsmen involved in work like that of Joseph's workshop. Galilean workers amassed arrow, spear, and javelin tips, shields and helmets, swords and axes. Monies dispersed and goods confirmed were the work of Joazar's agents. Nearly every Galilean village had financial stakes in the Jerusalem policies they hated. Public discussions were complicated.

At first, the group from Cana tried using Jugurtha's argument touting the economic benefits of Jerusalem's war to persuade each town and village to join their cause. It seemed to be a reasonable approach, but it did little to draw men to their cause. Then Joseph stepped forward one night and spoke about Little Sarah. Little Sarah's story was tangible and brought tears. He began to talk about Little Sarah at every stop.

She had awoken a month after the assault. After two months, she began to walk. Her voice, however, was wrong. Her words came out garbled and her thinking was slow. Her gait hitched and halted over short distances, after which she could not go on. She was just a child, and the Seleucid army had broken her in a way that no one could ever heal. Every time Joseph told the story, his audience wept. Men slapped their arms and hardened their faces. Some stood and sat and stood again. Then when the appeal came for Galilee to defend itself, to no longer rely on Hyrcanus but remember the days of David, each town and village responded with a wave of support. Men stepped forward to provide local organization and planning. Agreements were struck that spanned villages and valleys.

They stopped their northeastern march short of Gamla.

"It's time we returned to Cana," Joseph said.

Joazar said nothing.

"I need to see Little Sarah."

Joazar turned and put his hand on his brother-in-law's shoulder. "As do I, my brother. As do I."

The next day, they rode back towards the Sea of Galilee, to Kfar Nahum at its northern end, the quiet fishing village where Saul lived. The unusual riders looked dangerous and tired, their horses a dark omen. Without music, they contented themselves with Anna's conversation and cooking and with the noise of many children. After Saul's house, it would be one more long day to Cana.

"Two days," Saul corrected. He shook his head as Joseph tried to protest. "Two days. Detour to Nazareth. Assess the mood in the southern villages. See if Uri and Rehavam's message continues to hold sway in the hearts of the people there. Your time in Nazareth will be well spent."

Joseph studied his old friend for a minute in silence. Then he spoke. "Galilee is soon going to need you to lead in ways that a Galilean has not led in decades."

"You don't need to convert me," Saul said. "Kfar Nahum and the northern lake will be ready."

24

112 BCE

EARLY DAWN CAST long shadows towards Mount Carmel. Keziah, Moshe, and the three girls came out of Cana on the way to Grandma Sarah's as their shadows wrinkled and pulled back. Little Sarah rode the donkey to spare her back and legs. One of Joseph's carts would have been more comfortable, but Keziah did not understand the tack and would not let Moshe do it for her. He would marry within the year, but for now, he was just her boy. They walked to Grandma Sarah's.

"Father will be home next week," Moshe said.

Keziah looked up at the road ahead, at her son, at the three girls. "We'll be home first."

There came a moment on the road when that old feeling resurfaced. A lull had developed in conversation, and only the sound of their feet and the donkey's hooves disturbed the silence. Nothing warned her. The scene from her Judean village, starting with the murder of Little Moshe, came upon her. Her imagination raced beyond the scenes that she had personally witnessed. She avoided her abduction and stayed instead with her parents. She heard her mother's voice then, freshly remembered the warmth and the heaviness of it. The words were indistinct, but her mother's message still warned her of the vision's dangers. Yet the images pushed on, pushed past resistance, advanced upon a promise of new horrors. She felt again the waiting hammer, the darkness that lurked, the thing crouching in the dark, the thing with teeth. Something waiting to feast. She felt terror build within, a madness, a panic that welled and made her heart race, and then her mother's voice cut through again. One of the girls asked a question, and another answered. Moshe joined the conversation. Keziah disagreed with his answer.

They continued walking, discussing one thing and then another. After a time, her heart settled, and the feeling left her. The strange artifact of memory or imagination drifted below her thoughts and disappeared. It waited for another time. There was just the road again, her son, her daughters, the donkey.

At the grandparents' house, Ephraim seemed to have aged significantly in just two weeks. Grandma Sarah fussed with a stew. The place seemed smaller than it had in visits past.

"You have your own troubles now," Grandma Sarah said with a glance at Little Sarah. "How is she?"

"The seizures started again. Two nights ago was the last."

"Go down to the stream with the older ones," Grandma Sarah said. "I'll keep an eye on her."

"No," Keziah said. "You visit with the older ones. I want to take her with me."

Moshe came as well. The older girls stayed to help in the kitchen.

Little Sarah was eight years old, but she walked as if she were ninety and in great pain. The three of them took their time. They walked at her pace through a carpet of white almond blossoms and drifts of pomegranate petals. At the creek, Moshe lifted his little sister over the small stream, carried her the last few steps, and then set her down in one of the two seats carved into the great oak log. Keziah rested beside Sarah, and Moshe stood.

"Faher 'ade 'ish," Little Sarah said, touching the old, cracked recess of their seat, caressing the exposed end grain at the sides and putting her finger into a gap where bark still clung.

"Yes, he did," Keziah said. "Your Uncle Jacob and I hid over there." She pointed behind them and waited for Little Sarah to rotate her unsteady head and adjust her posture to look around. "Those bushes there. They used to be smaller, but they were big enough to hide Uncle Jacob and me. He was your age then. We hid all day and watched your father work. The old donkey stood there." She pointed again in front of them and waited for Sarah to readjust her posture and then her gaze. "It pulled that log all the way from Cana, and he carved it here."

"How did he move it by himself, from the cart to here?" Moshe asked.

"I didn't see that part," Keziah said. "Uncle Jacob did, then he came to get me. I never thought to ask your father.

Back then, I probably believed that he was strong enough to pick it up on his shoulders and move it himself."

Moshe laughed, and Little Sarah spoke indignantly. "He cooow."

"Yes, he could," Keziah said. "Somehow, he could. He did."

"You used to play the lute here," Moshe said.

"This was my place, yes. Sometimes I played in the house. Never at parties. Not like now. Back then, I just played for myself. It was with your father that I learned to play for others. With others."

"Does it seem strange to be here now and not play? And to be here with others?"

"No, of course not," Keziah said. "You're my family. I have come here with your father many times. I think at least one of you was made here."

Moshe shot his mother a flushed look, and Keziah laughed. "You're old enough, young man."

Moshe glanced at Little Sarah, but she no longer followed the conversation. The sound of the creek, the call of birds, and the whisper of leaves had claimed her attention. She might have been sleeping, but her eyes were open and her ears even more so. Just not to their conversation. She was awake to the land: it was Little Sarah's language. She was enthralled by trees, by light, by the sound of birds and water.

"It seems like you should play in this place," Moshe said.

"I should have brought my lute."

"I did," Moshe said. When his mother looked at him, he continued. "It's hidden in the sack of wood shavings we brought for the barn." Moshe smiled at his mother's expression. "Father told me that if we came here and the weather was sure to be dry, I should bring the lute. Give you a chance to play down by the stream."

"Oh, my boy." Keziah nodded, and he slipped away, leaving his mother and his sleeping-while-awake sister alone together. He hopped the creek and disappeared beyond a veil of blossoms.

When he returned with the lute case, she knew that Grandma Sarah and the girls had come as well and hidden—though not very well—in that place where she and Jacob had crouched so many years before.

The case usually went where Little Sarah now sat. Keziah hesitated, and then Moshe opened it and held it for her. She took the instrument out and tuned it slowly. It seemed naked without its case. She sensed Little Sarah coming back to them. She considered calling her other daughters and her second mother from their hiding place but then left them to their secrecy as Little Sarah's hand fluttered. The little girl reached out and touched the lute, a light-fingered blessing, and then she took her trembling hand back and waited. She did not settle the hand in her lap until Keziah began.

Keziah played a simple tune first, a lullaby she had once played for all the children when they slept. After that, she played a love song, but she did not sing. Basmat and Noadiah sang this song. It was a lovers' duet sung by two wives about their husbands. She did add secondary notes that sketched the lines her friends' voices would have sung had they been here. Joseph was on her mind then, the children far away. The creek was the same creek that had hidden them so many times over the years, had muffled their conversation and laughter.

After the love song, she played music from the synagogue and then something appropriate for the temple, a memory from a Judean childhood. After these came an innovation, just a series of scales with alternating finger patterns stylized to echo the sounds of this little island in the creek. With her children about her in this place, among the trees and blossoms and birds that had healed the trauma from her childhood and brought to her the first and only man she had ever loved, Keziah felt more peace than she'd felt in a long time. This special place now captivated her daughter as well. There were secret notes she wanted to insert into this innovation, a pattern within the strings that Joseph would hear and recognize, something that she had not played for him in a long time. But he was far away and would not hear, so she left the second tier of notes untouched. Then the music was just a memory travelling down the length of the creek, and there was silence again. Only the music of the water remained.

Back at the house, the older girls returned to helping Grandma Sarah. Little Sarah accepted Ephraim's invitation and sat beside him. She pulled her legs up against her chest, leaned into him, and started talking. Keziah could not hear the words. She did not know how much they understood each other, but they were happy together. They were each other's favourite, had been since before the Seleucids hurt Little Sarah and more so afterwards. The old man had come to see his granddaughter four times during her long sleep. Despite the distance and his health, he came, and it was on his fourth visit, with his agitated forehead pressed against hers despite Joseph's concerns and protest, that Little Sarah's eyes had opened for the first time. The old man did not notice, for his eyes were closed. He kept up his gravelly murmuring, and when her little hand lifted and rested on his face, the family was unsure if he understood the significance of that miracle. He stole all of that first waking, not leaving her forehead, never seeing her open eyes. He murmured his grandfather-words quietly to her until she slept again.

The family had been a confluence of emotions afterwards. The next day, Little Sarah had woken again, and this time Keziah was able to meet her eyes and speak with her. After she began to walk, Joseph left with Joazar and the others on their mission to spread the news about the renewed siege of Samaria and the new vision for Galilee's future. Little Sarah walked again, but she would never be the same in mind or body.

It was just before the evening meal when Moshe came back to the house. He had finished the chores and washed up at the creek. The older girls spread the dinner mat in front of Ephraim and Little Sarah and then laid the food out on the mat, and the rest made themselves comfortable on the floor around it. Moshe began the meal with the holy words as he had since his father had been away. "Blessed are you, Lord God, king of the world—" And then Ephraim broke in, not willing to be unmanned in his own home: "Who causes bread to come from the earth—" And then Little Sarah broke in with a too early and mostly garbled repetition of the key phrase. Next came the "amen" from the older sisters to cover the mistake. Moshe flushed, and both Keziah and Grandmother Sarah tried not to laugh.

Ephraim seemed unconcerned by the violation of roles and procedure and tore off a triangle of bread. He moulded it to his own design and then used it to pluck a particularly fatty piece of goat from the central pot. He was about to eat it when he caught Little Sarah's eye, saw her looking at him, frowned, nodded in surrender, and fed her the choice bit. She tore her piece of bread, didn't mould it much at all, barely dipped it in the sauce, and fed her grandfather the rather poor selection. Grandmother Sarah started laughing, then Keziah let a giggle slip, and finally, everyone but Ephraim and Little Sarah joined in the laughter. Ephraim frowned and proclaimed in a low mutter to Little Sarah the incredible tastes he was now enjoying, and she spoke back to him as well. While her words were incomprehensible, her tone seemed to communicate a similar report. They regarded each other with bright eyes and satisfied smiles. The laughter of the others did nothing to penetrate the high regard the grandfather and granddaughter shared for one another.

Keziah and the children left the little compound four days later. Keziah felt lighter. Ephraim stayed in bed, too tired from the visit to see them off.

They went as they came, with Little Sarah on the donkey. Sometimes she talked to herself, and at mid-morning, Keziah came up beside the donkey and carefully listened as they walked. She tried to pick out the words. The girl was talking to her grandfather, replaying a conversation or perhaps continuing it. She became aware of her mother looking up at her, reconnected with the present, and smiled.

An hour later, riders came upon them. The two men rode up on horses that were not Galilean farm animals. The men were foreigners. The edges of their beards were trimmed. They wore Egyptian helmets on their heads and Scythian shields on their backs but seemed to be lacking swords. At their waists, each bore a long knife and no other weapons. They came from the direction of the Jordan River. They rode up and then stopped, surveying the family with leering smiles.

"What do we want?" one man asked loudly. His smile was as crooked as his teeth. "You're supposed to ask what we want."

Keziah pressed herself against the donkey. Her oldest daughter took the reins while the second stood beside Keziah. Moshe stepped before the women. He had with him a sword he had looted from the battlefield trailing from Samaria to Scythopolis.

"What do we want?" the man shouted again.

"You'll tell us when you're ready," Moshe said.

"Moshe," Keziah said quietly.

"Yes, Moshe. That's no way to speak to your elders." The man boomed with laughter while his partner studied Keziah.

"You can have the young ones," the quiet man finally said. He spoke quietly, but the sound did not translate as gentle. His nose, deformed in a manner that suggested frequent abuse, seemed to characterize his demeanour better. "I'll have the mother. She looks fine to me."

Moshe pulled his sword out slowly. The men seemed to notice it for the first time. Keziah did not say anything. She had not wanted him to bring it—thought it ridiculous that a woodworker's son would have looted any sword, let alone one of this workmanship—but as he stood there before her, she was suddenly glad he had it. The way he held it made her wonder if there had been incidents on that Samarian trip that Joseph and her son had not shared with her. He held the sword like someone who had used it.

The girls moved around Keziah, but they did not come into her line of sight. She sensed them behind the donkey now and was afraid for them, but she kept her eyes on her son and the two men. She did not know how to help or what to do.

"What in Zeus's name is wrong with that one?" the loud man said, gesturing with his reins at Little Sarah.

Little Sarah was talking. At the sound of the man's voice, she began talking louder, louder than usual. Her words were incomprehensible even to her family, and she kept staring at the two men on their horses as she sat on her donkey. Keziah looked up at her in alarm and saw spittle running down her chin. Little Sarah stuttered her words through some previously buried anger that looked close to a new seizure. She was just short of shouting. Her broken half-words mixed Aramaic and old Hebrew and other incomprehensible sounds with syllables missing and passion overflowing.

Keziah put a hand on Little Sarah's leg. The girl did not pause in her speech but put her hand on her mother's and pushed it away.

The two men seemed disturbed by Sarah's performance. "Has she got a demon?" the broken-nosed man finally asked. "She looks like she has a demon."

"What in Hades is wrong with you?" the loud man suddenly barked. He backed his horse up, not looking at Little Sarah now but glancing right and left at the two older daughters as they appeared from the front and rear of the donkey. They bore their father's javelins. Each held their weapon as she had been taught to throw it, with a second ready in the spare hand.

"Zeus in Hades cursed!" the loud man shouted as the

girls came up on either side of the men. Moshe stepped forwards, close to the broken-nosed man who had threatened his mother. He extended his sword and laid the tip against the rider's thigh. Both men held their horses very still.

"Somebody shut that girl up." Both men seemed genuinely alarmed by Sarah.

"My sisters can throw faster than you can ride. Once you're gutted, I'll cut your heads off and feed your bodies to the golem that haunts this country."

"We're going north."

"Why?" One of the girls was now behind the riders, and the men could no longer see the entire family at once.

"Cyzicenus is recruiting a new army to replace the one you Jews destroyed."

"And you thought you would ride through our country to him," Moshe repeated. The men's visible panic continued to rise as both girls disappeared behind them and out of their field of view.

"Cyzicenus already has six thousand soldiers from Egypt."

"And you thought you would ride through our country to join him?"

"Judea. We avoided Judea. We didn't think Galilee would be a problem. We're just passing through."

"Do all mercenaries go looking for work without their own weapons? Or are you too stupid to work out what you need for war?"

The broken-nosed man stiffened. He raised his reins as though to advance his horse and then stopped himself as the sword tip pressed meaningfully against his thigh. "I wish you would shut her up," he said again.

"She'll stop when you've left our country. I suggest you move with speed, or her words may track you down and do what they threaten."

"Zeus," the man said again, though he was not loud anymore and did not finish his thought. He pulled his horse around, circled off the track, and then went back onto the road some distance ahead. His companion followed. Soon only dust lingered.

Sarah stopped talking. There was no seizure, no explanation, no conclusion. She just stopped and stared off into the distance with a line of saliva from chin to chest. Moshe reached for her, and Little Sarah dipped her face to him, and he wiped it clean. He could not catch her attention beyond that. She seemed lost in thought. Her older sisters gathered around their mother and burst into tears, and then when the group started out again, the girls kept their weapons at hand.

Keziah continued with the group, but she had less to say. Her children felt to her now like strangers.

Some time later, Sarah started talking again, quietly replaying her conversations with Grandfather once more.

25

112 BCE

On the new moon, the mercenaries descended from their northern assembly grounds outside Apamea: six thousand Egyptians, four hundred Greeks, and a dozen mixed-race. Cyzicenus led this motley force. After the previous summer's debacle, his damaged reputation clung to him like flies plaguing a slat-ribbed dog. The elephants went east with his co-regent half-brother, Grypus, to deal with the endless Parthian war. Cyzicenus took on the Jewish problem. No elephants.

Cyzicenus and his troops passed through northern scrubland and stumbled through late spring streams on legs made wooden by cold. They slid down rocky hillsides and crossed treacherous fields that gave the appearance of an easy passage, but the turned ground was not solid at its tilled surface, and it sank away below them. None in command had been farmers. The sown soil was more difficult to traverse than the desert's shifting sand. Progress crawled on its belly, their intended whirlwind of military redemption replaced with a dull burn. Wet mornings and heavy clothing created problems of foot and crotch for which no general had a cure. They were over-armoured and under-rationed. Supply wagons grew light. The passing of difficult days bred dangerous rumours.

Dusk saw them set up camp without the familiar instant-town miracle. When it came to tent locations, temporary thoroughfares, designated latrines, and common areas, the Egyptian mercenaries took few orders from their Greek paymasters, and it seemed that they had no other training to fall back on. Each did as he saw fit and did it wherever he pleased. Cyzicenus cursed what he saw, but he did not know how to fix the situation. All he could conclude was that a standard Seleucid army in some theoretical dysentery retreat would show more discipline than these Egyptians with their chaos. The Egyptians could lead a fight, but they could not make a camp.

They did not have enough men for a second attempt directly against Judea's army in Samaria. The plan was to draw Hyrcanus off from their siege by raiding towns throughout Upper Galilee. The deaths of farmers and the destruction of the nation's harvest would eventually break Jerusalem's will. Cyzicenus wondered why no general before him had thought of it. It would be a siege without war machines. There was no need for elephants. Starve Judea, and it would kneel. He smiled, showing his teeth. Soft ground and rain and Egyptian camp incompetence were no matter—he would succeed, and the Jews would suffer and start paying Seleucid taxes again.

The Seleucid army advanced upon a ridge early in the evening. Scouts reported that there was a village in the valley below. From the cliff, they could see smoke from the village's cook fires and some animals close to the buildings.

The invaders divided into predetermined companies. This task the Egyptians could be relied upon to execute with Seleucid precision. Men on foot crested the ridge, split off the trail, took to the forest on either side, and advanced unseen and unheard to the outskirts of the village. The buildings smoked their evening fires through black basalt chimneys. Every family was indoors.

"Assemble quietly," Cyzicenus had said. He had stayed back with the wagons, horses, and cavalry, but his instructions were clear. "When I give the signal, begin. All at once. Together." Cyzicenus could not suppress the enthusiasm in his voice. They were about to execute a plan he had come a long way to enact. He had his own name for it: Cyzicenus's Revenge. He foresaw the histories that would be written. He had smiled another toothy grin and savoured the moment as his men had crept away.

The Jewish houses had been built on stone foundations with basalt walls matching the chimneys. The carved and mortared stones were topped with pole and thatch roofs. The only way to breach the homes was through wooden doors of squared timber. A sharp-chinned Egyptian led a group of men to assemble at one such house. He was missing his ears, which had been crudely sawn-off in some adventure he recounted to none. There were eight in this group, all familiar with one another from countless Ptolemaic battles in Africa and Arabia. They had been lured away from their service to the Egyptian military by promises of treasure. Most of the other Egyptians, who were now surrounding other homes in the strangely quiet village, had come for the same reason.

The leader of the assault waited until all of the various groups were in position, and then from the edge of the village, he gave the signal, and the boy beside him let out a startling trumpet blast, and the army burst through Galilean doors as one. Each of the invaders expected to see startled households and hear the cries of war, the screams that advertised impending rape, the clash of precise instruments of war against kitchenware and flesh, enough opposition to bring a thrill. A few attackers might sustain unlucky injuries to feed later campfire mockery, but nothing here could dissuade the mercenaries from enacting their worst intentions.

The village remained quiet.

The earless Egyptian signalled his second and third to investigate the back rooms. A meal was heating on the fire. The aroma of a savoury stew filled the house. Their violent expectations met with confounding silence, and their uncertainty heightened their attention to more distracting senses. Freshly baked bread lay on a warming stone beside the oven. The pot amid low coals simmered but did not burn. Heads turned. Mouths watered. There was food, but no eaters and no cook.

There were four rooms, all empty: no rear entrance, no upper level.

"Gone," the earless man said.

"I could eat."

"We'll miss the looting."

There were sounds from elsewhere in the village, but the voices were Egyptian and Greek. No victims were fighting or pleading. The village held only the murmur of cruel men, disappointed.

"Useless peasant village."

"The food is good."

"Take what is here."

Eight gathered around. They tore loaves of bread apart and took turns at the bubbling pot, dipping the bread and sucking the spillage. They used knives to spear meat and vegetables. They licked their fingers and trailed juices down their beards and flicked excess to the floor. The pot of enough stew to satisfy a family for two days was emptied and left on the coals, where it blackened and smoked.

They left the house, searched the courtyard, and found only an old, blind goat with ribs in high relief and skin hanging. It looked diseased. The earless Egyptian swung with his sword, hacked halfway through its bony neck, pulled the blade free, and left the animal where it lay, leaking weakly into the dark earth.

The story was much the same in the other houses. They did not find even one of the village's inhabitants and found only a few animals. What they did find was unfit for consumption.

They set up camp for the night in the village. Some groups took the beds and floors of the village homes. Others set up in the courtyards and others in empty fields, attracted to the softness of turned ground.

It was during the second watch that the moaning began. Within an hour, the first Egyptian began to vomit, and forty-five of the soldiers were dead by daylight. Their stomachs had bloated, and their faces and necks had turned purple. They died in great pain. Of the sick, only ten were alive in the morning, but they were still curled in agony, sweating, panting, retching. They vomited aggressively and tore muscles doing so. Then almost all of the stomach violence ceased; the surviving victims were faint-voiced during the reprieve, speaking in stunned awe as if some wave of evil had come among them and just as suddenly vanished. Then a new wave began. When the agony resumed, it came with blood.

Cyzicenus ordered the company to move on. Ill riders unable to mount their horses cried out to not be left behind. Cyzicenus ordered a halt, and the company watched as the weak laid forearms on wagon decks and crawled up amid roped supplies. Those watching offered no help. When the army set out again, one living man was left behind. He stood alone, his body twisted like a wind-ravaged tree: a hip cocked one way, the ribs another. He looked like a scarecrow sliding down its pole.

New victims showed signs of illness by noon. Four more died before evening; three, unable to ride, were abandoned. One victim was a suicide at nightfall. The earless Egyptian survived. None of his companions lived to the third day. Cyzicenus gave new orders regarding discovered food, a direction needed by none and heeded by all.

On the fourth day after leaving the poisonous village, Cyzicenus passed into the shade below a stand of tall oak trees. He paused in the dappled sunlight, thin lips pressed together. The warmth and freshness of this light looked beguiling when in Antioch. Now it taunted him. He had not won the war with his half-brother. The murder of each of their wives simply prompted a settling of differences in favour of a co-regency. Cyzicenus's kingship was owed as much to his opponent's lost appetite as it was to anything of military consequence.

Cyzicenus's personal history and accounts of the previous year's incursion into Jewish territory now circulated among the Egyptian mercenaries: the failed rescue of Samaria, the destruction of Cyzicenus's retreating army, and the escape to Scythopolis were topics that received the most attention. The Jewish king's other priorities always ended these stories; Hyrcanus had not found Cyzicenus worth pursuing beyond Galilee. Finally, some informed captain let slip that the Jewish king had not even led the previous year's defence. The king's untried sons were the leaders of that victory. The king had gone back to being a priest rather than bother with Cyzicenus and his army. With these details circulating, exaggerations and fabrications gradually entered the conversation as well. Common to all versions was the theme of failure.

For the next two weeks, they raided empty places devoid of people, livestock, and wealth. The land seemed to empty itself ahead of them. When darkness and drink loosened tongues around the fires at night, discontent found increasingly fertile ground and began to spread even to Cyzicenus himself.

"We're too small to go against Jerusalem or lift the siege at Samaria," Cyzicenus complained. "And you cannot burn a field in the spring."

"We're doing the right thing," Callimander, his second-in-command, said. "Lure Hyrcanus north to us."

"We're acting like bandits raiding villages. But we're too numerous to raid a village. They see us coming. So how is this the right thing?" Cyzicenus made no mention of his former confidence in this brilliant scheme.

The next morning, the dense fog that had been blurring their vision lifted. In the far distance, sharp-eyed early risers spotted Galileans fleeing towards the forest line. The cavalry quickly mounted up and galloped ahead in pursuit. They pounded across the hard road onto softer fields, left Cyzicenus and the main force behind, passed behind a swell in the land, and disappeared. The rest of the army followed. Cyzicenus's teeth slowly reappeared as he grinned in anticipation of battlefield redemption.

The riders rode back into view with a large group of men and horses missing. They veered off at an angle away from the woods with their shields shifted to cover their backs. Arrows protruded from desperate survivors. Slings and javelins appeared from behind a row of bushes in front of the cavalry, and to Cyzicenus's horror, stones and shafts flew, every shot was true, and the remaining cavalry scattered.

Of the forty that had pursued the few running Galileans, twenty-four men returned. By the time the full army caught up to the dead, the Galileans were gone.

"I have no oath sufficient for my disgust," Cyzicenus said.

They dispatched the dying horses and came up short in the count. Horses were missing, which led to further debate.

"The missing horses' tracks lead towards the valley, that way," one adviser said, pointing to a gap between distant hills. "But I don't know what's there. The map isn't complete in that direction. It's probably just forest."

"There has been nothing but poison in the villages," another advisor said.

"No more villages," Cyzicenus said. "We follow the horses. We will find out where they are hiding. Somewhere in these mountains. Follow the horses."

For the next week, they followed the hoof trail. The fresh tracks indicated that they were always close, but the Seleucids never saw their quarry. At night, the watch reported hooves echoing in the dark canyons beyond their camp. In the morning, tracks were hard to discern.

Achaeus, a popular member of the scouting unit, approached the command circle. "I can find them," he said.

"There are men in your unit that can track these Galileans across pine needles and bare rock?" Cyzicenus sneered.

"No," Achaeus said. He was not a tall man, and he was thinly built, but he had won his fellow scouts' respect through age and experience. He could keep up with the youngest among the company across the longest distances. His face was lined, but his eyes were alert and clear. "But I can. I can find them."

He was sent off, and before Cyzicenus had finished his morning meal, Achaeus returned. A light sheen of sweat covered his face and neck, but he looked otherwise untroubled.

"They went east," Achaeus said, pointing. "A group of other men on foot have joined them. I'd say we're closer to the main force than we've ever been."

Cyzicenus burst out laughing, and when he finished, the smile lingered. He nearly embraced the small scout, caught himself, and dismissed the man with a gesture.

"Let's go," he said to Callimander. "Get them all moving."

They followed Achaeus's lead for the rest of the day and camped that night in a dark forest. The next day, the horse tracks disappeared completely. Cyzicenus turned to look back the way they had come, but they had lost the way. His army of six thousand stretched out behind him and had trampled any hope of discovering an off-trail.

"Bring me Achaeus," Cyzicenus commanded.

The scout was in the woods, and it took some time to find him. When found, he was brought straight back to the command group.

"I want you to find their path," Cyzicenus said. Achaeus stood before the command group, breathing heavily and sweating. There was no warmth in Cyzicenus's expression now. "We are done with following you aimlessly through this country. You find me these Jews. Today."

Achaeus nodded and said nothing. He did not walk out of the camp but ran, waving for the other scouts to follow him. Still within sight of the camp, the scouts broke up into three parties and disappeared into the forest.

The entire day passed while Cyzicenus and his men idled. Two of the scouting groups returned with no news late in the day, but Achaeus's group did not. The scouts were interrogated after dark, and it was confirmed that Achaeus and the two men with him had planned on searching in a southeasterly direction.

In the morning, Cyzicenus gave the army orders to march in the direction Achaeus and his men had taken. "The fool is chasing the Galileans instead of leading us to them," he grumbled to Callimander. "So, we'll do this ourselves."

It was midday when they found the small, lean scout and the other two men. They had been strangled and strung up in two oak trees. Achaeus was alone in his tree. The witless captains allowed the entire army to view the bodies before Cyzicenus ordered them brought down.

It did not take campfires and a dark moon for the men to talk among themselves that night. After Achaeus's death, discontent grew in open sunlight.

Early the next morning, they crossed a barren section where the land sloped up to the south, the trail pointed east, and a ravine lay off to the left. The right flank rose up a steep mountainside. The sun ahead blinded. Wagons skidded sideways on the slope, and the horses used quick steps to maintain minimal progress. They could not find water here. Precious sweat soaked every man, and concern floated in light heads.

When the rockslide started above, the company reacted slowly and then suddenly succumbed to full-blown panic. Men, horses, and wagons fled pointlessly down the slope as though to outrace the rocks. The most alert ran at an angle to escape the boulders' path, but several hundred men, a dozen horses, and three wagons ran off the edge of the small ravine. One man jumping might have made it to the bottom with recoverable injuries. On this day, men and animals and equipment swept over the edge and fell together. They hit the stone floor in a mass of broken bones and wood. There were screams of every variety, from both man and animal, and then came a final stoning by the avalanche. A dozen survivors were retrieved, bandaged, splinted, and squeezed into the remaining wagons.

Cyzicenus rode up to the open-air ward and cursed the men in bandages. "We've little food and few wagons, and so what little we have we'll use on these wretches?"

Three more weeks passed, the days filled with seemingly

minor misfortunes that cumulated into a wearying, deadly journey with no compensating tokens of success.

One night, thousands of shadowy lines appeared against the stars as a flock of arrows interrupted their camp's disorder. When the Seleucids picked through the field's population in the morning, they counted the dead and killed those near it. Every arrow found was fitted with small tri-blade heads—a precious commodity in any army.

"These are supposed to be just farmers," Callimander said.

Some of the Egyptian archers were perversely elated by the field of dead and dying. They set to gathering what could be recovered, both whole arrows and just arrowheads.

Only once did the Galileans give a proper invitation to open battle. A few days after the night attack, they appeared out of the treeline, numbering perhaps five hundred or a thousand. They charged from a great distance.

"Go!" shouted Cyzicenus. "Yes! Go!" The Seleucid army countercharged. They outnumbered the Galileans some five times or more, and the Galileans had no cavalry. They charged, then they disappeared. It was so sudden that the Seleucid advance halted without a command.

"Go! Go! Go!" shouted Cyzicenus, but to where was unclear.

They sent the scouts ahead, and half an hour passed before they returned. There was a dry riverbed ahead with steep banks. Except for occasional pools, the riverbed was empty. The Galileans were gone.

"Half one way. Half the other," Cyzicenus said.

"Probably," Callimander said.

"No! Us! Us! Divide your men. Half go one way and half the other. Find them!"

They sent scouts to run the riverbed while the army marched the upper bank. A total of four scouts were lost to pit traps in the riverbed. Crude spring traps in the tall grass killed three cavalry members and ten of the foot soldiers.

When both groups had returned, its commanders gathered on the riverbank edge with Cyzicenus and Callimander.

Cyzicenus looked west, where the sun sank low. He knew he should move his men well back from this dry channel before dark, or they would be vulnerable to assault during the night. Something flickered across his vision, and a strangled cry came from the man beside him. The man staggered back with an arrow lodged in his throat.

Seleucid archers immediately stepped forward and fired into the far side of the channel without a visible target. The sound of arrows striking solid wood and metal suggested that there were men with shields and armour hiding there, but the Seleucids could see nothing in the far side's tall grass. How many Galileans were there was unknown.

There was no time to stage a crossing this late in the day. There would be more traps in the long grass. Cyzicenus made a quick decision, and the Seleucids marched two miles in retreat before setting up camp. The field they chose was one of new green grass amid the previous year's stand of dry stalks. It was an unfarmed waste. Layers of flattened stalks from older years formed a mat below. New shoots struggled through this dead layer. It was like walking on a sprung floor. The Seleucids made camp here with the natural mats as a comfort.

A wind came up in the night. The fire that followed

came as a wall, bearing down with such speed that though the watchmen had time to raise an alert, the gap closed alarmingly fast while they did so. The Seleucid camp was a quarter mile from the forest. The heat pressed the army's back as they quickly marched their way ahead of the roar into the rocky forest land. They choked on smoke and dragged their kit farther into the treeline.

Exhausted and fearful, the invaders studied dark fire, sheltered by the shifting shadows of the trees. Some men noticed arrows embedded in companions' packs, the shafts standing proud like isolated porcupine quills. There was hasty lighting of torches and a search for further signs of assault. In the morning, they found eighteen blackened bodies in the field, with charred arrows standing erect like nails in a board. Those not killed by arrow strikes directly had been consumed by fire. The earless Egyptian used his knife to pry a metal arrowhead from the thigh of one such corpse. It was one of their own two-bladed heads from the day before, used back against them hours later. The archers again recovered as many of these arrowheads as they could find.

In daylight, the Seleucids retraced their steps from the day before. The burned field sagged below them. Ash billowed and formed a low cloud that was as tall as a man on horseback and obscured the land. The foot soldiers walked through a dim haze. When they came out of the field, men, animals, and equipment wore a layer of soot, and some men wore boots partially burned by still-smouldering fires in the lower thatch. Men coughed and spat up black phlegm. Black strands hung from horses' mouths like a gruesome webbing and continued to hang there as they passed into green country again.

They came again to the dry riverbed and expended hours of effort in unhitching the horses from the wagons, guiding the beasts down and back up the far side, unloading the wagons, lowering them into the channel, hauling them up the far bank, and then reloading and rehitching them. There were no signs of any Galileans.

❧

The next day Cyzicenus made a decision.

"You're in charge of the army," Cyzicenus said to Callimander. "Epicrates will be your second and successor. Move the battle south, engage the Galileans closer to their population centres, and use Scythopolis as your base for operations."

Callimander nodded.

"Draw Hyrcanus's attention away from Samaria. You'll find that the southern Galilean cities have more wealth. I didn't have time to exploit them last year."

"Where are you going to go?"

Cyzicenus showed his teeth and then slowly shut them behind thinly pressed lips. "I'm done with scrambling across mountains and rivers in search of empty-pocketed phantoms. The cavalry will come with me. There is business in Antioch that is a better use of my time. You keep the Egyptian foot soldiers."

Callimander protested.

"You can keep thirty of the cavalry," Cyzicenus relented. "None of the officers. You'll lead from your own mount."

❧

A sensible commander would have understood that this new commission was no promotion, but Callimander had a plan: he would make a name for himself where Cyzicenus had twice failed. Galilee would be Callimander's rise. Three days later, he mounted an all-out assault on a party of Galileans who exposed themselves on the edge of a woodland. It was the sort of assault that Cyzicenus had never led well.

Callimander commanded the men to pause before recklessly pursuing. An approach was agreed to. Only then did he unleash his force. Unlike Cyzicenus, Callimander would ride with his men and adapt his orders as required during the battle. It was an altogether different approach. The foot soldiers were to follow the cavalry charge immediately.

The men were inspired, and Callimander dared to smile. Their first victory was at hand. As his horse galloped, he felt the rush of blood, the excitement of the horse, the new lust of the men around him. He was achieving everything he had hoped to feel, see, hear, and then he felt the clobbering of a stone slung from a distance. It connected with his right eye socket, destroyed that eye, and broke the cheekbone. Inexplicably, the horse went down as well. While the stone drove him backwards, the sudden falling of his horse pitched him forwards. He barely managed to free himself of the animal, and by mere chance, he landed upright with his feet pressed hard against the ground. While he struggled to understand what had happened to his face, he felt immediate pressure and pain in his side. The ability to register such extreme pain was itself a surprise. With his one remaining eye, he looked around to discover what was happening and saw a boy of about twelve standing before him.

The boy pulled back his crudely fashioned sword with

hesitation, as if there were a polite way to perform that motion, while staring at Callimander's broken face. Callimander held the wound closed with both hands and spent his final moments still trying to understand. Some hours later, he was found by men who recognized him by his clothing, if not his face. He was propped up against the dead horse, having bled out alongside the beast.

Epicrates took over the command, and there were no further attempts to accept Galilean invitations to chase. He consulted the maps that Cyzicenus had left behind and charted a course for Scythopolis, away from Galilee and its murderous phantoms.

26
112 BCE

In the workshop, Keziah watched Joseph carve one last tightly controlled stroke. A curl of olive wood arced into sunlight. The thin and wide slice of the tree's heart became translucent before them in alternating dark and golden hues. He was working on refinements to an ornate case that had been recently commissioned by Saul.

Sweat beaded his arms. The blade was steady, but his movement revealed a stiffness. There was a scar at one shoulder that skipped across his upper arm and then dragged a thick ridge down his forearm. The wound was only two months old. Galilee had seen victory on the day that Joseph's arm was opened. The Seleucids had fled south to Scythopolis, that traitorous city along Samaria's border. Time was left for the Galileans to tend wounds properly, and so Keziah's husband lived. Moshe had looked after the dressing for two weeks. Eventually, father and son had returned with the rest of the men of Galilee.

Moshe. He was married now. The wedding had happened mere days after the men's return. It had been an irregular wedding, the final details handled in a rush. Avigail had married just before the war. Esther was engaged to be married next year. Soon they would only have Little Sarah with them.

When Joseph looked at her, for a moment it seemed that he did not see her, but then his eyes adjusted, and he smiled. They came together in a place in the shop with a raised wooden floor. Keziah spread out the mat while he watched, and then he reclined on it as she unpacked the meal.

"How is Sarah?" he asked.

"She was sleeping when I left," Keziah said. "She helped me with the bread first."

Silence took over the space. Dust motes hung in shafts of sunlight as they always had. It was a golden space where light and shadow conspired to produce alternating bands across Joseph's work. There was a kinship between the heart of the olive tree and the late afternoon sunlight in these shops. Keziah had come to this place many times when the men were fighting in Upper Galilee. While Joseph, his brothers, and Moshe had been gone, the same fine grains had stayed suspended in emptiness awaiting their return.

"It's nice to be working again on something that isn't designed to kill," he said. He spoke to Keziah, but his eyes were on a yoke, half-carved, propped up on the opposite side of the shop.

"I had an uncle who tripped over a chest about the same size," Keziah said. "He cracked his skull and died."

"Well," Joseph said with a wry smile, "it's not designed for that purpose."

Keziah followed his gaze to the half-completed yoke, then looked over at the case for Saul. "The box is beautiful so far," she said.

"I've got to get to work on more crates for Uri's quince as well," Joseph said. "Another batch will be ready for bottling soon, and Rehavam has already started on the bottles."

Two doves flew into the workshop and then back out.

"They've been doing that all afternoon," he said.

"Playing?"

"A kind of playing." He looked at her.

She laughed. "The answer is no. Not here. Your brothers."

"They're away."

"The answer is still no. Not here."

Three days later, Joseph and Joazar, with the other Galilean men, passed between Gerizim and Ebal. The clear water, black earth, and green foliage of the valley were not welcoming but cold. An eerie emptiness dwelled in the land. There were no signs left of Cyzicenus's first army from the previous year, no ghostly remains of the dead men's march. Cyzicenus's second army never made it this far. The city of Samaria lurked as a distant shadow slumped about the base of its mountain, empty of all souls. The Samaritans of the city and much of the valley were gone. The citizens of Scythopolis were gone now as well. In contrast to this quiet, across the Great Sea the slave markets would soon boom with sound and the diverging fates of the traders and the traded.

The missing people of this land were now profit for Jerusalem's treasury. According to Jugurtha's ledgers, selling the conquered brought a quicker return but, in the long run, less revenue than increased taxes. Nevertheless, Hyrcanus chose the slave markets. The choice was made in part by greed and in part to prevent future rebellions. A sold and deported people could not be disruptive in the future.

"No one brought in the harvest," Uri said.

The fields lay overgrown, untended, trampled. They passed by the closed gates of Shechem. None of the Galileans tried its bars. This Samaritan city still stood and was still populated, but outside its walls, only Galileans passed—Jews en route to Jerusalem.

Joazar's legs grew heavy as they climbed beyond Shechem. He needed something to break the gloom. "Jugurtha sent me a financial summary of Judea's campaign against Samaria," he said to the Galileans around him.

The men gave him quizzical looks.

It was a poor attempt at a mood change, but now that he had started the conversation, he felt the need to keep going. "It includes Scythopolis in the accounting. The money spent on the army, the supplies, the training, and Joseph's wagons and weapons. Arrow points. Provisions, and transport of those provisions, to keep up a one-year siege at Samaria. The supply train to both Samaria and Scythopolis. Slave transport to Joppa. Ships. Crewmen. Guards. All of it in the cost column.

"Then, in the income column, he put the territory gained. He made some assumptions about next year's taxes on whoever is left here. Accounted for any notable treasures captured. Estimated for one-time slave auction proceeds."

"What did they get?" Matthias, a neighbour of Joazar's, asked.

"He gave only a summary. I'm sure Hyrcanus got the full accounting."

"Like a business," Rehavam said.

"Yes," Joazar said. "Exactly like a business. Jugurtha calculated that, in the first year, Judea lost money. But two years on, with the new territory, maybe some repopulation growth if we can bring Jews back from Egypt and elsewhere, and then the taxes, the campaign starts to make money. He counted the costs from five years ago when we started building up the military's gear and weapon supply chain. So, it took over seven years for this enterprise to make money, mostly because of the upfront expenses and the delay in slave market revenue."

"We started working on the gear and weapon orders more than a decade ago," Joseph said.

"They ignore that," Joazar said. "They do accounting for five years only."

"The Samaritan and Scythopolis wars took seven years to make money?" another neighbour asked.

"Because of the long build-up," Joazar said.

"And he's still paying the mercenaries," Rehavam said.

"Yes."

"Then he needs to have another war soon," Rehavam said, "or he's going to be accumulating an expense on the books that will weigh down the profitability of the next war."

Everyone looked at Rehavam.

"Well? Isn't that how it will work?" Rehavam asked.

"It's true," Joazar said. "The quicker he has a war, the sooner he can make a profit on it."

"Did he count the money we raised to pay off Epicrates to hand Scythopolis over?" Uri asked.

There was a very long pause. Everyone looked at Joazar.

"I didn't see it in the summary," Joazar said. "I'm pretty sure it's not on the books."

"The king doesn't count Galilee's money, except for Galilee's taxes."

"Nor the loss of my son. There's no accounting for the loss of my boy," said Matthias. "Who is this Jugurtha friend of yours?"

Hard eyes looked at Joazar.

"Don't be angry with the man who tells you the king's secrets," Joazar said. "This is the same king that looted David's tomb."

"That's just a story," Matthias said.

"I was there," Joazar said. "I saw those who did it."

None seemed willing to ask the next question. They walked on to the Ingathering, the Festival of Booths, Sukkot, the festival designed to commemorate Israel's freedom from Egyptian slavery and their long-ago journey to Eretz-Israel. To get to this year's festival, the Galileans walked through the territory of Samaria. At the same time, thousands of Samaritans now travelled away from Eretz-Israel to their own new slavery. This message of opposites crossed more than one mind, but none of the Galileans spoke of it aloud.

Later, Joseph spoke quietly to Joazar. "In all the time I've known you, this is the first time you've come to the festival."

"I've been before."

"Yes, and you're going to the king's dinner with the rest of us. But you're talking like a man who hates the king."

❧

Joppa, the Judean port a long day's journey away from Jerusalem, reflected the sun like no other city. It was a jewel.

There was a gate standing within the city that still bore the name of Pharaoh Ramses from a thousand years before. There were homes in Joppa built by the Philistines, the conquerors that had come after the Egyptians. The city had been one of King David's prize conquests, and he added it to the tribe of Dan when there had been such a people. It was through this port that Solomon had shipped his cedars from Lebanon for Jerusalem's first temple. It was this port from which Jonah had fled God's direction. It had been the home of Sennacherib of the Assyrians in the days of Hezekiah when the ten tribes had been conquered and lost. Later, it was the port through which cedars again passed to build the second temple.

The Greeks designated it as the place where Andromeda had been chained to a rock in the sea as a sacrifice to the sea monster Cetus. Then Perseus, that half-human son of Zeus, had rescued her and married her while turning his rival to stone with the weaponized head of Medusa. The sea creature Cetus was now a submerged mound outside the port of Joppa. It would only be discovered again if the sea were to shrink and the depths forced to reveal their hidden, petrified terror.

Jewish legends attributed the place to Japheth, the son of Noah, in the days after the flood.

The old scribe knew all of this and more. He sat outside

the city, beyond the gates. Here he was away from the traffic of commerce and the tedium of council, from the gossip and the exchange. His daily routine was to walk slowly to this place and spend time in the sun with a few avian visitors and his memories. His back was no longer burdened by books and inks, the tools of his trade from his younger days when his eyes could see close up and his hands were steady. None would entrust him now with the expense of a blank page. He no longer had cause to read books. Everything was within memory now and his memory was sound. None studied under him anymore. He had outlived his students.

The old man came to his stone, the stone that time or some ancient mason had carved to suit his back and support his knees. He wore a broad hat of his own design. It protected him from the sun. He tilted it so the warming rays could bathe the one shoulder that needed warmth.

Three birds arrived, the same ones that always came to him. They never multiplied. It was always just the three hopping around his feet and the surrounding stones, shifting positions like a tiny gang of brigands intent on robbery. He offered them nothing at first. He watched them hop and wait and twerp their questions. He sometimes spoke back to them, but their responses were only avian. He sometimes went days now without uttering any sound at all. He found it remarkable after his years of teaching to say nothing for an entire day. It was a miracle to go for four days in silence. When unused vocal cords were occasionally struck, the notes were coarse and reminded him of someone much older than he believed himself to be. He wondered how others could understand him with the gravel that now infiltrated his speech.

When the time was right, he reached for his pouch. The three birds struck a noisy chorus, and then, with an effortful, protracted lean across the stone edge to his right, he deposited half a palmful of wheat grains on the ground. He was unbalanced now and used his emptied hand against the rock to push himself back up. He watched the three birds swarm the offering. They took more than seemed reasonable for the diminutive creatures, and then, with rounded bellies, they took to the air and were gone. The old man was left alone.

At midday, he shifted in some discomfort. He had once been able to sit here for hours without moving. His bones were closer to the skin now.

Hyrcanus's mercenaries came down the road to Joppa in the later part of the day, with a collection of captives in tow. The mercenaries numbered a dozen, the same size other parties on other days had been, and they looked to the old man like Thracians, the Hellenized savages of the northeastern world. They had olive skin like the Greeks, with matted and curled hair like any Seleucid. The difference between the Greeks and these mercenaries was their heavier features. They looked more like Pericles, the shipbuilder, harbourmaster, and mercenary recruiter—that brutal Cretan who somehow owned Hyrcanus's commission for the port at Joppa.

Hyrcanus no longer referred to his own family as Maccabees but as Hasmoneans, a name taken from further back in their family history and one that somehow justified Hyrcanus's command of both throne and temple. How the name justified an overthrow of Jewish laws the old man did not know. It was evident that the arrangement forestalled opposition: you could not decry the high priest to the king or complain of the king to the high priest when both were the same man.

There were no longer any prophets in Israel. This last fact troubled the old man the most, but he steered his mind away from it. He kept himself physically away from Jerusalem completely; he had no desire to try to penetrate the labyrinth that David's city had become. The old man's Greek mythologies and Egyptian histories were as much a comfort to him now as the Jewish Torah had ever been. Joppa was his city. It was a place where a sage could find encouragement for doubt.

He pondered the nature of change and isolation as Hyrcanus's mercenaries advanced towards him. He felt no fear though he knew fear was justified. He trusted the distraction of the mercenaries' youth and the power of their greed to leave him unmolested on his stone perch, abandoned by the birds, warmed by the sun, distant from the city that hardly knew him anymore. He had nothing to offer or threaten these men committed to hired violence.

Waiting for the dozen and their captives to arrive, he contemplated friends lost. They had each gone to some Greek, Egyptian, or Jewish afterlife or eternal death. If these mercenaries were to amuse themselves with his thin frame, they would find him to be a brief source of entertainment. It was hard enough to breathe in the heat. He would suffer only a little abuse before being transported to the mysteries beyond, and he was more curious than afraid of what he might find there.

He did not smell the mercenaries until they were upon him. The reek of old sweat and unwashed leather arrived just as rough faces came into focus. Some looked serious, some looked dull with sullen eyes, and all seemed slightly drunken. Their weaponry was packed away. Their mostly barefoot captives staggered on tired feet.

The slave train of Samaritan men, women, and children followed behind the soldiers. Their hands were bound, and each captive's neck was tied to the next one's. Some necks were bound by chains, others with rope. The majority of the prisoners were women, and they bore signs of abuse. The few men were shells—their heads bowed and faces distorted with swelling and dried blood. Two carried broken arms that would reduce their value at the auctions if the bones were not set before the end of their upcoming voyage across the Great Sea to the slave auctions there. The old scribe presumed that the damages were either from the war or from a failed defence of the captured women. The children did not cry but walked mute in this new reality, bereft of everything but horror.

Each captive looked empty as though they had nothing more to give or lose, but the old man knew they were wholly unprepared for what awaited them. Across the water, they would be stripped and sold like meat to a people whose language they did not know in a land they had never imagined, and such a fate would only happen if they were resilient enough to survive the ships and the sea. The old man decided that frailty held an advantage; he pitied those slaves who were healthy and would survive to meet the end of their journey.

The troop passed without a word. Alone again, the old scribe took a drink, ate a small piece of bread and an even smaller bit of sweating cheese, and then had another drink.

There was a small shoe in the road that had not been there before. It lay in front of him, half-buried in the dust, its worn straps dark with sweat. It seemed to accuse him, as though witnessing the terrible trade had made him complicit in it.

He resolved to take his silent sunshine walk and rest along the seashore tomorrow and in the days that followed. The breeze was stronger there, and the sun not as warm, but he knew some places where the rocks created a natural windbreak. He would find some comfort there. He would miss the birds.

27

112 BCE

After the festival came the feast. While there, Joazar heard something wrong with the music. It was Hellenic—Antioch in Jerusalem but without the scented women—and it made him uneasy.

"It's been many years," Jugurtha said in greeting when he saw Joazar.

Joazar looked closely at his friend. "Years full of letters," he said with a smile.

Joazar introduced Joseph to Jugurtha. The three discussed equipment and materials but said nothing about Little Sarah.

The first day of the feast was awash with gluttonous boasting. Through this, the Galileans learned of a new myth, a lie, an infection of misinformation that had started in Jerusalem and spread throughout the Judean south. It was a fresh account of recent events: Hyrcanus's sons had not only conquered Samaria with their mercenary army, but they had also become the sole victors over Cyzicenus's second invasion as well. The valour of Galilee's makeshift army and the months of unaided self-defence were completely missing from the accounts. This new tale so confounded the Galileans they were unable to form an immediate response.

Hyrcanus rose later in the evening. He teetered, steadied himself, drank from the cup at hand, and then began to speak about Egypt.

"Cyzicenus came to this land with his Egyptian mercenaries and suffered at our hands for it. But how was it that these Egyptians came to fight in the Seleucid army to begin with? Have the Egyptians turned against us?" He surveyed the room, took a deep breath, and then roared, "Are we at war now with Egypt?" He towered up on tiptoes. He roared again, this time without words. It was a mad roar, which descended into breathless laughter. The room stared at him.

"When Pharaoh Cleopatra was in need, Jews in Alexandria were her most loyal supporters," he continued. "She gave Onias leave to build a Jewish temple in Egypt—at Heliopolis, which others call Leontopolis, a reward for Jewish loyalty. Later, when her kingdom was endangered again, our brother Onias rallied our people in Egypt a second time. Jews keep Pharaoh's throne secure.

"Then six thousand of her soldiers went over to Cyzicenus to invade our country! Has Egypt's pharaoh now turned against us?" Hyrcanus leaned in, hands on his knees, nearly spilling his wine on the dining cloth before him. "No!" he roared, belching and tossing the contents of his glass half a man's length down the table. "No! That is not how Pharaoh rewards our people! This was done without her knowledge. The generals who concocted such a betrayal, this bleeding off of her forces to harm us, they have been subjected to such tortures that, if I were to describe half of them to you, I would ruin this feast! A betrayal from Egypt is not the news that I shall announce at this feast. Instead, I tell you this—" Hyrcanus stopped and looked around the room. "That same Onias who built the temple for our people, his sons . . . his sons . . . " Hyrcanus seemed at a loss for words.

"Chelcias and Ananias," said Jugurtha.

"Chelcias and Ananias. Chelcias and Ananias! They are now the queen's generals. Our Jewish sons are now the pharaoh's generals! We lead Pharaoh Cleopatra's army, and we have the backing of Egypt's empire, and thanks to my sons"–Hyrcanus stamped his foot and raised his hands in a kind of victory celebration–"the land of the Samaritans is once again ours as well. We have peace within our borders, and the Seleucids will never dare return! God bless my sons and the sons of Onias. The sons of two families have secured peace for our two great nations!"

The background music was overwhelmed by the cheering of the crowd, and Hyrcanus beamed at his guests. He glowed with manic pleasure while the Pharisees and Sadducees were united in their rejoicing. Only the Galileans seemed slow to embrace the news.

Hyrcanus waved his hands to quiet the crowd. He made his youngest son, Alexander Jannaeus, stand. He was the only son who had not been involved in military adventures, Egyptian or Seleucid. Joazar recognized him from outside the Samarian siege, the king's son that was younger than Moshe. He looked thirteen. Maybe fourteen.

"Another announcement! My youngest son has yet to wed," Hyrcanus said. "But a bride has been selected. Next year he will assume his duties as a man. He will marry my cousin Salome Alexandra, and she will bear him mighty sons."

The roar of the crowd rose again. The cries of celebration were as loud as before, and Joazar struggled to hear as Jugurtha pulled him close. "A strange match," Jugurtha said. "She is nearly thirty. More than twice the age of the boy. Never wed."

Joazar looked at his friend in puzzlement, and Jugurtha pulled him in again. "He is going to train as high priest. After Hyrcanus dies, they will make the kingship and the high priesthood separate again as it is in the law. The oldest brother, Judah Aristobulus, will be king. Alexander Jannaeus will be high priest."

That night, the Galileans went to foreign beds. They were unsettled and confused, and the clear-minded among them were angry. The rupture did not occur until the second night.

The second day of the feast was much like the first. The music was the same. Hyrcanus began boasting early, and his audience warmed to the act. He retold the exploits of southern mercenaries as though they were the heroic acts of actual Jews, and when there was still nothing said of Galilee, the Galileans became restless. At one point, Joseph pulled back his sleeve and left the angry snake-like scar to stand in silent testimony. Matthias, still grieving the loss of his son, was stilled by men from Cana when he tried to rise.

Hyrcanus held court with new plans to invade surrounding kingdoms. "We're going to expand south into

Idumea," he said. "Take over Petra of the Nabataeans. The whole of the east side of the Jordan River. And Iturea."

He wore a lecherous expression, like a man who had thrown raw meat into a pit of dogs and waited for the beasts to recognize their prize. "Gentile against gentile," he said. "Our mercenaries against the enemy. If ours die, we don't have to pay them. We just hire more men with the savings."

Conversation rose in the room. Assessments of this strategy confronted practical and theological protestations, and then a murmur rose among the king's own Pharisees. "The borders of Eretz-Israel are clearly defined in the Torah," a voice called from the crowd. "There is no provision for expansion!"

Several Sadducees tried to shout down the Pharisees' objections. Galilean voices rose in support of the Pharisees.

"I am offended, my brothers!" Hyrcanus shouted, drowning out the room and drawing all eyes to him. "Am I not also a Pharisee? And yet, I hear my brothers opposing the visions given to me by God!"

"God gave you no vision," said the elder Pharisee, Eleazar.

"Speak not!" the king shouted. He glared at the room. "What offence have I committed against my brothers?" He patted his chest as though looking for something missing. "I lost my father and mother and brothers to free this country from our Seleucid overlords, and I have accomplished what they began. What offence have I committed that you would oppose me?"

He stayed standing, dominating the room, and flattered his dissenting Pharisees. Finally, he acknowledged the great work of the people of Galilee. He invited Joseph to stand

and tell the story of his arm but moved on before Joseph had an opportunity to accept or decline. He complimented his generals for their training and leadership of the army. He talked in this way until Joazar despaired. Antioch's moon dimmed over Jerusalem. He sensed a cloud enter the feasting hall, dimming not the room's light but its purity. Pillars were suddenly too close together, the roof too low, the air too still. The only things missing were Pericles and the obvious whores. Otherwise, this was now Antioch.

Hyrcanus made a grand gesture. "It is the way of a Pharisee only to do the things that might please God, and as a Pharisee, that is my sole devotion." He smiled in a manner both unhinged and utterly sincere. His eyes were too bright, bright with wine and with anger. "I ask you, brothers, all of you, if there is any point of law where I have come up short, any matter in which I have offended, please correct me! I am your perfectly humble and righteous king."

The music had stopped, but Joazar could still hear the echo of Seleucid chords. From the crowd came a wave of commendations. The Sadducees declared their unswerving belief in Hyrcanus and his family. Two Galileans inexplicably rose and praised the king. The Pharisees were also inexplicably complimentary until it came time for the impolitic Eleazar to speak again.

Eleazar rose and looked steadily at the king. The room waited. He said, "If you desire to know what is true and on what matter you offend both God and his temple, then know that it is the matter of the high priesthood. If you would not make a mockery of our religion, then lay down the high priesthood and be content with the civilian government of our people. Leave the high priesthood to one who is not an offence to that office."

The room went quiet. Hyrcanus stared at his accuser. Finally, he spoke. "On what grounds am I an offence to the high priesthood?"

"We heard from our fathers and their fathers before them that your mother was taken captive by Antiochus Epiphanes in the time of the great persecutions, and that you were born a natural season thence. Neither the bastard, nor the child of rape, nor the child of an adulterous woman, and certainly not a halfbreed Greek may serve as high priest over God's holy people. Whatever the nature of the union that made you, you are unqualified for the office."

The volume in the room exceeded any previous outcry. Hyrcanus gasped and turned red. The Pharisees stood and, in the tumult, rushed Eleazar from the room. The feast emptied. No more dishes were brought in. The mugmar's aromatic spices remained unburned.

The Galileans left that very night and crossed into Samaria's empty land before they stopped to rest. Something was following them that invaded dreams. It coloured the texture of the next morning's grey sky. Jerusalem became a foreign place to them where many things were wrong, even the music.

28

111-110 BCE

PALE WAS THE moon that passed over Galilee. It lit the meeting place where Cana's people discussed Jerusalem's controversies and the Pharisee's charge, the new rumours and refutations and bitter memories.

"Bastard or son, Hyrcanus is a terrible king," Rehavam said to a small gathering at Joseph and Keziah's home. "He's a drunk who invents new histories."

Night after night, they covered the same ground. "About Jerusalem" one conversation might start, and so a new night of controversy began.

"We need a letter," Saul said one night when he was visiting. "I'll be in Jerusalem in two days. Give me one for Jugurtha, and I'll come back with a reply."

Jugurtha's reply came a week later.

Eleazar's accusations have torn up the city. Jonathan the Sadducee is stirring up a rebellion against the Pharisees. He has the king's ear. In the meantime, Hyrcanus is planning an assault on Medeba.

"You need to explain to him about Medeba," Rehavam said.

"He's not from here," Uri said. "He won't know."

And so Joazar wrote to Jugurtha. A few weeks later, another letter arrived:

You did well to inform me of the Hasmonean family's history with Medeba. I had no prior knowledge about what had occurred in that city. It seems that Hyrcanus seeks to settle an old score in which the Jews are perhaps the most guilty party. A massacre at a wedding more than repays for the loss of one son.

Hyrcanus has broken from the Pharisees and formally adopted the Sadducean party as his own. He won't accept a divide between his roles as high priest and king. He has chosen the party that supports him.

Another letter arrived some months later:

After a siege, Medeba has fallen. A garrison will remain to collect the new revenues. The rest of the army marches to Samaria to complete unfinished business there. The City of Samaria and Scythopolis remain subdued, but other cities in the Region of Samaria have yet to pay the tribute.

The letters continued to flow as the Judean forces kept pressing their way through the Region of Samaria. "Shechem has fallen now as well," Joazar reported. The men of Cana were a study in frowns as they sat in a circle near the long shadow of the dovecote.

"Maybe the winter will cool Hyrcanus's lust for war."

There was no cooling of the king's appetite. Jugurtha's next letter came in the spring:

Hyrcanus has sent the army south of Jerusalem, this time into Idumea. They travel with a strange auxiliary: over one hundred priests armed with surgical knives.

"What does that mean?" asked Uri.

"Convert and be circumcised," Saul said, "or die."

Salome Alexandra has given birth to a son with Alexander Jannaeus. We have discussed her older age, but now that she has produced an heir, she has nothing to worry about. They have named him Hyrcanus in honour of his grandfather.

Finally, a letter arrived that resolved the Idumean story.

The army has returned victorious. Only Maresha and Adora gave real resistance. Other cities surrendered early, and the rest of the region accepted Judea's terms without protest. And independent Idumea is now no more. According to reports, the blades of the priests saw more blood than that of the soldiers.

❧

Joazar dreamed that night of a small house somewhere in the south. A line of men and mothers with young sons stood outside. Men entered the house alone, and boys entered with their mothers. The men exiting did so in grief, holding themselves in pain, unmanned and unable to walk steadily, not helped by their friends who came to submit themselves to the same fate. The youngest boys were carried away by their mothers and wailed in the streets. In families with many boys, the sisters helped their brothers too. Men and mothers were ashen as they made their way home, the boys red-faced with outrage. The oldest of the elderly men hid for fear that they would die from the procedure. None of the boys were hidden lest they be discovered later.

Joazar awoke from his dream and wondered what strange swell of festivalgoers there would be in Jerusalem in the coming year.

29

105 BCE

SHEETS OF VERTICAL rain fell from an impenetrable, featureless miasma of grey, and a slow, rolling fog erased the distinction between ground and sky. Smoke from an invisible chimney slid along the slate roof and then rose to stain the world's new ceiling with a particulate counter grey. Water from the sagging sky poured off the roof in a constant stream. It concealed the features of the house with a liquid veil.

A goat, bound to the gatepost near the well, swam with just its eyes and ears visible through the mist. Staring out at the world in *tayish* terror, the animal's eyes bulged like those of a nearly drowned victim. Drifting mud rose to hock-level, where long hair swirled and teased like persistent insects. The small creature bleated urgently, but no one came.

❧

The royalty's visit to Galilee had been moved to the remoteness of Grandma Sarah's house, for it was the only one both large enough to house the guests and far enough away from the town to avoid sparking gossip. The winter rains isolated each building from the other and the farm from the region. Everything came to a pause. Cattle huddled in the centre of open fields, and sheep formed soggy masses in stone pens. The roads, impassable for wagons and treacherous for hooves, became places of careful wading for those desperate to reach a neighbour and the shelter of a conversation.

Grandpa Ephraim's barn, left to Jacob when he had passed, sheltered the wagons, the horses, and the royal guard, who were made as comfortable as possible with straw mattresses and coarse blankets. A safe place on the stone floor was cleared for a fire where it would not set the straw and barn ablaze. Smoke filtered out through gaps at the gables.

The house itself was full. Joseph and Keziah served as hosts. Jacob, his family, and Grandma Sarah were staying in Cana and looking after Little Sarah. Joazar was the unofficial leader of the Lower Galilean contingent with his wife, Noadiah, beside him. Saul represented Upper Galilee. Uri and Mahlah; Joseph's brothers, Peretz and Oren; and finally Rehavam and Basmat completed the number of Galileans present. Ebed had come from Jerusalem with his wife and others, both friends and Pharisees, to accompany the royal visitors, Alexander Jannaeus and Salome Alexandra. Jugurtha did not make the journey.

Grandma Sarah's house was built for a large family, but not for a conference with more than twenty delegates. Alexander Jannaeus was the youngest present, fifteen years his wife's junior and she much younger than the rest of those assembled.

"Give him time," Joazar said.

The women made no reply. They treated their future high priest as though he were injured in some manner.

"Moving Salome and Jannaeus to Galilee is less about making amends with the people here," Ebed said quietly to Joazar, "and more about keeping Jannaeus away from the political fray in Jerusalem."

"Jugurtha's last letter suggested more turmoil," Joazar said.

"None of the sons will be king after Hyrcanus after all. The will is changed. Hyrcanus's wife, Mariamne, will be given the throne when her husband passes. Mariamne will be queen, Jannaeus high priest."

"What about the older sons?" Joazar asked.

Ebed looked about as though confirming their privacy. "Not happy," he finally said.

"Mariamne is a Pharisee," Joazar said.

"The Pharisees are happy," Ebed admitted.

"The Sadducees are not?"

Ebed nodded.

"Has Hyrcanus become a Pharisee again?"

Ebed shrugged. "No, but he's set things up for the nation to go back to its old order after his death."

They stopped talking as others joined them. Unimportant matters were discussed, and then Joazar spoke again, this time to the whole room.

"Jerusalem stirs up trouble and doesn't pay for it because Galilee is its northern buffer," he said. "We are Jerusalem's unsupported northern guard."

"Jerusalem paid for your weapons and supplies," said Jannaeus.

"With Galilean taxes," Joazar countered, ignoring Jannaeus's status as their future high priest. "Our regular trade with Samaria falls because large sections of Samaria have been deported to the slave markets. Our regular trade with Jerusalem falls because Jerusalem chooses to bolster its new Idumean economies and direct spending south. Galilean income drops, but the taxes remain the same."

Joseph caught Joazar's eye. Joazar paused for only a moment before continuing, "The Seleucids to the north are becoming increasingly hostile. Judea's expansion into Idumea does not make them more at ease."

Joazar took a drink, avoiding Joseph's eye.

"Every one of the new fortifications is in the east and south," Joazar continued. "I was there when we made plans for those fortifications. They were to be at the borders of our land, not the borders of Jerusalem. Jerusalem diminishes our revenues but demands full taxes. Jerusalem stirs up the Seleucids and does nothing to fortify our borders, sends none of the troops we pay for north, forces us to send our sons on defence." He lowered his voice and looked at Jannaeus. "Jerusalem schemes, and we pay."

❧

Salome Alexandra watched Keziah as she turned the loaves over, centring them on a slate that rested on coals. The upturned crusts glowed. "I used to bake with my mother," Salome said and then continued after a long pause. "Your brother says things that have not been given much consideration in Jerusalem."

Keziah adjusted the loaves again. One tumbled off the slate and skittered across a black seam of charcoal. Salome's hand darted out quickly and caught the hot package. She brushed it clean against her skirt with juggling hands and returned it to the slate.

"Palace life has not ruined your hands," Keziah said. "He has said these things before, over and over again, but no one seems to listen. He works for Jerusalem, but I'm afraid sometimes he doesn't like it."

"That's your brother," Salome said. "Your husband, though, he was one of Galilee's warriors."

"One of, as was Joazar and my son as well," Keziah said. "Joseph is a reluctant warrior. He rallies Galilee because it must be done, but in battle, he remembers—" She stopped what she was doing and looked away for a moment before returning Salome's gaze. "He remembers Dagon and much else. We all do."

"It's different in the south," Salome said. "The boys of Jerusalem and Judea are soft."

Keziah gave her a puzzled look.

"Mercenaries fight their battles. They focus on the temple and politics. They learn the intrigues of the city. The separation of the high priesthood and the throne will satisfy the law and our traditions when it occurs, but it also creates a delicious new paradigm for our young men to digest."

"I don't understand."

"Who will truly lead our nation in the future: my husband as high priest or his mother as queen? Who will hold the most influence? Hyrcanus is not even dead yet, and this is what they debate." Salome looked out at her husband, who sat among older, poorer men more accomplished than he. "I've been told that most expect the power to reside with the priesthood, with my husband, because Mariamne is a woman."

She looked up as though an explanation might lie in the rafters of the house, and then she turned back to Keziah. "War has been the source of the Maccabees' success, but none of this generation of Maccabees has touched a man in battle. They pay other men to fight for them. Jerusalem's men bear no scars."

In the barn, a man born of a whore's womb, birthed in the dark hold of a ship rolling on a black sea, who found redemption first in thievery and then in soldiery, held a set of curiously carved bone cubes and red-veined stones in a four-fingered hand. He stared at the mat from under a rim of black eyebrows shot with silver strands while his companions watched, revealing varying degrees of expectation. One soldier sighed, an exaggerated effort of his chest and shoulders, but the four-fingered man was unmoved. Another drank a long, burning swallow and feigned a loss of interest while others simply waited in a silent, collective trance, their eyes trained on the hand, waiting only for the throw. The Jewish captain sat apart, unwelcome in the farmhouse, unwilling to mix with his gentile men. Finally, the four-fingered man cast bone and stone, and the soldiers came to life. There was a collective sigh as the score rolled back to even. Rain fell outside, and mist seeped in at every opening. Water pooled at the entrance. The animals in the barn's rear moved in muffled languor.

The great door remained closed. A smaller side door

opened, and Joseph came in, towing a sodden goat by one horn. With him came the quiet man, Anat, a member of the Jerusalem mission. The goat's eyes rolled wildly, and it bucked against Joseph's grip. The carpenter walked past the soldiers with a firm hand on his charge.

"Was he trying to swim for it?" the captain asked, standing up.

"Forgot him at the gate," Joseph said. "Do you have what you need in here?" He kept walking past the captain, fumbled open the rear stall, and ushered the goat in with his dry companions. He forgot the captain and studied Grandma Sarah's little flock. They were here while the sheep were in the rain. He considered Grandma Sarah's peculiarities, which included special treatment for the goats.

Some of the goats would need to be milked before nightfall. He and Keziah would look after it, and he guessed that Salome would come, but Alexander Jannaeus would not. Then he remembered his question for the captain. He turned back to the man, but he was already engaged with Anat, who was taking down a few requests.

The captain's bed was apart from the others. Joseph considered the separation. In recent Galilean campaigns, fathers and sons, brothers and neighbours fought, fled, slept, ate, and sometimes died touching one another. The Jewish captain would not touch his gentile men. He would not eat with them nor sleep near them. The stain of the uncircumcised gentile could easily be transferred. Still, the division between the leader and his troops was a flaw.

The alternative was to raise a permanent Jewish army. Then he thought of Moshe within such a system and knew he did not want that for his son. Mercenaries were the solution. With that compromise came this disconnect. It made the captain eager to talk to any son of Abraham who drew near.

Joseph joined Anat and the captain and so absorbed a different view on the developments in Judea. Joseph and Anat returned to the house later with little enthusiasm.

After the main meal, the conversation drifted. Topics were exhausted, and new ones were entertained. The conversation moved like a dragonfly that sought an ideal perch. It settled, moved, settled, hovered, moved.

There were no instruments present. Eventually, Noadiah began to sing. Mahlah joined her, and then Uri's red brow started to move rhythmically. Salome was entranced, Jannaeus curious. After another verse, Uri joined the women. Surprising everyone, two of the Jerusalem women contributed as well. It was a Galilean song known in Jerusalem, the melody light and beautiful. They had only rain on the roof as accompaniment.

Joseph looked over at Keziah and could see her frustration. She could only make music with her fingers. The lute lay quietly in its case so many miles away, up roads hidden by creeks that were running free across the land. Her consternation intensified when Basmat joined the singers. Basmat's voice was bright, a high reed above the others, drawing eyes to her in wonder as she created something new above the known melodies and harmonies. None of the singers faltered. They sustained their part while Basmat did with her voice what Keziah often did with her fingers. She improvised and captivated, invented illumination where her audience had not before seen the need and now none could do without.

Jannaeus stared at Basmat as a man might at a treasure to be possessed. The singers moved on to other songs. Mistakes and laughter halted some songs midway through as the singers took new directions. They handled some songs traditionally and added new parts to others. The singers sat scattered about the closely packed room, yet a unity formed between them as they passed the melodies back and forth across the space. The non-singers watched, listened, smiled, nodded. Some occasionally made suggestions, and then, surprised and embarrassed by the sound of their voices, abandoned the intrusion.

It was late when Joseph reminded Keziah about the goats. Noadiah offered to help, and Salome wanted to participate too. Joazar stood to help Joseph get the women across the yard. The five slipped and waded out to the barn, carrying extra supplies for the captain and his men.

The women looked after the goats. Joazar and Joseph visited with the captain while the soldiers tore into the delivered provisions. Salome's laughter was heard over that of the other women as she tried her hand at milking and exclaimed in embarrassment at her initial failure and then in delight at her triumphant success. Her eyes glowed as the party prepared to exit back into the night. Joseph had one arm around Salome and one around Keziah, an intimacy justified only by the treacherous ground, and she turned to both of them in excitement and said, "I should have been born here. The daughter of a Galilean farmer."

"You are the only Hasmonean ever to say such a thing," Joseph said

"My mother-in-law would say such a thing," Salome Alexandra said. "Mariamne is a true Israelite. I love her as much as I do my own mother. She will be a beautiful queen for this country." Water flowed about their ankles. "She will bring back what the Pharisees want. Hyrcanus knows this. My husband will do what is right in the temple, and Mariamne will unite our kingdom as it was always meant to be."

They began walking again, feeling their way forwards, and so came to the stone steps alongside Joazar and Noadiah. The last glow of daylight faded. In the eastern sky, stars were seen for the first time in days. It was not the full array, but it was an opening and a sign that the heavens were once again upright. The clouds would relent. The land would drain, and Galilee's rivers would return to their ordered paths of domestication and calm.

30

104 BCE

THE FOLLOWING SPRING, Joazar travelled the mountain roads of Galilee, attending to a waning king's commission. It was early summer before he returned to Cana. Noadiah heard his steps climbing Cana's stairs and met him in the courtyard.

"Do you know?" she said.

"Yes, I heard two days ago," he said.

She handed him a letter. He broke the seal and read out loud. "John Hyrcanus is dead. Alexander Jannaeus and Salome Alexandra have been recalled from Galilee."

"I thought he might say more," she said.

A few weeks later, a runner came up the hill with a letter from Jugurtha.

> *When read, the king's will was different than expected. Mariamne has indeed been made regent,*

but rather than Alexander Jannaeus becoming high priest, Judah Aristobulus, the oldest of the brothers, has been given that office. Alexander Jannaeus and Antigonus have no role in the kingdom. It seems unlikely that Judah Aristobulus would willingly surrender the military in favour of a priest's robes. Antigonus and Alexander Jannaeus having no role at all is an invitation for future trouble. It would appear that each brother has received what he did not want.

Cana's men were of one mind about this development: Jannaeus would have been the better high priest. Hyrcanus should have left Aristobulus with the army.

Another letter came.

Fears I did not imagine have come to pass. Judah Aristobulus and Antigonus have executed a coup in Jerusalem. Judah Aristobulus has kept the high priesthood but also made himself king, like his father before him. Antigonus supports him. He is second to the throne and has been given the army. Mariamne and Alexander Jannaeus have been imprisoned.

When Joazar finished reading the letter aloud in Joseph's house, there was silence among those present. Sounds of the children playing outside drifted through. Uri was the most stone-faced. Rehavam seemed about to ask a question but then chose not to.

Two weeks later, another letter arrived, and the group in Cana again came down to Joseph and Keziah's home.

"It's not any better," Joazar said as they settled in to hear him.

"Just read it," Joseph said. "Don't summarize."

> *Mariamne and Jannaeus remain in prison. Judah Aristobulus intends for their imprisonment to be permanent. Salome is free with their sons but remains under house arrest. There are rumours that Mariamne is ill-treated in prison, but I cannot verify these accounts. What is clear is that Judah Aristobulus intends to remain as both high priest and king. There are even reports that he will mint new coins for the realm promoting himself with both titles. His father, for all his flaws, was more modest. Judah Aristobulus not only defies his father's will and the instruction in the Torah but makes a boast of it.*

"God have mercy," Uri said.

"On who?" asked Joazar.

Uri looked up. "I don't know. Maybe I should say, 'God take vengeance.' "

"The Maccabees finally free themselves of the Seleucids," Joseph said, "and then become their own oppressors."

❧

There is a place of natural darkness relieved only by lamplight. Day and night, there is no indication of time or season. It is cool yet close, feels warm with a chill as though the underground air and stone were suffering a fever.

Very few venture to this place willingly. Soldiers sometimes appear with provisions and bring new tenants, but they rarely bring messages. They never linger.

Very few are here.

~

The reedy jailer, bony-shouldered and sweating, transferred a smear of goose grease from his mouth and beard to his sleeve. The air was cold in these underground tunnels, yet he was always overheated as though an unnatural fire burned within.

He grimaced over what was left of his meal. He considered the disembowelled loaf, tore another wedge away, dragged it through the remnants of oil, and then pushed it between his always wet lips. He employed his sleeve once again and nodded in satisfaction to no one in the empty room.

With the passing of Hyrcanus, Judah Aristobulus had begun a purge that impressed the jailer. His jaws worked, and the swelling in his neck bobbed. This was a good time for his profession. The prison was receiving new faces, and none sent to him now were common.

He decided he was done with the meal and stood. None came to take the waste away. He would attend to it later or graze through its wreckage once more. He was always eating, never fat, always sweating, never cooled. He drank nothing but water, and for that, he was considered incorruptible within his lair. He was the principled master of the lamp-lit underground.

He turned his back to the meal that looked like the evidence of a calamity. It was a frequent scene, easily mistaken as the product of feral children or rats. He always cleaned up the mess himself later. Cleaning before the arrival of the next ration was itself a pleasurable ritual. None would work with him because of his habits, and he needed no assistant. He received no compensation for his increased number of charges, and he asked for nothing but the opportunity to pilfer the delicacies delivered to his wealthier guests. No one reprimanded him for this habit, for no one was able to report it. In any event, his masters would only have approved.

There was only one rule for the so-called queen: Judah Aristobulus ordered that no rations were to be given to her but water. The jailer was under strict orders not to succumb to mercy in this matter. His paymasters came personally to the lower gate to communicate this, and such was their trust that they did not reappear again for nearly two weeks. When they did return, they came through the gate and inspected the former queen briefly. It was evident that he had been careful to obey. They hurried from the lower chambers and did not return, though messengers began arriving more frequently, looking for news. He had none, but he knew the time would be soon.

Having turned his back to the pools and bones, he focused his mind on impudent female rulers. The Seleucid queen Cleopatra Thea had perished some fifteen or so years prior, poisoned by her son for standing in his way. There had also been a Cleopatra in Egypt, one who had dared to rule Egypt as pharaoh, but she too was dead. Had been for a decade. Her daughter was another Cleopatra: Cleopatra Euergetis. She now held the throne in Egypt, and Egypt bore the shame of enduring two female monarchs with none able to overthrow them.

Jerusalem handled Mariamne's quest to follow the

Seleucid and Egyptian examples more nobly. Judah Aristobulus deposed her in short order; she had not lasted a week. Jannaeus, loyal to his mother, was also imprisoned here. Jerusalem would have no queen, and it would have no queen sympathizers. Aristobulus was a man the jailer could call a real king. A true Maccabee. The Hasmonean.

"Did Avigail or Bathsheba get the throne?" the jailer asked the empty stone room. "Did Solomon compete with his mother?" The jailer snorted before an imagined court. "Sons follow fathers, not mothers." He used his sleeve to wipe the sweat from his forehead and inadvertently left a streak of goose grease there. It was time to look in on his most senior charge. Her time was close.

He entered the room. She was on her back, the thin straw mattress insufficient for her bony hips. Bedsores suppurated and gave off a foul odour. Her pointed jaw was bird-like in high relief. The bones in her neck and the striation of her arched windpipe were visible in profile like a surgeon's study. Her cheeks were concave, her eye cavities darkly bruised. One arm was outside the thin blanket, bare from the elbow down, skeletal, like brittle branches wrapped in the lightest papyri. She was younger than her husband Hyrcanus had been. She had been beautiful in her time, her husband's joy. She looked like an apparition now.

As the jailer studied her, he saw the cage of her chest shakily rise and fall. He was disappointed. He used to eat in front of her. She no longer begged him. She no longer said anything. She had taken no water for the past day. If she suffered another day, he would be surprised. The chest rose and fell again, and he turned away in disgust.

ঌ

This is the path the shadow took, leaving subtle footprints that exposed its passage: it came up the Beth Netofa Valley and over Grandma Sarah's house in silence, the change unregistered by the old woman in her blankets. It stirred the sheep near the house, bent the grass tips, and made the leaves down at the creek tremble. Near the hill of Cana, it began to release a mist of rain. Following a tight and unyielding path, it passed on to Jotaparta, to Chabulon, to Akko, and finally to the sea, perhaps to pass over those waters and spread the news to kingdoms beyond.

What it left in Cana was more than mist. It left the waking of a long-buried beast.

ঌ

Near the base of Cana's hill, in a small house near Joseph's and his brothers' workshops, there rose a wail of anguish, a rattling of glazed cookware, and then a smashing of clay. A woman terrorized pottery with a wooden mallet. Shards reduced to slinger's stones of red centre and glaze spun wildly through the air, and her loosened hair flew as she screamed and swung the mallet again. Ceramic arrows jutted from the walls and littered the floor as new fragments exploded from her hand and flew across the room. A bright red streak painted one cheek. It lightly wept blood in response to a shard that had narrowly missed her eye. She paused in her assault, panting and moaning, with wet hair falling around her.

Joseph looked back in on Little Sarah, but she stayed asleep. He closed his eyes tightly, summoning control.

He returned to the common room, to what his wife

had become. Her fists rested on the work table before her, and blood coalesced to create one narrow track down her jaw. The broken mallet handle lay in a drift of cookery dust. He came up to her from behind, put his hands near her shoulders, hesitated, and then set them down. He had believed she was finally calm until he touched her. He felt her weeping from somewhere deep within.

He had once worked with a beautiful, strangely grained board that he believed to be dry. He had cut it to his liking and fit it for purpose. The next day, as he shaved the barest layers off to smooth an imperfection, the wood suddenly began to bend of its own accord. Before he could prepare himself, it exploded, the sound deafening, a deep rent in the board longer than a man's leg opening in one sudden shot like the passing of a wood spirit. The wood spun wildly from his grasp like a living creature possessed by something malevolent now violently freed, and within seconds his project lay ruined before him. One torn hand bled into the wood shavings at his feet while he watched. The damage had been unforeseeably sudden and utterly irreversible. Now, Joseph began to fear for Keziah.

She began to sob normally again. The sound was a relief to him, and he felt the pent-up coil relax beneath his hands. She turned into him and buried her face against his chest. She held not him but his clothing as she pulled herself against him.

"Tell me," he said, holding her head and hair to him.

"I'll never touch Greek pottery again," she said, looking up. "Don't you understand?"

He calmed himself and worked to maintain a quiet

voice. The wet and drying wood within her was gripped with hard, scarred, experienced hands.

"No, Keziah. I don't understand. Our queen—" He stopped as her eyes filled with drowning desperation.

"She died by starving!" Keziah shouted it into his face. "Don't you understand? She died by starving!"

Her breath was moist and foul in his face, her eyes terrified, her grip nearly enough to tear his shirt from him.

"I know, Keziah! I'm the one who told you!"

"Not her! Not her!" She began to fade against him. He held her up, hands at her back as she sank to her knees. He knelt with her. "Not her." Face to his shoulder. "Not her."

She pulled back. Her complexion was grey, flattening and distorting such that he feared something was breaking within her. When she looked at him, it was as if through dead eyes, and she was ugly in his arms, unrecognizable, a medium for some other voice. "My mother," Keziah said, "that is how my mother died."

He saw in her eyes what the consequences of recognizing the ultimate cause of her mother's death had unleashed, and it scared him. He could see the bones at her forehead as though the skin there had suddenly thinned.

Joseph knew the story of the village. When Joazar had first arrived in Galilee, he had told them about the burned and abandoned house, Moshe's grave, their lost parents, all that he had learned from the villagers. Joseph had first learned of the leprosy from Joazar's report. Keziah had confirmed it, filled in the details she had seen. Both men had heard once more her account of the abduction—her life had been saved, but the saving was its own act of trauma.

No one in Galilee had speculated about the fate of

Keziah and Joazar's parents. They understood that the couple's deaths had been related to the disease, for her father had surely been infected as well, but they did not seek out the particulars. Weather, animals, or starvation usually killed the leprous long before the disease did its worst. In those days of war and violence in Judea, it would have been starvation that claimed Keziah's mother. Joseph now knew that tomorrow, or the next day, she would recognize that as her father's fate as well. She could not grasp them both together. She would stage it out. Joseph knew what tomorrow would bring and braced himself.

Keziah slumped into him. He lifted her to her feet, led her into the back room, laid her down, and tucked her in the way he had Little Sarah. He smoothed her hair, the brown-black waves with many white strands intermingled. She put her hands to her eyes to stem tears, shook her head with her eyes closed, and then turned away. He put out the lamp and left her, passing out the door and into darkness.

The nighttime mist shaped itself into thin clouds that passed between Cana and the sky. It was a torn and tattered veil, a shape that could only be discerned by the pattern of stars appearing and disappearing in ragged lines across the night's expanse.

Joseph contemplated the broken sky above him. He flexed his hands in the dark. He felt an ache in one shoulder and deep anger within and a kinship with his son's reckless rush down Galilean hillsides, the catharsis of a physical opponent, the blood-rush of action. He remembered the brotherhood of the Seleucid war, the men and boys sitting around a fire or a cold meal in a dark forest, where the day's deeds were not just recounted but made real by the telling.

It was time again for action. A different kind of action. An action he believed he could perform better than Moshe and his young companions.

His son would be among those who would want to go to Jerusalem to fight for Alexander Jannaeus's release and Mariamne's revenge, to overthrow Judah Aristobulus's horror-inaugurated reign. But Antigonus was in the field with the army. Any fight would have to take both brothers into account. There were things that Moshe's generation knew nothing about. The Galileans would have many allies in Judea, but they were not well suited for marching through Samaria's valley like a formal army. Galilee had no elephants.

31

103 BCE

THEY MET AT Joppa by the sea. Massive waves rolled onto hard stone edges and broke into translucent fans. Loose grains tumbled through miniature channels across a rough surface unsmoothed by a thousand years of water and salt.

"You've seen the letter from Joseph?" Ebed asked.

"Yes," replied Jugurtha.

"Is there a way?"

"There is always a way. I just cannot imagine what it is yet." Jugurtha looked out past the nearshore waves. In the distance lay a treacherous calm. "Aristobulus is no longer with his army," he said.

"Why?" Ebed asked.

"He's ill and hiding it. Salina thinks . . . well, we'll leave that unsaid."

"What does the king's wife think?"

"I won't repeat it."

"What about Mariamne's murder? What does she have to say about that?"

Jugurtha stretched his hands out in front of him and studied his long fingers and clean nails. The scars of his childhood had faded and been replaced with the scars of time and the beginning of that papery skin he never imagined coming to his limbs. "She hides her feelings well. She does not support her husband, if that is what you're asking. She would help if we were to find a way."

"I've never learned how to play political games," Ebed said. "It was never part of my role in Hyrcanus's staff."

"Leave it to me," Jugurtha said. "I know this world well."

⁂

Sunlight streamed aslant. Two women sat on a mat on either side of a milk *shekhar*. Around them, Salome's private residence in Jerusalem was nearly empty.

"I miss Galilee," Salome Alexandra said. Salina looked up and took a prim drink. "If only we could focus on something other than fear," Salome said.

"It's natural for me to be afraid," Salina said. "What have you to fear?"

Salome frowned. "I live under arrest in my own home. The man who put me here, your husband, has my husband in prison. And he starved his mother to death. What have I to fear? What have *you* to fear?"

"Aristobulus is a threat to my life."

"How? He's your husband."

"He could die. He will die."

"How is that a threat to you?"

Salina took another drink, not so prim this time. "Antigonus has the army. He's very successful. He's taking the same approach as their father. Hyrcanus gave the Idumeans a choice: conversion or death. Antigonus is doing the same now in Iturea. Priests travel with knives. The Itureans are expected to heal and then make the journey to Jerusalem. Antigonus will be a huge success."

"At the Festival of Booths," Salome said.

"Yes. Antigonus is even more successful than Hyrcanus. He's not lost a battle yet. He doesn't even have to fight half the time. They just surrender to the priests."

"Antigonus is successful in the field," Salome said. "He is much loved by Judah Aristobulus. I don't see how this puts you at risk."

"Your husband is in prison because he threatens the validity of Aristobulus's rule," Salina said.

"The murder of his mother threatens the validity of Aristobulus's rule," Salome shouted. "His father's will refutes the validity of his rule."

"Shush," Salina said. "There is no need for others to hear." She lifted the cup to her lips and then set it down again, untasted.

"Fine," Salome said. "Arguably, if the Sanhedrin ever were to try the case with a balanced court, your husband has invalidated his claim to the high priesthood through matricide. Hyrcanus never left him the throne to begin with. Antigonus would be made king. My husband, Jannaeus, would be restored to his original position as high priest. Your husband, Aristobulus, would be stoned for the murder of his mother if justice existed in this country."

There was silence in the courtyard for a few moments.

Children could be heard beyond the wall. The guards were silent.

"But no one is going to stone Aristobulus," Salome continued. "I am no closer to understanding why you think you are in danger."

"My husband is ill," Salina said.

Salome looked up and contemplated her sister-in-law for a moment. "I may be imprisoned in my own house, but his illness isn't a secret."

"He's more ill than people know. He's not in Iturea because he would probably not survive the journey. He is bleeding when he passes stool, sometimes a great deal, and he has a burning in his throat and pain in his chest. When he throws up, it comes with blood."

"So, he may die," Salome Alexandra said.

"Yes."

"I hope it's as painful and slow as the death he chose for his mother."

Salina picked up her glass and took a serious drink.

"I make no apology for hating your husband," Salome said.

"My feelings aren't particularly warm towards him either," Salina said, "but he keeps me alive."

"How?"

"When my husband became king, he made me queen. His will names me as his successor. The throne passes to me."

Salome Alexandra snorted and finally took a drink herself. "He would try to do for you what he denied his mother?"

"He would attempt to, yes. When he dies, I will be

regent. What should I do with Antigonus? Make him high priest? Leave him in charge of my army? Imprison him?"

"Yes, imprison him. Put him on trial for complicity in the murder of his mother."

"Precisely. And he has the army."

Salome Alexandra sat back. She heard her sons' high voices echo off stone. "I see," she said. "I have been focused on my husband and children. And our future."

"I live in fear."

"Then you need to start doing something about it. If you're going to be queen, then you'd better deal with Antigonus before your husband dies. Or it will be your turn to . . . "

"To starve to death in a Jerusalem prison."

"Lord God of Heaven," Salome Alexandra said.

Salina held the cup to her husband's lips. She was his only nurse at this hour. "The priests should have reached Iturea by now," she said.

"Victory," said Aristobulus, "repeating my father's deeds in Idumea. Antigonus's reputation now conquers ahead of him. He doesn't even have to lift his sword."

"Yes. Antigonus's reputation conquers. That is what everyone is saying."

Aristobulus tried to catch her eye. Failing that, he turned on his couch to see her better. "Jugurtha has told me slanders about my brother. The doctor has passed on a rumour. Now my wife is trying to suggest something?"

She shrugged. "Whoever takes victory in the field is the victor. The Galileans drove Cyzicenus's mercenaries into

Scythopolis and paid the bribe to have the gates flung open. The victory was theirs. They offered you the open gates, and you took it—"

"With Antigonus."

"With Antigonus. You and Antigonus took Scythopolis. Hyrcanus was the king. The Galileans did the hard fighting and raised the bribe, but Scythopolis is counted as the conquest of Aristobulus and Antigonus because you entered the city together."

"We took the city!"

"You entered the city. But, yes, you took the city while Hyrcanus was king in Jerusalem. And so Scythopolis is Antigonus's and was never credited to Hyrcanus or any of the Galileans."

"Antigonus's and mine."

"Perhaps."

"Wife, there is no '*perhaps.*'"

"There is a '*perhaps*' if Antigonus keeps conquering region after region based on his reputation alone. In time, it will be Antigonus who entered Scythopolis and Antigonus who conquered Samaria, and you just happened to be there."

Aristobulus coughed. A spume of blood followed in a rush. "Lord God," he groaned as she carried the rags away.

"You cannot officiate as high priest at the festival this year," Salina said.

"I never had any interest in that fussy office anyway."

"You will have to designate someone to take your place."

"Well, by Sheol, you've made it clear that it can't be Antigonus. Conquering general and high priest as well.

I might as well drown in my own blood and be free of this earth."

"You cannot let him continue beyond Iturea either."

"You would have me bring him back here and make him idle?"

"Tell him to stay where he is and install the new government in Iturea."

"We have men who can handle that."

"Tell him to oversee it himself. Make it a model for the future. Make him stay in Iturea until it is time for the feast. Then he can escort the new Iturean Jews down to Jerusalem for their first festival. The way is long, and it will be a great victory for Jerusalem to see the Itureans present in large numbers."

"He'll be just as furious about being made idle in Iturea as in Jerusalem."

"Enforce your will as king and make it clear that you have interests beyond simply conquest. Let him show his respect for your leadership. If you doubt his willingness to submit to you, then that's all the more reason to force his hand. Expose him."

"There is nothing to expose!" Aristobulus protested.

"Then prove it!" said Salina. "At the very least, avoid giving Jerusalem's gossips another Antigonus victory to write songs about."

"Nobody is writing songs about Antigonus, wife. Not yet, anyway." He sighed and settled back on his couch. "It's late. Do it tomorrow. If you still feel this strongly, then write up the orders tomorrow and leave them for me to mark. And pick someone to be high priest. Write that up as well. I'll mark them tomorrow."

❧

"What do you think?" Saul asked.

"How much did it cost?" Joseph asked.

"It was—"

"Liberated," Uri said. "We needed to give a certain person a few expensive bottles to help him remember where to find it."

Oren circled the pieces with undisguised greed.

"Can you repair it?" Saul asked.

"Repair it? It's beautiful!"

"We want it to be awe-inspiring," Saul said.

The piece of armour—a muscle cuirass—stood unsupported on the workbench at Cana. Crafted in the Greek fashion like an idealized male physique, its hammered iron was shaped with great detail from the nipples and navel embossed with gold to the silver bands at the edges. Leather straps held the breast and back plates securely together. The inside padding was stained, and the leather fringes were worn.

"We want the padding replaced. The scars buffed out of the metal. The silver details need to be polished. Either fix the one strap to match the others or replace them all if you cannot get the colour to match. Make it look new."

"The helmet needs work as well, I presume?" Joseph said.

"Yes. We want no marks there. Replace the inside padding. Clean and polish it."

Joazar picked up the helmet. "Phrygian," he said.

The men looked at him for a moment before finally Saul spoke. "Sometimes I forget you spent time with the Seleucids. Phrygian. What does that mean?"

Moshe was impressed with both the armour and the helmet. He accepted the helmet from his uncle, handling it with the same awe that Oren bestowed on the body armour.

"A place up north. The cavalry tends to prefer the Phrygian-style armour," Joazar said. "They said in Antioch that Alexander himself preferred this style."

"I've seen the type with feathers on top. Outside Gischala and Meronoth and at the ambush at Baca. The metal crest?"

"Typical for a Phrygian piece."

"Will it do?" Saul asked.

"Yes. Yes!" Joseph finally let himself laugh out loud. "Yes, Saul, you've outdone yourself. You and Uri are the best finders this country could ever hope to know. Not even Solomon had something like this. I wouldn't be surprised if you two entered heaven and borrowed Gabriel's armour."

⁂

They kept news of the kingly armour restoration quiet. News of the finished prize, however, was publicized widely. Messengers were sent into Iturea to proclaim its splendour to Antigonus.

On his journey back to Jerusalem and the festival, Antigonus took the route through Galilee. Messengers assured him that the gift of armour was a fitting tribute after his conquest of Iturea and was a bold way for him to forge a bond with Jannaeus's former Galilean allies. It was worth the detour. He could not puzzle out his older brother's new strategy of conquest restraint, but forging internal alliances seemed wise. He accepted the Galilean offer.

He tried the armour on in the brothers' workshop. All

three brothers were big men, veterans, impressive specimens. There were a few others present, including Joazar, who worked for Jerusalem. Antigonus flushed with pleasure at the unprecedented suit. He had never seen its equal.

He and his guard departed and quickly caught up to his new Iturean pilgrims. He hid the Galilean gift amid his baggage.

❧

Months of rumours fostered a fast, dry rot within the creaking mind of the king. Like an eroded stream bank, his surface stayed together, but a slow, internal collapse began. Many were the voices that contributed to his fall.

"Antigonus has come with his entire army to the festival."

"Jerusalem is filled with mercenaries."

"Why has he not yet come to the Citadel to see the king?"

"The Galileans have gone over to Antigonus's side."

"The Itureans were promised something more than a festival. Theirs was an alliance of more than blood." This last rumour came from a priest upon his return from the north, having spent time with Jugurtha before reporting to the king.

To the king's ear, the news of the surrounding mercenaries and new alliances was ominous. He wiped blood from his mouth. What he encountered issuing from his mouth and in his stool bled into the fear of what this news might mean.

On the last day of the festival, Antigonus clad himself in the new Galilean armour. He paraded before the people as a conqueror. He walked about the temple's outer courtyard with Iturean Jews as faux captives in his wake. Many proclaimed how he achieved his recent victories by the power of his name alone. He was the conqueror and converter of the gentiles; the incarnation of both kingly and priestly qualities; the lord of Samaria, Scythopolis, and Idumea; the liberator of lands east of the Jordan River and now Iturea.

The news of Antigonus's celebration in the last days of the festival came to Aristobulus in unfiltered accounts. Additionally, the noise of the nearby temple's crowds sounded like rebellion. Jugurtha and Salina had to do little to keep the narrative moving.

"He acted today not like a civilian or even a loyal Jew," the acting high priest reported to Aristobulus as darkness came to the city, "but like a king. Like a Seleucid king. I don't doubt he intends to seize the government."

The priest had rehearsed this last line, and Aristobulus flew into a rage, sending the terrified man running out of the Citadel. Salina appeared at her husband's side to calm him. His mouth was frothing with pink foam.

"They say he wears Alexander the Great's armour," Aristobulus muttered. "The Galileans had it. Gave it to Antigonus. Not me."

"Perhaps they have gone over to him as the people say," Salina said. "They were close to Alexander Jannaeus and loved Mariamne."

Aristobulus wound up for an outburst. Then he stopped. "There is one way to end this. Bring Antigonus to the Citadel. Early tomorrow morning. I wish to see him and settle the accounts of what occurred in Galilee and Iturea."

"I can write up the order in the morning when you've rested."

"Write it up now!"

"It is late."

"Wife! Write it up now!"

Salina bowed and departed. She returned, papyri and ink in hand, and wrote out the instructions as he dictated, including instructions that Antigonus should come with his new armour to show the king. "You should see the suit that's made such a strong impression upon your people," she explained.

"Yes. Tell him I want to see him in all of his conquering glory." He was nearly drunk with emotion, lack of sleep, and pain. "I want him humbled by his own grandeur while I suffer here in this stinking room. I want him to see why people mistrust him."

Salina nodded, finished, and then gave Aristobulus the papyrus to mark. He did so curtly and turned away, curled on his couch.

Salina left the room and placed the orders in a safe place. After a brief time, she returned with fresh papyri covered in newly written words.

"My lord," she said quietly.

He turned to face her, groggy and in distress.

"I fear your brother."

"Which is why I will meet with him in the morning. Go away."

"I have advised you poorly," she said. "I am ashamed of how careless I have been."

"What is it?"

"I don't believe the worst rumours, but I do know that this year's festival is not like previous years. There is an ill wind within the city."

"There is an ill wind within my body, and when it comes out, the stink is like death."

"If there is the slightest chance that even some of the rumours are true—"

"There is not."

"Even just part of them. It seems very unwise to bring Antigonus into the Citadel, into your private chamber, fully armed and armoured. You cannot appoint a guard to watch him here. That would suggest you do not trust him. And you certainly cannot meet him in public. They must not see you like this. If you are to talk as brothers and put things right between you, he should come without his armour. He should come unarmed. You can see this Galilean armour some other time. Perhaps he even means it to be a gift for you, and he wore it at the festival impulsively. You know how he is . . . enthusiastic now, thoughtful later."

"Sometimes thoughtful never," Aristobulus said. "Often a fool."

"Then send for him to come to you unarmed for a conference between brothers. Nobody goes to visit someone they love in battle armour. That would put a strain on the conversation from the beginning."

Aristobulus looked as if he were going to sit up straighter but thought better of it. "You are a good woman," he said finally. "I know you love Antigonus as much as I do. I look forward to tomorrow morning when I can embrace my brother and we can put aside these months of rumours. Write it up."

"I did," she said, presenting him with the papyri.

Aristobulus regarded his wife with kind eyes and barely took them from her as he marked the orders. "You are a good woman," he said, returning the package to her. "I wish that I were in health and could treat you as your body deserves."

"You will be well again soon," Salina said. "Everything passes."

"Yes, it does, though this passes slowly. Leave me now. In the morning, we will clear this up. God willing, we will discover that my illness is as fleeting as these foul rumours. Tomorrow both I and this kingdom will become healthy again."

❧

To the messenger, Salina showed the first set of orders and commanded haste. "He must come in the morning in full battle armour—the new armour he received in Galilee. The king desires to see it. Go."

To the captain of the guard, she showed the second set of orders. "You are to appoint a guard in the passage. If Antigonus comes unarmed, then he comes in peace, and you will let him into the king's chamber. Only Antigonus. No one else should see the king while he recovers.

"But if he comes armed, he is to be killed in the passageway. He must not be allowed to escape the Citadel and launch his rebellion. Are you clear on this?"

"The king's brother, if he comes armed, is to be killed in the passageway."

"On pain of death—your death—he is not to leave that passageway alive. Not to go up to the king's chamber and not back out to where he may rally supporters. The city is full. There are far too many of them for your guard to suppress."

"I understand. My best men will be in the passageway."

32
103 BCE

SLAVES LABOURED IN Antigonus's room, applying a final oil and polish to the metal masterpiece. It shone from every angle. Afterwards, they buckled Antigonus into the muscle cuirass and left him alone. He was resplendent.

Antigonus concealed the masterpiece under a modest cloak. Preparing for a dramatic reveal was unnecessary, but he appreciated the Greeks' taste for presenting glory gradually and theatrically. His brother was as much a Hellenist as Antigonus. The king would appreciate the theatre.

The walk to the Citadel was brief though crowded. Antigonus took pleasure in seeing people part before his men. They walked without breaking stride. When they got to the Citadel, they went straight through the doors and on into quieter, echoing halls.

The captain of the guard met him inside. His quick eyes

went to the stunning Phrygian helmet Antigonus carried under his arm. He took in the hints of chest plate beneath the cloak and the tip of the sword sheath appearing below.

Antigonus noted the man's naked curiosity and resolved to display his prize to the entire Citadel guard when he returned. For now, they would have to wait.

The captain signalled a barefoot messenger, who darted into the passageway. Antigonus smiled. The king was ill. He wished to be alerted so he could prepare for his visitor. His absence at the temple, his appointment of a substitute high priest, and the formality of sending a messenger to the king's bed-chambers all told the same story. Antigonus decided that the visit would be brief. His brother could be such a bore with his illnesses.

The captain escorted him to the passageway.

"Enjoy the garden," Antigonus said to his men. "My business with the king will soon be over. The captain will send for you when I am ready."

He gave the Citadel captain a conspiratorial smile. The man paled and nodded. He stood aside, and Antigonus strode through the dark archway at the same pace he had taken down Jerusalem's streets. He descended the first flight of stone steps and walked quickly across the level passage through dim light towards the staircase beyond.

Steps down the passageway, from a dark alcove to his right, came a sword. It sliced through his heavy cloak and glanced off iron, revealing a dazzle of silver and gold. Antigonus fumbled with his sword handle, and his left hand shot out, using the helmet as a small shield before him. From the opposite side, a second sword flashed and violently struck his left arm. The chunking sound of a blade striking bone echoed, as did the helmet as it bounced down the stone floor.

Antigonus stepped back, a gasp in his throat. He pulled back from his opponent. The stubborn bone refused to release the blade, and Antigonus wrenched the sword from his enemy's grasp. The helmet clattered to a stop, and there was a second of strange silence. He inhaled deeply to cry out, but the first sword came a second time. It plunged between the leather straps at his side, slipped between his ribs, and emerged from his far side. His chest froze mid-breath, skewered like a young goat. The assassin withdrew the sword, and this second act felt worse than the first. He tried to shout and felt his half-cry fade, expelling blood and air from both sides.

He was born a Maccabee, a proud Hasmonean. He did not fall but backed up one step. He heard the sword buried in his left arm drag against the wall beside him, and then someone tore it from his arm. He backed up two more steps and tried to get his own weapon out, but his torn ribs and lungs betrayed him. He could not get the sword higher than his waist. His assailants came at him again, and he died, never having raised more of an alarm than the clanking of his helmet down the passageway and the final ring of his cloak-padded backplate on stone steps.

The action on the Citadel's ground floor was also short-lived. Twelve armed guards had come with Antigonus. Three died during the arrest, and the remaining nine laid down their weapons before the sixty that confronted them. They were taken immediately to the jailer, who was amazed at this influx of new residents.

❧

The king's rage that morning was loud, but not loud enough to be heard below. Only those who ventured up the tower heard him.

The queen came ashen-faced to the lower levels, shooed away those who were still trying to remove Antigonus's blood from the passageway, and warned the servant girls to stay away for the rest of the day. A man was brought at midday to remove the king's bowl of bile and blood. He carried the stinking bowl down stone stairs, holding it away from him, fearful of what lurked in the vapours. Just past the twin alcoves, he stumbled, bumped into a wall, sloshed the bowl, and shouted aloud as it spilled over, slapping the first two stairs with filth, the very stairs where Antigonus had died.

Soldiers came running and found the man backing away from the mess he had created.

"I fell," he said.

The soldiers stopped short of the shimmering stains. The captain pushed his way through and surveyed the scene. "Clean it up," he said, pointing at the shaking man. "Clean it well, or I'll send you to the jailer next."

For the rest of the day, the king demanded news, but none would tell him anything. He had heard shouts below, heard running, muffled voices, the ongoing sounds of activity. The king became more and more agitated. A fever consumed him, and thoughts of fratricide racked his mind.

Finally, Salina reappeared at his side and told him all: she described how Antigonus had made his stand, trying to fight his way to the king's chambers alone; how his soldiers had died on the lower level, trying to take over the guard in the Citadel; and finally, how the bowl of the king's blood spilled in the very place where Antigonus had died, their blood now mingling together in the stone.

"Those sounds now are the cleaners," she said.

Aristobulus grew even more grey. "Murderer of my brother," he moaned. "He and I murderers of our mother. God will not let me live. He has tortured me these many months while my brother enjoyed his victories. Now God has mixed my blood with his, his crimes with mine. He will bring us both to the grave in judgment. If only my blood would leave me all at once and not drip so out so slowly." He looked at his wife. His face and neck were blotched and bloated, and bloody spittle flecked his chin. "Why did God exact vengeance on my brother so swiftly while he continues to draw the life from me so slowly?"

Salina looked at her husband, reached out her hand as though to touch his face, and then took it back. "You killed your mother by starvation, you fetid swine," she said. "Let God claim you however he chooses. You are despised throughout all Israel. You will die with less than a year on the throne, and the nation will rejoice at your passing. Your will makes me queen, but am I foolish enough to try to maintain the throne in a country that starved its last queen to death, the very wife of John Hyrcanus?

"My first act as queen will be to free your brother from prison and sever myself from your cursed fate. Your brother Jannaeus will have the high priesthood that your father willed for him, and he will have your throne as well! The histories of this year will remember only your crimes. You will rank as the worst of Israel's rulers. You will be remembered as a drunken commander who took credit for other people's victories, a putrid king who vomited on himself, smeared blood and filth on his own legs, and could not properly clean himself, who could not stand unattended, who whinges after murdering his brother."

"I will be none of those things," the king whispered hoarsely.

"Wipe your face and see why I won't touch you," Salina said. She snorted and spat across the space between them. "You couldn't even produce an heir. When I am finally free of you, I shall go out and find a man, and by his body, I will purge all memory of you. I will find not a creature like you, but a man. A man who will give me *sons*."

She stood, trembling, picked up the wine she had brought with her, and cast it into his face. "Find your own way from the bed to the couch if you can. I will let the guard know that you do not wish to be disturbed. When they find your body here in this stench, they will know you died in madness."

She walked to the door and then turned and pointed to the other cup she had brought for him. "Or you can drink from that cup and join your brother more quickly. When I made enquiries for such a mixture, the nation provided me with a thousand samples. Die quickly or die slowly, but either way, I will see to it that no one visits these chambers until I call them to carry out your body."

33
103 BCE

IN JERUSALEM, IN Ebed's upper room: throat clearing and coughs, a din of voices, the clink of adjusted copper, a gravelly scrape of baked clay, laughter, the human bark that signalled some hybrid of humour, recognition, and surprise intermingled with genuine laughter. All these sounds commingled with the smell of a meal half consumed, of wine in the room's heat, of sweat translated through linen and hair, along with the smell of smoke from the fire, incense from the lamps, and the still bough-laden air of the post-festival season that drifted in from temporary rooftop tabernacles—the clean scent of olive, pine, myrtle, and willow.

Only men occupied the upper room. The Galileans and Judeans present had all been at the unofficial Galilean conference at Grandma Sarah's house two years earlier. The women were not welcome. This was Jerusalem.

The conversations drew to a pause, and Joseph spoke into this silence, addressing Jugurtha in a voice that filled the room. "I usually get my news through Joazar as he reads your letters to us. Listening to Jerusalem's crowds and heralds myself has been an unusual exercise in sorting truth from rumour."

Laughter filled the room. "You'll have to write all of this down, Jugurtha," said Saul. "If you don't simplify it and send it to Joazar for us to hear secondhand, it's not real."

There was more laughter in the room, a common sound this night. Excitement and good humour flowed through the company as an excess of wine lubricated each tongue. This energy, though, was the product of something wilder than wine. They were as men on a plain before a Davidic bonfire. They celebrated the unspeakable yet wondrous: the death of a king.

"God bless Salina!" someone said, and all the men shouted at the bold and welcome sentiment.

"She was the most radiant widow I've ever seen."

The entrance below opened. Unbeknown to the men in the upper room, two formally clothed figures entered the house, escorted by several guards. The figures silenced the women below, and so none alerted the men above.

"No more wars beyond our borders," Uri said.

"The temple will go back to the Pharisees," said another. "The country to its people."

"The Hasmonean madness has ended."

"God bless Salina."

"God bless Jannaeus and Salome!"

The three guards stayed with the women on the main floor. Only the two distinguished figures mounted the stairs to the upper room. It was into a moment of unbridled joy that these two emerged, unheard amid the noise of Judean and Galilean men celebrating.

Candles flickered. The fire crackled, and then the noise in the room stopped. The celebrating men rushed to stand up as they recognized their guests: Alexander Jannaeus with his queen, Salome Alexandra.

A series of small snaps from the fire marred the silence. The light shed by the oil lamps around the room suddenly seemed inadequate. The silence stretched, and none seemed capable of doing anything to disturb that frozen atmosphere beyond standing and waiting for who knew what.

Alexander Jannaeus finally broke the silence, and his movement caused a ripple to spread through the room. He identified Ebed among the group and went to him. Then he embraced Ebed and took the man with him to Jugurtha, who he embraced as well. He stood with these two, one in each arm, and surveyed the room.

"These two men are true friends of the king," Alexander Jannaeus said.

Alexander Jannaeus noticed Joazar and moved in his direction, causing men the king did not recognize to part out of his way. He embraced Joazar and then Joseph as well. "These two hosted my wife and me when we were forgotten exiles in Galilee. That man," he said, pointing at Uri, "can sing. And his wife with him. And someone else's wife, an utterly beautiful woman—" He looked around the room as though trying to find a spy among them. Finally, he started and pointed at Rehavam. "Him! You! It was your wife. Her name is Basmat. I will remember Basmat always. As long as I live, I will remember Basmat."

They did not stay long. Salome Alexandra spoke only a few quiet words to Joseph about Keziah.

The royals departed, and after they left, the spirit in the room had difficulty recovering its previous level of celebration. Conversations were subdued. Laughter lacked its former light.

On the road back to Galilee, Uri asked, "Why did he call us 'friends of the king'? That's a Hellenistic expression."

None answered but the terebinth trees. The few remaining leaves rustled an untranslatable reply that stirred dark birds of fall. Their silhouettes rose against a low autumn sun accompanied only by the rough scrape of the travellers' shoes on the road.

Oren finally said what the others would not. "I don't like the way he spoke of Basmat."

The next day they passed over the limestone ridge, filled their skins at Jacob's well, and continued down past Shechem and into the valley.

They walked in silence until they came to the Valley of Jezreel and turned northwest. Joseph began to talk again. He spoke about the iron chariots that the original Canaanite inhabitants were said to have used. A discussion commenced about the nature of those ancient chariots, whether they had been solid iron and impossibly heavy or if the wheels alone were iron. Or perhaps only the fittings and armoured shields were iron or the oiled axles and hubs, or perhaps they bore iron skins like moulded shields over wooden frames. The men agreed that this last idea was most likely, though the image of an all-iron chariot still captured their imagination.

The oak and the terebinth trees were indistinguishable from a distance and even less distinctive this time of year.

In contrast to their uniformity stood the occasional sycamore, their bifurcated and leprous trunks covered in white and brown patches of scaly bark. Naked branches were contorted and cast in white against a darkening sky that exposed strange orbs of ripe, woody fruit hanging precariously. There they would hang through the fall, and in the winter, they would open and scatter their hidden cache of fine-haired seeds into cold winds. For all its flamboyant and even disturbing outer appearance, Joseph liked to work with sycamore wood. Bizarre shapes could be found when the grain was spalted. When the right sample could be found, it was full of illusory movement like the wood grain of an olive tree.

As they walked, Joseph carried on a historical discourse with any who would join him. It was a habit he had started with Moshe. Without Moshe on this trip, the other men humoured him, and it made the hours pass.

They spoke of the battle between Deborah and Jabin in this valley, the king of Hazor defeated by Israel's prophetess, judge, and reluctant commander. They spoke of King Saul and the Philistines meeting here, of Pharaoh Necho coming from Egypt, advancing beyond Jerusalem to engage the Babylonians, and of King Josiah unwisely interceding on behalf of the Babylonians and dying somewhere on this plain. No man in that company knew on which side of the Kishon River the great king had fallen. They crossed the river, which flowed from the Gilboa Mountains to the sea. Joseph returned to the beginning of his chronology. He spoke of how Joshua had been saved as the Kishon floodwaters had swept the Canaanites to their death and how centuries later, downriver towards the sea at the base of Mount Carmel, Elijah had executed the multitude of Baal's prophets. Their bodies had been cast into the same river and sent out to sea just as the defeated Canaanites had been centuries prior. The bodies of all the river's dead were said to eventually wash up on Akko's shores.

The travellers turned away from the next village's abundant cisterns and grain pits and continued climbing over hills with tired legs. They passed more villages and high mountain homes suspended and lit in the evening air like beacons. It was dark when they arrived at Cana. The local men scattered. Uri continued in the dark with Saul.

Each home in Galilee stayed lit late into the night as families celebrated the news from Jerusalem. Cautious hope stirred where none had been for many winters. An age had passed: the age of war for profit, the age of forgetting purity. So many ages were now in the past: the age of forgetting the wisdom of the Pharisees, the age of Hellenism, the age of forced conversions, the age of provoking foreign powers. All this—the stain of Hyrcanus's later years and the obsessions of his firstborn son—were behind them. Many were rejoicing in Jerusalem and throughout Judea. In Galilee, joy burned like deep coals, heat coaxing greater heat. Before the night was finished, after Sarah had gone to sleep, Joseph found Keziah looking for him as she had not for some time. They did not need secret notes from her lute to find each other in the dark.

Israel's king and high priest was dead. Long live Jannaeus and Salome after him.

Israel was a kingdom finally at rest.

34

103 BCE

Across Uri's farm, bleak lines of cold rain froze to stony ground. Small icicles formed in the cliff face above against the shapes of coiled sea creatures—ribbed, shelled, and petrified. They were fossils, reflecting the weak dawn in silver and scarlet through prisms of temporary ice. These relics of water and flood had witnessed the drowning of the land with their great stone-clad tails curled in a hard death. When it rained, the unsteady imagined the creatures reanimated and crudely flexing through the floodwaters. They haunted the dreams of old men, steady or not, who had observed their strange shapes in years past and remembered them with wonder and fear.

There were stories of a long-ago prophet who crawled up the cliff face with a hammer and chisel, not to release the stone-bound creatures but to chip them into oblivion, as no graven image was permitted in the land. All agreed that the prophet was mad. He fell, struck his head, and died some days later, and none had dared to climb that limestone wall since. The fossils still hung from their stone perch overlooking Uri's land.

As long as the trees and the vines prospered, Uri considered the fossils to be giant unknown flowers coiled for centuries in hard hibernation. He believed that the land was made to grow wonders such as these and that as long as they remained unreleased by water, man, or angel, the soil was free to produce other crops in uncontested fecundity.

❧

Mahlah, Uri's wife, stepped into the shed on quick feet. The other women behind her followed in a tumble of wet clothing and shining eyes. The shed nearly smoked with the heat of its hoofed residents, the layers of pungent straw, and now the panting breath of women. There was a mist about the doorway that rolled out into the vertical stream of rain. The heat escaping from the shed was made invisible in the endless downpour.

"How long until one of them comes, do you think?" Keziah asked.

"Do you need someone to come?" Mahlah asked.

"It would be nice."

Mahlah laughed. "Uri will stick his head out of the house and just call, 'Woman? Are you lost? Are you coming home, or have you moved in with the goats?' "

"I see someone there," Basmat said. She squinted through the rain.

No one came. The women waited and watched the curtain of falling water and a small flood advancing before them like a translucent carpet moving left to right. They stood with shoulders overlapping and leaned against one another. Mahlah rested one hand on a weathered doorpost as though she were raising a signal.

Finally, Joseph appeared, pacing beneath the overhanging roof of the nearby house. He spotted the women, disappeared back into the house, and then reappeared. With his cloak slung over his head, Joseph tentatively ventured down from the house and into the stream, discovered that it only came to his ankles, and then walked confidently across the yard. He smiled and led Keziah from the group. He wordlessly walked her back to the house, his cloak slung over both of them.

The other men came out of the house then, shamed into action. They advanced as a group, Saul with Joseph's coat, Rehavam with his own, and Uri with nothing, arriving with his bald head now a red and glistening dome. His eyebrows and beard were bejewelled with water droplets that were constantly collecting, falling, and then collecting once more. Saul and Rehavam escorted their women as Joseph had, and Uri just stood grinning out in the rain, looking at his petulant bride of three decades.

"Of what use are you?" she asked.

When he strode back to the house, he carried Mahlah in his arms while she protested and slapped a wet hand against his sodden chest. He set her down graciously. They were both soaked.

"I suppose you got hungry," Mahlah said to Uri and indicated the men in general.

"Joseph said you might be lost."

"I am sure he did."

"I told him you had moved in with the goats."

"One day, I will."

They ate then, men and women together at breakfast, as on one of Keziah's music nights, as during the flood days at Grandma Sarah's when Jannaeus and Salome had been among them. They spoke of many things, from the weather to the flooded conference at Grandma Sarah's, which in turn led to talk of Grandma Sarah's recent passing.

"She understands," Keziah said.

"The first thing—" Joseph started.

"The first thing she said was 'I'm not Little Sarah anymore.' " Keziah looked like a woman freshly wounded. "The second thing—"

"Keziah." Joseph put his hand on her arm.

"—she said was 'I don't want to be the only Sarah. I want Grandma Sarah to come back and be Grandma Sarah, and I can stay as Little Sarah.' She said it the way she talks now. Most people would not understand her, but I knew what she was saying. I thought after her grandfather passed . . . "

❧

There was an aspect to the cliff-face fossils overlooking Uri's gate that appeared only in winter when the sun had risen halfway to its zenith. Shadows were erased in that light. Instead of warming in the sun, the seemingly featureless stone had a cold appearance. Cold stone radiated cold. When it then rained, shadows appeared in sheets of ripples flowing down the cliff, and in this way, water betrayed what the falsely placid stone previously concealed. The shapes could be seen most clearly in that light through water. From across the room, Uri saw the same manifest in Keziah's features: hurt was made clear by tears.

༄

Five days later, Joseph came into the house from the workshop with a streak of blood across his arm, though he showed no distress. "Peretz and Oren both left already," he said by way of explanation.

He sat, and Keziah washed the arm, revealing the long, old battle scar and beside it the splinter from which welled the darkest red. Her nails were adequate for the task, but she feared a shard would still break off inside his arm. Keziah fussed and took longer than needed. Joseph grew restless. "Shush," she said. "You're like the children when they were babies."

He swivelled his head and looked at her.

"When they wanted milk, and I could not act quickly enough."

He arched one eyebrow at her and then looked back at the floor while she worked.

"Sarah came to the shop today," he said just as she exhaled in victory and presented the unbroken miniature spear for him to inspect. She washed the wound and then wrapped it.

"She said she was the only Sarah now."

Keziah hesitated before tying off the wrapping.

"She said that she would do a good job of it."

Keziah finished, held his arm, touched the old scar.

"She wants to start making the bread. Like Grandma Sarah."

"She can't stand long enough. She doesn't have the strength to knead the dough properly."

"She wants me to build her something she can use while she's sitting. Something with a lever to multiply her force the way I lift logs with a lever but working in the opposite direction. Make it push down."

"You can do that?"

"I don't know. Maybe Oren can help me make something in metal. Rollers to push the dough through. A hammer on a lever, maybe? I don't know. She wants my help."

"You will help her."

"Of course, I'll help her."

"You have to do it."

"I said I'd do it."

"No, I mean, you have to do it so it works perfectly."

"You don't want to knead bread anymore?"

"For her!" Keziah said. There was an edge to her voice.

Joseph pulled her in. She sat on his leg, leaned against him, arms wrapped around him. "I'm sorry, but you have to do it."

"Keziah."

"I know."

35
103 BCE

JUGURTHA WALKED FOR hours on a flat plain with Joppa behind him. Spires of wind-borne dust appeared as sudden witnesses over the land, spying over the fields, spending themselves, and then ceasing to exist as the grains fell back to earth with a faint staccato. A residual haze drifted slowly away, and he walked through and onwards. He passed the desiccated skeleton of a horse or donkey, freed of its harness and picked over by the ceaseless polish of wind. Brilliant white arcs of bone pierced a slow drift of silent sand.

He came to Gezer. With its casemate walls and half-restored Philistine gates this city had once been the ancient conquest of a pharaoh, and after him the Assyrians, the city of Solomon's chariots, the Seleucid stronghold, and finally Simon Maccabeus's conquest. It was perched over a vast system of caves that were filled with its dead. The city, formed over its ancestral dead, was now neglected, uncontested, bypassed—it was as dead above ground as below, a reservoir for hollow bass notes, subject to a reverse siege, its inhabitants not bottled up within but poured out, the entire city like a drained vessel.

He had quoted Nahum years ago during the siege of Jerusalem. Something about the city being emptied like a pool. Gezer was empty now. All that was left was a shell that bore witness to the art and toil of prior centuries, but only where those efforts were inscribed in stone. Its former homes and public buildings now lay abandoned and half-buried in windblown debris and dust.

He climbed the slopes before Gezer and stood outside its crumbling walls, looking west over the way he had come. The wind whistled in his ears, and his vision blurred. He could see the sea's blue line in the distant west, its farthest reach marked by white on the horizon, and above that the same blue sky he stood under.

He descended from Gezer and continued east towards Jerusalem. He walked for hours through the Low Shephelah foothills of marlstone and soft chalk and continued over the High Shephelah, climbing and hearing his breath become ragged. This higher land was an accumulation of the same marlstone and soft chalk as before but was also mixed with windblown sand hardened by a thousand winters. The ground was fractured by bony roots, the illusion of fragile cracks that would bloom green in a few months but now were merely a low forest of gaunt and blackened branches in a brittle waste. When he came to hard chalk and limestone, he decided he was in the Judean mountains proper.

He paused again to drink, the water skin tilted, his

throat working with effort. A funereal vulture rose on a current of air above Jugurtha and circled higher than the dust spires outside Gezer, but not failing and falling as they had. The creature hung in the sky as a silhouetted witness in wait.

There were rumours of active shadows in Gezer's caves behind him, the lost ghosts of poorly buried souls, life ever pending in each mountain's dry branch, the suspended sun scouring each rock, deadly hailstones forever falling, the betrayals never ceasing, and famine's vengeance never satisfied, the slain masses left like the forgotten donkey to whiten beneath a yellow sun.

The pack he carried held all he needed to persuade Jannaeus to pursue the new campaign against Akko. His ledgers forecasted wealth and so advised in favour of war. If the coastal city on the western edge of Galilee could be conquered with a siege of one year or less, the revenues from the city would make the campaign profitable with the collection of just one year's tribute. The Akko campaign would secure a fortress in the north, which the Galileans wanted.

Jugurtha felt a wave of anticipated regret. He would, by this counsel, bring war again to Galilee's doorstep. He had not spoken the truth to them when they met in Ebed's upper room and celebrated the end of Hasmonean wars of speculative expansion. Kings were made for war. Jannaeus's ascension did not change that. If they could not read that truth in their holy books, he could not teach them.

He paused again, looked up, and found the vulture still waiting above. He drained his water skin and moved on against his body's protest, eyes and ears watching for signs of a spring.

If the king had known he would walk the road alone,

he might have had Jugurtha arrested for his own protection. Even Pericles would have resisted such foolishness. Jugurtha left Joppa early and in secret, knowing his old friend would otherwise have sent an escort. He took to heart the words of the old scribe he had met along the seashore. The old man held to Greek and Egyptian philosophies mixed with Jewish lore. He spoke of the afterlife as an inevitable and approaching adventure that brigands could only hasten but not alter. He said that this was the only certain truth to be found, and there was no cure for it. Jugurtha felt the same about kings and war and told himself he bore no personal responsibility for what might come to Galilee.

Evening approached, and he was short of his goal. He was well into the Judean mountains now. All around him were sudden rises and falls of vertically jagged white and grey rock that was weathered, carved, and pocketed with channels, hollows, and caves. In low-lying sections, the accumulated soil was red, rich but shallow, drifted into the natural terraced borders of bright limestone in deep cuts formed by some ancient violation. On the downward slopes, he encountered evergreen forests instead of the lifeless black limbs that thrust up from Gezer's surrounding plains. He came to a spring before dusk, quenched his thirst, filled his waterskin, and settled on a spot off the trail to sleep. He did not see his companion as he started a small fire. It remained a silent overseer of his quiet meal, a secret watcher in the dark.

Later, he lay on his back under the stars with a blanket wrapped around him and another one lying on top for warmth, using his diminished pack for a pillow and keeping his small sword at hand. He felt his sixty-three years in the thinness of his hips, the ache in his back, the way cold permeated his bones.

Before sleep took him, a story came to mind from the days of Jannaeus's grandfather, Simon. Simon's brother Jonathan had been the high priest and king in those days. King Jonathan had been captured by the Seleucids and taken to Akko. Just north of Mount Carmel, the city had been a wealthy and powerful port, and it still was. It had resisted Joshua. Resisted David. When Simon Maccabeus sought the release of his high priest, king, and brother, the Seleucids proposed a devil's bargain: they required the price of a king's ransom and Jonathan's children to be delivered as hostages in Akko in exchange for Jonathan's freedom. The hostages were to ensure Jerusalem's compliance with future tribute payments. To not pay the ransom would mean death for the king. To pay was to gamble with King Jonathan's children.

Jugurtha looked up through the gap in the pine trees above to the black sky beyond. The darkness he saw was pinholed with stars that moved across his narrow field of vision like points on a steady wheel that rolled through the night without slowing, removed from the cunning deliberations of men. It was a realm altogether distant and reserved for the gods or, if the Jews were correct and his conversion not in vain, for the one true God. He knew his sleep would be fitful in this place, and he knew his ledgers were mere justification. Jannaeus was determined to avenge Jonathan's captivity at Akko. The cost did not matter.

In the days of Jonathan's captivity, Simon had refused to abandon his brother. He sent Jonathan's children to Akko along with the ransom. Within the walls of Akko, the Seleucid generals counted the gold. Then the officers brought Jonathan's children before their father and one by one executed them before his eyes. The generals waited until Jonathan's grief rose to its peak, and then they killed him as well and congratulated themselves on the art of their performance. The Seleucids loved theatre, and there was nothing more captivating than what was real. Enriched and entertained, they departed north for Antioch.

Judea's coffers had been emptied. Their king and high priest and his descendants lay murdered and improperly buried at Akko. Israel was impoverished, disgraced, and in despair. It was into this void that Simon Maccabeus stepped so many years ago. He provided new leadership. And so Jannaeus's grandfather, Hyrcanus's father, became high priest and ruler, and as it always had been, the Maccabees only succeeded to power on the blood of their brothers.

To this day, Akko remained unbowed. Now it was Jannaeus's first wish as king to see Akko fall. Jugurtha's ledgers were of no account.

In the morning, Jugurtha rose in bright light and encountered what he had failed to see in the night. He had made his bed near the bottom of a short cliff face. Around eye level in the uneven rock, the morning light revealed the face, or rather the skull, of an ancient creature. The sight took Jugurtha back to the childhood stories his father had told him about his grandfather and the creatures found in his African homeland. These creatures were not found anywhere in the Greek lands, neither east nor north of the sea. The skull now before him was larger than a horse or donkey. One cavernous eye socket was visible. The toothy visage emerged in a crude grimace, and two stout horns rose from the creature's face, one from below its eyes and another from its snout. A rhinoceros. Father had drawn the creature for him, and he would not have believed his father had he not already seen elephants, proof that such strange beasts existed.

Farther back in the stone, where a section had collapsed, there were signs of another bone, perhaps a shoulder or leg. The rest of the creature remained encased in rock. Jugurtha looked closely at the leering, demon-like skull. Nearby, he found the fossil of a stony shellfish, and he wondered what history or magic had led these two creatures to be cursed together in this place so far from Africa and the sea.

He wished to pull the skull from the rock, to trample and scatter it into a million pieces and ensure that it no longer loomed over the passage of any future traveller by this stream, but it was only partially revealed, and there was nothing for him to grip. He tapped at the revealed horn with the butt of his sword but could cause no damage. He did not have a mason's hammer. There was something evil here. This demonic observer must not remain so close to Jerusalem. He resolved to come back to this place with a mason's hammer and chisel.

He set out after a light breakfast with his mind inflamed.

In Dora, along the sea, a man's great head tilted and studied the room and the sea beyond. From the chest up, he looked like a general. He looked too virile for just a king and was a mythic hero in his own eyes. Below the chest, he was built like a boy with thin legs and a disappearing backside.

The Seleucid abandonment of their southern lands around Eretz-Israel had left Dora with a strange freedom.

The Jewish nation reformed inland. Egypt worked through their royal intrigues while the Parthians fought mysterious, distant wars, and the Nabataeans kept to their desert trade routes. None claimed Dora until Zoilus did.

One day, after much planning, Zoilus quit his market stalls and ships, stood on his boyish legs, swung a sword powered by his manly chest, and kept swinging until he found himself to be master of the city. From Dora, he went down the coast to Strato's Tower and took that port as well. Then he consolidated the territory between the two cities and began to plan his next conquest. Joppa was the next city to the south, but it was too closely tied to Jerusalem's shipping interests, and Zoilus had no appetite to take on the Maccabees. The north was a desolate coast until the base of Mount Carmel, beyond which lay Ptolemais, which the Jews now called Akko, a city-state as independent of any king as Tyre and Sidon farther north. Like Joppa and Jerusalem, Akko was beyond the former merchant's power. The only other direction led across the sea, and he was not about to attempt invasions into Egypt or Rome or Macedonia. He just wanted one or two more nice cities to control, but there were none to be had. So, having retired from his merchant business, he now retired as well from war. He lived a luxurious life as the ruler of Dora, Strato's Tower, and the nine miles of coastline between. He had a wife in Dora, a wife and a mistress at Strato's Tower, and a young widow halfway between with two children who lived a frugal life near the main road. He stopped there and abused her and her children en route between his two cities when the mood struck him. His ability to do so proved his absolute dominion within his small kingdom. The widow was a microcosm of his whole little empire. What he could not practically do to every resident individually, he did to her personally.

When the sickly king in Jerusalem, Aristobulus, died, Zoilus considered travelling to Jerusalem to pay his respects. He thought about it, but he did not leave Dora. The Jews did not welcome gentiles in that manner.

What he did do was try to learn what he could about the new king and queen: Alexander Jannaeus and Salome Alexandra. He wondered what compelled the world's royalty to name all their children Alexander, Alexandra, or Cleopatra, with the repetitive Antiochus designations. Many Salomes would follow this one, he was sure. He was proud of his name: Zoilus. It was distinct, and distinction was true royalty. All the world's Alexanders were named after the first, and Zoilus was the first of his name.

The new king and queen in Jerusalem were a puzzle. She was much older, which was not the usual Jewish custom. She was rumoured to be a devoted Pharisee, but her husband was a Sadducee. They had taken the throne from the previous queen, Salina, but somehow Salina still lived.

His spies circulated through the region and reported all they learned. The master of Jannaeus's fleet sailed from Joppa. Jannaeus had ordered a new army be raised, though as far as Zoilus could tell, there was nothing wrong with the old army. Jerusalem was fat with revenues from its new territories. Galleys sailed from Dora empty, and the implications chilled Zoilus in his palace: they would return, as they had before, with new recruits for the Jewish army. Spring was coming, and with spring came war. Those ships did not sail for any current conflict. They sailed for the one that was expected. Zoilus needed to know who Jerusalem's next target would be.

From the open window, a great insect entered the palace. The segmented creature hummed and bumped blindly about the interior walls, obscenely flexing its lower body. The insect irritated him, and he did not know the name of its ugliness. He supposed that the ancient Jewish Solomon knew its name. There was undoubtedly a book in Jerusalem to explain its lifecycle or features. "Bah!" he blurted and spat at the insect in frustration. It buzzed when it bumped into the walls and then was gone out the window, flying in a straight line. Zoilus's gaze followed the insect until it disappeared, and then he continued staring across the sea toward Egypt.

The Jews would not be mobilizing to invade Egypt. Jews were in command of the Egyptian army. The two countries were allies. His spies reported that Salome and Cleopatra had some form of friendship.

The Seleucids to the north were also an unlikely target. The Jews were no match for the Seleucids far from home. The Jews had no elephants. Nabataea to the south and east was a valid target, but his spies made it plain that Jannaeus's attention was not directed towards Nabataea. The Parthians were not worth considering. Even the Seleucids had yet to tame the Parthians.

That left only three targets. The Jews had reclaimed everything that their holy books called Eretz-Israel except for these three coastal cities. The largest prize was just north of Mount Carmel: Ptolemais. The Jews had called the city Akko in their ancient books and, with the Seleucids gone, were once again calling it Akko. It had been an impossible target when Zoilus had established his little empire, but for the Maccabees, it was a plum that might be plucked. The other two cities were south of Mount Carmel, and they were his.

Zoilus looked again for the invading insect. He stared in the direction it had gone, but there was no sign of the thing.

36

135-102 BCE

A SHORT WALK FROM the fossils overlooking Uri's gate, a two-men-tall section of the cliff bowed out in a great arc topped by a rubble-strewn plateau. Its perfect size beckoned for someone to build a house upon it. The cliff continued to rise higher behind the plateau, but this curious base offered a foundation, a sure protection against flood, a view over the rest of the farm, and a defensive position. Uri had been enthusiastic. Mahlah would not have it. She had envisioned climbing a sloped ramp each day, children falling from the front door, and many other trials. The master's house overlooking all was never built, but Uri could not let the space go unmarked.

When they were young men in the days before Keziah, Uri built a ladder up to it as a temporary measure, and Joseph laughed at Uri's endeavour. Loose material from the cliff face above littered the platform. This rockfall further entrenched Mahlah's resistance. Still, Uri could not let the platform be.

Two years had passed when Joseph returned to the farm to discover a tunnel cut into the rock base. It was as tall as Uri, caught Joseph at about eye level, and was wide enough for a broad-wheeled cart. The tunnel sloped gradually upward and curved to open onto the plateau.

"Wouldn't it have been easier to build a wooden ramp rather than cutting stone?" Joseph asked.

"Stone is forever," Uri said.

Over the next few years, in the vintner's off-seasons, foundations rose. Stone and mortar were dressed with thick crossbeams as the structure continued to climb, and Uri built a semicircular tower four stories high and melded with the irregularities of the cliff face. Once completed, the tower had three oversized stories floored in loose planks. He set large, square holes into the masonry at regular intervals. The beams projected through some of these holes, pinning the walls to the cliff with exaggerated joinery and anchors. Most of the holes were left open as unshuttered windows.

The tower's exterior walls were as smooth as he could make them. Inside, the masonry was a honeycomb of rock ringing the entire interior with the largest recesses the size of a man's head. On the cliff side of the tower, a similar pattern of crude recesses was painstakingly carved into the limestone. It was hammer and chisel work that took years to accomplish. With sweat pouring from his bald, flushed head even in the shadow of the tower's interior, Uri removed the loose floorboards as he worked his way down, leaving only the structural beams in place. When he was finished, it was an empty tower with no levels but the crossbeams.

Three final tasks drew the project to its conclusion. First, he built a tightly sealed door at the bottom of the tunnel ramp that, when closed, would admit no creature, however small. The second task was outside the tower. At about shoulder level, he plastered a cubit-tall and utterly smooth band around the base of the tower. He sanded and painted the band to protect it from the weather, and he shaped a matching band along the joint where the tower met the cliff. No snake, fox, or weasel would find purchase on the plaster's smooth surface. The dovecote was secure.

For the last task, Uri brought Mahlah into the finished dovecote. They stood together in silence, looking up at the crossbeams and shafts of light intersecting high above. From one of the highest beams hung two strands of a great rope strung through a large pulley. He motioned to Mahlah, and she positioned herself immodestly as he passed pads between her legs, under her arms, and across her back. He secured the pads in place with tight knots and then attached her harness to one of the ropes from above. When she was ready, he hoisted her into the air. Suspended just a foot off the ground, she looked at him with wide eyes, wiggled roughly in her harness, and then gave him a quick nod. He looped the rope about himself and began to pull even lengths down from above. The higher she went, the harder he pulled, and higher still she rose into the tower's shaft. Past the first beam, then the second beam, she came nearly to the third beam.

"That's it!" she shouted down to him. Her voice rolled around inside the tower and reverberated back in lower tones. She unhooked the small jar that had been raised with her. She spoke the words, poured some of the contents into one palm, and scattered it to the walls, repeating the ritual again and again until the jar was empty.

"Don't drop it!" he shouted at her.

She put the empty jar away in a bag tied around her waist and then opened one of the small grain sacks. She flung handfuls at the nesting holes until the first sack was empty.

"Lower me down to the next level," she said.

Carefully, sweating from the effort and heat and a bit of fear, Uri lowered her to the second beam. She emptied another small sack at this level, stretching to reach recesses just above and below her. She came down again until her feet were just above her husband's height and scattered the remaining grains.

"Okay," she said.

He lowered her to the dovecote's floor. When she was safely on the ground, he crouched beside her, shaking and rolling his shoulders and arms and back as she untangled herself.

Her eyes were wide, bright, and alive. "You should go up there," she said.

"I built it. I've been up there."

"Have you been with no floors? Just you and the rope and the light coming in from all the openings and the hollow sound? It's beautiful."

"I put the floors in. I took the floors out," Uri said.

Her gaze was on the beams crossing the hollow spaces high above. She gave no indication that she heard him.

As Uri stood in the same place so many years later, ankle-deep in dove dung, slinging it by the shovelful into the wagon he had rolled up the tunnel, he wondered at the passage of time. The dovecote had been empty for nearly a month before the first bird found it and the bounty of grain inside. The first year it housed fewer than a dozen pairs, and then there were three dozen the following year. Now, the picturesque intersections of light were shattered by the wingbeats of a thousand birds. They made this tower their home and left their dung to pile at its base for Uri to shovel and wheel and spread across the fields. Most of the farm was subject to the dangers of flooding, but the doves were lords of all. They were protected, housed high above the weather, served by the same farm they fertilized.

When Joseph had asked the question, Uri looked at him for a long time before answering. "They don't eat grapes," he said finally. "You waited this many years until I'd already built and populated this entire thing to ask me that question? The whole time you were wondering if I was creating a community of doves that were going to then destroy my vineyards?"

Joseph smiled and showed his palms. "I just thought of it now," he said.

Uri laughed at the memory of that conversation as he rolled the cart down the long, sloping curve and out into sunshine. When he set the cart handles down and stood erect, he was surprised to see men standing in the yard near the house. The day labourers were in the vineyards, so these were visitors. Uri recognized Mahlah's shape with them. He closed and secured the dovecote door before moving across the yard towards the group. The visitors had almost surrounded Mahlah, and Uri picked up his pace. He had no weapon, not even a farm tool. Then some in the group turned, and Uri recognized them.

"Uri," the tall man said.

"Joseph! Moshe. Saul. Rehavam." He deflated and slowed down. The men gave proper greetings. Mahlah brought out a fresh pitcher from the well, opened a flagon of wine, and set small cakes out on a large cloth on the ground. The cakes were two days old and crumbled when the men tried to eat them.

"Why are you here?" Uri finally asked.

Joseph reached into his shirt and removed a letter, which he slowly unfolded.

"From Jugurtha," Uri said.

"Yes."

"The siege of Akko is over," Uri guessed.

"In a manner."

He saw the expression on Joseph's face. "Mahlah, go inside."

Mahlah reacted as though she had been slapped. "No, I'm not going inside."

Uri looked at his wife with a half-grave, half-numb expression.

"Has the dove dung gotten to your senses?" she asked.

He looked at her uncomprehendingly. It was not clear if he even remembered what he had said to her. "What is happening?" he asked Joseph.

"Zoilus came up from Dora."

Uri shrugged. "He was next, I presume. Might as well throw in his lot with Akko."

"Jannaeus abandoned Akko and chased Zoilus back to Dora."

Uri thought about that for a moment. "Jannaeus will go back to Akko when he's done with Zoilus, no?"

Joseph considered the dovecote before turning his attention back to Uri. "Lathyrus landed at Akko."

Uri studied Joseph a moment before speaking again. His head reddened. He waited longer and then finally said, "I thought the Egyptian rebel was dead."

Joseph shook his head. "Banished. Not dead."

"Banished," Uri said. "The Egyptians haven't landed at Akko, just Lathyrus?"

"And his army."

"His army." Uri took a moment to look at each of his other guests in turn. Rehavam made another attempt at Mahlah's cake. "He was banished. The Egyptians banished Lathyrus—with an army?"

"To Cyprus," Joseph said. "Drove him off. He was not really banished. The civil war against his mother failed, and she let him go, alive, with his followers. He escaped to an island. Probably Cyprus."

"Lathyrus. A bastard son born of incest between mother and uncle. Twice an abomination."

"I don't think he's a bastard," Joseph said. "I think they were married."

"She married him?" Uri asked. "Her uncle?"

"Okay, first Cleopatra Euergetis was born. Her mother and father were siblings. The father died. Cleopatra's mother then married her other brother, Ptolemy," Joseph said. He looked around at his friends to make sure they were following. "Cleopatra was already born. Ptolemy married his sister, Cleopatra's mother. So now, Ptolemy is Cleopatra's uncle and adopted father."

"Yeah, we got that part," Uri said.

"A few years later, Ptolemy married Cleopatra as well.

While the mother was still alive. He married both mother and daughter at the same time."

"Cleopatra Euergetis married her mother's husband while he was still her mother's husband?" Uri asked.

"Now you've got it," Joseph said.

The group of men all looked at Joseph like he was insane. "And Ptolemy has a baby with Cleopatra Euergetis, his wife's daughter, his niece, who is also now his wife as well."

"Yes," Joseph said.

"And that baby is Lathyrus."

"Yes," Joseph said, "and when Ptolemy died, Lathyrus started a civil war against his mother, Cleopatra."

"Who is a morally deficient, corrupt, strange woman married to her own mother's husband."

"And also a friend of Salome's."

Uri flinched. "Salome's?" A long pause ensued. The others said nothing. A flurry of doves left the dovecote behind Uri, and he turned to watch them swoop together and then disappear in the far trees. "Egypt's incestuous pharaoh is a friend of our queen?" he said, still watching the treeline.

"So says Jugurtha," Joseph said. "Cleopatra and Salome write letters to each other."

"Why would—"

"Let's not talk about the Egyptians," Joseph interrupted.

Uri considered that for a minute. He looked intently toward the gate and the cliff face. In this light, he could not see the fossils he knew were there watching. If indeed they had been creatures with eyes for watching and not flowers as he told others.

"Jannaeus is besieging Dora now, yes?" Uri said. There was an edge to his voice. Mahlah leaned in towards him, reached with a hand, and then retracted it.

"Yes," Joseph said. "Our king is dealing with Zoilus at Dora now instead of finishing the siege at Akko."

"And Lathyrus is in Akko," Uri said.

"Well, no. It seems the people of Akko originally sent a message seeking Lathyrus's help. To protect them from Jannaeus. But when Lathyrus landed at Akko, they changed their minds. They wouldn't let him into the city."

Uri stared at Joseph. Waited. Joseph said nothing.

"The people of Akko solicited help from Lathyrus," Uri said. "He leaves . . . where was he?"

"Cyprus."

"He leaves Cyprus. Puts his whole army onto ships."

"Horse and foot," Joseph said.

"Horse and foot. Onto ships. Sails to Akko. Disembarks. They change their minds and tell him they don't want him at Akko after all. 'Go home, please.' "

"That's about it."

"Are the people of Akko trying to start a war with a second madman?" Uri asked.

"Uri," Mahlah said. Uri ignored her.

"It would seem so," Joseph said.

Uri turned to Saul. "You know these people. You trade with them."

"I think they realized that if they ally themselves with Lathyrus, then Cleopatra Euergetis might think they've allied against her," Saul said. "Lathyrus is still technically at war with Egypt. Akko does not want the pharaoh marching on their little city. Our king was bad enough."

"So, Akko invited a new army to its shores," Uri said, "then immediately made it their enemy as well."

"I don't care about Akko," Joseph said.

"The situation then is that Jannaeus, who we helped put on the throne to stop pointless wars, is now besieging Dora, and Lathyrus is besieging Akko in his place," Uri said. He waved off Mahlah's reaching hand. "Presumably, Jannaeus and Lathyrus will meet each other in battle at some point when one of them is done with their respective sieges."

"Well, no. Lathyrus has gone to Zoilus's aid in defence of Dora. It's a way to save face," Joseph said. "Lathyrus came here as an ally. If not for Akko, then Dora. Our king will fight Zoilus and Lathyrus now at Dora. Akko is spared for now."

Uri sat stone-faced for a while. He poured himself a new cup and topped up those of his wife and friends. Finally, he spoke. "Our king marched out to conquer Akko, and instead, he's in Dora about to fight two different armies, neither of which has anything to do with Akko."

"The bird dung hasn't gone to your head after all," Joseph said.

Uri slammed his cup down. "I'd like to mix Alexander Jannaeus's blood with my bird dung and spread it across my vineyards as fertilizer where it might do some good for this country!"

"Uri!" Mahlah said.

"I don't disagree," Joseph said.

Uri considered the cliffs, the barns, and then the dovecote. He studied each of the four men and his wife with an inscrutable gaze. "Where is Joazar?" he finally asked. "If the four of you are going to come, you might as well all come."

"Joazar should be on his way to Jerusalem," Joseph said. "Or maybe he's at Dora by now."

"Dora?"

"With Ebed and Jugurtha. Salome's request. The queen wants to repeat history," Joseph said. "A negotiation instead of war."

"Like when Ebed and Joazar, when they were boys, worked out a deal with Sidetes and the Seleucids," Uri said.

"Yes."

"What about Jugurtha?"

"Ebed, Joazar, and Jugurtha are all on the same side now," Joseph said. "The three of them will represent Jerusalem and try to prevent a war with Lathyrus."

Uri contemplated this with his head down, his chin nearly touching his chest. After a moment, he raised just his eyes. "What else?"

"The queen has written to Cleopatra Euergetis."

"Why?"

"To get her to come and deal with her rebel son now that he's no longer somewhere at sea."

"Why would the pharaoh do that?" Uri asked. "He's our problem now. Our problem, thanks to Jannaeus, who wasn't supposed to be starting any war at all. I can't believe he's not even besieging the city he marched out to attack. What is wrong with the Hasmoneans?"

"Lathyrus is still Cleopatra's problem. Her son wants the Egyptian throne, not Israel or Dora or Akko," Joseph said. "But with Dora or Akko as an ally, he has a base. With them, he might be able to take Jerusalem and then the rest of the country. With Israel's revenues, he could buy the loyalty of Jerusalem's mercenaries. With all that, he would finally have an army strong enough to attack Egypt again. It's better she deals with him now before he re-establishes his power right on her doorstep."

"So," Uri started. Then stopped. He frowned, studied the crumbled cakes, and looked back at Joseph. "If Cleopatra is the solution to Lathyrus's threat, what's the point of Joazar, Ebed, and Jugurtha's mission?"

"Jannaeus needs relief now, not two months from now. Jugurtha thinks he can buy time. Joazar and Ebed and Jugurtha will bribe Lathyrus to abandon Dora. Maybe even betray Dora."

"And the four of you. Why are you all here?"

Three of the men looked to Saul, and he shuffled forwards to speak. "We came to talk about growing the quince business. We can use this situation to our advantage."

"Quince?" Uri said. "Lathyrus likes my quince?"

"I suppose he might," Saul said. A half-smile formed on his face. "We're not interested in Lathyrus. We're here for Cleopatra."

"You want to send her some of the quince wine?" Uri asked.

"Sell it to her," Saul said. "Introduce her to it. Get her to love it. Maybe designate a royal buyer in Alexandria we can distribute through rather than the usual channels."

Uri burst into laughter. "You came here to talk about wine? About business?"

"Of course," Saul said. "Jannaeus has yet to kill anyone in Akko or Dora, and he won't start now. War needs to stay in the past. We didn't help put him on the throne so he could restart his brother and father's *raca* wars."

"Does Joazar know about this?" Uri asked.

"He made sure we came to see you," Joseph said.

"Are we in agreement?" Saul asked.

"How many cases?" Uri asked.

"A dozen to start," Saul said. "If she takes them all, that will be a good sign. Agreed?"

The men nodded, as did Mahlah.

"Then we go to Kfar Nahum."

Before Joazar left for Jerusalem, he went to see Keziah. Brother and sister met alone in the courtyard. She did not want him involved with Salome and Jugurtha's negotiation scheme. His negotiation with the Seleucids years before had led him to captivity in Antioch. Making deals with the Egyptians could end the same way.

He had not told her about the plan to use Cleopatra to betray Lathyrus, but she already knew of it from Joseph. She confronted him on his intent to deceive Lathyrus, and when he flinched but would not admit to the details, she felt control slip. She brought up the shameful raid on David's tomb. She brought up how Joazar had avoided going to the festivals in Jerusalem for years. She brought up Antioch and accused him of hypocrisy, of unknown sins committed in the north and hidden from his wife. At this last accusation, Joazar finally reacted.

"I fought for Simon at Dagon!"

"And you watched his wife die on the wall."

"While you hid our mother's leprosy. Hid it. In the middle of the village. Risked the entire village."

"Our family was safe!"

"If they were so safe, where are Father and Little Moshe now?"

Keziah looked at him in shock, and the colour left her face. Her wide eyes focused elsewhere.

"While you found a nice, new, safe home in Galilee," Joazar continued, "I wore chains to Antioch. Was exiled from my own people. While you discovered a new home and a new family and a new husband, I sweltered in a dungeon in the north, and you dare despise me for going to Jerusalem to help prevent another innocent soul from going through the hell of banishment? Do you want Lathyrus on our throne and ruling the temple?"

He left Keziah then. He left without an embrace, striding off while she stood by the low wall outside the courtyard. She laid her hand on the cold stone to stop her trembling. She needed Joseph then. It was just her and Sarah in the otherwise empty house while Joseph was with the others to see Uri and likely go from there to Kfar Nahum.

News of the Jewish–Egyptian negotiations came to Zoilus after the siege of Dora was already over. He had no opportunity to opine on the arrangements. When the details were passed to him, Zoilus took the news badly. "Three hundred pounds?" he said in amazement. He held a wooden staff he had taken from his favourite widow's home as a memento from his last visit. He had beaten the woman with it before he left, and so it was special to him. "Lathyrus accepted three hundred pounds? Of silver?"

"Jannaeus will lift his siege of Dora," his spy said. "He can lay siege to us forever, and we can't lift it on our own, but with Lathyrus in the picture, the Jews were in trouble. Lathyrus gets paid. The Jews avoid a fight with Lathyrus. And our troubles are over."

"For three hundred pounds? Of silver?"

"The siege will be lifted!"

"Antiochus Sidetes accepted two thousand pounds, not three hundred," Zoilus shouted. He threw the widow's staff across the room. "Of gold, not silver!"

"This is Dora," the spy said, "not Jerusalem. Dora isn't worth as much as Jerusalem."

"You stupid man," Zoilus shouted. "This *is* Jerusalem. Dora and Lathyrus's armies against Jannaeus, who is not behind his walls but in the field and vulnerable—Jannaeus was finished! Lathyrus had the whole of Judea before him! Cursed of Zeus, he could have taken out Israel's army, Jerusalem would have been left open to us, and Akko would have been a simple conquest as well. Two nations were in his grasp! Instead, he accepted three hundred pounds? Of silver?"

Zoilus waved the man away and turned to look out the seaside window. Egypt lay that way. He thought again of the grotesque insect and the widow, and he knew he needed to visit the widow. The Jewish army camped outside his gates stood in his way. He looked back to where the spy had gone and then across the water again. Zoilus knew he was going to have to pay Lathyrus as well for this rescue. Dora had called out to the Egyptian for help. Rescue required a payment. Lathyrus was going to earn two commissions on this adventure, one from Jerusalem and one from Dora, neither one of which involved any actual fighting.

Zoilus felt rage rise within and worked to suppress it.

He decided that as soon as he could, he would go see the widow again. He would make her pay for the outrage of his failed bid to defeat the Jews at Akko, for the humiliation of his flight back to Dora, and now for whatever obeisance he was obligated to extend to Lathyrus for this salvation. He wanted to know how many days it would take before he could get back to being the master of his domain again. The widow would suffer much more this time. He walked across the room and picked up the wooden staff. He held it tight. He made plans for how next he would use it.

Once co-pharaoh of Egypt, Lathyrus stood before Dora's puny gates with an aggrieved and contemptuous expression. This countenance was so characteristic of the man that the sculptors in Alexandria had etched it into stone. He stood with his close-set eyes studying the city before him. His curled hair tangled into his beard. His thick neck expanded with each intake of breath as though his neck's lateral muscles were somehow engaged in the act. His guards stood behind him, followed by the horse guard and the footguard. The whole force totalled eighty thousand men.

Had he done all he could with the Jewish negotiations? The Jewish king's trio of ministers had been disarming in appearance and manner. Lathyrus set his misgivings aside and faced his situation with a pragmatic and private assessment: underneath his commander's physique, he was on this bloodless battlefield as a man whose own mother had made him divorce his first wife, a man whose same mother had then stolen his throne, a man who had married two of his sisters, as was the family tradition, and then was made to divorce both of them at his mother's command. He was a man who had been invited to these shores by a city that rejected him once he landed. His army of eighty thousand was beginning to question their present loyalties. They had lost a war in Egypt, lived in poverty on an island, come for action in Akko and been dismissed, and now marshalled for war at Dora. The Jew's capitulation and departure, at last, signalled some kind of victory. The amount and currency of payment was not public knowledge. Only the tribute's ornate chests were known. He could now pay his men. Soon enough, there would also be the spilling of blood and the looting that they lusted after.

When Zoilus invited him to dine within the palace, Lathyrus made it clear that he would dine on an outdoor dais with his guards and generals. It would be a feast in full view of his army, and Zoilus would join him with his generals and ministers only. Zoilus agreed to the proposition though he seemed hesitant to do so.

Lathyrus surveyed Dora's palace courtyards and selected a point of high visibility and great impracticality. Zoilus gave the orders and had the banquet moved. Squeezing a considerable portion of the Egyptian army into the square and the surrounding open spaces was a feat that required most of Zoilus's army to leave the grounds. Disorder prevailed. The kitchens, already under strain, were taxed further with transporting the banquet to the new location.

Eventually, the parties established their seating, and Lathyrus, after an hour of aggrieved and contemptuous impatience, accepted his place at the banquet with Zoilus at his side. Their officers intermixed across the dais and looked down on the assembled Egyptian army spread out below them. Half-naked slaves of the finest physicality served the wine. There was a rumbling among those who were forced to stand and observe what amounted to a show.

The servants were dismissed, and speeches began while the audience of soldiers demonstrated their collective boredom. Then the dishes came, and the servants were again fine specimens. They were dressed in a manner so provocative that they caught even Zoilus's jaded eye. There was a rumble of talking from the army below, gestures and grins and occasionally loud explosions of sound as the soldiers expressed their enthusiasm for new flesh as it appeared. After some dull speeches, the show resumed its extravagant display of human flesh and excessive consumption: fish, fowl, pig, and goat, grilled and baked in fruits with juices sloshing, coated tables and tongues as anxious servers settled trays, removed trays, and refilled wine jugs. Portions of the meal made their unauthorized way from the table to the assembled thousands watching, and soon the feasting had spread throughout the courtyard, a bottomless maw, a vanishing of sweet and spiced carcasses and a pilfering of platters and palace silver.

The kitchens panicked at the ever-changing logistics, at the spiked volume in demand, at the disappearing serving pieces and the bottomless appetites of what turned out to be not merely Zoilus's gluttonous retinue and the Egyptian command but an entire army come to feast. Cooks plundered Zoilus's cellars and replaced decorative flagons with clay amphorae, which circulated far beyond the official tables. The drinkers drained and broke jars and called for more and more as servants opened private cellars and raided farther and farther from the palace kitchens. Whenever they spotted tableware of even modest value, the kitchen messengers looted, foreshadowing the upheaval to come.

Initially submissive to the change in venue and circumstances, depressed and desiring to move past this distasteful state formality, Zoilus found himself left behind by the events of the feast. The celebration of the city's liberation quickly became the gutting of city order. He was unable to work out how to avoid offence even as Dora emptied around him.

A slave girl came along carrying a roasted pig, a load far too large for the child. She hurried, her bare feet sliding on spilled oils and wine. She stepped too firmly in a place too smooth, and she slipped one last time; the pig flew as she fell. She slid off the dais's edge, and her dish skittered down the length of the assembled guests and passed unfaltering into the open air. The roar of those below who caught the pig and those who caught the girl were indistinguishable but for the girl's screams. Neither the pig nor the girl was spared from that mob.

Lathyrus rose and with him his generals. Zoilus was utterly perplexed, wondering if the Egyptians were courteous enough to rescue the pig or the girl or both. Then it dawned on him that the Egyptians had drawn their swords. Zoilus looked up at his guest in surprise. The man's expression was as aggrieved and contemptuous as ever, but now it was also smeared with malice. Zoilus realized that malice had always been there, a latent potentiality in those Greek-Egyptian features. The Egyptian made another speech, and Zoilus was able to comprehend, on a delay, that his life and kingdom were forfeit, that this was part of Lathyrus's arrangement with the Jews. He had been betrayed for three hundred pounds. Not of gold. Just silver. And for this price the Jews bought not only the lifting of the siege but also Zoilus's life and kingdom. His whole kingdom. He was aghast at how cheaply he had been sold.

Lathyrus turned his attention back to Zoilus, and the Egyptian's sword entered the place between Zoilus's neck and chest, and Zoilus felt the shocking intimacy of his spine as it was severed. Shock remained in his eyes, and he had a flash of insight that somehow the widow had caused this. This was her recompense for his abuse, the penalty for his crimes against her, and that penalty would follow him beyond death into some grim afterlife where the shades of the underworld would bestow on him their tortures, be they the shades of Tartarus, Eurynomos, or the Erinyes of Hades, or whatever angels or demons the Jewish god controlled and commanded to inflict punishment upon him.

These last thoughts were chased away by the euphoric wonder of no feeling, of disconnection from the body he had known all his years as his eyes looked where his head lolled—a view of cloth, stone, the backside of a seated companion, and in a welter of blood and a view without dignity, the tyrant died. In the chaos around him, unbeknown to him, his body was jostled forward with the nearly severed head lagging, and then with a wet sound, his slackly jointed face landed in a slaughter of fish and pig and blood and sauces.

37
102 BCE

It was a strange conveyance back to Jerusalem: they rode three abreast on a war wagon, with their baggage mounded behind and the driver perched in front. The flat coastlands receded, and dry, rocky lands lay before them. What madness might prevail between the gentiles would be cleansed by a salt spray and did not concern the wagon riders.

"We've done this before," Joazar said.

"I remember. Pericles sat where you are now," Jugurtha said.

"You all rode three-wide like this?" Ebed asked.

Jugurtha nodded. "On our way to Antioch."

The journey back to Jerusalem offered none of Pericles's raucous laughter nor the embedded fear from that Antioch journey. This misadventure with Akko, Dora, and Lathyrus was behind them. These few weeks had been educational, a corrective event for the throne and the nation and, above all, Jannaeus. Joazar shuddered to think of Israel controlled by the Egyptians.

❧

Jugurtha rode silently and calculated. Dora and Strato's Tower would be Jewish again when Lathyrus was through. That was the agreement. None doubted that the Egyptian looting would be severe, but he had factored the lost wealth into his bookkeeping. They would get none of the typical up-front conqueror's reward; that would go to Lathyrus. Those losses, however, were offset by the efficiency of the conquest. Invigorated with Dora's loot, Lathyrus would seek to recover his pride at Akko, and the siege there would be lengthy. The Egyptians would remain on Israel's borders for some time, but they would be preoccupied.

"My wife will solve the long-term Lathyrus problem," King Jannaeus had said. "She's sent for the man's mother. Cleopatra will not let her son establish a base here. Let Lathyrus go from Dora to Akko and exhaust himself there. His mother will deal with him soon enough."

"What if the Egyptians don't leave?" Jugurtha had asked the king. It was not like him to be this cautious, but Jannaeus had a mad energy about him recently that Jugurtha distrusted.

"Lathyrus?" Jannaeus had asked.

"Or his mother after him."

Jannaeus had made a gesture, a peculiar fluttering of his hands that Jugurtha knew from Aristobulus and John Hyrcanus as a Hasmonean signal to end a conversation.

The wagon's creak was just like the discussion between

Ebed and Joazar: unceasing. The two were now men in their forties, men who had known each other their whole lives. Jugurtha reflected that he had no such companion. He was an old man, like the old wagon, and no one argued with him.

An hour passed. All Jugurtha did was reorder numbers and listen to Joazar's and Ebed's voices. Their conversation's content slipped through him unremembered, but that dialogue's nature left a mark like a wound. They talked in half sentences. They used familiar and understanding tones that could turn abrupt but were always smoothed by a tilt of the head or a slight gesture. Ebed handed Joazar a skin, although he had not asked for it nor indicated thirst. Joazar drank long and without thanks, and neither man registered the transaction nor remarked upon it.

Jugurtha began to think less of ledgers and more of the two he rode with, of what ran between them and not him. The dawning awareness of newly discovered absence stole through him.

They made camp that night within sight of Samaria city's abandoned ruins. Mount Ebal was far ahead.

The logs they burned that night were as thick as a man's thigh. Years' worth of growing girth turned white and black in the fire, forming into fractured squares and rectangles whose grooves writhed red before transforming into pure, colourless light, a dangerous and unyielding vapour. Deep coals glowed below; the flames above were invisible. Into this furnace was set a cauldron of hammered iron. The contents began to bubble. The men sat in semi-darkness and waited while the driver occasionally stirred the pot with a makeshift ladle. They were the king's emissaries dining with the common tools of Galilee.

The night was a metropolis of noise: frogs and insects made a relentless din. Night birds held side discussions, and an owl hooted afterwards. A muted response came from farther away, followed by a wolf's lonely howl, which went unanswered. The ghosts of the original people of this land had long ago departed. There were none to answer the wolf's cry, none to explain to the dead why this caravan of travellers was passing through the remnants of the Samaritan civilization.

Before he slept, Jugurtha thought about the wolf and his unanswered call. It took a long time for sleep to come.

A streak of impractical fatalism increasingly consumed the old scribe from Joppa. He had set out upon the road when he first heard that Jannaeus had laid siege to Dora. He arrived at Dora from the south at the same time that Lathyrus arrived from the north. The old scribe passed around the sealed city and through Jewish and Egyptian lines with the invisibility white hair afforded. To these young men in armour and good health, his posture and shuffle were foreign and uninteresting. He walked slowly. What had been a day's journey in his youth now took three. He was nearly at Akko when a stranger caught up to him on the road and passed on tales of terror. In this way, he learned of the looting of Dora.

When he arrived at Akko, some guards who knew him admitted the scribe through the gate's door. He was welcomed for his knowledge of Jewish lore and his willingness to share it with men of like interest. He was one of the few Jews known in Akko who would willingly discuss Homer alongside Jeremiah or Daniel and do so with enthusiasm.

Within the city, he was admitted into a courtyard that faced half a dozen doors. The rightmost opened at his knock. He was led to a room lined with columns, oil lamps, and scrolls upon lecterns. The floor was composed of great limestone slabs. The room's focal point was a small theatre. It was here that the old scribe found those he sought. He was tired and still wore a sheen of sweat from his journey. His hosts were unsurprised at his appearance and welcomed him with his eccentricities and odour. He dropped his road pack at his feet as though this were a common hostel. In Akko, a city between sieges, the old man's fatalism was welcome.

On legs frail as blown glass, the old scribe was introduced to a grizzled man from Jericho who looked like the sort who might have commanded a slaver's trireme—not as the ship's captain or drummer but as the man with the whip. Or he could have been a mason. A mule driver in a Nabataean mine. He looked like the sort of man who might save a young girl from going over the edge of the cliffs between Jericho and Jerusalem, and if not the girl, then the girl's father or uncle or some other stranger on that road. The old scribe had heard such stories about this man, all the things he might be or might have done or was believed to have participated in. Singular among his achievements was the respect that Akko's intellectual circle accorded him.

The man from Jericho shared news not from north or south or east, but instead from the west. News from the sea.

"Cleopatra will arrive within the month," he concluded.

"This far north?" one of the men of Akko asked. "Not in Joppa or Gaza?"

"No. Here."

The old scribe then told the group what he had observed

of Dora's siege and the events surrounding its fall. Afterwards, he accepted the hospitality of a bath and a meal from one of his Akko associates. A few days later, the old scribe pieced together a small supply that would sustain him on the journey back to Joppa, for he expected to find no nourishment in Dora or even in Strato's Tower.

Once the midday heat had passed, he left the city through the gate's small door and travelled down the strangely empty road that led from Akko towards Mount Carmel, where it bent around the peak and continue farther south.

When he was in sight of Dora, he met Lathyrus's satiated Egyptian army. The city backdropped that spreading horde as the men departed from a wreckage of their own making. They advanced towards the old scribe. He assumed that the Egyptians intended to lay siege to Akko next. The unarmoured cavalry led the way, spread across the plain in a broad line and raising a cloud of dust with their progress. The dust veiled the tens of thousands of infantry following behind. The old scribe stood silent and alone on the road. He took off his pack and set it at his feet. They advanced closer. When he could see clearly, he saw horses with wide and wild eyes like carnivorous beasts baited by rumours of blood, willing witnesses to sights that could not be unseen. The riders rode on old but unstained saddles strapped over mismatched blankets decorated with undamaged plaited fringes. The riders themselves were clean and shone in the mid-morning sun as though they were mere messengers of war and the bloodstains on their tunics were simply costume adornments unreflective of recent experience.

They rode around the old scribe, leaving him unmolested until a final rider thrust out one leg and toppled him below the cloud of dust from which he rose again, coughing. He waited for the infantry.

A contingent of foot soldiers arrived and surrounded him, guarding him as though the old man might flee in this wasteland that held no refuge. When he was presented to Lathyrus, someone confiscated his pack. The old scribe looked like an ancient madman come down from a cave on Mount Carmel's heights to testify or prophesy or drool.

"I have no fear of death," he said bravely to the outcast pharaoh who rode a wagon, upon which hung the stinking head of Zoilus. The Egyptian did not seem to notice the stench.

"What news, old man?" Lathyrus said. "What news of Akko?"

"I have no fear of the land beyond death. It holds wonders for me to discover."

"I don't doubt that it does," said the Egyptian. "But do you fear watching the vultures drag your entrails across the desert while you live? It is a terrible thing to see. The panic is like nothing else, chasing your innards as they rise to the sky. There is nothing in your stoic philosophy to prepare you for the raw instinct to try to gather those secret parts back into yourself. You will do it like breathing, and your heart will race like a child's as he tries to find breath underwater. No amount of philosophy will save you when your body betrays you. You will succumb to every indignity without control."

The scribe had never considered such a death. He felt light-headed from the heat. He felt ashamed. His first words to this violent man now seemed foolish. Before he could form an answer, a soldier struck him on the head with something made of wood, and he went down hard on the road before being pulled roughly back to his feet. The sky wheeled swiftly overhead. The hand that held him up was steady but not kind, and he fought for balance. He knew then that he would not be able to endure anything this man might inflict upon him. Everything in his life until now had been nerveless intellect, but as his stomach roiled and his head turned, he felt something new. It was not the fear of losing a debate or disappointment with some mild turn of fate, but a physical fear he had never known before. It ran in the blood, had a life of its own, despised the mind, made his stomach seize, caused heat and sweat to rush to his hands and face.

"Cleopatra sails for Akko," he exclaimed.

Lathyrus raised a hand. All activity stopped. "How do you come by this information?"

The old scribe told the Egyptian everything he knew. He told of the Jewish queen's letters to Egypt and the plan to betray Lathyrus's army. He tried to remember everything the stranger from Jericho had related. When he could remember no more, he exaggerated a Parthian alliance while mid-morning starbursts obscured the vision in his right eye.

The soldiers abused him no more than his thin skeleton could bear, left him with only his waterskin, and marched on to Akko. He lay still for much of the afternoon as one side of his face burned in the harsh sun. Later, his unburied body stirred like that of a quickened corpse. It rose slowly, oriented itself to the city's weak light, and then made its way towards Dora. It moved at a pace that gave little reward for the eye of a watcher, were there any watcher to mark its progress.

The city smelled of death. Mourning extended to every quarter. The old scribe passed through the disordered city, not stopping, not even seeking a wet rag for his wounds. He passed the southern gates and made for the road towards Strato's Tower at a quarter of his usual pace.

It was late the following day when the sky above him grew prematurely dark, and the Egyptian's words came back again and began to roam through his imagination. He put one foot down in front of the other. He failed to notice that one sandal was loosening. It would not take long for him to lose it, but his mind did not register the trailing leather, and none marked the peculiar track he left in the soft margin of the coastal road. He walked hungry and thirsty, and when he belatedly reached for his waterskin, he found that it too was gone. One cheek was swollen from abuse and the other burned by the sun. He stumbled forward, no longer confident in fused philosophies, having trouble seeing, unsure of his course.

A child found him. The old scribe was standing still and looking at the road. Strung muscles twitched as though remembering the act of walking from a dream. The child, a girl with one tooth missing and her hair unbound, took his hand and pulled him forwards. She did not understand what was wrong. She understood that he should not stand in the road. She understood that she should bring him home to her widowed mother. She took his hand and pulled him forwards and, by doing so, pulled him off balance. He would have fallen then had some part of his mind not alerted him. By chance, the old man lifted the correct leg and stepped forwards, and then again, and did so once more as though recovering the habit of something long forgotten.

⁂

Lathyrus's renegade army assembled outside Akko with his navy resting in the harbour. His close-set eyes seemed to change hue as he considered the navy man's question. "Take the ships to Gaza. Wait for me there."

"Where will you be?"

"With the cavalry. We will teach Jannaeus not to betray a real king." He looked past the navy man, past Akko, and to the mountains. "Half will stay here and finish with Akko. The rest will carve a path through Galilee and then into Judea and pay them back a thousandfold for the insults of this entire expedition. I will ally with the Nabataeans."

Lathyrus put one hand to his cheek and rubbed it, still looking at the mountains.

"We can divide up Jannaeus's miserable kingdom between the Nabataeans and us. With whatever is left of the Jewish army, we will reclaim our home in Egypt. I might even give all of Israel to the Nabataeans in exchange for that."

He turned and looked at the navy man as though seeing him for the first time. "We will go through Galilee like fire."

38

102 BCE

"HE JUST SAID he had to go home," Ebed said. "No real explanation."

Jugurtha found himself considering too many things at once: his report to Jannaeus, the expense of the king's celebration in Jerusalem, new ideas for new wars already under discussion, Joazar's abrupt departure from Jerusalem, Ebed as the closest thing Jugurtha had to a friend in the city. Pericles was his next closest friend, based in Joppa and now at sea, a man who was something like an object in Jugurtha's life. An acquaintance of long years was not the same thing as a friend. Jugurtha wondered why he had never understood this before. He remembered Joazar in Antioch asking the naive question, "Are we friends now?" and his rebuff. He was ashamed now. He had squandered an invitation. Decades of letters followed, but they had been mere transactions.

"I should go to Galilee," Jugurtha said. "I've never been."

❧

The forty thousand Egyptian foot and horse soldiers, Lathyrus's promise of fire, entered Galilee almost silently. Despite its size, the army blended quietly into the mountains. When it came to Baca, the force seemed to coalesce from the ground. It descended on the small hamlet with a great noise. A flood of armour and weaponry swept before it the elderly and young alike. The village burned. There was a roasting that night, and the army ate in abundance, leaving carcasses scattered about half-consumed and stripped of their choicest parts.

Baca's smoke signalled a warning to Bersabe, but this was not the time of the Galilean war against Cyzicenus nor the tense year of Aristobulus's rule. Few concerned themselves with rumours about Akko or Dora. This was the time of Jannaeus and Salome, and Galilee expected only peace. Bersabe was unprepared.

The Egyptians came to Bersabe's hill. They strode up its slopes with sword and spear and fire. The cavalry caught all who fled, ran them down from behind, impaled them without mercy. The cries from Bersabe should have been a warning like the flames from Baca. The next village, Selame, was also unprepared, allowing Lathyrus to obtain a threefold deposit on his vow for vengeance. Galilean blood paid the price for Judean duplicity.

From Selame, the army continued down the valley toward Cana. They came to the hilltop town with its skirting of layered houses and the manufacturing yards at its base. There was no pause in their assault, and they left Cana as a combination of both Baca and Bersabe: burning and weeping. The army passed from the city and went beyond the peculiar boulders, among which no child hid, while a great carpentry shop lit the sky. The oils and preservatives of that trade went up with the dried boards and drying timbers, the framing and roofing and projects finished and underway. It was the tallest fire any man of that company had ever seen. The Egyptians were delighted with their progress.

They turned in their quest back towards the sea. Bypassing Sepphoris, the bigger prize, they came to Shikhin next. They entered Shikhin in the darkness of a Sabbath morning. By the light of a complicit moon, tens of thousands moved through the pottery yards of unlit kilns, dull firing pits, barrels of clay slurry and barns of clay forms, threading mounds of red clay and sedimentary clay, kaolin and vitreous sand. The slinking soldiers were thinly veiled by wisps of predawn mist. In the near darkness, a dozen stumbled into a dye-mixing pit on the left flank, and ten more tumbled into its twin beside. As the dawn emerged and gave reluctant shape to the invasion, the two groups of head-to-toe red and yellow soldiers stood out amid those thousands as though they were monochrome mascots on parade.

Asochis, which the locals called Shikhin, fell on the Sabbath day, and it was here that Lathyrus began to regret the wealth he had been destroying until now. Word went through the companies, and they reversed sword handles and spears, their victims no longer cut but clubbed. By the end of that holy day, the Egyptian invaders added ten thousand to their number, bound hand and neck, huddled in misery and ordered to march. The road led them back to Sepphoris, where Lathyrus set in for this campaign's first siege. He sent word to the coast for news of Akko.

❧

Joazar did not take the Jericho road but the shorter route north past Shechem. He came as far as two hours past the beautiful city of Tirzah before he noticed smoke.

He approached Cana in the evening. From a distance, the lights on the hill gave him peace. He turned his mind to the weight of his legs and his hunger and desire to surprise Noadiah and immerse himself in the quiet of the town, but as he drew closer, Cana failed to reveal its shape. A coldness came over him. A large section of the eastern area where Joseph's home and workshops should have been was darkness. The darkness extended to the western edge of the hill. In the centre before him, the light was bright and in places too bright, as though he could see through walls and observe family hearths directly.

The first buildings Joazar came to were silent and roofless. The smell of old smoke reached out and enveloped him like wraiths with treacherous invitations. The spaces between buildings were bereft of order. Charcoal-stunted beams rose in his path, which turned out to be no path at all, and he stumbled in the dim light, trying to find his way. He felt disoriented as he climbed over the refuse of a great upheaval. He struggled through a pile of rags and leather harnesses and ropes. He fell and got up again. The smell of blood overwhelmed him. Finding his way blocked by a broken pile of half-blackened crates, the newly slivered wood set like spears barring his progress, he detoured through the shell of what had been a home.

He found the stone of the climbing street once more, the stairs between empty buildings. There was no sound despite the absence of doors and roofs. Then in the distance, he heard a cry of mourning and a voice of calm. There was a remnant of life in Cana. The lights he had observed had not just been phantoms luring him to an underworld.

He turned near the top of the hill, out of breath, not breathing. He paused. Finally gasped. The scent of charcoal and smoke entered his lungs, along with the distant smell of something dead.

He came upon and passed homes with light and life within, screened by temporary doors of hung cloth that vaguely revealed the flicker of shapes behind. The moon's glow exposed each building's nakedness, as though some great storm had swept through the town and removed every hat from every head, every roof from every home. He could see a few gable ends and ridge beams and rafters like a shattered thicket of collapsed wood by the moon and against the stars. Rain and sun would now be admitted, whatever the season. He did not enter any homes or ask the few passing, furtive shapes for an explanation. He let each soul make its progress through the cluttered waste in silence. He found himself repulsed by the idea of human articulation.

He came within shouting distance from where Noadiah had birthed four daughters and where they had raised them. He stopped then, not yet within sight of his home, just around the street that curved with Cana's hill, crouched, head down, a provisional grief welling within for what he was about to face.

He did not know whether it was the son or the mother or the son and mother together in an evil union, but he did not doubt that this was the work of Egypt. The destruction was too immense for merely a band of brigands. This was the work of an army. The plagues of Egypt had come to Eretz-Israel. A poisonous tension traced a path within him, and the feeling reminded him of the murder of the long-haired man in his childhood village. The feeling made him search for one last murder to commit. Something for vengeance. He did not doubt that his negotiations at Dora had caused this. His clever work on behalf of Jerusalem's importunate army had caused this. His work for that waste of mercenary adventurers in need of salvage. Jerusalem's royalty, caught in a pinch between Dora and Lathyrus's war horde, was somehow the spark for this fire that had consumed Cana. This was his fault.

She knew him by the sound of his walk, by his shape in the courtyard, by the way he breathed. She came at him out of the darkness in a rush and billow. She struck him with her full body and wrapped her arms around him, unmindful of the street, of propriety, of any that might watch, unthinking even of his fear or surprise and not noticing the reaction, the stiffening, the tension before he relaxed.

He took in the smell of her in the night, the smoke and sweat, and the scent he only knew as Noadiah.

"The children?" he asked.

"Gone."

39
102 BCE

FOUR MEN KEPT to the road with the Sea of Galilee on their left, Kfar Nahum and the low morning sun behind. Their shadows stretched ahead of them like strangely thin creatures that led the way home. When they came to the river, the shapes sank mysteriously underwater, rippling over golden stones in the shallows. The men took off their sandals, lifted their lower garments, and then waded across the ford towards the vineyards ready for harvest. With each step, they discovered either pebbles or mud. Sections of smooth rock showed the same golden hue as soft patches that swirled when a foot entered. A history of sediments rose with each step in these soft places, stirring up deep browns and greens. These new colours formed up into clouds that diffused downstream into the wilder lake beyond. They signalled their presence to any aquatic watcher that knew how to read the river's flow and its disturbance.

Drying their feet and legs, they looked around. Uri took in the stranger's ripe crops. "It's time to start harvesting my fields, too," he said.

"Are you working with the same crew as last year?" Joseph asked.

"Mostly. All the same pickers. A couple of new pressers."

"This harvest looks good," Rehavam said.

"Yes. Mine's the same. A surplus crop. With the new peace, we're going to keep Saul busy for years."

They passed through the fertile Kinneret plain and took in the smell of vine wood, the sweet, pungent undertone of fermented fruit, the scent of black soil, and the cleanness of lake air.

Later in the morning, Magdala loomed before them, the town that some still called Migdal and others dubbed Taricheae for the smell of smoke and pickling. The town was a veritable fish preserve factory so proficient at its trade that any approaching the town smelled no fish at all, only its preservatives. Its produce comprised a full half of Saul's export volumes. The town's smokers were in full force even this early in the morning. As the heat built, the air became heavy with the product of hundreds of small smoking operations. Wisps of escaping black vapour rose in straight columns all about the town before spreading and joining together into a thin film hovering at a steady altitude above the sprawling streets. That smoky layer lingered over the town like an ominous pool supported on black stick legs of the same oily substance.

Once they were under Magdala's oppressive cloud, the four men stopped to eat. Pickling dominated the centre of the town, and fresh catch was sold along the shore. They ate fresh fish, packed pickled ones, and then turned inland, ready to climb the mountains with their burdened bellies and packs. They passed through high valleys, villages of Lower Galilee, and lonely outposts of shepherds' huts and isolated farmsteads.

Late in the day, the meandering path led them down from the exposed rock summits and pine forests of the mythic great horned ibex, the elusive leopard, and the ubiquitous eagles and vultures. It then brought them into the thicker hardwood forests of wild boar, bear, deer, wolves, and owls. Tired and ready for rest, they approached the valley of Uri's farm. There they saw Magdala's smoke pillars re-emerge. Yet these were not the thin greasy pillars of Magdala's smokers. The smoke here was diffuse, and as the men crested the hill in silent dread, they discovered the source of the fire's fuel. The farm had fed the fire—remnants of roofs were fallen in, the main house, the family house, the barns, even the dolia barn. Each building's stone walls had together formed large ovens within which had burned everything that fire could consume.

"Uri," Joseph said, not a statement or a question but a groan. He put a hand on his friend's shoulder.

They stepped down the slope and moved fast, weariness from the day's hike forgotten. The valley flickered in disjointed images through the trees, snatches of tumbledown walls, derelict buildings, abandoned equipment all blurred with glimpses of destroyed vineyards that bled with the season's trampled production, the building-sized ovens still smouldering in corners and pockets. There was no movement in the landscape but the hesitant last wisps of apologetic smoke.

They came to Uri's house first, and Uri went through the vacant opening, stones cracked from the heat, lintel blackened but still intact. Inside was ash and mounds of half-buried houseware. Throughout the house, they searched and found nothing but the fallen ridge beam. Its centre had burned through with great black squares at each end.

The men moved on like four blackened spectres smoking with drifted ash. The ash falling in their wake made a fifth ghost that followed them out of that emptied stone oven.

"Uri," Joseph said.

They crossed a yard churned by the hooves of thousands of horses, trampled by the feet of infantry numbering in the tens of thousands, the very pattern of the ground itself reshaped. In the dolia barn, they found the great containers open and half empty. The remaining liquid reflected nothing but a floating layer of ash. Moshe thrust a long pole into one dolium and punctured the crust, revealing a thick, blackened liquid beneath. One dolium was empty and burned, the concentrated brew within having ignited an unbelievable cauldron of fire, overheated, and now cooled, cracked, and so ruined.

The men stirred each dolium, and Uri crawled down into the last burned and cracked container, shuffling through the debris at the bottom to satisfy himself. The men were black all over save for Uri's bald crown patterned with streaks where sweat bled bright channels. "There is no one here," he said. His voice was husky, and then they heard Rehavam's voice shouting from across the farm.

The shout seemed like an impropriety in that place where mourning was due. It was an offence that stirred anger as well as fear. Each man had only a moment to find a weapon in the wreckage. They stumbled out of the dolia barn's remains at a run and followed the shouting until they found Rehavam in the dovecote's open doorway. The door itself lay littered about the tower's base, unburned, torn apart by the blows of axe and battering ram and discarded in the long grass. The tower's base held a drift of plucked feathers and the remains of small feasting fires. Hundreds of doves had been slaughtered, plucked, and consumed. Little rib cages, skulls, wings, and feet were heaped in obscene piles.

They entered the dovecote. The air inside was pungent with bird dung, but few birds stirred in the heights above. However, the eye did not go to the birds but to the eight bodies hung from the first crossbeam. They had been abused nearly beyond human recognition. Uri collapsed in a crouch before this horror, but Joseph gave him no rest, hauled him upright, and made him look.

"Who are they?" Joseph asked. "They are not Mahlah. Who are they?" He held Uri's head in his hands and made him look. "Who are they?"

"David and Nava. Their children. Two are pickers. From Upper Galilee."

Then came a cry. It was a weak sound that travelled around the tower's stone interior and found its way to the four soot-covered figures. Each man looked to the other and then to the eight bodies before them, but none here were the source. It had been like a bird's cry. An involuntary sound, the distant howl of some creature beyond the dovecote penetrating through one of the many dozens of openings and haunting this ruin with misdirection and false hope.

The cry came again, like a voice trying to recover the

miracle of sound, a broken voice, a spirit resurfacing, uttering a single word. "Uri."

It was Mahlah, but none could find her in the dim light.

"Where are you?" Uri shouted, startling the men who had been straining to listen.

"Here."

The men looked in scattered directions, unable to locate the strange sound's source.

"Up."

Above was darkness, but Uri understood. "Fire," he said. "We need a fire. She's up high. Moshe, get the door. Get it started with the door. Rehavam, Joseph, come with me. Clear a space and build a fire. Get it started. Build a fire so we can see."

He said nothing more to the voice up high. It was like Uri to act, to be practical, to not tell her what he was doing. When the men returned, they came with armloads of branches and the remnants of a broken wagon. Joseph dragged it to the dovecote door, up the ramp, and dumped it beside Moshe's fire. They found the young man talking to the darkness above.

"I built the fire away from the . . . " Moshe gestured at the bodies. "Shovelled some of the floor."

"Yes, good. The light will reflect off the walls as well. Did she answer?"

"Not much. A couple of words. I think she's on the third level, at the highest beams."

"Yes. Of course she is."

"We need rope."

"We've got rope." Uri pulled Joseph to the exterior wall and positioned himself below the lower beam. Joseph bent to boost him. Tired and in his forties but suddenly spry, Uri swung up onto the wooden beam, shimmied out to the rope that supported all eight of the hanging bodies, and untied the knot. The friction of the rope around the beam caused the bodies to descend slowly. The men below caught each of them in turn, untying the victims and bringing them to rest on cleared patches of the floor. They coiled the rope in a looping pile.

"This is all we have for rope," Joseph said. "Not enough."

"Plenty," Uri called from above. "Throw it up to me! One end."

It took two throws for Uri to catch the rope's end. He tied the rope about his waist and then considered it for a moment. "Make the fire bigger," he said. He did not look at his friends but studied the rope, untied it, and retied it about his chest, making a second loop over one shoulder before letting the balance trail away to the floor.

"Uri," Joseph said.

"Make the fire bigger." With that, he began to climb. He had yet to say a word to his wife. She was three stories up in darkness. He climbed using the dove nest recesses and exterior wall's windows as hand- and footholds. "Second beam," he said. His shape was disappearing in the darkness above.

"The rope's end has just left the ground here," Joseph said.

Uri said nothing in reply. The floor-bound men tracked his progress by the rope's rising end. Some minutes later, they heard a sudden slipping sound, a grunt, and a slap of skin on stone. Mahlah made a high-pitched cry, and then

Uri grunted as he re-established his grip and began to climb again. He made no further comment on his progress.

As he started moving across the top beam, the three men below followed Uri's course by watching the rope's end bob and sway above their heads.

"Good God, Uri," Joseph muttered and then glanced at Moshe and Rehavam. Rehavam nodded silently at him. Moshe fed the fire and gave no indication of hearing his father's words.

The rope end had nearly reached the interior cliff-face wall when there was a sudden outburst above, a woman's cry in the darkness, and a weeping transmitted through a dry throat, through dry air. A murmuring followed that the men below could not hear clearly. The rope end jerked upward and disappeared. The shape of the couple above was only a suggestion in deep shadow.

"Joseph," Uri finally called.

"Yes."

"Climb up to the second beam. I'm going to lower her down to you."

"Uri—"

"She can't climb. She's been up here for days."

"I'll do it," Moshe said.

"Moshe!" Joseph protested, but the young man was already climbing, scaling the interior cliff face how Uri had the outer wall. He moved quickly up to the first beam and then slowed his pace once he was beyond it.

"I'm here. I can see you now." Moshe's voice carried around the inside of the dovecote the way Mahlah's first cry had, coming from all directions.

"Uri!" Joseph said.

"He just needs to steady her," Uri said. "When I lower her down to you, Moshe, you get her over the beam. She can hold herself sitting, but I don't trust her to stay there. She had tied herself up here. Without that, she would have fallen long ago. Keep her from falling until I get to you."

"Uri!"

"Joseph, there is no time. Moshe can do this."

"How have you secured the rope?"

"She's safe," Uri said. "I've lifted her before. I've used her clothes as padding. She can't fall out. I made a harness."

"No, your end. How have you tied it off at your end?"

"Around me."

"Tie it around the beam." There was silence from above. "Loop it around the beam. Leave a belly of slack, then tie it off. Hold the belly of slack and let the beam's friction slow her descent. If something goes wrong, her weight won't pull you. And less can go wrong if her full weight is not on your arms, pulling you down. Just listen to me. If you fall, you'll take her and Moshe with you."

Silence ensued, broken only by the fire's crackle. Then Uri finally spoke. "Yes. Someone here can still think. Good. Good." The wait for Uri to adjust the bindings seemed interminable, but finally, he spoke again. "Okay. Get ready."

There was a murmur in the dark followed by the sound of sliding, of something torn as cloth caught on the beam and ripped, and then came a cry from Mahlah. There was the sound of clothing sliding over the beam and a body falling, a grunting from Uri and a frightening hiss from the rope. Then control and descent and Moshe saying, "A little bit more. Her knee is on the beam. Gently now." There was no sound from Uri above but breathing and groans, and then Moshe again: "She's down. She's seated. She's straddling the beam. She's leaning back against the wall, and I'm holding her steady."

"Okay, I'm untying the rope now," Uri said. His disembodied voice fell as though down a well.

"You can't do it again," Moshe said.

"I've strength left in these arms."

"There's no way onto the beam. She's against the wall. I'm holding her steady. I can't let her go, and I can't pull her out away from the wall. You would have to leap over the both of us to get to the beam. You can't get here with us in the way." Silence from above. "Drop the rope down. I'll do the same as you and lower her down to the next beam."

"I'm coming," Joseph said. "You send her down to me, son."

From above: "Boy, you cannot lower a grown woman."

"Pass me the rope and get yourself down from that wall."

The two men below couldn't see the rope, but Moshe caught and gathered it in quickly. "Do you know how to tie it off, son?" Joseph asked. "Do like we did to lower the—"

"I know," Moshe called back and then muttered again before turning to Mahlah. "They have fat where they used to have muscle, and they've looked at their fat for so long that they think it's what muscle looks like." Something cracked and broken came from Mahlah, but neither the man above nor the men below recovered her words. "Are you ready?" Moshe asked her and then his father.

"Yes. Send her to me."

Uri suddenly appeared on the wall beside Mahlah and Moshe. He looked at his wife, his eyes white in a sea of shadow and soot. He stood with only one foot and one elbow jammed into nest niches, the extra foot and arm dangling in space. "You hold her with care," he told Moshe.

"You're in the way," Moshe said. "She's leaning that way. Get down to the first beam at least."

Uri's bald head disappeared below him, and then a voice rose from below. "Send her down, son." Uri was now on the first beam facing Joseph with his back to the wall and Joseph pinching the beam with his knees farther out, creating a space between them to receive Mahlah. "Send her down."

It was Moshe's turn to grunt as he slid Mahlah off the beam and worked hard to control the rope. The beam absorbed most of the friction, and he lowered her slowly, hand over hand.

"More. More. We have her. You're safe, Mahlah. That's Joseph behind you."

"Drop the rope, son."

"Rehavam is below. We're going to lower you down to him."

The rope dropped from above, but the two men did not tie off this time. Joseph passed a loose loop around and through his hands and then continued to wrap the rope around Uri's back and into his hands. Impatiently using themselves as anchors, they toppled her off the beam. She gasped and swung, and the men grunted and twisted as the rope snugged up around them and began to burn through clothing. They got control and lowered her slowly, length by length, until, from below, Rehavam said, "I've got her."

Moshe was the last down from the wall. Uri gave Mahlah water to sip as she held his other arm. Tears tracked her face. She looked at the three men standing, then to her husband, then at the tortured bodies on the dovecote floor. Her face was a pale mask in the firelight.

"I was up there the whole time," she whispered.

40

102 BCE

THEY STAYED THAT night and part of the morning at Uri's farm though all the men were anxious to leave. Mahlah could not be left alone and needed time before she could travel. When they set out on the road, she carried nothing but herself, and their pace was slow.

Rehavam led the three men and Mahlah to his secluded home, where they found Basmat and the rest of his family and the labourers and artisans employed at the glassworks. Basmat told the men everything she knew from the fragmented sounds and images she had glimpsed from behind the low rise and screen of trees that separated their home and yards from the invaders' path. The house, the workshops, the kilns, and the firepits, even the goats tethered in the yard, were unharmed. The invaders had passed this way, but they had not noticed, or at least not detoured into, this place.

While Basmat took charge of Mahlah, another witness, one of Rehavam's glassmakers, filled in her story's gaps. The glassmaker was a wiry man with thin, kinked hair. He could stand before the kiln fires for hours, spinning molten sand with his iron tools, blowing, shaping, creating magic, drinking and sweating the entire day, working shirtless in summer and winter. The man's report was fierce and factual: Cana was a ruin; Joseph's house and workshops were gone; the savagery had been brutal and complete.

The four men left Mahlah with Basmat and went directly to Cana. They walked through the ruins of Joseph's workshop and home, in and out of former buildings' frames, accumulating new layers of soot and ash. They kicked at half-consumed shapes in black drifts and identified the remains of great bending jigs, saws, and chisels, each blade liberated from its handle. They did not go through the house. It was empty. It was a home for shallow ash drifts and did not need kicking feet for the men to tell that none from the family were there. Rafters formed blackened lines against the sky. Rehavam and Uri stood apart. Joseph and Moshe, father and son, were husks around a dark tension.

"Maybe they live," Joseph said. "She and Sarah. Somehow. Despite what the glassmaker said."

They went up Cana's hill. They received subdued greetings from those who would meet their gaze. They found Joazar at his doorway and were brought inside. Noadiah was there.

"Peretz, Oren. Their families. Avigail and Esther. Their families." Joazar leaned back as though offended at his speech, as though ill. "All of the children. Their families as well. Moshe's wife and young children, too. They are all gone."

The dazed men listened in silence to the story of slaughter, of Noadiah's escape and Joazar's return, of collecting the dead and having no choice but to bury them without proper ceremony. Entire families had been found butchered. The friends shook as they learned the news. Tears tracked down worn cheeks and through wet, dirty beards, finally falling to create new black stains on their clothing. Unconquerable grief, the mere beginning of it, and the forfeit of all future hope welled up within them. Noadiah spoke as though her survival was an offence, and she flinched when anyone spoke of her good fortune. She was a woman who had endured until Joazar came home and now, in community, was unable to cope.

"She needs to go to her sister and Mahlah," Joseph said when he had a moment alone with Joazar. The brothers-in-law came to an agreement. "But you know nothing of Keziah or Sarah?"

"No," Joazar replied, "nothing. I searched through the bodies myself. I found every one of my mine. I found all of Moshe's and his wife. I found Avigail and Esther and their families. I did not find Keziah or Sarah."

"Perhaps they escaped."

Joazar was silent.

"Speak," Joseph said.

"Sarah cannot move quickly enough, and the assault was—"

"I understand," Joseph said.

"They are here either among the living or among the

dead." Joazar's face was stiff, and his eyes fixed on a nearby section of the wall.

"They are not among the living," Joseph said, a new tension creeping into his voice.

"And I did not find them among the dead."

Joseph moved like a man about to make anger physical. He calmed himself, but his voice remained tense with uncharacteristic gravel in its tone. "Then they are somewhere else."

"Brother . . . "

"What are you not telling me?"

"Some, many, were unrecognizable. Trampled. Burned. I can't know for sure. If they were alive, they would have come back and found Noadiah. Or maybe they were taken."

A stone lodged in Joseph's chest. "Don't say that." He paused and raised a hand to prevent Joazar from interrupting. After a moment, he looked up and caught Joazar's eye. "I thought you went to negotiate a truce."

"I did," Joazar said. "We did. We succeeded."

"Then why has Lathyrus broken faith?"

"I don't know."

The friends left Cana, Joazar and Noadiah with them, and returned to the untouched glassworks.

The days that followed were days of delayed ceremony. Days of mourning. Days of anger and days where the three women could be found in a close communion of tears. At that time, the men either formed pairs or stood alone, mostly alone, with eyes that stared a mile beyond the trees before them, eyes that saw nothing but what a drowning man sees, the glassy white beyond the skull that narrows and bows as light moves through a jar. Mealtimes brought a hint of suspended sanity. The three women and five men ate in the manner of people practicing a mindless ritual. Some took little and only when pressed. Grief poisoned the air. Mealtimes were the cord that lightly tethered each to the other and all to the ground.

Saul and Anna then arrived at the glassworks. The addition of friends was a dark welcome. The news was retold, and fresh grief plunged all back into drowning. It extended their season of isolated staring and mealtime regathering.

It took one of the glassmakers restarting the kiln and firing a new creation to wake the men. They stood as near to the heat as they could and watched a glossy mass glow and droop and twist. Questions were asked. They asked the glassmaker the *hows* and the *whys*, the trade questions of an apprentice even though none of the men would act on the information gleaned. They were the questions men ask when they seek a distraction. They made suggestions that were observations encased in curiosity but paid little attention to the responses.

Finally, Joseph spoke. "It has been a decade since we drove Antiochus Cyzicenus from these mountains and valleys."

The men nodded.

"I was a younger man then," Uri said.

The glassmaker spun his iron wildly, and the glass in the kiln evened out. He pulled the glowing orb from the fire and began to blow.

"Where will Cleopatra land if she comes?" Rehavam asked.

"Akko," Joazar said. "That's what we learned before I left Jerusalem."

"Lathyrus found out," Joseph said.

"That she was coming?" Joazar said. He did not look directly at any of the other men. "Perhaps. Perhaps that explains the raids."

"Galilee has to go to war again," Joseph said.

The glassmaker mishandled the tongs. They swung and bumped against the side of the kiln, the orb falling and melding into the blaze. Blackness spread across and dimmed its glow.

ɷ

Galilee, assembled in its native forests again, was a resolute aggregate, as solid in its disparate parts as stony mountain fragments and hard river rocks. It was an indivisible union. Fathers and sons, slingers, archers, and spearmen all assembled. Most carried a sword won with blood during the battles fought in these same hills a full decade before. Scythian, Seleucid, Parthian, Egyptian, and even Nabataean swords hung in scabbards—some plain, some elaborate, as suited to its former owner's rank and preference. Survivors of Baca and Bersabe were present. Selame. Cana. Shikhin. Men from Lower Galilee and east of the lake were present, and thousands came from Upper Galilee, as far as away as Kfar Nahum.

They made scattered camps about the siege of Sepphoris. The city overlooked the Beit Netofa Valley in southern Galilee. Lathyrus and his army still patiently waited out the trapped residents while Egyptian supply and communication caravans passed up and down the valley between Sepphoris and the now conquered Akko.

The Galileans positioned themselves in places where

they could spot any enemies approaching from the city. These were Galilean mountains, and the men could escape over the ridges if needed. In this way, the mountains protected the men and boys who formed raiding parties to harry the Egyptian camp.

The Galileans were a few thousand against Egypt's forty thousand at Sepphoris. Even if they were to stop this siege successfully, another forty thousand Egyptians were waiting at Akko. Expectations of success did not drive the Galileans. Many had nothing left to lose but their honour. They would gladly die fighting, but they would not live with themselves without trying. For others, this was a repeat of the Seleucid war: they would harass the Egyptians as they had Cyzicenus a decade prior; their success would be the success of small birds tormenting eagles until the eagles departed. Common among all was a fierce bond between neighbour and neighbour. Cowardice had no place among these men of the soil, animal herds, artisanal crafts, fishing vessels, and building trades. Death and injury were not prospects that altered their direction.

The Galileans came down from their aeries in loosely coordinated bands. As in the war against Cyzicenus, they agreed on a campaign of oblique harassment and erosion of enemy material and morale. Unlike Cyzicenus's, however, Lathyrus's invading forces were stationed in fixed formations about Sepphoris, which made it easier for the Galileans. The siege was focused inwards, on Sepphoris, when the Galileans began to trouble their perimeter.

The Egyptian cavalry was the primary threat to the Galileans. The small, makeshift stockades grouped around the camps' edges corralled horses that the men and boys of the mountains could not outrun. The first Galilean assaults were against horses. In late evening light, slingers had dropped thirty mounts before the Egyptians grasped the threat. A fusillade of arrows brought down a dozen more, and then the Galileans melted back into their woods. The Egyptians gave pursuit on the remaining horses, racing against the fading sun, and relearned an old Seleucid lesson: traps met them in the dim light, and a dozen riders and their mounts failed to return from the haunting forests about Sepphoris. The Egyptians pulled up their stockades and moved them inwards with a layer of infantry posted to the new perimeter.

A resupply trip from Akko went missing, and when the Egyptians went in search, they found signs of battle, the bodies of Egyptian labourers and the guard scattered about, the wagons and supplies missing. Tracks departed north. Rumours spread that Sepphoris's siege was itself surrounded, and unease began to run through Egyptian ranks.

Unaware of history and careless with geography, Lathyrus sent a phalanx from Akko to follow the northbound trail, determined to root out the Galilean camp and make an example of the country fighters. The phalanx found itself climbing into the forest, disbelieving that loaded wagons could have been pulled this high and far by anything short of the Pegasi of Medusa. On the second morning, they passed between trees that were too narrow for the wagons, yet they found scarring on the rocks, deep wheel tracks in soft places, and random discarded supplies, all of which indicated that the stolen wagons were smaller than they had expected. Satisfied with this evidence, the men continued climbing higher in their pursuit. They were gasping by the end of the second day, freighted with armour designed for fighting in an open field, burdened with great rectangular shields, and laden with long sarissas like a force of bristling porcupines. They came to a place where the land sloped steeply, and even the least imaginative began to believe they were following trails made by ghostly wagons and mythic horses. Then they found the wheel with a makeshift handle at each side and one set of horse tracks leading away across soft ground and onto bare rock.

The party was stunned and looked about for the rest of the wagon even as the deception dawned on them. The captain shouted, and the phalanx attempted to form, but there was not enough space for a proper square. The steep slope made the upper ranks half a man taller than the lower. The snap of a branch below prompted the command, and the soldiers shifted the massive sarissas to all point downhill. The soldiers struggled to lift and swing their great weapons without tangling them in surrounding trees. A bird flew past. Then a flight of arrows came from the left flank, and three soldiers went down with shouts. The captain gave orders to adjust shields and sarissas, but then a flight of stone struck down two on the right. A contrary order rang out, and the sarissas became entangled in trees and among themselves.

The formation had been designed for the open field, for an implacable forward advance, not for these blind responses to threats from multiple directions. The phalanx became a thicket of disarray. Unseen enemies downslope and on both flanks distracted them such that none saw the Galileans emerge above, lobbing stones more massive than a great man's fist that crushed tight helmets and broke shoulders. Stunned soldiers dropped in the middle of the formation, and unwieldy sarissas and shields clattered to the ground. There were no archers among the Egyptians, no slingers, no scouts. The usually fearsome force became a tragedy among trees.

When a slinger's stone caught the captain's throat, it crushed his vocal cords and sent him spinning out of the collapsing formation. He went down the slope, scrabbling at his throat even as his weapons dropped away, and his men interpreted this as flight. More soldiers dropped their sarissas and shields to draw their swords and begin a panicked flight back down the false wagon trail. Some broke off the trail, expecting a further ambush, and fled down the uncharted mountainside, crashing through a lower fan of dead branches. Two such soldiers found themselves launched off a small ledge, their bodies breaking on the rocks below. An unlucky Egyptian caught a branch in one eye that pulled the wet orb from its socket; the man fell screaming, and it seemed the forest itself now fought for the Galileans.

Of the one hundred invaders sent to punish the Galilean thieves, only twenty-three returned to Sepphoris. One unconscious survivor, pulled and carried down the mountain and across the plain by devoted companions, wore his helmet for the full ten days that remained of his life in the Seleucid camp. The dent in the helmet matched a dent in his skull, and none were able to remove the helmet without killing him. Rumours circulated of giant slingers among the Galileans in the mountains. These creatures were able to hurl stones the size of melons from their great slings, sending boulders to crash sideways through the tightest phalanx. The force of such stones could penetrate rows of shields and men for as deep as the Egyptians cared to stack them. That not a shield came back with the survivors reinforced the wild rumours. When the wounded man died, his friends buried him with the irremovable helmet. So fear broke Sepphoris's siege. The Egyptians left the small prospects of Galilee and made for Judea.

The Galileans watched the Egyptians move south from the ridge above the forest, and their leaders quickly gathered into a new council. They could harry the retreating army to support their southern brothers, but this path was not popular. The Galileans had broken the siege of one of their cities, but they had done little to dent the invading army's numbers. To follow would mean moving into open ground where the Egyptians would have the advantage. The alternative was to leave Jerusalem to taste what it had created, and there was a bitter will among the Galileans to leave the south to its fate.

"Jerusalem grows rich taxing our trampled fields," a heavyset survivor from Baca declared. "We have shed our blood time and again against Jerusalem's enemies who had never been enemies to Galilee before."

"Solomon himself said that to rescue a fool is to be a fool," a man from Migdal said.

"Will we do nothing?" Joseph asked. "Gentiles have desecrated the temple before, and if Lathyrus takes Jerusalem, he will do it again."

"We cannot stop the Egyptians," the man from Migdal said.

"Can Jannaeus?" Rehavam asked.

Eyes turned to Joazar.

"No, I don't believe he can," Joazar said. "Not if the forces from Akko join Lathyrus in the south."

"Then who can?" the man from Baca asked. His manner was abrupt, even dismissive.

"Cleopatra," Joazar said.

"Will she be a friend to Israel?" Rehavam asked.

"She has been. Her generals are our brothers."

"And she lands at Akko," Joseph said.

"She will land there," Joazar said.

"Then we need to ensure her safe landing," Joseph said.

All those gathered agreed that it would be impossible to liberate Akko on their own, and none found the path to at least try appealing. The gentile city on Galilee's coast was known for false trading, incursions into Jewish lands, and the murder of Simon Maccabee's brother and children. None cared at all for Akko.

The council nearly decided to quit the field altogether and to leave wars to the kings who revelled in them. They could begin rebuilding their homes and the homes of their neighbours. Winter would soon be upon them. Cleopatra might not come. The cement within the Galilean aggregate weakened.

In the end, the majority still favoured protecting Akko's landing sites. Akko's full siege was impossible, and harassing troops within city walls was beyond the Galileans, but they still had a chance to secure the way for Cleopatra. They gathered fresh recruits from Sepphoris's liberated inhabitants and then set their faces towards the coast to do what they could.

41

102 BCE

Joazar sat with his back to an old terebinth tree and watched the men together. The father was kneeling, and the son was sitting against a fallen tree with his back arched over the trunk, his arms raised, and his naked chest exposed. Across Moshe's lower ribs lay a poultice of milk and unleavened bread beneath a bandage of rags. Joseph unwrapped the bandage. The congealed sludge beneath was wrinkled and had moulded to the young man's shape. Joseph carefully peeled one edge of the bread back. "Ah," he said. "Good."

He slowly eased the rest of the poultice away from the wound and revealed several long splinters.

"Hidden no more," Joseph said.

Two of the small wooden shafts came out of Moshe's body, stuck to the bread. He held them up for inspection and flicked one toward Joazar, who leaned forward to retrieve it from the forest floor. The remaining two miniature spears stayed in the body but were now visible.

Joseph adjusted his position and pinched the first splinter between his knife's edge and his thumb, withdrawing it slowly and smoothly from his son's flesh before repeating the process with the second splinter.

"Unbroken," he said. "Done."

Moshe sat forward and lowered his arms. A trickle of blood flowed from four small holes, the surrounding area still inflamed but now clean. Joseph treated the area with a smear of honey and then applied a patch of soft, clean cloth, rewrapped the bandage, and tied it off.

"Would that all injuries were as easy to treat," Joseph said.

Joazar rose and walked into the forest. The trees creaked with winter's shifting winds. The forest floor was quiet and still, but up high, the air pulled at leafless limbs. It sounded like the wagon creaking from Dora into Samaria. The rafter-like branches above made him think of Cana's houses, roofless and cold and empty. Noadiah was with her sister Basmat and their friends Mahlah and Anna in Kfar Nahum, where they would be safe. The northern city was untouched, far away from the Egyptian army's path. In the event of attacks, its southern lake would provide advance warning as nothing could be torched along its shores without the surrounding coastal towns immediately raising the alarm. Even though she was a refugee, their children had been destroyed, and their home lay in ruins, the fact that he was able to send his wife somewhere safe made this company consider Joazar as one of the fortunate ones. Many, like

Joseph and Moshe, had no one left. They fought because it was right and for no other reason.

The Galilean campaign had not been able to recover the captives from Shikhin. Had they been transferred to Akko and the ships already? Had they marched somewhere in the throng that had left Sepphoris? The Galileans only knew that the captives were gone. They were lost among Galilee's missing. None could contemplate the captives' present fate without going mad.

Survivors buried their dead, and the permanence of the grave was a marker for grief. Some, like Keziah and Sarah, were not found.

It had been bitter to let the force at Sepphoris slip away to the south. The decision to focus on Akko left splinters that no poultice could draw out and no honey could heal.

Joazar raised his eyes to the sky. Grey and white clouds passed overhead like vast schools of slow fish undulating in a solid mass just beneath the ocean's surface, one substance formed of many, something both inert and alive. That he was blessed because his wife lived made him somehow feel that his losses were less. Yet he wondered if they were more. Noadiah was a woman bereft of her children and grandchildren. Would it be easier to have lost her as well? His wound then would be as bitter and clean as Joseph's and Moshe's, and the three would be equals in loss.

The thought felt to him like his memories of his enslaved mistresses at Antioch before Noadiah. Those memories had haunted him through the years, and he looked down from the sky quickly, the forest shimmering and wobbling before him. He thought he saw shapes then, dark spots before his eyes, the gift of advancing years that made his vision occasionally shudder. Then he realized the figures were real. There were fighters in the forest, coming on an indirect course, not yet having seen him, moving towards the Galilean camp. Joazar looked left and saw movement there as well. They were not coming from the plain this time, the direction of the city, but the interior. The Egyptians had learned not to drive the Galileans into the forests but to circle and push them out into the open flatland towards the coast. It was late afternoon, and there was still light. Joazar felt a chill.

≪

The morning sun revealed that the Galileans were nearly across the coastal plain. The rising sun sent their shadows on ahead into the sea. The men were bloodied, scraped, and encrusted with dirt. Falls in the night had left their clothing in rags, their haggard appearance only a suggestion of the men they had once been. Archers were without arrows. Slingers used whatever missiles could be scrounged from the broken land. The slingers then sent their roughly scavenged projectiles on erratic arcs, their wild shots posing little danger to the forces following them.

The Egyptians were on foot and had been similarly ill-used by the terrain. They were rags chasing rags.

When the Galileans reached the sea, they turned south towards Mount Carmel and away from Akko. The Egyptian conquerors of Akko followed.

42

102 BCE

IN AN AGE before Akko had been raised, before humans had explored its rocky shores, a scallop in saltwater quickly closed one of its shell valves and shot across the ocean floor. It disturbed a drift of skeletal coral fragments and settled amid deposits of fresh sedimentary silt from the shore's freshwater stream. The scallop's fan-shaped shell of golden brown was ribbed with sixteen ridges and cross-hatched with bands of dark burgundy and traces of white so thin it was as though an artist had stroked it not with a brush but with a single hair, satisfied with only the most delicate effect. With its gills, the creature drew in and expelled seawater, moving, feeding, and breathing with one combined action.

The stir of sediments revealed in the murky water a substrate of stone beyond the small creature's understanding. The scallop continued to feed, mindless, frequently moving, and in doing so, it perceived the changing of the light but not its significance. From above, a thick cloud spread a vast expanse of the surface's disturbed sand into the ocean depths. Sensing too late the concentration of silt, the creature tried again to dart across the ocean floor. The scallop attempted but failed to escape as its efforts drove it inadvertently deeper into silt clouds. The sand's weight gradually bore down and choked the creature. Further escape attempts continued to make matters worse until it and countless others like it were enmeshed in a blanket of silt that continued to grow and bury them.

The community of scallops died, and smaller creatures moved in and hollowed out their shells. As centuries passed, layer upon layer of shells, sand, and organic debris accumulated. Over a millennium, the mixture combined and compressed and became cemented into limestone. The cycle repeated and repeated until one age shifted to another, and the layer of limestone began to rise on torsos of chalk, legs of marl, feet of clay.

The mountain nature built from the ocean's tombs became known as Carmel. Various pagans had worshipped their different gods on Mount Carmel without restraint until the Jewish god smote his rivals' prophets. Then an ancient people quarried the limestone to build a wall for a growing northern city. The city was called Akko. One such cut block contained the fossilized remains of that white and burgundy scallop, its rich colours leached to a nearly uniform tawny white. The fossilized shell lay in an upper corner of the block, and the block itself was placed high up on Akko's outer wall.

During a siege in the time of the Assyrian kingdom, a hurled stone of granite struck that outer block, and a fig-sized piece broke off. Severed from its stony home, the scallop was soon trampled and kicked aside.

Some centuries later, a young boy found the stone and

used it in his sling just once during a time of peace. It sailed towards the sea and fell with a clink onto the stones before the water. Then all was silent save for the sound of the sea. Sometime later, the fossilized scallop was slung again, the stone's short arc ending this time in the sea where it sank below the shallow water. There, the tide pounded it for centuries more, rolling it over and over again in the surf, pushing it up the shore, grinding at its shape until it formed a nearly perfect small egg on the beach. Then a new set of gnarled older hands picked up the prize and thrust it into a sack of similar stones, and what remained of the scallop jostled with its peers in the bag's darkness. It did not stay there for long.

The stone was thrust again into sunlight and again into leather for its third circular flight from a sling. Then the release came, but instead of a stony click on the beach or a watery plunge, the stone struck flesh, broke through a skull, and sank into softness. The Galilean named Joseph went down before his son, down before his brother-in-law, down before his friends. He was dead before his great shape fell into the waters they were trying to cross: the shallows of the Kishon River as it entered the sea.

Moshe cried out, but he could not stop, for two men's hands held him up and pulled him across the current where they entered the hard land at the base of Mount Carmel and continued to run. The shape that had been Joseph took a different watery course. The Egyptians waded where his body had been, and the history of that place continued without him as his body bore the ancient creature's fossil once more back out to sea.

43

102-101 BCE

AS THE ROOFS of Cana were restored, tales flowed north into Galilee. The Judean war with Lathyrus went poorly. Thirty thousand of Jannaeus's gentile mercenaries were lost in one encounter. Other reports said fifty thousand. Reports came of Judea's rural villages raped and plundered. The Egyptians only suspended their habit of slaughtering for the sake of the slave markets. Chained Judeans trailed the conquering army into Idumea, where they added Jannaeus's southern Jewish converts to the slave-chains. Then the mass moved back into Judea and towards Jerusalem. It seemed inevitable now that Israel would receive new masters and that the Hasmonean line would end. Renegade Egyptians were ascendant, and there was no sign of Cleopatra.

The Galileans had nothing further to do with Jerusalem's war. Half of Lathyrus's forces remained within Akko's walls, and the Galileans could do nothing but die on nearby beaches or the broad plain before the city. They had no navy for the coast. Instead of continuing to fight, they retreated to their mountains. They brought home those of their dead they could find and stayed home. Joseph and Keziah's circle of friends regrouped at Rehavam's glassworks, but there stood a void in the centre: missing voices, their presence, her lute, all the others. Gone.

They were in the house by the glassworks one night. Discussions centred on the memories of those lost in recent battles.

"The armour," Uri said in near darkness. Spare light fell weakly between the human shapes gathered this night.

"Uri," Mahlah said. She reached for him, but he sat on the far side of their circle, and her hand was a mere gesture. It settled back in her lap.

"He remade that armour with his brothers," Uri continued, "to help send away a corrupt king and lift Jannaeus out of prison. Put Jannaeus on the throne. Put an end to Maccabean wars."

"Uri," she said again.

"Joseph and his brothers did that," Uri continued. "And another Maccabean war put them in the ground."

"And Joseph in the sea," Joazar said.

"The sea," Uri exclaimed and made as if to throw something, but he had nothing in his hand. "Not even the ground. The sea."

"Idumea is gone," Saul said. "So is the area east of the Jordan. Whole tracts of Judea."

"New lords," Uri said. "The temple will be stripped.

Again. Egyptians instead of Seleucids. Jannaeus has ruined everything we built."

"Cleopatra finally came," Joazar said.

"And let Lathyrus's troops escape Akko while she sorted out unloading her ships," Uri said.

"Akko threw its gates open to Cleopatra," Saul said. "Gave no resistance at all."

"Is it confirmed?" Joazar asked. "Lathyrus went to Gaza?"

"Yes," Saul said, "he had ships waiting for him there."

"He planned to lose?" Rehavam asked.

"He gave himself an escape route in case he lost," Saul said. "Not something our king thought to work out."

Spring days grew longer. Uri and Mahlah went back to rebuild the farm. Rehavam and Basmat tidied the glassworks, but they had little motivation to restart the kilns with few prospective commissions. Joazar and Noadiah stayed at the glassworks along with Moshe.

Saul gathered the remaining store of Uri's quince wine from its various depots and began to rebuild his contacts. He negotiated new contracts for what would be the last of the quince. The invaders had cut down Uri's trees. The vineyards were nearly ruined as well, but the roots were recoverable. Uri focused now on reviving the grapes and the winery. He would not make the quince again. The elevated price for the final vintage of quince would fund the rebuilding of many homes and the feeding of many families.

A massacre at Akko sent a shudder through Galilee. They may have been Galilee's neighbours, but the people of Akko were still gentiles. Though violence close to home made them uneasy, the Galileans left it to Dionysus or Zeus to avenge Akko and did not concern themselves with gentiles fighting gentiles. News of Lathyrus's final atrocities also filtered north. Shamefaced messengers brought reports of disaster upon disaster in the south, but it had all become too much for Galilee's valleys and mountains to absorb. News from beyond Galilee was deflected at its borders. There was enough within Galilee to occupy its people without worrying about the south. The region became a place apart, isolated and alone, shut off from the nation beyond, just as before the Maccabees.

Rumours circulated about survivors lost in the mountains. There were reports of Shikhin's captives coming back from across the sea. Having escaped from their captivity, they had landed at Gaza and were pursuing Lathyrus onto his ships, but these were the fantasies of a people gone mad. There were also reports of a ghostly regiment from Bersabe: veterans of the old Seleucid wars were outside Tyre guarding Upper Galilee against any Tyrian adventurism or a new Seleucid incursion. There may well have been bandits operating in the north, preying on gentile travellers, but they were not a mysteriously resurrected remnant of the fallen.

One morning at Kfar Nahum, the sun shone brightly on the water, and a group of men met along the shoreline. They packed jars into boats and carts. Saul walked among the men. "Put that one in the big wagon," he said, pointing at an oversized crate. "You'll need another man."

Reports had been circulating that Joseph had been seen, a demon of revenge around Akko, Mount Carmel, and as far south as Dora. But Saul had seen that stone enter Joseph's skull. As he had stepped onto the river's far shore and looked back one last time, he had seen the big man's body sinking where the fresh water met salt. The false stories made him angry.

"No, that one's for the boats," he said, redirecting the path of a smaller crate. "The big wagon!" he said to the first group of men. "The big crate goes in the—"

"We've got it," one of the labourers said. He brushed against Saul as he passed, and Saul registered the offence in silence.

Saul made his way down closer to the boats and discovered that none had been loaded. The crates had been stacked haphazardly on the shore, and a debate seemed to be in progress.

"I saw him," one of the labourers said. Deep creases marked the back of his neck where his hair curled wet and oily. No one was working.

Saul tried to move to the front of this gathering and was pushed back by one of his men. "I'm trying to hear," the man said, not looking to see who Saul was.

Saul pushed in again, frustrated by the necessity of a second attempt. Men parted slowly. They were focused on the argument, which the oily-haired man seemed to be winning.

"He's a big guy," the oily-haired man said. "You can't mistake him."

"Mistake who?" Saul asked. He stood in the middle of the clearing and did not recognize the man before him. A new guy. Day labour.

"Joseph. The carpenter from Cana."

Saul stared at him. He had come primed to end a debate about loading boats. "Joseph?"

"South of Akko. Killing Egyptians like there's nothing to it."

"Joseph is dead."

"Awfully alive from what I saw. Tearing up a mess around Dora. Sampson reborn."

"A stone went through his head," Saul said in a deep tone that threatened fury, but the labourer was oblivious.

"I don't know anything about a stone. Whoever says he got a stone doesn't know anything."

Later, Saul did not remember deciding to swing. His right fist took the man in the face, and he was dimly aware of the strange feeling of gums and a nose sagging below his knuckles. His left fist missed its intended target and struck the man in the throat, and then Saul swung again and again, and the two were down on the wet sand, Saul straddling a barrel chest and pummelling a bloody face. The victim's hands blindly shielded his face, and Saul's fists continued to fall until other hands caught him and pulled him up off the body.

"He's done, he's done," voices said, and Saul stood panting before his boats and his men, the sailors and cartmen. He realized he had been shouting only when he stopped. Standing there, panting, looking at the mud mixed with blood before him, Saul began to cry. Hands now lay lightly on his arms, no longer holding him back. No one spoke.

Many here had known Joseph. Some owned boats built by his cousins.

Kalev, Saul's right-hand man, pulled the oily-haired worker to his feet with the help of a wiry boatman. The beaten man swayed before he opened his eyes, found Saul, and said, "I seen him."

Kalev's reaction was immediate, as was the boatman's, and their coordination was either accidental or deliberately savage. The boatman grabbed a fistful of oily hair and hauled the man towards the lake while Kalev grabbed a leg and pulled in the opposite direction. Together they hoisted the barrel-chested man into the air and slammed him face-first into the sand. Kalev came down on the man's back, punches landing on skull and neck. Then he stopped. He stood up, panting. He and the boatman stood over the body and waited. It stirred, shifted onto its elbows, lifted its head, and then vomited onto the beach. A misshapen face turned and found Saul again. "Been drinking all night," he said slowly and with difficulty.

"He's not from around here," a voice in the crowd said.

"He's from Bersabe," said another. "Lost everything and everyone these last few months. He was in the mountains with us during the war. Fought like a demon."

A man beside Saul leaned forward and looked into his eyes, his hand still lying lightly on Saul's arm. "He just wants it to be true," the man said.

Joseph was not the only subject of the stories told in Galilee that spring. A rumour spread about a woman. Two women. They were living in the mountains. Some said they lived in caves near Nazareth, and others said they had been sighted near Sogane. Some suggested that the women were Keziah and Sarah, but any who had known the two dismissed these accounts as simply more wild tales. Later reports said the women were lepers and avoided anyone they encountered. Then news came that one of the women, the younger one, was a cripple. She walked, but haltingly, and the older one cared for her. The stories disturbed Saul.

"They're nothing," Moshe and Joazar would say when Saul passed on the tales. "Too many people living alone, away from everyone else. They make up hope."

Later, a different version of the story was brought to Moshe's attention while he and Joazar and Noadiah were at Rehavam's glassworks. This story was consistent with the other tales but for one detail: the older woman sometimes carried the cripple in an ingenious sling that allowed her to move the younger one through difficult terrain. The storyteller described the sling in detail, and it was exactly like the one Joseph had made.

"She only used it around the house," Moshe said to Joazar and Rehavam. "It was for bad days." His eyes were brimming. They told the women, and their tears came with the sound of pain reborn, and they left the men alone.

"Send someone for Uri," Moshe said.

Rehavam nodded and went looking for his fastest man.

"Saul is somewhere north of Akko," Joazar said.

"I'm not waiting for Saul," Moshe said.

"Nor will I," Joazar replied.

None of the men said what they planned to do.

Late that same day, Uri arrived at the glassworks. It was late spring, and he had left the crew management to Mahlah, who had practically whipped him down the road, past the gate and the overlooking rock-face fossils.

"She said not to set foot on the farm again until I had Keziah and Sarah safely home," Uri reported to Moshe, Joazar, and Rehavam. "She's going to work the labourers on the farm like a madwoman while I'm gone." He was trying to be light-hearted, but there was nothing light about the expressions worn by the four men meeting at Rehavam's place. Later that day, with little other conversation, the four men took to the mountains.

The late spring sun and rain brought brightness to the land and the chorus of birds. Every bush and deciduous tree sprouted leaves of the brightest green that filled in all the spaces between the evergreens and woody thickets. The thickened foliage foreshortened both sight and sound, and only in bare, rocky places could the searching men see for a distance. Even the night was noisy with insects and bird calls. They might have passed those they sought in the darkness and never heard them calling for the racket of the night's population.

The three men let the rumoured sightings lead them into the woodland north and west of Cana. Twice they found abandoned camps that could have been the lair of bandits or wanderers or lepers, but the two they sought remained elusive. They came down a rocky channel following the deafening roar of a spring river. They stepped and slid with uneasy feet where the moss grew slimy and slick like long green hair on the rocks. The streams were cold. They searched the shorelines for a sign, for the women would need water as well as shelter.

At night, the stars above appeared as the distant fires of angels. The four men discussed the heavens, and they prayed to their God that had created those fires and kept them lit from age to age. In the morning, they moved on. When they came out to where the river emptied onto the plain, having found no sign of the women, they began to debate. Had they searched far enough up the slope beside the stream? If the women were hiding, had gone mad, or believed the Egyptians still terrorized Galilee, might they have been hiding back in the woods as the men passed? Should they return upstream and try again or go over the next ridge and continue the search there?

They resolved to continue their search valley by valley, ridge by ridge, stream by stream. Were it not for the story of the sling, they never would have believed and ventured forth. The story sent them out, and the story would not let them stop.

Weeks into their search, they stirred up a nesting pair of black francolins near the borderland between the forest and plain. They felt the pounding of the wings as much as they heard them, and though the birds aggressively swooped back down to protect their nest, the men had already taken the eggs, and they ate well that night.

As they continued their journey, the men heard the chuckling of a swamphen but never saw its grey head. Later, as they traversed through a new pocket of hills, a moorhen hissed them away from a dense thicket by a quiet pond, the red beak raised in defiance until Uri's sling stopped the bird's display. Again, the men ate, and so they made their way through the mountains.

They encountered migrating groups of stone curlews, strange little birds that some called thickknees, their feather coats patterned like the debris of sticks and last year's dried leaves. Having finished their wading and feeding, the birds shuffled from creek edges and back into the forest itself, disappearing against the ground before taking to sudden, changeable flight.

The search party fed mostly on rock pigeons and wood pigeons, turtle doves and collared doves. They even killed and ate Namaqua doves, which would have been too small to target had they not gathered in large groups around pools and on the forest floor, making them easy prey for the slinger.

"When the doves return to my dovecote, they will be safe," Uri said. He looked down at Rehavam, awash in grey and white and brown feathers. A stack of small carcasses sat beside him from which projected tiny reddish-brown legs, and the glassmaker laughed. His long beard rivalled that of the oldest sages now. All the men now looked like mountain hermits with their untamed hair, and still they climbed and searched.

They came to a meadow high and dark below late-afternoon clouds. Flashes of lightning revealed black stone shot through with glints of mica. Frazzled-looking nightjars lived in the place. The birds took flight in the low light, dipping and twisting in violent manoeuvres as they fed on insects the men could not see. Their frantic dance seemed overdone to the men at the forest's edge. It was a violent, energetic performance.

The travellers camped in that meadow, tired from the climb, and at night they debated the source of the surrounding chorus: nightjars sounding like crickets and the cries of bright blue rollers indistinguishable from crows. It seemed strange that either bird was calling in the semi-darkness when the men only expected owls. Moshe claimed he could identify different owl species by their call, but he was at a loss when he tried to describe which type the men could hear that night. None in that party could draw, and they did not have the scribe's kit needed to try.

They came down again from the mountains, slumped against wind and rain. They passed through foothills covered in tall grass and climbed again. The band had now become a source of new rumours: tales told of Galilean hunters combing through Lower Galilee's hills looking for lost Egyptians, of guardian angels that did not stand at crossroads or on promontories but rather patrolled the hidden places—the caves, gullies, and high canyons—seeking the sources of rivers throughout the territory.

The staccato alarms of small wryneck woodpeckers followed the wanderers into a place where the trees had died, their inexplicable grey and leafless trunks and limbs now home to a vast community of birds. The men felt an eerie awe in that stand of columns. The place disturbed the men, and they had seen enough to know that no human hid there, so they moved back into dense greenery with relief.

They descended again down the path of a stream that they had nearly overlooked in the thick foliage, following its course for the sake of thoroughness and not with hope. As the men waded through the shallow brook, they stumbled across an unusually large pile of rocky sediment and discovered a small rill running through a narrow cleft in the leftward cliff. Its water seamlessly mixed into the stream. Joazar paused, tired and hungry. He sat down on a rock and drank from the brook, waiting for his friends and nephew to notice and return. They assembled around him without words, each as tired as the next.

Uri's bald head was marred by a scar received during their escape along the beach south of Akko. His brow also bore the patchiness of age and numerous fresh scratches from their push through thickets along countless stream beds and low places like this one. The others wore their hair long and untamed, each man becoming a fright and a stench even to himself. They would often bathe and dry their clothes on bushes, but by the end of each day, they again had a disreputable appearance and odour, and they could never find a place where they could sleep soundly on the crowded forest floor. The men always refused the hospitality of the villages they encountered and pressed on, relentless in their search, indifferent to how their appearance fuelled rumours in the places they passed.

When their search had led them back to the wilderness near Cana, the men had sent a messenger to run to the glassworks and inform the women that they lived. That had been all the news they could send. They stayed under no roof as spring turned into summer and heat found its way into the mountains.

Rehavam broke the silence that hung over the little creek. "Are you sure about the rumours we're chasing?"

"It's the sling," Moshe said.

"I've never seen it," Rehavam said.

"Your father carried her if she needed carrying," Uri said. "She usually just walked."

"Sometimes, they took her about with the donkey," Rehavam said.

"Mother did not use the sling outside the house," Moshe said. "If she needed to leave the house and Sarah couldn't walk that day, Father carried her. Or I did. No one else outside of the house would know about the sling."

The three then discussed the places they had searched, identifying each valley and stream by its adjacent human settlements. They talked about the areas yet to come, the endless mountains they had yet to search, and the places they had already explored that perhaps held overlooked secret hollows that warranted a second search.

Joazar did not participate in this discussion. He sat on his rock, weary and empty of will. Parallel rows of brilliant greens overhung the channel and framed the blue summer sky above. The air contained a cleanness that contrasted with the four grime-coated men. Their clothes were torn and roughly mended. They would have to return soon to Cana for new clothes, if for no other reason. Joazar wondered how long they would search for the ghost of his sister, the phantom of his niece. He, too, had seen Keziah use the sling. Only once. He had come to the house and surprised her as she was moving Sarah from a bath to her bedroom. It was enough for the strange story to ring true, but their search had come to nothing.

He turned away from his nephew, from his friends. He knew the quest was futile, and they were exhausting themselves chasing a memory. Even if Keziah and Sarah had somehow escaped the Egyptians, they would not have survived the fall and winter alone. None of the stories spoke of the strange women seeking supplies. If they were found, they would be found starved.

As he looked upstream, the image of both his parents and his sister left to starve crept through Joazar, and he wished that whatever torrent had worn these stones smooth would come again and sweep him away the way Joseph had been swept out to sea. Once again, the weight of surviving seemed worse than the loss of dying. He wished to go down the mountain and throw himself at Lathyrus with abandon, to die and be free of the pain within. But the villages had passed on the news: Cleopatra had met with Jannaeus, Lathyrus had fled Israel, the Jewish king had prostrated himself before the pharaoh, and she had spared his kingdom because of Salome's gifts and her Jewish generals' counsel. Cleopatra had departed. Jannaeus remained in Jerusalem, discredited, impoverished, hated but secure on his throne. There were no invaders left in Israel for Joazar to throw himself against.

Staring upstream, he spotted a waxwing pecking at some berries. The austere bird was quite the opposite of the previous night's scruffy nightjars. When it darted off, its wingtips glinted yellow and red before it disappeared to the right, seeming to fly straight into the rock face. It was such an abrupt and violent manoeuvre that Joazar started, and the men behind him stopped talking.

"What is it?" Uri asked.

"Nothing," Joazar said. "Just a bird and a stream."

"To the side, through the crack," Rehavam said. "I saw it as we passed."

"We should look," Uri said.

None protested. Searching without hope was what they did. They had initially overlooked the opening out of weariness, not an intentional lack of thoroughness, for the narrow ravine was still wide enough to be a refuge.

Moshe stood first. "I'll go."

He walked away from the two men who had been his father's friends, who he now called his. He walked past his uncle. Moshe was the youngest of the group. Unlike the other three, he had no one to return to, none he still called his own; this search was all he had. Joazar feared the young man would go mad in the mountains. As Moshe passed and went on, Joazar turned to the others to raise his concern but, looking at the two pairs of eyes following Moshe, he saw that there was no argument to be made. He and Uri had wives, but there would be no future children. Rehavam had his full family, and his path would diverge in the years to come as he and Basmat focused on their grandchildren and connections with Saul's family. For Uri and Joazar, there would only be subtraction. The same would hold for Moshe unless he found a way to start again, but that could not occur as long as this search continued. Joazar opened his mouth to speak but still found nothing to say. Then Uri rose and followed Moshe, and after a few moments, Rehavam did the same.

Joazar found himself alone, looking downstream. The footsteps on loose stone behind him faded.

He was not there when Moshe pushed himself through the crack in the rock and found a clearing.

He was not there when Moshe found the olive trees in that place, the strange, gnarled transplants picked clean of last year's crop and brimming again in summer with developing fruit in the small valley.

He was not there when Moshe found the whitened skeleton of a donkey, when he saw the drying racks for meat, the natural poles tied into place by rawhide straps from the donkey's reins.

When his companions did not return, Joazar trudged back up the stream. When he entered the crack, barely the width of a horse or donkey, he was surprised to see how quickly it opened up beyond, and then the following sight hit him as if the sea had reared up and pounded him down. He fell to his knees, imitating what he saw before him—the grizzled and haggard Moshe suddenly become a boy again, weeping loudly against the breast of an old woman who was cleaner than the men, her hair streaked with grey, her dress in tatters, holding her boy against her with a fierceness that was primitive and threatening. She looked up and took in the men about her and spotted Joazar in the distance. Her eyes spilled tears.

There was a babble of voices in that place. Joazar could not distinguish hers, and he stayed where he was, unable to move until Uri and Rehavam made their way towards the shelter beyond. Keziah leaped to her feet, suddenly a madwoman, her hair undone, her clothing the colour of dust. She shouted, "You cannot! You cannot!"

Joazar started to his feet, moved past an unsteadily rising Moshe, past Uri and Rehavam, and stood before his sister. She swam before his eyes. She looked wild—like both a child and an old hag—and he could see terror there and pain and madness and a wild longing. There was something dangerous in her, something fierce and unholy and afraid, and he spoke before she could reject him. "Keziah."

She looked at her brother, and the expressions that crossed her face made him even more fearful for her sanity and intent on reaching her. He said what he should not have to cut off whatever led her to this place and to get out what he feared most to say. "Joseph is dead. He was killed at Akko. He was killed saving Moshe. We have been looking for you ever since." And then, just a whisper: "Keziah."

It was not the news that did it, though the shock on her face showed that she had registered what her brother had said. It was the last word, spoken so quietly, spoken the way her father would have said it, that broke her open. She began to weep, then to sob, and as she sank to her knees again, it was her brother that went down with her and held her to his chest, and she was no longer an old woman or a mother. She was a little sister held by her older brother, who was now himself an old man. Though he looked little like their slight father, he sounded the same, and he spoke her name the same, and Moshe saw his mother transformed.

After some time, she spoke again. "You cannot go in there."

"Sarah?" Joazar asked.

"Yes."

"What is it, Keziah?" Joazar asked.

"You cannot go in there."

"What is wrong with her?"

"Nothing is wrong with her!" She was defiant and angry again. "She is the same."

"Why can't we go in there?"

She would not answer.

"I don't care about disease," Uri said, striding forward. "I would see that girl again if it cost me my life."

"No. No. Please. There is no disease!" Keziah shouted. "You cannot go in there!" As Uri strode towards the hut, Keziah rose, and Joazar tried to hold her back while Rehavam and Moshe stared in confusion. Then there came a sound designed to stop an adult in their tracks, a sound pitched to irritate, to call, to warn, to stir the milk in a mother's body and demand the attention of both sexes. In that place of rock and greenery and water, amid the brook and the leaves and the adult voices, there came the cry of a baby.

All stopped. Shock rippled across the clearing like the sound of a boulder shifting underwater, a spasm within that flushed the face and loosened limbs. Keziah looked like a woman stripped and gutted before a staring public.

"The Egyptians," she said, all air, no voice. "The Egyptians." She let out a shattering cry. Each of the four men understood then what took place during that horrible assault on Cana and what transpired afterwards. Each man stood horrified. The child, of mixed race, brought forth in blood and condemned to die by hatred, by custom, by shame, had not been killed but cared for through the long, lean winter.

44

101 BCE

THAT FALL, ONLY the men went to Sukkot, the Ingathering, the Festival of Booths. Moshe with Joazar, Rehavam, and Uri sat in their fragile shelter outside Jerusalem's walls and looked up through gaps at the stars above. In this way, the fall reminded them of their time of wild searching earlier in the year.

Saul joined them, as did Jacob. On the second night, Ebed left his family in the city and found the Galileans under the stars. He and Joazar spoke of the festival in the days of Simon. The next night, Pharisee friends of Ebed's came from Jerusalem. The Pharisees spoke of a sage's passing, of the state of Jerusalem, and the men from Cana reported on news from Galilee, avoiding the story all cared most to hear until Jugurtha came. The old man came late and quiet in the night, looking even older than his years. Only when they were all assembled did the four men from Cana share their story of the mountains, of the wild searchers of Galilee, of the months under rain and sun, and finally of the discovery of Keziah and Sarah and the infant.

Joazar spoke of her silence and Moshe of her pain, neither specifying whether they were referring to Keziah or Sarah. The listeners understood that by saying *her*, they were speaking of both women. They decided then and swore by Jerusalem's gates that there would be a second Ingathering this year. It would be in one month, at the full moon of the month of Cheshvan, in Galilee, at Grandma Sarah's home, which had now become Jacob's. The women and the children would have the house. The men would sleep in the barns as soldiers once did so many years before. There would be a gathering.

⁂

Keziah and Sarah sat in that old and cracked place made for two, the small island of rock with the creek on either side. The almonds had long passed, but the pomegranates were still ripe. Keziah would bring some of the children down later to pick the fruit, but for now, it was just she and Sarah at the creek. The others, so many others, were up at the house. The men had slept in the barn because of the rain, but it was dry now. The air was clean and still warm, but the harvested crops forecasted the coming cool of winter.

There was a heron downstream, the first such bird that Keziah had seen at Grandma Sarah's farm. It stalked something swirling in an indolent eddy at the water's edge. The great bird's chest bore black and grey feathers below a white neck. Its yellow beak extended past yellow eyes, and a mass of blue and ashen grey feathers swept behind its head like unkempt hair sculpted by the wind. It struck Keziah as a tall blend of the scruffy nightjars she had seen in the mountains and the formal waxwings that had hovered near their hidden home the previous winter and spring. It was a creature both elegant and dishevelled, perfectly embodying how she felt now.

She wished for Joseph to be buried in this place, here with her people. The little of him that lived at all now lived in Moshe and Little Sarah and the baby. This made the Galileans accept what was otherwise an abomination, this child of rape, Jewish blood mixed with gentile. All agreed that he would be Joseph's and Keziah's. Egypt would be banished from the child's history, and he would never know his true origin. With the silence of one generation, his bloodline would be as pure as that of Abraham's own sons. Keziah, her family, and their friends would raise and protect the baby for Joseph's sake.

Keziah looked over at Sarah, who was enthralled. The crowd at the house was almost too much for her. They had spent a year in the mountains. The two were now attuned to the sound of birds, leaves, and modest fires. They were used to hearing each other breathe. The crowd at the house was so loud that no one's breath could be heard. Laughter and tears were everywhere. In the mountains, only the creek laughed. Sarah had been Keziah's reason to survive that long winter.

The two had learned to talk in a new way. They spoke now with gestures and a form of face reading. None but the family had understood Sarah's speech a year before. Now only Keziah understood her daughter, but they understood each other perfectly.

There was music coming from the house. A trick of the

air carried the sound across the field, over the stone wall, and through the trees. She could just hear it above the sound of the gurgling water.

Her lute was gone. It, along with Joseph's case, had burned with everything else in Cana. Saul had found a new lute for her. At the first touch, she could tell it was superior to Grandma Sarah's lute. The case, of course, was inferior. Saul had taken the lute to Jerusalem and left it with Ebed, who commissioned a better case. Joseph's case was something that could never be recreated. It had been the product of constrained hunger for love redirected and poured into the wood and joinery—an expression of focused passion, hidden, concealed in craft, brought forth as a gift. It was a promise spoken without words.

Music came again from the house, through leafless trees, and Sarah turned to speak silently. *You should play.*

Her hands fluttered to her lap, and Keziah watched them settle. She looked up at her daughter's face, took in her eyes. She thought of the new case and the instrument within and the music that could be made, and she knew she could not do it. She thought of Joseph, remembered his arms and his back as he cut this log into their current seat with only his donkey as a companion. She saw him drinking from this stream, and she remembered making children with him in this place, the dangerous outrage of it, and she thought of the times she had played just for him and the times she had played in a crowd but had given him those secret notes, the first time he caught her eye across the room, recognizing the language she spoke in public but only to him so only he could hear.

"I can't," she said. "I don't think I will ever play again."

They were quiet then. They listened to the creek, to the snatches of sound from the house, and they watched the heron which seemed to be not fishing but sleeping while standing, head cocked and unmoving in the stream's deeper current, on long, thin, brown legs.

There was a different sound then. Keziah looked over at Sarah and saw that she was crying. Keziah tried to speak to her, but Sarah would not turn and kept looking downstream. Keziah knew it was not the heron. She was avoiding her mother's eyes, tears tracking her face, hands firmly in place.

"What is it, Sarah?"

Sarah would not move. Keziah wanted to take her hands, to make her form words with them, but she waited. The girl could be stubborn.

Finally, Sarah spoke.

Now it was Keziah's eyes that flooded, and her daughter turned to her and repeated the request with her hands and her glistening face. *I need you to play. Please.*

Then the moment froze. A splash downstream went unheeded. The women ignored the whoop-whoop of the heron's great wings as it lifted from its place in the water, and neither did they hear another snippet of sound drifting down from the house through the red pomegranates and over the little island. Sarah held her gaze, would not relent. She said yes, and Sarah put her head down. Keziah kissed the girl's offered forehead, and a smile formed behind the girl's tears.

They made their way across the field very, very slowly. Moshe met them before they reached the low stone wall, helped Sarah over, and carried her the rest of the way to the house. Inside, the music continued. Basmat was singing with Noadiah. Uri played his lyre; Mahlah played the pipe and sistrum together. Jugurtha was there too, and he seemed overwhelmed. It was his first trip to Galilee.

The group acknowledged Keziah and Sarah's return but did not stop playing. When the song was over, they began a new one, one that did not need the lute but still welcomed it.

Keziah went over to the case and opened it. Her back was to the room. She knew that each eye followed her, but none openly stared. She trembled as she lifted the lute from its case.

She sat quietly, on the edge of this group of friends, her true family, and rested her hands on the body of the lute, felt its smooth skin, let one hand follow the arc of its long neck, its tight strings. Her trembling eased. Her arms and fingers grew calm. There came a pause between the music's phrases, and when the sound picked up again, she slipped into the flow like a spring leaf dislodged, bright and green and pert at the top of the flow, carried along and giving shape to the translucent surface.

The music picked up the pace. Her fingers were slow, and twice she dropped out as her movements sought to be light once more. She did not give up. Each time she rejoined the music, and then came a transition when suddenly her fingers were what they should be, they became her young fingers again. Then they became lighter and faster yet, and soon she was leading the music, and she changed the song. Those from Galilee and those from Jerusalem followed her as she drove bass notes and the high melodies; the music came louder and faster, and then it haunted and slowed and accelerated again. It was the creek in the mountains and the river in the plain; it was the stream below the pomegranates, and it was the wind, and then, before she recognized what she was doing, she added the secret notes, the notes that only one heart could hear. The tears came fast and hard, and she knew they stained not just her face but ran down her neck and soaked into her dress. Still she kept on playing the main melody and the secret notes, angry and yearning and calling and calling with her fingers.

A cry from Galilee to the sea.

A Note from the Author

Over several years I fell in love with Keziah and her Galilean community. By reading her story, I hope you have grown to care for her as well.

A Review Request:

If you enjoyed *Keziah's Song*, please consider taking a minute to leave a review wherever you are most likely to buy books. Reviews help other readers find my work, and it would mean a great deal to me if you took a moment to tell others about your experience.

To Experience More:

If you would like to know more about the creation of *Keziah's Song*, access deleted scenes, read the author's commentary on unusual features of the novel, pose a question to the author, sign up for my newsletter or find out about upcoming publications, please visit my website at:

darylpotter.com

In this life, I have made friends equal to Keziah's Galilean community. May you find the same kind of community: every one of them a character–fierce, loyal, and loving.

Daryl Potter
Oct 20, 2020
Oakville, Ontario, Canada

ACKNOWLEDGEMENTS

This ambitious project would not have succeeded without the help of many generous hands. I would like first to thank my beta readers: Sam Medeiros, Caleb Lightening, Debbie Vazirali, D'Arcy Delamere, and Lyra Fletcher. You all helped me immeasurably by providing early encouragement and constructive criticism on some, admittedly, very rough drafts. In addition, Alex Duimstra, Ilse Lightening, Margaret Grimm, and my wife, Carolyn Potter, read select portions to help me assess specific aspects of the novel. Their comments provided either the goad or the encouragement most needed in the moment.

Diane Young provided generous editorial support. In addition to prescribed editorial tasks, Diane sourced valuable insights on second- and first-century BCE Israel, Judaism, and the proper use of Hebrew terminology by consulting her colleague Bob Chodos (the former editor-in-chief of the *Canadian Forum*), which proved to be an immeasurable help. Stephanie Fysh provided early editorial feedback, as well as a valuable orientation to the Canadian publishing landscape. Dania Sheldon likewise provided early editorial feedback that stayed with me throughout the rewriting process. Amelia Wiens delivered the final, detailed edit of this entire manuscript. Her work was a showcase for editorial excellence, covering everything from grammar to timeline continuity, historical fact-checking to stylistic and readability considerations. Lastly, S. Robin Larin stepped in and proofread the final draft. Her detailed critique went beyond the standard proofreader remit and was a valuable contribution to this project. I owe the final polish of *Keziah's Song* to Amelia and Robin and their remarkable and talented efforts. Any errors that might persist within this work are mine.

The folks at Damonza were a joy to work with on both cover design and typesetting. A truly outstanding team of engaged and talented individuals.

Many reference materials were essential for my research. For the basic historical outline, I am indebted to Flavius Josephus, the first-century CE Jewish historian. I found insight in his works *The Antiquities of the Jews* and *The War of the Jews*, which were both published in his lifetime for a Roman audience. *The Story of the Jews: Finding the Words* by Simon Schama was helpful, as were many other reference works to help me tie Josephus's passages to recognizable dates in our Gregorian calendar. Works that went beyond the dates and provided a more intimate view of the era, places, and people were also vital, such as Seneca's letters from the first-century BCE Rome, the diaries of Julius Caesar, and the works of Philo Judaeus of Alexandria, a Jewish philosopher from the first-century BCE to the first-century CE. Modern works in this vein included *Galilee: From Alexander the Great to Hadrian 323 BCE to 135 CE* by Sean Freyne and *Queen Salome* by Kenneth Atkinson. Countless other texts, websites, and educational aids, including the works of Alfred Edersheim and portions of the Talmud, were also invaluable background material.

I would like to thank Dr. Douglas Jacoby, an adjunct professor at Lincoln Christian University. Dr. Jacoby led trips through Turkey, Greece, Egypt, and Israel, which were educational and experiential milestones that helped make this book possible. Mike Luzine organized my participation in these trips, and for that, I am grateful.

Lastly, I would like to thank my wife, Carolyn, and my children, Jackson and Mackenzie. They put up with me spending seemingly endless hours, evenings, and weekends for years, in coffee shops. I would slip out of the house to read and write where I could work undistracted by household affairs. Without their support, this project would not have been possible. An unusual artifact from that period now lives in our family's favourite room: two tables and four chairs. They were gifts from my local Starbucks, the Dorval location in Oakville, after that location completed a renovation. In part, they were given to me because I asked and in part in recognition of my near-permanent place at one of those tables over many years. My first two novels were written and researched at those tables, and to have them now in my home is an unusual pleasure.

www.ingramcontent.com/pod-product-compliance
Lightning Source LLC
Chambersburg PA
CBHW030828110726
47900CB00006B/1787

* 9 7 8 1 7 7 7 3 0 7 3 0 1 *